Montagnard

A JD Cordell Action Thriller

D.C. Gilbert

DEDICATION

To the brave men and women who run toward danger when
everyone else runs the other way.

ACKNOWLEDGMENTS

I would like to offer my sincere thanks to Eric Ewald, Carol Piser, Martha Knapp, Evan Wagoner, and Curtiss Gilbert for their fantastic help and hard work in reading and reviewing this work and providing me with their valuable feedback and support, and to Bob Starr, former USAF pilot, for his review and comments and help in making sure my flight communication were authentic. I must also thank my four clandestine readers who prefer to remain anonymous but provided great subject matter expertise. In addition, I would like to thank Angie at pro-ebook covers on Fiverr.com for the awesome book cover design and my editor, Beth Kallman Werner, for helping bring this book to completion. I own any mistakes found in this novel.

PROLOGUE

The history of the Degar people begins in the Central Highlands of Vietnam. The term *Montagnard* has its origins in the French word for "people of the mountain." The Montagnard people existed as a loosely allied group of about thirty tribes. The largest tribes were the Jarai, Rade, Bahnar, Koho, Mnong, and Stieng. During the French colonial period, the Montagnard tribes enjoyed a certain level of autonomy.

In 1954, the Viet Minh—a communist guerrilla force founded in 1941 to fight the joint Japanese and Vichy French occupation of Vietnam during World War II—defeated the French at Dien Bien Phu. A meeting in Geneva between opposing sides resulted in Vietnam being partitioned off, with the Central Highlands falling under the control of the newly formed Republic of Vietnam. Soon, the Degar people began to lose their freedom. Vietnamese replaced the Degar languages in their schools. Persecution for practicing their now illegal Christian beliefs soon followed.

When the communist North Vietnamese began their intrusions into South Vietnam, the Montagnard found themselves directly in their path. For self-preservation, the Montagnard tribes began to form military alliances with each other.

The French defeat at Dien Bien Phu had another result. When the French withdrew from Vietnam, the United States took over the training and support of the South Vietnamese army.

By the 1960s, the Central Highlands had become a critical region in the fight against the invading communists. The South Vietnamese government agreed to let U.S. Special Forces units start training the Montagnard militias to defend their villages and patrol the border. The U.S. Special Forces, or Green Berets, discovered the Montagnard to be exceptional jungle fighters. They had great personal courage and loyalty to their allies. About 40,000 Montagnard served with the U.S. military as soldiers, scouts, and interpreters. American Vietnam veterans have provided many tales of the heroism and loyalty of the Montagnard warriors.

America ended its involvement in Vietnam in 1975. In April of that year, the Republic of Vietnam fell to the North Vietnamese Army. The irony of the situation was that the U.S. military had defeated the North Vietnamese Army. The Tet Offensive was their last gasp. Later interviews with high ranking NVA officers revealed that they were stunned when the United States pulled out. The U.S. had won the war but somehow did not know it. The truth is, the American media fed the American people a very different story, and too many bought into it. Public support dwindled. The American military won the war, but the media and politicians gave the victory away.

The American withdrawal was the beginning of a very dark time for the Montagnard people. During the final days of the war, Montagnard leaders attended a meeting held at the U.S. Embassy in Saigon. U.S. military leaders asked the Montagnard to fight as rear-area guerrillas against the communists. In exchange, the U.S. would provide food, arms, supplies, and eventually, sanctuary. The Montagnard agreed.

For several years after their American allies left, the Montagnard continued the fight against communism. Sadly, the U.S. government turned its back on the promise to its former partner. Their steadfast loyalty and willingness to help their American Special Forces allies sealed their fate.

Because of their strong support for the U.S. military, the Socialist Republic of Vietnam exacted a terrible vengeance on the Montagnard people. The communists instituted a policy of systematic repression and genocide against them. This program continues to this day. Following the communist victory in 1975, the Montagnard people, including non-combatants, were forced into restricted areas or re-education camps, and often denied medical care and supplies. Anything written in any of the Degar languages, including Bibles, were burned or destroyed. In 1975, there were about seven million Montagnard living in Vietnam. Today, there are about half-a-million.

The U.S. military veterans did not forget their loyal Montagnard allies. But, with no support from their government, there was little they could do. Retired Special Forces soldiers, as well as other special operations warriors, have long fought to keep the promises made to their Montagnard allies so long ago. Then, in 1986, two hundred and twelve Montagnard refugees were discovered living in a camp in Thailand. With the intervention of President Reagan, those two hundred and twelve refugees were resettled in North Carolina.

While *Montagnard* is a novel and a work of fiction, it is also a tribute to these brave mountain warriors and loyal American allies. I hope that their future as a people will be brighter when more understand just what they sacrificed.

CHAPTER 1
VIETNAM

17 September 1967

Dish leaned his back against a tall Dalat pine and struggled to quiet his heavy breathing, listening for sounds of enemy pursuit. The ambush had been perfect. As point man, Dish had been allowed through the kill zone. Somehow, he'd missed it, which meant that whoever laid that ambush was damn good; because Dish was also damn good.

The terrain hadn't allowed for the typical L-shaped ambush or the Viet Cong's favorite, a V-shaped ambush. Still, the Green Beret A-team was now caught in a deadly crossfire from both sides of their position. Separated from his team by a dense hail of bullets from both the ambushers and the Green Berets returning fire, Dish tried to circle back and rejoin them. He was unsuccessful, running directly into a group of a dozen VC moving up to reinforce the right leg of the ambush. Spotting Dish, the group opened fire, and he could do little more than turn and flee back down the trail. The excited VC, forgetting their mission, took off after him, following in hot pursuit.

Reaching up, he removed his Boonie hat to wipe sweat from his brow with the sleeve of his olive drab jungle fatigue jacket. Listening, he heard nothing.

There's no way I lost them, Dish thought. *Maybe I outran them?* He doubted that was the case and was sure they'd be along. More likely, they were moving cautiously.

4

Finally, he risked a swallow of water, relieving the dryness in his throat. Placing the canteen back in its pouch on his left hip, Dish returned the Boonie hat to his head. Crouching down, he shifted his grip on the M-16 rifle he carried and listened for several long minutes.

Could I have lost them? It still seemed unlikely.

The sound of a snapping twig a short distance to his left answered that question. Dish froze, hearing a hushed but angry admonishment in Vietnamese.

Then, his eye caught a movement. Dish held his breath as two of his pursuers stepped out of the brush into a small clearing; they were just a few yards down the slope from where he stood pressed against the Dalat pine. The black-clad VC carried AK-47s and wore bandoliers with extra ammunition hanging sash-style over their shoulders. Each wore the trademark conical straw hat as protection from the sun, which luckily at this moment was directly behind Dish.

Dish felt a bead of sweat run down the back of his neck. More sweat stung his eyes. He could do nothing; even the slightest movement might give his position away. To his surprise, the two enemy fighters never glanced his way. Their attention seemed focused on something downslope. Seconds later, the two began to work their way down the hill carefully, moving away from where Dish was trying to become part of the tree. Then, like two jungle ghosts, the VC were gone.

Turning, Dish began running along an outcropping of rock, partially concealed by the Dalat pine against which he'd rested. There was a shout. An AK-47 fired, and a spattering of bullets ricocheted off the rock just behind him. They were right on his tail. Spotting a cut in the rock just ahead, Dish raced toward it. With his pursuers moving to close in behind him, he ducked into it.

I hope this isn't a dead end!

There was no place to hide. The crack created by the outcropping was narrow and not very deep. Perhaps five feet wide at its opening, it narrowed to about eighteen inches where it ended at a rock face. The split in the rock was seven or eight feet deep at best. Dish saw only a thick growth of leafy scrub brush at the base of the rock face. It was a dead end.

At twenty-three years old, Dish had been fighting the North Vietnamese and their VC allies for seven years; he had witnessed their evil brutality and was determined not to be taken alive. Moving quickly to the rear of the crack, he pressed his back into the brush and checked the action of his M-16 rifle. Dish carried ten fully loaded 30-round magazines in his rucksack but doubted he'd get a chance to reload. He was resolute that before he died, several of them would precede him.

Pressing the release, he quickly checked and reseated the magazine. It was full. Dish moved back into the split in the rock as far as he could. Turning to face the opening, he leaned back into the brush, wanting to feel something substantial behind him. There was nothing. He shifted back just a bit and pressed back again. Still, he felt nothing. Crouching, he worked himself farther back into the scrubby growth and suddenly tumbled over backward.

Getting to his feet, Dish looked at the rock face, but he was now standing on the other side. The elevation in front of him was solid, but there was a hole, probably cut by water at its base. Stooping, he peered into the hole and estimated the rock wall to be several feet thick. The scrub brush concealed the opening, and he had luckily fallen right into it. Listening carefully, he couldn't hear anything. The VC were cautious in their approach. Suspecting they had him trapped, they were in no rush to get themselves killed. A trapped rat will turn on its pursuers, and Dish was no rat, he was a jungle tiger.

Quickly taking stock of his situation, he could see he was in a big bowl cut by falling water. There was a rocky wash on his right that led up a steep, almost vertical bank.

The only way out of here is up, he decided.

Slinging the rifle across his back, he started climbing, making as little noise as possible. At about a hundred feet up, the path suddenly turned out onto a rock ledge. Flattening himself out, Dish lay on the shelf and listened, trying to quiet his ragged breath. He now could hear the VC below, searching for him.

"Fan out! He didn't just disappear. Use your bayonet and check that brush." There was the sound of a bayonet snapping into place on a rifle barrel and then being thrust repeatedly into the brush.

"I tell you he isn't here!"

After a time, the perplexed group of Viet Cong moved on, their voices fading as they drew farther away. They'd completely missed the hole into which he'd fallen.

After lying still for several minutes, making sure the VC had indeed left the area, Dish got up and began to reassess his situation. His hands, scraped and bloody from climbing the rock wash, hurt, but he ignored the pain.

Let's see where this leads. Dish was in no hurry to head back down toward the VC search team. Working his way along the narrow ledge, he rounded a corner on the mountain and found himself standing at the edge of a large rock shelf about eighty yards long and thirty yards across at its widest point. Many trees provided a canopy of shady coverage, and a spring formed a pool near the rock wall that continued upward toward the mountain peak. A small stream flowed from the pool over the edge of the shelf some twenty yards away.

Cupping his hands, Dish scooped water from the pool and drank. The water was cold and refreshing. Ignoring the stinging of the cuts and abrasions covering his hands, he washed the blood away. After a second drink, he unslung the M-16 from his shoulder and leaned it against a tree. Shrugging out of his rucksack, he dropped it to the ground before sitting down and leaning back against the tree to rest. Reaching over, Dish dug into the ruck and came out with a ball of sticky rice wrapped in green leaves. He began to eat.

The shelf seemed safe enough for now, and it was already getting dark. Deciding to spend the night where he was, Dish stuffed the remainder of the rice ball into his mouth, shifted into a more comfortable position, and closed his eyes. Exhausted, he was asleep in moments.

It was still dark when he opened his eyes. He got to his feet and, picking up his rifle, returned to the spring, where he splashed water on his face and quenched his thirst, then refilled his canteen.

Feeling somewhat awake and refreshed, Dish began to explore the shelf in the early morning light. There was a great view of the valley below from several points along its edge. It became clear that the only way on or off the ledge was the rocky wash he'd scrambled up the night before.

A perfect place to hide, a stroke of luck to discover it.

His pursuers long gone, his stomach reminded him of how hungry he was. Making his way carefully back down the wash, he climbed back out onto the outcropping just outside the crack in the rock. It was no wonder the VC had missed the hole. The opening at the base of the rock wall, entirely hidden by scrub growth, could not be seen. Dish had been fortunate.

Adjusting the sling of his M-16 on his shoulder, he began to backtrack toward the trail that would take him back to the original ambush site. He wasn't sure what he'd find and suspected the twelve-man team would no longer be there, but he could track them through the jungle readily enough. Dish never forgot that hidden rock shelf.

Present Day

The morning sun had not yet burned through the dense fog that hung over the central highland peaks. A heavy dew covered everything like a wet cloak. There was a chill in the air, the dampness making it feel colder than it probably was. The sun would soon take care of that.

Dish stood in the doorway of his longhouse, peering out into the dense fog. There was little to see. The cold made his joints ache, a reminder of the many injuries sustained during past battles with the North Vietnamese Army and the Viet Cong. All in all, he was in pretty good health for a crusty old Montagnard warrior, but he was no longer a young man. Time didn't seem to have much meaning in these mountains, and he hadn't seen a calendar in some time, but Dish knew he had to be at least seventy by now.

The sounds of his woman beginning to stir inside reached his ears. Chanmali was a Laotian woman who certainly made life in these remote mountains much more bearable. He'd discovered her lying along a mountain trail several years ago. Alone and severely injured, she was being stalked by an old tiger in search of easy prey. Dish decided he could not very well stand by and let the tiger have her, so he unslung the old M1 carbine he often carried and shot the big cat. Chanmali, grateful for not being the tiger's next meal, decided to stay. Dish had not been sure how he felt about this at first, but soon learned to appreciate the benefits of having her share the longhouse he'd built on the rock shelf he'd stumbled upon during the war.

The communists did have long memories, and they'd placed a bounty on his head that would make anyone who could collect it a wealthy man. So, as remote and desolate as the shelf was, it was infinitely preferable to death, or at minimum, confinement in a re-education camp or prison.

The closest Vietnamese village was Dak To, about twenty-five kilometers to the east, a good day's hike. The Laotian village of Xayden sat to the west, a little closer. Near Dish's hideout, the three borders of Laos, Cambodia, and Vietnam came together. This tri-border region of Vietnam's central highlands was once an area of great strategic importance to both sides during the Vietnam War.

After the war, the border region became home to many needing to avoid contact with agents of Vietnam's new communist government. Many inhabitants of the region were former South Vietnamese, guilty of supporting the Saigon government and its U.S. allies during the conflict. They'd fled to the area to avoid a life of hard labor, torture, starvation, and disease. Unfortunately, others also found the remote region useful. These were often nothing more than criminals—thieves, murderers, rapists, and drug dealers.

Vietnam had become a key trafficking hub for opium filtering down from the Golden Triangle to the north. Since the Americans pulled out of Vietnam at the end of the war, many former Viet Cong commanders had discovered the lucrative drug trade. When Thailand began cracking down on drug trafficking, they happily began to pick up the slack.

Like most Montagnards, Dish hated the communist regime now running Vietnam. A younger and impressionable Dish had seen first-hand the evil savagery and violence of the North Vietnamese Army, especially their VC allies. He carried an intense hatred of them permanently seared into his being. The war in Vietnam had forged him into an instrument of vengeance, and he hunted his enemies implacably and without mercy. Working with the U.S. military during the war, and now, leading his small group of men, Dish considered himself a freedom fighter. Despite his age, like a tiger in the jungle, Dish was still a formidable adversary.

CHAPTER 2
NIGER

The West African country of Niger has a long, painful history of lawlessness and violence. With eighty percent of its landmass contained within the Sahara Desert, Niger is a scorching, dry country that holds little in the way of attraction for most sane people. Nevertheless, it was precisely where Ellen Chang found herself.

Ellen had flown into Diori Hamani International Airport in Niamey just three months earlier. A physician working for Doctors Without Borders, she was out to change the world.

Born in 1982, Ellen grew up in Chicago, Illinois, the second child of three and the only girl. Separately, her parents both immigrated to the United States from China in the early 1970s. The couple met at the Chinese Christian Union Church in Chinatown. Ellen's father, Henry, worked hard, saved his money, and soon opened a small Chinese restaurant a few blocks from the church, but it was her mother, Grace, who was the real driving force behind their business success. Ellen's two brothers joined the family restaurant business, but she wanted something more.

With several scholarships and working nights at the family restaurant to fill in the gaps, Ellen majored in Pre-Medicine at the University of Illinois in Chicago. Completing her undergraduate degree, she enrolled at the Pritzker School of Medicine at the University of Chicago. Upon graduation, Ellen served a rigorous three-year residency in internal medicine. Now, she was ready for the next challenge.

Being a member of a traditional Chinese family had both pros and cons. Ellen's mother was soon playing matchmaker and announced she'd found the perfect husband for their daughter. Gordon was the son of family friends and a respected urologist at Chicago Lakeshore Hospital. Grace had it all arranged. Ellen, however, was having none of it. Life in an arranged marriage was not the reason she had worked so hard in medical school. Her independent streak kicked into overdrive, and she contacted the international humanitarian medical organization, Doctors Without Borders.

Passing through the gate at the airport, Ellen spotted a man holding a small cardboard sign on which someone had printed Dr. Chang. She headed toward him. The man saw her coming.

"Dr. Chang, I am Bram Alderik. I am here to drive you to our temporary base of operations in Agadez." The man had a strong accent, perhaps German or Dutch.

Ellen extended her hand. "Please, call me Ellen. Let me collect my luggage, and I'll be ready." On the way to the luggage claim area, Ellen asked, "How far is it to Agadez? It's been a long flight."

Bram gave Ellen a funny look. "It's about a fifteen-hour drive into the desert from here, provided we don't run into any... uh, problems."

"Fifteen hours into the desert?" Ellen repeated. Shock and fatigue registered on her face for a microsecond before she managed to replace it with a look of calm assurance that she didn't feel. "Okay, then. I'll need some water."

"I have all that," Bram replied as they made their way down the escalator to the baggage claim.

After collecting Ellen's luggage, Alderik led her out into the short-term parking lot, where they approached a dust-covered Land Rover. Ellen could see four gas cans strapped to a bracket on the Land Rover's rear hatch. Alderik tossed her suitcases into a metal mesh carrier on the vehicle's roof and strapped them down. In the back seat were several cases of bottled water and what looked like boxes of freeze-dried foods and canned goods. While not an expert, Ellen thought she also spotted a couple of ammo cans.

Alderik motioned Ellen to get in on the passenger side and went around to open the driver's door. Reaching in, he pulled a web belt with a holstered gun from behind his seat, securing it around his waist before settling the holster comfortably in place.

"Is that necessary?" Ellen inquired.

'Yes, Ma'am, it is. We are heading into some rough country. I'm not just your driver. I guess you could also say I'm your bodyguard." He laughed. "Or, whatever you want to call me. I sometimes work for Doctors Without Borders when they have people in the more dangerous regions."

"I see." Ellen's eyes had just spotted the military-style rifle also stashed behind his seat.

"Don't worry, though," Alderik continued. "I'll get you there. The nasty areas are northeast of Agadez."

"So, just how bad is it, Mr. Alderik?" She was now beginning to wonder if she'd made a mistake coming here.

"Call me, Bram. Well, as bad as Agadez is, the region to the north and east of Agadez is much worse. Lots of carjackings, kidnappings, murders, rapes, and robberies. The area is hugely desolate, with a few rough roads and a lot of terrible people running around." Bram paused to open a water bottle before continuing. He indicated Ellen should help herself. "Recently, we've received reports that al Qaeda has a growing presence in the area. Supposedly, both ISIS and al Qaeda are moving into the region after suffering big losses farther north." He grinned over at Ellen. "Don't worry; you'll be safe enough. The U.S. Air Force began constructing a new base for its MQ9 Reaper drones just outside Agadez. We're operating from the base for the time being."

That's reassuring, Ellen thought.

"If you don't mind my asking, I'm just curious, Bram. Are you of German descent?" Ellen wanted to change the topic of conversation.

"Close. Dutch."

A few weeks after arriving at the new drone base, Ellen readied her supplies for a trip into the area just north of Agadez. There was a severe Hepatitis E outbreak in the region, and the humanitarian response was sadly lacking. There were several reasons for this: insufficient resources, poor coordination between humanitarian organizations, and the fact that the Agadez region was a dangerous place to be.

This danger no longer worried Ellen. Somebody needed to go in there, and she was here. She'd been pretty fearless her whole life. Besides, she'd already made several uneventful trips into some pretty desolate areas to provide medical services. This time she would have Norman, her assistant, with her as well as that Dutch mercenary, Bram

Alderik. She should be safe enough.

This outbreak was taking a heavy toll on some of the area's most vulnerable people, especially pregnant women and refugees. These people needed her help, and helping was the reason Ellen had become a doctor.

CHAPTER 3
VIETNAM

Dish shivered in the cold; damp morning air crept through to his bones. As he turned back into the warmth of the longhouse, his thoughts went to his adopted sister, Mai. He'd not seen her in many years. Chuckling to himself, he remembered the American soldier who'd fallen from the sky and crashed to the jungle floor, maybe forty yards from where he had been eating his lunch.

It was now many years long ago that Dish had been squatting there eating his sticky rice when he heard the chopper fly over. Shortly after that, the sound of the chopper's engines changed; it was taking evasive action. Suddenly, something crashed through the branches some forty yards away, and he'd looked up to see the American hanging there, his rucksack tangled in some vines. The American finally broke loose and fell to the jungle floor with a thud, lying still.

Dish carried the young American officer, injured and unconscious, back to his village where Mai tended to him. Mai, who spoke excellent English, later told him that the American, whose name was Cordell, was thrown from the chopper when it banked hard trying to avoid a rocket-propelled grenade.

It was several weeks before the American was well enough to try and make the trip south to the closest military base camp. He had no map, compass, or radio. On his own, Cordell would be lucky to avoid the NVA or the VC. He would need a guide.

Unfortunately, an increase in VC and NVA activity in the area delayed his attempted return to his unit. When the enemy movement died down enough for Cordell to make a try, Dish was ordered north on a scouting mission with a Green Beret A-team. He could not guide the American soldier to the basecamp. Mai had immediately offered to lead him to a special forces camp a couple of days hike to the south of the village.

Dish was proud of his adopted sister. He knew that his sister was fond of the American. He came to like the quiet American soldier as well. And, it was clear to him that Cordell had grown very fond of Mai. Dish hoped they were still together. He liked to picture Mai in America, married to the American officer. She would not have had much of a future in Vietnam. Suddenly, Dish snapped back from his reminiscing.

"Here is your breakfast," Chanmali spoke in Laotian, smiling as she handed Dish a steaming bowl of Cháo. Dish grunted his appreciation and sat down to eat. It was delicious. He often wondered what Chanmali added to the porridge to make it taste so good. This morning, she made boiled coffee as well. While serving with the Americans, Dish had developed quite a fondness for the strong, black drink. So much better than tea. The combination of hot porridge and strong coffee slowly began to drive the chill from his bones.

Dish and several of his men were departing the village that very afternoon on a dangerous five hundred and fifty-kilometer journey to Sisaket, Thailand. After completing their business in Sisaket, they would make the same trek back, albeit by a different route. He and his men would travel lightly, carrying only the food and water needed for the journey. They would all be well-armed.

A twenty-kilometer hike to the Laotian village of Xayden made up the first leg of the trip. Once in Xayden, Dish and his men would pile into several beat-up old Toyota Land Cruisers for the fifteen-hour cross-country drive to Sisaket. To avoid any official entanglements, they stayed off the main roads and tracks traveled by regular tourists. In this way, they also avoided many of the border checkpoints, toll booths, and possible searches by Vietnamese authorities. On this trip, he and his men would cross the Mekong River using the ferry at Muang Champassak.

Dish was quite friendly with the family running the ferry. He'd helped them out of a tight spot when a younger family member ran afoul of one of the local loan sharks. The young man had tried to start a business of his own. Having no access to startup funding, he turned to a local thug. With interest, he had quickly owed a large sum of money, and the consequences were rather severe. Dish negotiated a lower settlement and paid it. Over time, the grateful parents repaid Dish with their friendship and considerably less scrutiny when he used the ferry.

Dish was a gun smuggler. It was how he continued his war against the communist government that now ruled his country. He sold guns purchased from his source in Thailand to the anti-communist rebels in Vietnam.

An additional danger to avoid was drug smugglers. The Golden Triangle, formed by the intersection of China, Laos, Thailand, and Myanmar, sat to the north. When Thailand cracked down on the drug trade, the smugglers shifted their shipping routes through Laos and into Vietnam. Dish had little use for drug smugglers who were usually closely tied to the prostitution rings. He viewed them as dealers in human misery and degradation. Reinforcing this view was the fact that many of the drug smugglers were former VC. After the war, they'd found a way to earn a living that provided a means for satisfying their urges for brutality and subjugation.

Dish had no problem with killing any drug dealer he met along the trail, but it was better to avoid them. His gun-running business relied on maintaining an uneasy truce. However, clashes did sometimes occur. He had not set out to be the leader of a band of outlaws. Despite that, several new longhouses appeared on his remote shelf of rock, built by other Montagnard and South Vietnamese outcasts. A few had served with him during the fighting around Dak To. They were not technically criminals; they just happened to be on the losing side in the war and lived in this desolate region to avoid government reprisals. They, too, needed to make a living.

Dish's fierce reputation as a Montagnard warrior attracted like-minded followers. His small village now boasted forty-three men, several with wives and children. Tight security was essential to ensure their survival. Dish's rules were inviolate, placing the continuation of the group over the concerns of any individual who ignored his rules.

In Sisaket was the source of the arms he bought and sold. Major Anurat Detphong, a retired Thai army officer, had served in South Vietnam during the war. Anurat had witnessed the brutality of the communist North Vietnamese and their Viet Cong allies and did not want that evil to spread. He preferred to help the anti-communist rebels in Vietnam fight their battles and to keep the fighting out of Thailand.

While the Thai-Cambodian border was teeming with arms and drug smugglers, the major only did business with a select few. Dish was one of the few he trusted, and their relationship grew over many years. Both Dish and Major Anurat had good reason to hate the Vietnamese communist government. Neither man would have anything to do with the drug smugglers. However, they avoided crossing them simply because they were a murderous lot. Many powerful warlords were former Viet Cong leaders who found smuggling opium easier and more lucrative than working for the communist government.

Dish never knew what weapons the major would have for him. Mainly, it was whatever Anurat could get his hands on. This time, the shipment consisted of twenty-nine AK-47 assault rifles, four 7.62mm Russian-made machine guns with five thousand rounds of 7.62mm ammunition, and a case of Chinese-made grenades. The exchange was made in an old abandoned warehouse just north of Sisaket, while several of Anurat's men kept watch for Thai police or other intruders.

Dish was pleased with the weapons. They were in good shape and would bring a reasonable price back home. His men disassembled the guns and packed them into wicker pack baskets, covering them with rags and rice straw. They loaded each pack into the back of a Land Cruiser. Once they reached Xayden, each man would carry a pack basket the remaining twenty kilometers through the mountains and into Vietnam. They didn't mind. Dish, being a good businessman, compensated them well.

The retired Thai major stepped close to Dish as they prepared to leave.

"Be careful, old friend. There is trouble among the opium smugglers. Someone is making a move to eliminate competition. There have been many killings." Dish nodded.

"I have heard of this. Any idea who it is?"

"I heard the name Trần mentioned, but I do not know." Dish looked up, hearing that name. Anurat noticed his sudden interest.

"Do you know this Trần?" the major asked.

Dish did not immediately respond.

"I don't know. I remember a Trần from the war. The man was a

Viet Cong butcher. But it may not be him. Trần is a common enough name." Anurat nodded.

"Until the next visit, my friend," he stated, turning to leave.

"Until then," Dish replied.

South of the town of Sisaket, the Dângrêk mountain chain cut along Sisaket Province's southern border, eventually adjoining a section of Thailand's border with Cambodia. Dish and his men followed a paved road toward the mountains and then turned east, following a dirt track that would eventually lead to the border. Dish sat in the passenger seat of the lead vehicle. He left the driving to the younger men. His job was to lead and keep an eye out for trouble. He was good at that.

It was a long drive, and his men needed to remain sharp. Riding with the windows down helped. The men also took turnabout, alternating between watching the countryside through which they traveled and dozing. This remote area was not heavily traveled, and on occasion, could be dangerous.

CHAPTER 4
NIGER

The white Toyota Hilux turned down a dusty alleyway between two empty, mud-walled buildings and pulled to a stop just before the alley ended. Telling his driver to wait with the truck, Khalid Rehman opened the passenger door and got out. Moving toward one of the few entrances that still had a working door, he knocked. A rag that served as a window curtain shifted slightly in a window with no glass. A few seconds later, there was a scraping sound of a bolt sliding back, and the door opened. Khalid stepped inside.

The room was dim. There was no electricity. The only light available was what could pass through the few remaining filthy windows. Two other men were already in the room, waiting for Khalid's arrival.

Khalid didn't have time for pleasantries. "Well?" he demanded. "What have you learned?"

Frightened, Saheed hurried to answer. Everyone knew Khalid's reputation.

"The woman is making a trip through the outlying villages to the north tomorrow. Her assistant will be going with her, as well as the Dutch mercenary. He is good and will be heavily armed, but he will be alone. They are expecting no trouble since things have been quiet, and it is a humanitarian mission."

Khalid nodded, turning to Mustapha. "Your men will intercept the doctor and her team as they visit their last village. They will be tired. Kill the mercenary. I want the woman doctor alive and unharmed. Do you understand?

"Certainly. It shall be so. What about the woman's assistant?"

'He is inconsequential." Khalid turned to Saheed. "Your work on the American base has been beneficial to our cause. Allah rewards those who serve."

Saheed nodded his head enthusiastically. "Thank you, Khalid! You are most kind."

"The Americans will pay a good ransom for the doctor. If not, she will die an infidel's death for all the world to see. Either way, her abduction will benefit our cause."

Khalid was satisfied. Turning, he walked to the door, then paused to look back at the two men.

"Saheed, return to the American base. See what else your ears can uncover. You know what to do."

Saheed nodded again but said nothing.

Khalid continued. "When you have the woman, bring her here. Remember to tell your men; the woman is to remain unharmed. See if you can learn anything from her assistant. I doubt he has any useful information, but you never know."

With that, Khalid exited and climbed into the Toyota. His driver navigated the narrow, dirty streets and moments later; the small truck sped off into the shimmering desert.

Mustapha glanced over at Saheed, glowering at the man in a warning. He did not trust spies, even their own. Saying nothing, he left the building on foot. A little way down the block, he ducked into the empty doorway of a building that, during better days, had housed a restaurant frequented by oil workers. Passing through the building's empty main room into what was once the kitchen, he went out the back door and climbed into his beat-up older Toyota Hilux. Then, he too was making his way through the streets of Agadez until he was outside the city and heading north into the desert. Mustapha had preparations to finalize for tomorrow's planned kidnapping.

As Saheed made his way back toward the American base on foot, he could not help but feel a little sad. The Chinese American doctor was always pleasant and friendly toward him. It was too bad. Saheed shrugged. *I am merely a pawn, an implement of Allah's will.*

Abardek village was the last stop before the team would head back to the drone base outside Agadez. Exhausted, Ellen had treated seventy-three patients so far. There were another seven waiting in

Abardek. Ellen saw each one in turn. The hardest to see were young children. The look of hopelessness and hunger in their eyes was almost unbearable. Ellen frowned as her mind drifted home for a minute. So many people in her generation had no idea how damn lucky they were.

People protest over such stupid stuff. They should experience a little of this life. Life or death, out here, was real.

After Ellen treated the last patient, Norman threw her medical kit into the back of the old Land Rover, relieved that the hot, dusty day was drawing to a close. Bram stood nearby, keeping a vigilant eye on the surrounding desert. Ellen hadn't met any mercenaries before and didn't know what to expect. He seemed quiet and polite enough, very professional, but there was a detachedness in him that discouraged much in the way of pleasantries.

What makes a man do what he does? Ellen wondered.

It was so hot and dry; you didn't even sweat. Or at least, it didn't seem like it. Any sweat evaporated immediately. Ellen took a sip of water from the bottle she held in her hand. She always carried one; hydration was vital in Niger.

And to think I volunteered for this shit! She almost laughed.

Ellen suddenly became aware that Bram was waving her frantically toward the Land Rover and yelling something. With his Dutch accent, it was hard for her to make out his words. Then, from nowhere, Norman grabbed her arm.

"Come on, Ellen! Run! We've got to go. NOW!" Ellen heard shots fired and turned to see Bram on one knee, firing the Galil Ace assault rifle he never went without. Her eyes looked in the direction the gun pointed, spotting a group of pickup trucks racing toward their location.

"Oh shit!"

Ellen needed no more urging. She turned and raced the few yards to the Land Rover, climbing into the passenger seat as Norman jumped into the driver's side and pressed the ignition switch. The Land Rover's old engine sputtered to life. He threw the transmission into gear and spun the wheel, swinging around to pick up Bram. Bullets were flying everywhere. Ellen could now see men standing in the back of the speeding pickups, firing their weapons.

As the Land Rover moved toward him, Bram dashed toward it, reaching for the rear passenger side door as Norman momentarily hit the brakes. Reaching back, Ellen tried her best to help him in. Bram was almost in when several AK-47 rounds tore into his back. Ellen screamed as his blood splattered over her arms and face.

"Get the fuck out of here!" Bram yelled as he fell back, several more bullets striking his body. He was dead before he hit the sand.

Norman stomped the accelerator, heading for the road that led back to Agadez. Bullets slammed into the side of the Land Rover. A pickup truck cut wildly across their path. Instinctively, Norman swerved to avoid hitting the smaller vehicle. The Land Rover skidded to the left, glancing off the side of an old mud-walled hut and careening wildly in the opposite direction. Norman fought to regain control of the wheel, correcting for the skid. He overcompensated. The Land Rover flipped over onto its passenger side.

The last thing Ellen felt was her head hitting the windshield, hard. Everything went dark.

CHAPTER 5
WASHINGTON, DC

President Steele entered the situation room accompanied by his chief of staff, Martin Sansby, and senior counselor, Miriam Randolph. With a solid build and standing just over six feet, Steele possessed an air of quiet confidence forged during his years of military service. It was easy to see why he'd emerged as president after the embarrassment of the last election. The arrest of his opponent, Josephine Warren-Brookstone, on election night—on charges of campaign fraud and attempted murder—had shocked the nation, creating a political firestorm.

Adding fuel to the fire, California did not go to Brookstone. The Hispanic vote swung the state, and California's fifty-five electoral votes went to her opponent, Benjamin Steele. There were cries of voter fraud and demands for recounts. Three times, California's ballots were recounted. Each time, Benjamin Steele emerged the winner. It turned out that the Hispanic voters, a staunchly Catholic population, were a bit more conservative than the 'experts' had predicted.

Steele survived the political chaos, proving himself to be a solid man of integrity and honor, and finally took the presidential oath of office. He'd since earned the respect of everyone in the room.

Already seated in black leather chairs at the long conference table were his national security adviser, William Braddock; the homeland security adviser, Jacqueline Hamm; the CIA Director, Mike Connors; and the outgoing chairman of the Joint Chiefs, General John F. Dunning. Dunning was retiring at the end of the month; the president had tapped General Clay Ellerson to replace him. Ellerson was, at this moment, meeting with members of the Senate in preparation for his confirmation hearing. Dunning would later brief Ellerson on what transpired during this meeting.

The president unbuttoned his jacket and took his seat at the head of the table, then waited until his chief of staff and senior counselor had settled themselves to either side of him. Steele directed his attention to General Dunning. "I have the impression that whatever you have for me is not good news."

General Dunning nodded and cleared his throat. "That is correct, Mr. President. Yesterday evening, a humanitarian mission based out of our new drone base in Niger failed to return. The team for this mission consisted of two American citizens, Dr. Ellen Chang and Norman Holley, as well as a Dutch national, Bram Alderik. Ellen Chang is a physician working for Doctors Without Borders, Holley is her assistant, and Alderik was a Dutch mercenary hired to provide security."

The president raised his head. "You said, 'was...'?"

"Yes, Mr. President. When the mission failed to return, the base commander sent out a squad of Marines to investigate. They found Bram Alderik dead at the last stop along their planned route, shot several times. It looks like there must have been quite a firefight. Alderik may have gotten some of the attackers. There was a lot of scattered brass and blood, but no other bodies."

"Probably carried them off," Braddock observed.

"Probably," the president agreed. "Continue, John."

"It looks like Dr. Chang and Holley tried to get away in their vehicle, but somehow lost control. There was no sign of them at the site, and their Land Rover burned. Kidnapping is the most plausible conclusion. We aren't sure by whom at this point. This region around Agadez and Base 201 is like the wild west.

"Perfect place for a drone base," Jacqueline Hamm commented with a wry smile.

"Exactly," agreed Braddock. "Providing security for our base will give us a great opportunity to put a damper on some of this activity."

The president raised his hand to stop the discussion. "So, what was Dr. Chang doing there?"

"They were out treating people for a Hepatitis E outbreak at several nearby villages."

President Steele scowled. "So, she is out there helping those people, and they kidnap her? Not a lot of sense in that scenario."

The CIA director spoke up. "Mr. President, I have a feeling we will soon learn that al Qaeda is behind this. I suspect we'll receive a ransom demand; either that or, God forbid, we will shortly see videos of their beheading posted on social media."

"That would make sense," the national security adviser added. "We've knocked al Qaeda back on their heels. They are hurting and strapped for operating funds. That Sahara Desert is a tough place to be. They need resources, and ransom would be an obvious choice."

"You're probably right, Will." The president leaned back in his chair. "We cannot and will not pay a ransom. That will only encourage more kidnappings in the future. What kind of assets do we have at Base 201? Can we put together a rescue operation? I need some options."

Dunning handed the president a folder. "I've had my staff put together an initial rescue plan. If we receive a ransom demand and get enough intelligence, there is a good chance we can pull it off. However, staffing on Base 201 is mostly engineers, support units, and a lot of civilian construction contractors. There is only a small contingent of Marines and a handful of Air Force security police for the landing strip."

Connors turned toward the president. "I have an asset on the base, named Rick Hahn. I know Rick, and the man is handy in a tight spot. He could coordinate local support for any rescue operation, and he has a pretty good team of contractors working for him."

"Could they handle a mission like this?" Steele seemed doubtful.

"This is not their area of expertise, and we don't need any bad headlines," Dunning interjected. "I would suggest using a covert team, maybe Delta Force or SEALS. They go in, kill the bad guys, grab the doc and her assistant, and get them the hell out of there. If this man, Hahn, can provide logistical support, that would be a big help."

"Al Qaeda will still know it was us," Hamm suggested.

"True. But, there will be no proof," Connors observed. "The locals will not be able to point to anyone on the base. As far as al Qaeda goes, if they believe it was us, that may be good for us long-term. It will send them a strong message. If you attack Americans, you will pay a heavy penalty."

Steele's expression indicated he had made his decision. "I like that idea. We have tiptoed around these terrorists far too long. It has not slowed them down in any measurable way that I have seen. Do they now think they can attack Americans with impunity? I say we alter that thinking." He turned to General Dunning. "John, I am leaving this in your hands. You have my complete confidence. If you need anything from me, give Will or Martin a shout. Do you have anything else for me at this time?"

"No, Sir. Not until we have a lot more information, and a ransom demand arrives." Dunning's gaze shifted to the CIA director. "Mike, can you get in touch with Hahn at Base 201 and see what he can do for us?"

Mike Connors nodded. "No problem."

"Again, if you need anything at all, contact my chief of staff. I want this Doctor Chang and her assistant rescued if possible, and a serious message sent to these terrorists either way. Let's do this right," Steele made his point clear.

Next, the president turned to Sansby. "Martin, has anyone contacted the family of either Ellen Chang or Norman Holley?"

"No, Mr. President. We were waiting until we had some real information."

"Please see to that for me, Marty. Give them our sincere condolences and tell them we are doing everything we can and will keep them informed. Get me their contact information. If I get a chance, I will give them a call myself in the next day or so."

Sansby nodded. "I'll take care of it, Mr. President. I'm sure a call from you would be appreciated."

With that, President Steele, followed closely by his chief of staff and senior counselor, left the room.

Dunning caught the CIA director at the door. "Mike, let me know what your guy on the base has to offer. I'll call Admiral Spence and see what he thinks. This mission is something a SEAL team would handle well."

"I'll get right on it, General, and should have an update for you later today." Connors paused. "You know, General, my son, David, is a doctor and also works with Doctors Without Borders. He's in Sri Lanka right now. That makes this hit pretty close to home for me."

General Dunning reached up with his right hand and clasped Connors' shoulder. "I didn't know that, Mike, but I understand. Let's get that lady out of there."

CHAPTER 6
VIETNAM

Word of trouble along the border region trails occasionally reached the small village on the rock shelf. Often it was a story of a military-style ambush in which a group of smugglers would die, and their cargo of opium was seized. It seemed to Dish like somebody was making a play to take over all the drug smuggling operations in the tri-border region around Dak To. Most of the heroin that found its way into the big cities with their red-light districts and brothels originated from this region.

The efficiency and success of these raids began to make Dish wonder about who was behind all this. Whomever it was, the man was efficient as well as ruthless. There were rarely any survivors. Could it be that this drug lord named Trần and the brutal Viet Cong colonel named Trần were the same?

It isn't possible, Dish thought. *But I should look further into this.*

The man responsible for so many deaths among the Montagnard and South Vietnamese villagers during the war in Vietnam was a man with whom Dish still had unfinished business to address. Dish cultivated his own short list of contacts. Certainly not as extensive as some of the drug smugglers, but many knew who Dish was. They remembered him as a hero during the war. Since then, there had been several acts of kindness and generosity to those people, both Montagnard and South Vietnamese, who were victims of brutal treatment or oppression by the communist government. Dish always helped when he could.

I will have Hai get the word out. There would be people willing to help.

Late one October afternoon, near the end of the rainy season, a lone man carrying a small sack of belongings over his shoulder wandered into the little settlement of outcasts living on the rock shelf.

There was no outdoor activity in the remote village. Most of the inhabitants stayed inside, avoiding the torrential downpour. A few, whose longhouses had porches or verandas, sat on benches, watching it rain. The air was cold and helped cut the humidity.

The stranger made his way toward a small roofed structure centered between the longhouses. The pavilion served as a communal gathering place for the villagers and offered cover for a few benches around a low table. There was a water barrel in one corner that collected rainwater. The barrel was full, and water overflowed the sides and splashed to the ground. The stranger took a seat on one of the benches. Setting his bag and his conical straw hat on the table, he waited for a break in the rain.

To those sitting on their porches, the man appeared to be Laotian, perhaps a bit larger than average. They did not often have visitors to their small village, especially since it was nearly impossible to find. With the heavy rain, the older children who served as lookouts along the single trail that led up to the rock shelf must have missed the man. Hai, who considered himself to be Dish's second in command, spotted the stranger sitting on the bench. Leaving his porch and splashing through the puddles, he dashed to the structure and joined the stranger at the table.

"Good day to you, Sir. Beautiful weather we are having. I think it has rained for three days continuously. My name is Hai." The Laotian stranger looked up but said nothing.

"Bad weather for traveling. Where are you headed? Are you just passing through?" Finally, the stranger spoke, his voice surly.

"Where I am going is my business and nobody else's. Now leave me alone. Go back to your porch." Hai, caught off guard by the brusque tone and rude manner of the Laotian, stepped back.

"Not many find our little village. How did you happen upon it?" Hai inquired. The stranger seemed ready to make another rude retort, then shrugged.

"There are rumors, he replied. "And, though it is well-hidden, there are signs of the trail to those who know what to look for." Hai nodded.

The stranger went on. "I am wanted by the government and need a place to lie low. I decided to look for this place."

Hai considered this for a minute, then turned to leave. Dish would want to know of this newcomer.

The Laotian looked up, spotting a woman crossing the space between two longhouses. Letting out a bellow of rage, he pushed past Hai, stepping out into the rain. The woman he'd spotted coming out of one longhouse and carefully making her way around the puddles toward another, was Chanmali. The stranger strode angrily toward her. The loud sound of the pouring rain muffled the footfalls of his rapid approach. Chanmali never saw what hit her. The man struck her hard with his fist in the back of her head. She fell to the ground. Several who were sitting on their porches stood, angrily yelling at the stranger to stop. But the enraged man took no notice. He was too busy cursing the fallen woman. As Chanmali tried to roll over and get to her knees, the man kicked her in the ribs. It was a powerful kick. Chanmali let out a groan as she felt the air leave her lungs. Her midsection felt like it was on fire.

The stranger drew back his leg for another kick but never got the chance to deliver it. A forceful blow struck his right hip, knocking him off his feet and to the ground a few feet away. Dish, stepping out on his veranda to see what the commotion was about, saw the stranger kick Chanmali. He'd rushed forward, launching a powerful side kick that struck the stranger's hip.

Dish knelt to check on Chanmali. She was hurt badly, but she was alive. Dish stood and turned to face the stranger who got to his feet, his face a distorted mask of fury.

"How dare you interfere? This ungrateful woman is my wife! She ran away. I will do with her as I please!"

"So, you are a man who beats his wife?" Dish replied, the scorn in his voice evident. "She is no longer yours. She is my woman now, and you will answer to me."

Cursing, the stranger rushed Dish, coming in low, trying to take him to the ground. Dish side-stepped, drawing his left leg back as the hard knuckles of his right hand slammed into the stranger's jaw; the loud crack heard over the noise of the rain. Dropping to his knees, the stranger shook his head. He got slowly to his feet, turning to face Dish; his jaw broken.

"The way you fight, it is no wonder you only beat up women," Dish stated, the disdain in his voice ringing clear. Bellowing incoherently, the stranger rushed in again, swinging a right fist toward Dish's chin. Dish shifted slightly, parrying the strike with his right palm. Reversing its course, the edge of his right hand smashed upward into the stranger's throat. The force of the blow caused the stranger to reel back, exposing his liver to the knuckles of Dish's left hand, which slammed into their target. The stranger doubled over from the force and pain of the strike, and the calloused edge of Dish's right hand struck the base of his skull. The man dropped and did not move. He was no longer breathing.

Dish moved to kneel beside Chanmali. She was clearly in pain.

"Chanmali? Are you okay, woman?" Chanmali tried to move. A gasp escaped her lips.

Gently lifting her into his arms, Dish carried her into their longhouse. He laid her carefully on the sleeping pallet. There was no doctor, but several in his group had rudimentary medical skills acquired by necessity during the war. They could handle broken ribs.

"Lie still," Dish ordered. "I will get Hai's wife to come and look after you. I must see about that man." Chanmali reached up and took Dish's hand in hers. She spoke in a whisper.

"I was never that man's wife. I was the oldest girl in my family with no husband. My father gave me to him to have one less mouth to feed. That man is a horrible monster. I refused to marry him. He beat me often, and he raped me. One day he beat me more than ever before. I wanted to die. I ran into the jungle, and I just kept running. It was that day you found me and saved me from the tiger. I owe you my life." Chanmali let go of Dish's hand. There were tears in her eyes.

In all this time, she'd never told him how she came to be injured and alone in the jungle that day. Life had made Dish a hard man, but this woman was good to him. She kept his house clean, cooked for him, was kind to him, and asked for little in return. And, she was loyal. That meant a great deal in Dish's world.

"Do not worry, Chanmali," Dish replied gently. "You are a good woman..." He paused. "I am happy that you are here with me." He got up and left the longhouse.

Several men stood around the body of the Laotian stranger. They looked up as Dish approached. He motioned toward Hai, who took a few steps forward.

"Hai, would you be kind enough to ask your wife to check on

Chanmali?"

"Certainly. Is Chanmali hurt badly?"

"I don't think so, but she may have a few broken ribs." Hai nodded and headed off to get his wife.

Hai quickly returned, his wife already on her way to see what she could do for Chanmali. He approached Dish and placed his hand on Dish's shoulder. "Go, see to Chanmali. We will take care of this."

Two other village men were already grabbing the wrists and ankles of the dead Laotian. They would find a place to bury the dead man in the valley below, some distance from the village. Dish nodded and turned to walk to his longhouse.

CHAPTER 7
CHICAGO, IL

Henry Chang sat at the desk in the small room he used for an office in their quiet Chicago suburban home. Scratching away at some budget figures for the physics department, he reached for the cup of hot tea his wife, Grace, had placed beside him moments ago. Being a physicist and a damn good one, Henry hated this part of his job. Administrative work bored him to death. But he was the physics department chairman for the University of Chicago, and this needed doing.

He heard the phone ringing in the background but ignored it. He knew Grace would get it. She was already in the kitchen, where the phone hung on the wall. As if on cue, the phone stopped ringing. Henry went back to his figures.

Several minutes went by. Henry looked up from his desk to see Grace standing in the doorway. It was hard for him to discern the look on her face, which was now quite pale.

"Grace, what is it? What's wrong?"

"It's Ellen." Grace's tone was hushed, her voice shaking.

Henry stood. "Ellen? Did something happen to Ellen?"

Grace took a step forward. Henry moved around the desk to his wife and took her arms in his hands. They were shivering. "Grace, tell me. What has happened?"

Grace blinked. "That was the government, someone from the State Department. She said Ellen is… missing. That nice boy, Norman, is missing too. They believe someone kidnapped them, but they aren't sure yet. The lady on the phone said they are doing all they can."

Henry caught his wife as she collapsed into his arms. He gently helped her to the old wingback chair he kept in the corner of his office. "Are you sure? Our Ellen?" He couldn't believe it.

"Yes, Ellen was giving Hepatitis vaccines to women and children in a village near that base in Niger she works from, and now she's missing. Norman is missing. That is all they know, at least for now."

Reaching up with his hand, Henry gently wiped a tear from his wife's cheek. "She will be alright, Grace. She will be alright. Ellen is a good woman, a strong woman. God will not let anything happen to her. God will protect her. You will see."

Grace did not reply. Henry wrapped his arms around her as she buried her face against his shoulder.

"It will be alright, Grace. I promise." Henry hoped with all his heart that it was true.

CHAPTER 8
FT BRAGG, NC

JD threw his duffel bag into the back of the jeep and reached down to give Ajax a scratch behind the ears. Ajax's crate, kibble, bowls, and other assorted gear were already loaded up. Ajax gave a soft woof of appreciation.

Golf Platoon, SEAL Team 5, finished up their two weeks of advanced specialized reconnaissance training at Ft. Bragg near Fayetteville, North Carolina. The platoon training involved working in close cooperation with Ajax. Over several years of deployments, the team had already developed quite a bond of trust with the dog, but the SEALs always welcomed the refresher training.

After the initial introduction period with Ajax and the team getting to know each other, Ajax had quickly become a hit with all the platoon members. Ajax, for his part, accepted each of them into his "pack." Even Maddux had been won over by Ajax's intelligence and abilities.

Just a few months after JD returned to Afghanistan with Ajax, they'd gotten orders to check out a sector north of Camp Shaheen, an Afghan army base near Mazar-i-Sharif. Intelligence reported an increase in Taliban activity in the area. After a recent, well-coordinated Taliban attack on the camp during which more than one hundred Afghan soldiers died, they were taking no chances.

JD and Ajax were on point, slowly working their way along a section of road used by both military and civilian traffic. Jackson and Sweeney handled communications with an AC-130 gunship that served as their eyes in the sky. Working with them was a Marine Corp Lance Corporal named Jennings, an explosive ordinance disposal specialist. The EOD specialist regularly assigned to their team was temporarily out of action with a severe case of food poisoning.

Suddenly, JD saw Ajax's ears shoot straight up. Something had him on alert.

"What is it, boy?" JD whispered, releasing the dog from his leash. Ajax worked better off-leash, and JD had learned to trust his canine partner's instincts. Ajax started forward, nose to the ground. JD followed, with Maddux and the rest of the team fanning out behind them. About twenty yards farther, Ajax's tail stood straight up and started to wag. It was one of his tells.

"Explosives," JD relayed back to the rest of the team. JD moved forward a bit behind Ajax, with the rest of the SEALs following about twenty yards behind. Suddenly, Ajax sat. JD marked the spot and called Ajax back to him. Jennings moved forward while the SEAL team covered him. Ajax had alerted on a well-hidden trigger switch. There was a second trigger switch a few yards away. Jennings carefully marked them and then located the improvised explosive device, wired and also well-hidden on the opposite side of the road. It was big, too big to move. Jennings disarmed the bomb. After a short discussion, they decided to blow it in place before finishing their patrol. Sweeney radioed back the bomb's location while Jennings set a charge to destroy it.

After moving back to a safe distance, Jennings gave a warning. "Fire in the hole!" The explosion was impressive.

Maddux let out a low whistle. "That is one smart fucking dog! We could've been fucked up!" Maddux moved over and gave Ajax a heartfelt pat on the head. "I owe you one, Ajax." After the pat on the head, Ajax and Maddux were buddies.

Now, months later, the team engaged in the training at Ft. Bragg. You could always improve your skills, and while the team sharpened their abilities with Ajax, they also got a chance to see how the two new guys handled themselves. Carlos Vivas replaced Jonesy, who'd retired a few months back. Vivas had immigrated from Puerto Rico when he turned eighteen and immediately enlisted in the Navy. Natural ability and hard work had landed him in the Basic Underwater Demolition/SEAL program. After completing training, Vivas got assigned to Golf Platoon, SEAL Team 5, where Chief Whitley appointed him the duties of primary driver/navigator, shifting Jackson permanently to communications. Jonesy had been the team's last communications expert, but Jackson had filled the spot for the last several months and seemed to have a real knack for it.

Axel, too, had called it quits when he reached his twenty years. Axel's replacement was Joe Palazzolo, the newest member of Team 5. Joe was of Sicilian descent and proud of it. He loved to regale the other guys with stories of growing up Sicilian in the Bronx. They had some difficulty coming up with a suitable nickname for Joe, finally settling on Pallie. Joe slipped into Axel's position as the team's heavy weapons operator, a job he seemed to delight in and took very seriously.

Both rookies had performed well during their unofficial probation period. While Joe was still the new guy and got the shit details, the other team members had already accepted him. He just needed a new 'new guy' so he could pass the shit details along.

The only sour note during this training exercise had occurred while taking a short break out on one of the ranges at Ft. Bragg. Sweeney squatted down near a log, leaning back against his rucksack for support when he suddenly let out a loud curse.

"Sonofabitch!" He jumped up, looking down where he'd just been squatting.

"What's up, Sweeney?" Chief Whitley asked. Sweeney was clutching the left cheek of his butt.

"Sonofabitch!" he repeated. "A fucking copperhead just bit me in the ass!"

"Are you kidding me?" the Chief responded. Maddux and Pallie started to laugh. Jackson, who had been closest to Sweeney, jumped up, moving away.

"Where?" he asked. "I don't see any damn snake." Sweeney pointed at the ground. JD followed the line of Sweeney's arm and moved over toward where he was looking, getting there just in time to spot a copperhead slithering off into the underbrush.

"Ajax! Zit!" Ajax had made a move to follow the copperhead into the brush, and JD did not want Ajax to get bitten. Ajax sat, but let out an excited whine. JD laughed. "Yep! It was a copperhead, alright. A big one too, maybe three feet!"

Vivas laughed. "Somebody's going to have to cut Sweeney's ass and suck the venom out."

'What kind of *chooch* would sit on a copperhead?" Pallie interjected, trying to conceal a broad grin.

"Ain't nobody cutting my ass!" Sweeney retorted.

"Belay all that shit!" Chief Whitley ordered. "Maddux, get on the radio and call this in. See if we can get Sweeney a lift out of here. The snake bite probably won't kill him, but we better not take any chances." Trying to suppress his grin, Maddux reached for the radio handset. Forty minutes later, a Humvee pulled up, and an embarrassed Sweeney cursed as he climbed into the back for the short ride to the aid station.

"Shit!" Sweeney muttered. "Right before we start a thirty-day leave. This sucks!" As the Humvee drove off, Pallie looked at the chief.

"Will Sweeney have to use his leave while seeing the medics for a snake bite? That does suck if he does."

"That would serve his dumb ass right, but no. I don't think he'll be there long; day or two, maybe. They'll probably give him some anti-venom shots and send his sorry ass on its way. Sweeney will be okay; he's a frogman." Pallie nodded, satisfied.

The rest of the day went without incident. The squad completed their final tracking exercise with Ajax leading the way, then humped the seven miles back to their temporary barracks, training over.

JD was tired. While he was in great shape, at forty-years-old, the pace was beginning to take its toll. Ajax was starting to have digestive issues, and JD was pretty sure it was a sign of stress from so many deployments. He was worried about what might happen to Ajax if they drew another tour in Iraq. JD knew Ajax loved to work, but their work was highly stressful for both two-legged and four-legged operators. Thankfully, JD only had seven months left in this last commitment. Then he and Ajax would both be done. He had already submitted the paperwork to take Ajax when he retired. Chief Whitley assured him several weeks back that it would be approved.

"Ajax is too damn good a dog to do anything else. If they make any other decision, SEAL Team 5 will declare war on those assholes. We've got his back like he's had ours so many times." Whitley promised.

Completing their training at Ft. Bragg, JD called his parents to see about driving up to spend a week or so with them in Knoxville. After that, he figured he and Ajax could spend the remainder of their thirty-day leave driving from Knoxville back to San Diego, with plenty of time for sightseeing.

Of course, both Curtis and Mai were excited about seeing JD Mai put the phone on the speaker before telling JD she would let Annie and Robert know he was coming in. The two had settled in Nashville after they were married, where Robert practiced sports medicine at Vanderbilt Medical Center. Annie worked part-time for a successful CPA firm, allowing her to spend more time with their two young boys, Allen and Jimmy.

"They can't wait to meet their uncle; a real, live Navy SEAL," his mother went on. JD heard his dad laughing in the background.

It was a pleasant call, but JD could tell something was not quite right. He chose not to press the issue over the phone, but his dad sounded tired.

The next day, the team had their equipment stowed and ready for transport back to Coronado on a C-17. Pallie naturally drew the shit detail and had to escort the gear back to Coronado, then secure it before he could begin his leave. There was a little grumbling, but it was mostly good-natured. That was just how things worked. Pallie wouldn't be the new guy forever. JD, who'd driven out to Ft. Bragg for the training, was packed and ready to head toward Knoxville.

"Okay, Ajax. Let's load up." Ajax leaped up into the back of the jeep and settled down in his crate. JD secured the gate and closed the tailgate. Going around to the front, he slid into the driver's seat, cranked the engine, and pointed the jeep toward Tennessee. It was a pretty good drive, and JD was anxious to see his dad.

It took about six hours from Ft. Bragg, NC to Knoxville, TN. Shortly before crossing the state line, JD wheeled the jeep into a rest area and stretched his legs while Ajax watered a few bushes. Following the brief bit of exercise with a drink of cold water for Ajax and a diet Mountain Dew from the vending machine for himself, they continued on their way. A few miles later, they passed a sign, "Welcome to Tennessee."

It was another hour or so before the jeep pulled into the driveway at the Cordell home in Knoxville. JD killed the engine, opened the door, got out and stretched. He went around to the back of the jeep to let Ajax out. Ajax bounded out of the vehicle and happily made for the front door. JD's mother opened the door just as Ajax leaped up the front porch steps. Mai dropped down to meet Ajax with a big hug, laughing happily as the dog joyfully licked her face.

"Hi, Mom," JD greeted as he stepped up on the porch. Mai stood and gave her son a warm hug, kissing his cheek.

"It's so good to see you, JD" Mai stepped back to give him a look. "You look tired. Come on in and sit down. Your dad is in the den, and your things can wait a few minutes. Let me get Ajax's food, and I'll feed him in the kitchen. Then I will join you." JD started to protest, but Mai stopped him. "It's no trouble, and I want to do it. Can I bring you something to drink when I come?

Resistance was futile. "Sure, Mom. A glass of unsweetened iced tea if you have it, or even water would be fine. Ajax's bowls and food are in the back of the jeep. It's unlocked."

"Okay. Now, go see your dad." Mai started toward the back of the jeep with Ajax trotting happily along beside her.

JD made his way to the den, where he found his dad sitting back in a recliner.

"Hey, Dad!" Curtis pressed the lever and sat up in the chair. He got up, gave JD a big hug, and sat back down.

"JD, it's good to see you. How are you?"

"I'm fine, Dad. How are you doing?" JD was a bit shocked. His dad not only looked tired, but it looked like he had lost some weight.

"I'm fine. Have a seat. You look good. Tired, but good." Curtis paused. He could tell his son wasn't buying it. JD stood there, waiting. Finally, Curtis shrugged. "Well, the truth is, JD, I am not doing well."

"What's the matter, Dad?" JD asked, waiting quietly for his father to go on.

"Well, it started a few months ago. I was feeling tired, you know, just not myself. And, I was losing weight. Then I started itching, like a rash. Figured I had a virus or something, so I went to the doctor and got a check-up. The doc wasn't sure what was going on, so she ran some blood tests. The short version is that it turns out I have cholangiocarcinoma, which I guess is a fancy way of saying liver cancer."

"Oh shit."

"Yeah. It's a real bitch. Turns out what I have is caused by some parasite I picked up in Vietnam. It's some critter called liver flukes. From what I've learned, it's a parasitic flatworm that lives in the rivers in Vietnam. You can get it from eating undercooked or raw fish, and you can get it through cross-contamination, whatever the hell that means. You know, sometimes on those long-range patrols, the rations would run out. We ate what we could. I guess you'd understand that."

JD nodded. He certainly did understand that. Fortunately, they now had more options than when his dad was in Vietnam.

"A fair number of Vietnam vets are now turning up with it, according to the doc at the V.A. She said this problem could remain undetected for decades and you won't know you have it. The damn worms can be killed with a few pills if you catch it early, but I never knew I had it."

"So, what does all this mean?" JD asked quietly.

"Well, with the symptoms I have, it is pretty much in its final stages. It isn't good, son. I am getting treatment, but the prognosis is not good."

JD sat down on the sofa, not sure what to say.

"What is the prognosis?" he finally asked.

Curtis sat back in his chair. "The doctor thinks I have maybe a year, maybe less."

JD nodded and said nothing. The two men sat quietly for a time. Nothing needed to be said. What could either man say?

A short while later, Mai entered the room and handed JD a glass of unsweetened iced tea.

"Would you like anything, Curtis?" she asked.

"No thanks, babe, I'm fine." Mai went over and sat on the couch next to JD, giving him a pat on the arm. A few minutes later, Ajax, having finished his supper, entered the den and made himself comfortable, keeping Mai's feet warm. JD reached over and put his arm around his mother.

"Your dad told you?"

"I told him," Curtis answered.

JD found himself at a loss for words; he could only nod. Mai reached over and patted his knee.

"It's okay. We can talk later. Maybe we can find something good to watch on the television." Curtis retrieved the remote from the table by his chair and started surfing the channels. There wasn't much on. They decided to watch an old black and white movie starring Cary Grant called *Arsenic and Old Lace* that started in about twenty minutes. JD excused himself and quietly left the den. He went out to the jeep, got his luggage and Ajax's traveling gear, and moved it to his room, which now served as a guest room. He returned to the den just as the movie was beginning.

The week spent with his father was a good one, despite the bad news. Curtis refused to discuss his health situation. Few people outside the immediate family knew. Tuesday was family night at Coal Creek Armory, so the three of them headed to the range to do a little shooting. Curtis and Mai both enjoyed going to the range and maintained a family membership. Mai was an excellent shot due to Curtis' coaching, but both were very impressed with JD's prowess with his Glock 19.

"Damn glad you're on our side," Curtis commented with a grin when JD's target came back to the shooting station. There was only one, slightly ragged hole, about an inch in diameter, where the center circle had once been. JD had set the target out fifty yards.

JD laughed. "I get lots of practice." JD looked at his mother's target and whistled. Her pattern was not much larger and with just a few outlying holes. "Dang. Mom. You're a regular Annie Oakley with that MP9."

"I have an excellent teacher," she replied, giving her husband an appreciative pat on the shoulder. "Besides, I was only shooting at ten yards... not fifty!" Mai, done shooting for the day, waited while Curtis and JD both shot a couple more magazines before calling it quits.

"Let's go get some lunch," Curtis suggested.

"Where do you want to go, JD?" his mother asked.

"Oh, I don't know." JD thought about it for a minute. "Is the Stock and Barrel still open?"

"It sure is," Curtis replied enthusiastically. His father liked the great little bourbon and burger bar as much as JD did. "Let's go."

All three were quite hungry and started with an order of crispy 'shrooms as an appetizer. The fried mushrooms came with a dipping sauce made with Tennessee honey, grain mustard, and creamed horseradish. They were delicious and one of Mai's favorites.

Mai ordered the Ring of Fire, a spicy burger with great flavor. Curtis settled on the Steakhouse burger with barrel-aged cheddar cheese and mushrooms. JD decided on the bison burger, but kept it plain, with American cheese, ketchup, and mayo. He also ordered fries, paying two dollars extra to have them fried in duck fat. It gave the fries a wonderful flavor. All three settled on ice water with lemon, not wanting anything to take away from the burgers.

There was little discussion during the meal. When the three finished their burgers, JD and his father each ordered a bourbon on the rocks, choosing the Corsair Triple Smoke. Curtis liked its smooth, smoky flavor. Mai settled back with a glass of Raeburn Chardonnay.

"When are you and Ajax leaving for San Diego?" his mother asked.

"I was planning on leaving Sunday morning," JD replied. "There is no real hurry. Ajax and I could take our time and do some sightseeing on the drive out." He paused. "But I can stay longer, I mean, under the circumstances."

"I appreciate that JD, but there is nothing you can do. Stick with your plans. You and Ajax should leave Sunday and enjoy a nice leisurely trip back to San Diego. You can both probably use the break, and it'll be a chance to unwind. Your mother and I will let you know if anything changes. I promise."

Mai nodded. "Yes, JD. Your father is right. If anything changes, we will let you know." She took a sip from her wine glass and smiled. "Annie and Robert wanted to drive over Friday with the twins. The boys were so excited to meet you. Unfortunately, both are sick with some kind of bug, so it will have to wait."

The pleasant conversation continued for some time. It was nice to catch up. There'd been so few chances for them to talk because of the intense schedule SEALs maintain.

Finally finished with their drinks, Mai paid the check despite JD's protests, and the three strolled back to the car, checking out the storefront windows on Market Square, mostly bars and food establishments with a few clothing shops and gift shops. Market Square had changed a great deal over the years JD had been away. Crossing Gay Street, they cut down beside the Riviera Cinema and were soon back at the State Street Garage and on their way home.

CHAPTER 9
VIETNAM

Dish led his men along a trail that ran just below the top of the ridge overlooking Xayden. The Land Cruisers were back in their shed, the weapons and ammunition now carried by Dish's men for the remaining hike back to their rock shelf hideout. They encountered no travelers while climbing the ridge. It was late and beginning to get dark. The men were all tired from the long ride on bumpy mountain roads. The stress of maintaining constant vigilance during the fifteen-hour drive from Sisaket also took its toll.

They came to a small clearing in a secluded cut along the ridge. It would be a dry camp, but they carried water, and it was a place to rest. The clearing was known to gun runners and drug smugglers alike and was utilized by both. In an honor-among-thieves arrangement, the camp was neutral ground, and trouble typically avoided.

Entering the clearing, Dish's men set their heavy wicker baskets down and began a simple evening meal of rice cakes, drinking water from their canteens. Tomorrow would put them safely back in their village. A couple of the men, already stretched out and using their wicker baskets as backrests, were trying to get some sleep.

Dish was suddenly alert, and a few of the men sat up. They heard voices coming up the narrow path to the clearing.

Three men stepped into the clearing. From their appearance, they were drug smugglers. They were unkempt and dirty, with eyes red from sampling too much of their product. Dish looked them over with an indifferent eye. All three were heavily armed and carrying wicker baskets similar to their own. The only difference being the contents.

The three newcomers lifted their hands in greeting and moved to an empty spot in the clearing. Setting their packs down, two men stepped over to the edge of the clearing to urinate. The third man pulled a small metal container and a pocketknife from his pants pocket. Opening a lid on the metal box and using the knife's blade, he carefully scooped a small quantity of white powder from the metal box and held it to his right nostril. He snorted loudly and then licked any powder residue from the knife. Closing the container and the pocketknife, he slipped them back into his pocket. Only then did he focus his attention on Dish, who was watching the man's every movement. Dish's right hand rested casually on his right hip where it was only inches from an old Browning BDA .45 he carried in an equally old leather holster on his belt.

The man grinned at Dish. "It's been a long walk today. Do you have any food you can share with us?"

Dish paused a few minutes before answering. "I am sorry, but no. We have little enough for ourselves, and tomorrow's trip is long."

Dish had little regard for drug smugglers and would not have shared food with them even if he had plenty. He considered them to be the lowest sort of scum, dealing in human misery.

The leader of the smugglers glanced at Dish and smiled. It was not a warm smile.

"You would do better to share what you have. Don't you know who we work for?"

Dish shrugged, having no idea and not caring.

"We work for the biggest warlord in the region. He will swat you like the pesky insect you are."

Dish chuckled. "And, just who is this powerful man who makes his money turning women into prostitutes and selling poison to children?"

"Surely, you have heard of Colonel Trần," the drug smuggler continued boastfully. "A brilliant leader of our Viet Cong brothers during the war against the foolish Americans."

Dish's reaction was instantaneous, recognition bringing the rage he carried suppressed in his heart to an instant boiling point.

"Say that name again," Dish ordered, his voice now ice cold, emotionless.

"You heard me, Colonel Trần..."

Dish shot the man through the heart. The smuggler standing to the dead man's left tried to slip the battered AK-47 off his shoulder and bring it up to fire. He was too slow. Dish shot the second smuggler twice in the chest. The third smuggler stepped back, both hands raised in the air. He did not want to die. Dish pointed the barrel of the Browning pistol at the third smuggler but did not pull the trigger.

"What is your name?" Dish's voice was devoid of any emotion.

"My name is Phan. I am just a smuggler. I know nothing of these things," Phan replied, his voice betraying his fear.

"Phan," Dish repeated. "You go back to your Colonel Trần, and you tell that piece of cattle dung that the Montagnard, Dish, is going to come for him. You tell Trần that Dish, the Montagnard, is going to kill him."

The smuggler, shaking and desperate to remain alive, nodded. "Yes! Yes! I will do as you say." The terrified man took a last glance at Dish, then turned and fled back down the path toward the main trail.

A couple of Dish's men dragged the two lifeless bodies into the jungle, rolling them into a ravine some thirty yards from the clearing. A newer member of the group approached Dish, who was now reloading the old Belgian Browning's magazine from a bag of cartridges he kept in a pouch at this left hip.

"Excuse me for asking, but who is this Colonel Trần of which you spoke? It is clear you have some history with this drug lord."

Dish looked up at the man. While new to the village, Poh had shown himself to be trustworthy and did not shirk his responsibilities. Dish respected this in any man and decided to answer the question.

"Trần is a former Viet Cong commander. He is an evil, wretched dog responsible for killing many Montagnard and South Vietnamese people. Trần massacred the women and children of my village because our village men fought for the Americans during the war. I believe Trần is responsible for killing the family of my adopted Vietnamese sister, Mai, who now lives in America. Now, Trần kills our people with drugs, turning our women into prostitutes and our children into criminals. I swore long ago to kill this man when I got the chance. Now, perhaps, his time has come."

Poh digested what he'd just heard. He was South Vietnamese and had fought in the war against the communists. Poh had taken a Degar woman as his wife. He understood.

" I will help you if you will let me." Poh turned and walked back to

45

where his pack lay and sat, leaning back against it. It was time to get some sleep.

Dish finished loading his Browning, holstered it, and leaned back against a tree. His smaller pack was not suitable as a backrest. He closed his eyes to rest but couldn't sleep. Thoughts of his adopted sister Mai and the American soldier returned and swirled through his brain. The American he'd found injured in the jungle had been a good man. He had carried the American to his village on his back, where Mai had tended to his injuries.

Dish absentmindedly fingered the hilt of the Buck General, a bowie-style knife the American had presented to him as a gift the day he and Mai left the village. Mai had guided the American safely to a U.S. military base. Dish had wanted to go himself, but could not. He later received word that Mai had indeed married the American officer and left for America with him. He smiled again. That was good. His sister would have a much better life in America than if she had stayed in Vietnam.

I wonder if they have any children.

Dish rolled over on his side and grabbed his pack to use as a pillow. He needed to get some sleep.

Sleep did not come easily. Hearing Trần's name again had stirred up old memories. Dish's brain kept cycling through the events surrounding the Battle of Dak To, where he'd learned of the massacre of his village.

The Battle of Dak To, later known as the "border battles," had been a series of military actions. The North Vietnamese launched several offensive operations during the second half of 1967. These operations targeted Loc Ninh in Binh Long Province, Song Be in Phuoc Long Province, and Con Thein and Khe Sanh in Quang Tri Province. The goal was to draw the American forces and their South Vietnamese allies toward the border region, away from major cities in preparation for their primary objective, the Tet Offensive. The resulting battles were some of the bloodiest and hardest fought battles of the Vietnam War. While they were considered tactical victories for the U.S. and South Vietnamese forces, they were strategic victories for the communist North because they achieved their goal.

Dak To was the location of one of the camps in a chain of Civilian Irregular Defense Group (CIDG) camps advised by U.S. Special

Forces personnel. Dak To sat in the west-central region of Kontum Province. Dish, leading a thirty-man Montagnard platoon based in Dak To, had played an essential role in those bloody border battles. His detachment of fierce Montagnard fighters, armed with a hodge-podge of American-made weapons, fought valiantly beside their American allies. Dish had also made efficient use of his Buck General bowie knife.

With seven members of his Montagnard crew, Dish had just returned from accompanying a four-man recon team on a scouting mission. The team, led by Lieutenant Steven Kulwicki from the 3rd Special Forces Group, consisted of the radio operator, Corporal David Sawinski, Staff Sergeant Ed Manning, and Sergeant Leon Haywood. During the mission debriefing, Lt. Kulwicki got word that the Viet Cong had recently slaughtered all the men, women, and children living in a Montagnard village located northwest of Dak To. There were few survivors, only a small number who managed to flee into the jungle and hide. The VC spared no one, not older men and women, young women with children, or even babies.

A well-organized and especially brutal unit of Viet Cong had moved into the region surrounding the village, to tax and terrorize the local populace into submission. The slaughter was in reprisal for the villagers' support of the American forces. Some of this information came from a Viet Cong soldier captured by a platoon from the 2nd Battalion, 503 Infantry sent to survey the damage to the village and render aid. Lt. Kulwicki passed the info on to Staff Sergeant Manning. During one of his conversations with Dish, Manning had learned the name of his village.

Dish had received the tragic news from Manning stoically. Manning placed his hand on Dish's shoulder, a genuine gesture of sympathy and understanding.

"I am very sorry, my friend," Manning said. Dish nodded, his dark eyes remaining impassive. The Staff Sergeant nodded and turned to walk back to his quarters.

Dish appreciated Manning's sincere sentiment but had no words to express his feelings. Sorrow and rage welled up inside him. One good thought that managed to pierce through the violent storm raging in Dish's mind was that Mai no longer lived in the village.

A few days later, there was additional information. Dish learned from Manning that the leader of the Viet Cong unit that conducted the slaughter was known. While interrogating a second captured Viet Cong soldier, a South Korean intelligence officer learned that a Viet Cong Colonel named Trần Nam Tin, had ordered the raid. It was a name Dish would never forget.

Eventually, Dish fell into a short, fitful sleep. Morning came way too early. He and his men had a light breakfast of rice cakes, washing them down with water. As Dish ate, his mind returned to his thoughts of the previous night. He had few regrets considering how his life had unfolded. Perhaps his one big disappointment was that he would never see his sister, Mai, or the American officer again. He would have liked to see them both, but that was now impossible.

CHAPTER 10
CORONADO NAVAL BASE

The sun was rising as JD and Ajax finished their early morning five-mile run along Coronado Beach. JD had always enjoyed being fit, but now, as he got older, he felt additional pressure to keep ahead of the newer, younger members of the team. It would certainly not do to be shown up by a new guy. So, Ajax and JD both worked extra hard to keep their edge.

It was a beautiful morning for a run. The temperature was a pleasant seventy-five degrees, and there was a steady breeze blowing in off the Pacific. JD loved the taste of the salty ocean air.

Both man and K9 worked to get their breathing back under control as they trotted from the beach to the parking lot. By the time they reached the jeep, both were breathing a bit more regularly. Piling in, JD started the engine and pointed the Jeep toward the off-base housing he and Ajax now rented. JD had recently taken the Jeep's top off, allowing Ajax to enjoy the wind when they were on the road. Ajax loved riding in the Jeep and sat up tall in the back, his keen nose busily analyzing whatever wealth of information the wind carried. JD's recent promotion to Senior Chief made living off-post a lot more affordable. He and Ajax had recently moved into a two-story duplex not too far from the base.

Being single, JD had spent most of his career living in on-post quarters to save money but had finally decided off-post housing wasn't such a bad idea. It afforded him more privacy and provided more opportunities for a social life. Over the years, JD had wandered in and out of various romantic entanglements but never seemed to find the right woman with whom to settle down. He was beginning to wonder if a family of his own would be in his future. His recent promotion to Senior Chief meant that he would probably soon be assigned to another SEAL platoon as a Platoon Chief, that is unless Chief Whitley retired. JD wasn't sure he wanted this. He enjoyed working with Ajax and the men on his team. And besides, he planned to retire shortly anyway, just as soon as he could take Ajax with him.

The Jeep turned in to the driveway on their side of the brick two-story duplex. Ajax bounded toward the door with JD close behind him. Unlocking the door, JD stepped into the foyer followed closely by Ajax, who headed straight for his water bowl in the kitchen. JD dropped his sweat towel on the floor of the laundry room and made his way through the bedroom to the bathroom. He was looking forward to a hot shower when the ring of his cell phone caught his attention. Glancing at the phone's display, he recognized the number.

"Cordell here."

"JD, grab Ajax and get your ass in here. Something just came down from Special Operations Command."

"Yes sir, we're on the way. We'll be there in twenty minutes."

"Good. See you in twenty." JD ran upstairs, quickly changed, and, grabbing his war bag, was back at the door in just a few minutes. The shower would have to wait. Ajax's war gear was already at SEAL Team 5's headquarters on the base.

"Let's go, Ajax. Duty calls!" Ajax knew what the tone in JD's voice meant. His ears perked up, and he trotted to the door, ready to go. Exiting the duplex, they climbed back into the jeep, and JD drove as rapidly as possible to the Operations and Logistics Support Facility at Coronado. Seventeen minutes later, they parked and made their way into the building.

The Operations and Logistics Support Facility consisted of three stories. The first floor was constructed of concrete masonry. The second and third were both composed of Kynar-coated insulated aluminum panels. The facility housed storage rooms, where Ajax's gear was stored, a gym for physical training, a space for specialized hand-to-hand combat training, individual personal lockers, classrooms, offices, and administrative areas. JD opened the door and entered with Ajax walking on his left side.

It was unusually quiet in the classroom where the men of Golf Platoon, SEAL Team 5, began to gather. When JD and Ajax entered, only a few fluorescent lights were on. JD spotted Joe Palazzolo—aka Pallie—seated in a chair in a dark corner, leaning against the wall, sleeping. Vivas and Jackson sat at a table playing gin rummy with a deck of old worn-out cards Jackson kept in his locker.

JD grinned. "Damn, Jackson, when are you going to replace those old cards? Do they even shuffle anymore? "

"Can't replace them, JD," Jackson replied. "These cards are marked! Shit! I'd have to start all over again, marking a new deck." Vivas frowned and looked carefully at the backs of the cards in his hand. Jackson broke out laughing.

"Just fucking with you, Vivas! They're good."

A few minutes later, Pete Sweeney, closely followed by Jim Maddux, entered the room, dropped bags near the door, and took seats at one of the tables. Sweeney opened a can of Pepsi and swiveled around to watch the card game in progress. Maddux called Ajax over to him and began to vigorously ruffle the dog's neck, which Ajax seemed to enjoy immensely.

Maddux called over to JD, who'd taken a seat at another table. "Hey, JD! How's Ajax today?"

"He's good," JD replied. "Same as always. Ready to rock and roll!" The ruffling completed, Ajax trotted back over to where JD was seated and lay down near his feet, waiting.

Chief Mike Whitley, the Team Leader, entered the room, followed by another operator they all knew well. Leroy Washington was a damn good SEAL and a respected member of Echo Platoon.

Grinning, Maddux jumped to his feet, "Hey Chief, what's up?" Typically, within their group, the team was a bit more casual in attitude, but Maddux felt it was a special occasion, seeing how they now had a visitor from Echo Platoon.

"Settle down, Maddux," Chief Whitley responded. "You all know Leroy here. He's volunteered to help us out, bring us up to full squad strength for this mission."

Whitley stood at the podium in front of a large whiteboard and dropped some files on the table. He flipped a switch, and the projector mounted on the ceiling began to warm up, casting a map of Northern Africa on a screen beside the whiteboard.

"Let's get to business." The cards quickly disappeared into their box and then into Jackson's pocket. Pallie moved from the corner where he was dozing to the center of the classroom and took a seat. The levity from a few moments earlier evaporated. SEAL Team 5 was now all business.

"Gentlemen, we have a rescue mission." Whitley pointed to a spot on the map. "We are going to Agadez, Niger, to rescue a doctor and another possible surviving member of her team. They were kidnapped two days ago by an al Qaeda-associated group in northern Niger. The doctor's name is Ellen Chang."

The picture of an attractive young Asian woman in a medical jacket appeared on the screen. Whitley went on.

"She had an assistant with her, one Norman Holley, also kidnapped."

A picture of a young man with longish blond hair in a dark t-shirt and jeans appeared on the screen. The young man was grinning happily.

"There was also a Dutch mercenary, Bram Alderik, who was providing security. He was killed in the kidnapping but managed to take out several of the kidnappers." There was a quiet moment as the team absorbed this information.

"What the hell was this doctor doing in that Godforsaken part of the world?" Sweeney asked, finally breaking the silence.

"Dr. Chang is a member of Doctors Without Borders. She was trying to contain a Hepatitis E outbreak among the locals, working from Base 201—the new Predator drone base being built just outside Agadez. The team had almost completed a sweep of several villages and were ready to start back when the kidnappers hit. Al Qaeda is demanding a $5 million ransom for Dr. Chang's safe return. They have not mentioned Holley. These assholes have given the U.S. ten days to comply, or they are threatening to cut off her head and stick it on a pole in Agadez. We are taking them at their word." Whitley paused. "You all know the official policy on negotiating with terrorists."

Heads nodded around the room.

"The president wants to make an example of these assholes. Snatch an innocent American citizen, especially one doing humanitarian work, and there are consequences; you get whacked."

"Shit," Sweeney replied. "It's about damn time!"

There were several murmurs of agreement.

Whitley continued the briefing. "Through a local CIA asset, we have learned that Dr. Chang and Holley are currently being held in Agadez, in a section of the city known to be populated by al Qaeda sympathizers. That source has been inside the location and saw both Chang and Holley alive. The location is being monitored, and we will be updated when we arrive on the scene."

Whitley paused, looking around the room. "Gentlemen, this part of the city is not under positive U.S. control. The president does not want another Mogadishu. This rescue will be a clean operation. In and out, no fuck ups!"

"How good is this source's intelligence?" Maddux asked.

"According to the CIA, this source has always been reliable. He has a special hatred for al Qaeda. Something personal, but I am not privy to what."

"Do we know the strength and capabilities of the opposing force?" JD asked.

"The same source estimates this group currently has about twenty-five to thirty members, but the odds are only a few will be guarding Doc Chang and Holley. No way to tell exactly. They are, however, well-armed."

JD nodded.

Pallie spoke up. "What's the plan, Chief?"

"Glad you asked, Pallie," Chief Whitley replied. "There isn't an easy way to get to Base 201, especially if we want to avoid detection. The team will leave this afternoon and fly, compliments of the U.S. Air Force, to Italy, and from there to Camp Lemonnier in Djibouti. From Lemonnier, we fly into Base 201. Unfortunately, there are no carriers currently in a position to assist with this operation, and it would take too long to get one there. Camp Lemonnier is the only base we have in Africa, so it will have to do."

Whitley paused a few seconds to make sure everyone was still with him. They were.

"Once there, we will be shuttled to Base 201 on cargo jets flying the regular supply runs for the new base. The base employs local labor, so we can assume al Qaeda will have eyes and ears all over. The idea is to come in on an already scheduled supply flight. This way, there should be nothing out of the ordinary to arouse anyone's curiosity. Once on base, we will hook up with the CIA operative and his local asset to finalize plans.

"Four Humvees will be available to us, as well as two Blackhawks.

The choppers will be placed on alert when we go in for quick extraction and support if needed. The Blackhawks at Base 201 currently fly security missions as well as supply runs."

"Sounds like a plan," Vivas commented. "What time do we leave?"

Whitley looked at his watch. "Wheels up at 1300 hours. Get your shit together." With that, the chief turned and walked from the room.

"Alright! You heard the man!" Jackson quipped. "This is what frogmen get paid for. Get your asses moving." Sweeney threw his empty Pepsi can at the grinning Jackson, who easily ducked it as they filed out the door and headed off to collect their gear.

Both the flight from Coronado to Aviano Air Force Base in Italy and the flight from there to Camp Lemonnier in Djibouti were smooth and uneventful. The eight men slept, listened to music, checked over their gear, and chatted quietly.

During the stopover at Aviano, an Air Force Colonel approached Chief Whitely and spoke quietly with him for a few minutes. When the Colonel left, Whitley called the team together and announced they had a few hours to kill while they serviced the transport jet and loaded some additional cargo for Camp Lemonnier. The Colonel had welcomed the team to use the dining facility to wait, but given the time they had, suggested that they might take advantage of the situation to try one of the great restaurants in the city of Pordenone. The team liked the sound of that and, with orders to be back in three hours, caught a couple of taxis into the city.

While it was not Sicily, Pallie was very excited to be in Italy again and took charge, leading the team to Due Lune, one of the best local Italian restaurants, for dinner. He'd lived on Aviano airbase for two years while his father was stationed there during his years in the Air Force. While it had been a few years, Pallie still remembered his way around. Most of the team wanted spaghetti and meatballs and, at Pallie's suggestion, ordered ragu bolognese, which was unanimously declared "amazing." Joe Palazzolo had a dish that contained mussels and a variety of other seafood. While a few others were intrigued, none were brave enough to try it. Pallie feigned being disgusted.

"Damn! A bunch of snake eaters scared of a few mussels. What a bunch of freaking polli!" he exclaimed. Vivas threw a meatball at him.

"Alright, guys. Don't get us thrown out of here!" JD interjected. Pallie deftly took his fork and stabbed the meatball, which had bounced off his chest and landed in his mussels, and popped it into his mouth.

"Yeah! Wise up..." he added while chewing. They all enjoyed their dinner, even with limiting themselves to just a few glasses of vino. When coffee was over, they paid their checks and caught two more taxis back to the airbase. A short time after they arrived on base, the SEAL team loaded up and, once again airborne, continued toward Camp Lemonnier.

As the team settled in for the flight, Vivas shifted over to where JD was sitting, scratching Ajax's ears.

"Hey, Cordell," Vivas began. "Let me ask you something."

"Sure, Vivas. What's up?"

"I heard you are pretty damn good with some karate or something. I mean, not that tippy-tap tournament shit, but real old-fashioned take-no-prisoners shit! Is that real?"

JD sat quietly for a few minutes, weighing his response. Vivas, while still a newer member of the team, had paid his dues and earned the respect of his mates. He was solid. JD made up his mind.

"Yeah, I guess you could say that. What I do is a blend. My father studied a Vietnamese martial art when he was in Vietnam. My mother is Vietnamese, and she was the daughter of a village elder who was a well-respected practitioner of that system. It's called Nguyen-Ryu. Both my father and mother were pretty good at it, and I learned a lot from them. Then, as a young kid, I studied Isshin-Ryu with an Okinawan instructor in Knoxville, Tennessee, and he was excellent." JD paused. "It was no-nonsense. Real personal combat stuff. What I do is a blend of the two systems." JD paused to scratch Ajax again. "They have a lot in common."

"Cool," Vivas replied. "I grew up studying Escrima. My father is an Escrima instructor. He trained for years with a guy he met while in the Marines. His instructor's name was Advincula. Advincula was a drill instructor with my dad. Anyway, Advincula taught Lago Y Mano Escrima and Isshin-ryu Karate, I think.

"Yep. You're right. I've met Sensei Advincula." JD responded. "My instructor, Tokumura, and Sherman Harrill and AJ Advincula all trained on Okinawa together. Tokumura was one of Tatsuo Shimabuku's top Okinawan students. All three were good, but Sherman Harrill was truly scary. It was amazing how hard he could hit." JD paused, remembering the several times he'd been the recipient of some of Sensei Harrill's strikes, in an informative manner, of course. He went on. "I've heard of Escrima. Isn't that Spanish for fencing or something like that?"

"Sort of, " Vivas replied. "I guess you could say it is a Filipinization of the Spanish word for fencing, esgrima. We often use sticks to train, but they are knife or machete techniques. They also translate very smoothly to empty hand techniques. Like what you do, it's efficient."

"Interesting," JD observed. "We should compare notes sometime."

"Yeah! I'd like that," Vivas replied. "The hand-to-hand training we get is not bad, but it pales in comparison to what you can learn from a real combat arts system. Let's do that sometime—train a little bit. See what comes out of it."

JD smiled. "Sure. That would be interesting."

Djibouti sits on the Horn of Africa, directly across the Gulf of Aden from Yemen. It is home to mostly French and Arabic-speaking people and consists mainly of dry shrublands, deserts, and volcanic formations. Djibouti is also home to Lake Assai, which sits in the Danakil Desert, and is one of the saltiest bodies of water on the planet. The country boasts a beautiful shoreline with many amazing beaches on the Gulf of Aden, but unfortunately, there was no time for the team to enjoy a day at the beach.

Camp Lemonnier is designated as a United States Naval Expeditionary Base and is headquarters to the Combined Joint Task Force-Horn of Africa. It is currently the only permanent U.S. military base on the continent of Africa. The 474th Air Expeditionary Group, based at the camp, is tasked with airlifting supplies and materials into Agadez, Niger, during the construction of the new drone base.

The team, carrying their gear, disembarked the aircraft and were met by an Air Force Captain who, from his uniform insignia, was with Air Force Special Ops. Captain Everett escorted them to a hangar where they could relax. In the shade provided, the team found bottled water and a crate of oranges, compliments of the U.S. Air force. The group sat around on boxes, sipping water and peeling oranges as Captain Everett filled them in.

"Welcome to Camp Lemonnier. Sorry for the crude accommodations, but your stay will be brief. It is now 0400 hours local time, and the next supply flight for Agadez is scheduled for take-off at 0630 hours. The flight will take just under seven hours, so you will arrive at approximately 1330 hours, which is good. You will be flying on a C-17 carrying an assortment of supplies, including construction materials and some other items. You can load your gear in a cargo crate we have provided for your use." Everett looked over at Chief Whitley. "Are you guys okay with helping unload the cargo?"

Sweeney looked up at that.

"Don't worry," Captain Everett laughed, "the labor is mostly done by local hired help, with forklifts and other equipment. Essentially, you will stand around and act like you are supervising, inspecting the electronics, stuff like that. Just look like you belong. This secret squirrel stuff is just in case some of our local help happens to be friendly to al Qaeda. We don't want them to see anything out of the ordinary and report it to anyone."

Vivas chuckled at that. "I think we can handle that."

"Good!" Everett replied. "Once the cargo is offloaded and the local labor released, you can hang around the C-17 until it is refueled and takes off again. Of course, it will leave you behind. Beyond that, all I know is that some spook named Rick Hahn will contact you."

Captain Everett paused a few minutes while his eyes took in the men he'd just briefed. They looked exactly like what they were, a badass bunch of world-class warriors.

Even the dog looks badass, Everett chuckled to himself. He'd worked with men like this before.

Everett spoke again. "I'm with Air Force Special Ops, Tactical Air Control Party. Officially, I don't know a damn thing. I haven't even spoken to you men. But I do know what you are and where you are going. And I watch the news. I hope you get that lady doctor out of there. Many of us have met her and like her. Good luck and good hunting."

The members of SEAL Team 5 looked up and nodded. They had relied on men like Captain Everett on past dangerous missions in places they weren't supposed to be.

With that, Captain Everett turned and walked out of the hangar, promptly forgetting everything that had just transpired.

The flight from Camp Lemonnier to Base 201 took exactly six hours and fifty-three minutes. The crew of three, Pilot Joe Stavaski, Copilot Colleen Sharp, and Loadmaster Kevin Johnson, welcomed the team on board, and they were quickly in the air. Chief Whitley chatted a bit with the pilot, while Washington made a brief and unsuccessful attempt to engage the copilot in conversation. For the most part, the conversation was minimal, with both the team and Ajax trying to get some sleep wherever they could find a comfortable spot on the transport.

Shortly before landing, Johnson made his way around and stirred them awake. The eight SEALs prepared to play their roles as supervisors and technicians, ready to check the state of the offloaded materials and equipment.

As the C-17 prepared for its final approach into Base 201, it circled over Agadez. JD's thoughts turned to the woman being held hostage in one of the mud-walled ramshackle buildings.

What would ever possess a woman to volunteer for a job like that in such a dangerous place?

His thoughts turned to his sister, Annie. He could not see his sister doing something like that. But, his mother? He chuckled at that. She'd be first in line. Hopefully, they would get the doc out of there in one piece.

The big cargo jet set down on the short runway. Fortunately, the C-17 handled such conditions nicely. The highly versatile aircraft could land on and take off from old dirt roads in some harsh environments. Success only depended on the skill and intestinal fortitude of the pilot.

The aircraft taxied to a stop near some large storage hangars, and the loadmaster opened the rear loading ramp. JD and the rest of the team jumped to their feet and assumed their roles. Within minutes, a crew of locals hired by the Air Force began unloading the cargo. Vivas kept a close eye on the crate containing their gear as it was unloaded with a forklift and moved to a storage hangar near the C-17. It was labeled "Test Equipment." Vivas stayed close to it for the remainder of the unloading operation.

Maddox made a great show of checking the condition of the crates marked "electrical equipment" as they were offloaded one-by-one with the forklift. One of the forklift operators, a surly Arabic-speaking young man, kept up a constant jabbering at Maddux as the work progressed. He did not like being delayed while Maddux inspected the crates and made a mark on his clipboard. It was all for show, with the paper on the clipboard being a preflight checklist. Maddux was enjoying himself.

A few of the locals were interested in Ajax, but they stayed well away from him. JD had put Ajax on his leash and was leading him around to sniff each crate as it was offloaded. To any onlookers, it looked like the dog might be sniffing for explosives or drugs.

There was a loud crash as one of the locals dropped a smaller box he was carrying. The container was marked "Office Supplies." With a twinkle in his eye, Pallie immediately began to curse the clumsiness of the poor man in Italian, loudly. Not understanding a word, the man tried to lift the crate back onto his shoulder. Pallie stormed over and helped the man get the box settled on his shoulder, pointed him toward the hangar, and with a slap on his back, sent the confused man on his way. Pallie turned to grin at JD.

"Man, ain't this fun!" JD only shook his head, a look of bemusement on his face.

A short time later, the unloading was complete. The cargo was secured in the hangar under the watchful eyes of a couple of Air Force Security Police and was now quite safe. The local laborers had been released and went home for the evening. Chief Whitley, who'd left to check-in with the base commander, returned and led the team to the hangar where they collected their gear before proceeding to a Quonset hut off to the right of the hangars. The Quonset hut had a couple of air conditioners mounted in the walls, about a dozen bunk beds down one side, and a few tables with folding metal chairs down the other side. There was also a refrigerator with bottled water in it, as well as a lavatory and shower area. Each man chose a bunk, set down their gear, and grabbed a bottle of water. Then, seated around the tables, they waited. Ajax made himself comfortable on the bunk where JD had set his gear.

CHAPTER 11
NIGER

A few minutes after they settled in, there was a knock at the Quonset hut door, it opened, and a man stepped in. Dressed in Columbia River hiking boots, gray cargo pants, a black cotton button-up short-sleeved shirt, and a khaki cargo vest, he looked to be in good shape. Oakley tactical sunglasses covered his eyes. The man had curly, dark hair partially hidden under a khaki Boonie hat, and a matching beard.

"Who are you supposed to be? Indiana Jones?" Sweeney asked. The other seven team members smiled but said nothing, waiting quietly.

The man laughed. "Hell no! I suck with a bullwhip! My name is Hahn. Rick Hahn," he grinned. "I'm your friendly neighborhood CIA paramilitary man."

The introduction elicited no response from the SEAL team. "You know... a spook!" Maddux and Pallie chuckled at that.

"A spook," Jackson replied. "Now, that's more like it."

Chief Whitley stood and approaching the man, held out his hand.

"I'm Mike Whitley, the proud leader of this ragtag group of social misfits."

The spook shook Whitley's offered hand, taking a seat at one of the tables. The Chief introduced the rest of the team, including Ajax, who, after raising his head to check out the team's reaction to the newcomer, had gone back to sleep on JD's bunk.

"So, what's the situation?" Whitley asked. Hahn leaned back in his chair and responded.

"I know where al Qaeda is holding Dr. Chang. Her assistant is probably there as well, although my source has not seen him in a few days. We don't know if the assistant is dead or alive. However, we are fairly sure he's not left the building."

JD spoke up. "Your source has seen the woman... what's her name? Ellen Chang?"

"Yes, hc has, several times. He is a member of the group of thugs that are holding her hostage. He has carried food to her."

"He's one of them?" Pallie asked. "Can you trust him?"

Rick Hahn turned to face Pallie. "Some years back, Bin Laden had my source's father, his mother, his brother, and two sisters brutally murdered because he thought the father was working for the CIA. I am not sure where Bin Laden got his information. Anyway, my source vowed vengeance on Bin Laden and al Qaeda. He has been working for me for some time. He infiltrated the group while they were still in Afghanistan and fled here to Niger with them when things got too hot. He is a trusted member of the team, and we work hard to ensure he stays so."

"How do you know the story about his family is true?" JD asked.

"Because his father was working for the CIA. I was his handler." JD leaned back in his seat as Hahn went on. "I don't know how Bin Laden found out. We were cautious. It must have been something random. Just bad luck. The kid only survived because he'd gone on some quick errand for his mother, and somehow the killers didn't realize they'd missed him."

"I'll say," Vivas interjected.

Hahn shrugged. "Shit happens! I am certainly sorry about it, but what can I do? Their deaths turned this guy into the best resource I've ever had. While I'm sorry it happened, there is still a war going on here."

Chief Whitley nodded. "We have all seen our share of bad shit happen. So, what else do we have? We need a plan. We only have a few days left until the time these assholes have threatened to behead this lady. We aren't going to let that happen."

Hahn nodded. "I have a plan."

"Let's hear it," Whitley replied. Hahn reached down and pulled a map out of the right-side pocket of his cargo pants, then spread it out before them. The whole team gathered around the table as Hahn pointed to a building on the map. It sat on the outskirts of the east side of Agadez.

"This is where they are keeping Doc Chang. Most of the surrounding buildings look like Berlin after World War II. This one is in pretty good shape. It is a one-story structure with a large front room. There is a hallway to the left that leads to the back where there are four smaller rooms. The room at the end of the hall is the only one with a solid door. Doc Chang is in there; the door has a sliding bolt lock on the outside. The other three are storage rooms full of assorted crap. Also, there is an exterior door at the end of the hall that leads out to an alley. The guards bar that door from the inside. My source has never seen it open, but he has been in the alley."

"What about this guy Holley? The doc's assistant?" Whitley asked.

"The last time my source saw him, he was in the room with the doc, but the last two times he's been in there, Holley was no longer in the room. Holley may be dead or badly injured. We don't know. They might have him stashed in one of these other three rooms." Hahn indicated the three storage rooms. "Those rooms only have curtains over the doors, so if he is in one, he is probably dead or incapacitated somehow."

Maddux nodded. "Makes sense..."

Hahn continued. "See the main drag here?" Hahn's finger traced a street on the map. "It's a straight shot, maybe half a kilometer from one of the old hotels to the building where they have Dr. Chang. The hotel is in ruins now, left over from better times, but it is in a relatively safer neighborhood. We can control access to it easily enough. It's on the edge of town, so we should be able to get to it unobserved if we time it right, say, early morning while the locals are sleeping?"

Hahn paused. Sitting back in his chair, he looked around at the SEAL team operators. They were paying close attention.

"Once we turn down the main drag toward that building, we are leaving the relatively safe part of Agadez and entering an area controlled by al Qaeda. There's no wall or line, but there will be few if any friendly faces."

"Sounds like Somalia all over again," Maddux commented. Sweeney and Washington nodded in agreement.

"It's not that bad," Hahn interjected. "Nowhere near the number of hostiles Delta force and those rangers stirred up. But we will have to keep our eyes open and stay loose."

JD nodded. "Okay. Then what happens?"

Hahn continued. "Once we get the doc and Holley, it's a quick, straight dash down this main drag to the hotel. Getting out is relatively easy. The problem is getting in without tipping the bad guys off that we are coming."

JD and Pallie both muttered their agreement. That was clear enough for everyone to see.

"How do you propose we do that?" JD asked.

"My plan is this," Hahn continued. "My source sometimes delivers stolen supplies to al Qaeda sympathizers in that part of town. He has an old truck with a canvas-enclosed bed. The truck is loud and it smokes a bit, but it runs. He does this pretty regularly, so it will attract no attention." Whitley nodded.

Before Hahn could go on, Jackson cut in.

"Stolen supplies?"

"Yep," Hahn replied. "I supply a lot of them to him. Mostly food; old MREs, bottled water, old tools, batteries, occasional leftover building materials. Sometimes some basic medical stuff like bandages, tape, and shit like that. I gave him a few old cell phones once that I had bugged. Unfortunately, the phones were never activated. Anyway, it helps his cover and keeps him in their good graces."

"I see," said Jackson. "That does make sense in a twisted sort of way."

"That's the CIA for you," Hahn laughed. "We are a twisted bunch."

"So, we ride to the building in the back of this guy's truck," Whitley observed. "Then what?"

"Then we go in and kill all the bad guys. We grab Doc Chang, and Holley if he is in there. That is more your team's area of expertise, but I don't think we should leave him there, even if he's dead. I'm sure he has a family." Everyone agreed to that.

"How do we get out?" Pallie asked.

"We position the Humvees with drivers out of sight; here, at this old hotel." Hahn indicated the hotel on the map, then continued. "We do this early, while it's still dark... maybe 0300 or 0400. I have some contractors who are willing to drive and serve as turret gunners. They are good men and understand the situation. We go in with the truck just after daylight. That would be our driver's normal routine."

Whitley nodded. "Makes sense."

Hahn went on. "When we enter the building and the shooting starts, the Humvees will race down the street to the building. All the bad guys should be dead and the doc safely in our hands just about the time the Humvees pull up. We all jump in and haul ass back to the base. We will have the black hawks on standby for air support should the shit hit the fan. It's simple enough."

"What if they get to the doc first?" Sweeney asked.

"My source says the guards are fairly relaxed. The doc does not know where she is, and they keep her restrained. The guards are usually in the main room and only check on the doc occasionally. The odds are excellent that they will all be dead before they can get back to the doc and do her any harm. Since they've had her stashed there, there's been only two or three guards at any given time, usually sleeping." Hahn sat back in his chair. "Anyway, that's my plan."

"Sounds like as good a plan as any, given the situation," Whitley concluded. "Two questions. You said 'we.' Are you planning on joining us? And, when can I meet the guy driving the truck?"

Hahn laughed. "Yep, I said 'we.' I am going with you. You can't have too many guns on your side when you are heading into a gunfight with al Qaeda. Besides, I have a dislike for assholes who kidnap and torture women. Most of us on the base have met Doc Chang, and we like her. As far as the truck driver, you've already met him. Or at least he has ..." Hahn indicated Maddux. "He's the guy who was cursing you out when you were unloading the cargo from the plane. He was operating the forklift."

Washington grinned at Maddux, who just shook his head. "I'll be damned! That loud-mouthed little shithead?" Maddux muttered.

Chief Whitley stood up. "Okay, then it's settled. It's too late to do much now. So, we will get some sleep tonight. Tomorrow we check our gear and coordinate for the air support. I'll also want to meet these contractors you have lined up as volunteers for the Humvees. Everybody on the teams knows their job, so we will layout the details for assault and breaching that building tomorrow. Hahn, if you go in with us, I want you to stick close to JD. He's the one with the dog. You can help him cover our asses. We are all going home alive. We are not leaving anyone in the damned building except dead al Qaeda. Everyone gets some sleep. Tomorrow's going to be a busy day."

Hahn left for his quarters, and the SEALs settled in for the night. After trying to catch naps during their flights, the bunks were like feather beds. Soon the Quonset hut echoed with the sounds of snoring men.

The next day, plans for the rescue operation began in earnest. By 0800, Chief Whitley had already met the command and flight crews to coordinate with the two Blackhawk choppers tasked for their use. When the truck started toward the building where the doc was being held, the helicopters would be on standby alert. They could be over the site in a matter of minutes.

Whitley also met the truck driver who would drive them up to the building. With Rick Hahn serving as an interpreter, Whitley got a good read on the man named Abaeze. The extent of his hatred for al Qaeda was unmistakable, almost palpable.

Abaeze showed Chief Whitley the picture of his family that he carried in his old, worn leather wallet. Chief Whitley took the picture and looked at it. When he looked back up at Abaeze, the pain and grief in the man's eyes were evident. He handed back the picture.

"I am sorry," was all Whitley could say. Abaeze nodded, and the pain in his eyes was gone. His expression was now impassive, unreadable.

"No matter now. We will fix these bastards good, yes?"

Chief Whitley nodded. "Yes, we will fix them good."

Chief Whitley found himself impressed by the fact that Abaeze could control his rage enough to remain calm and unaffected, never mind friendly, when associating with the al Qaeda operators, and said so to Hahn, who nodded.

"It's got to be some survival mechanism. I'm not sure how Abaeze does it, but he does. He has been a great asset after what al Qaeda did to his family."

Whitley told Hahn he'd see him a bit later and started back toward his team's quarters. He was hungry now and wanted to grab some breakfast, then pick up JD and Ajax before meeting with the contractors. Whitley had come to rely on Ajax's reaction to people as much as his gut instincts.

After breakfast, Whitley, accompanied by JD and Ajax, met with six contractors employed by the Red River Services Group. Red River Services, a private military contractor, provided highly trained security personnel and services for several non-government organizations, multinational corporations, and prominent individuals. They certainly looked like a salty bunch.

Hahn had given Whitley a rundown on the team. They consisted of a former Delta Force operator called Slim, two former SWAT officers from New York City, and a retired Special Boat Service operator who'd decided he'd retired a bit too soon. The last two were former Navy SEALS. Chief Whitley recognized one of them he'd met a few years back.

"I am curious. Why are you volunteering for this mission?" Whitley asked.

"Shit, man! We like the doc. She's a nice lady. She even helped Roy over there."

Slim pointed at one of the former NYC SWAT guys, who nodded.

"Roy had a God-awful boil on his ass. Hurt like hell, didn't it, Roy?"

"Yep," Roy grinned and agreed. "But, the doc took good care of it."

Slim cut Roy off. "Seriously, we didn't know where she was, or we'd have rescued her ourselves." The former Delta Force operator glanced over at JD and Ajax. Ajax was sitting by JD's left leg; his attention sharply focused on Roy. "Nice looking dog! Does he bite?"

JD smiled. "Only on command."

Slim laughed. "That's good!"

JD looked the men over and then asked, "Why'd you let her get kidnapped in the first place?" He just wanted to see their reaction.

The retired SAS operator scowled at JD. Slim just shrugged.

"Well, she wasn't our job. We got underbid by that Dutch group. If Doctors Without Borders had gone with us, we wouldn't be having this fucking discussion. The doc would be just fine. It's too bad. Bram was a good guy. But, he was by himself out there. Seriously understaffed, you might say. We wouldn't have let that happen."

JD seemed to accept that. Whitley turned to him. "Well, we do need drivers and turret gunners. If these guys want to help out, we could use it."

"I agree," JD replied. However, he was a bit concerned over the fact that Ajax's attention had never strayed from the former SWAT team member named Roy. Roy had noticed this as well.

"What the fuck is wrong with your dog?" Roy asked in a less than polite tone.

"Not a thing," JD replied in a matter-of-fact voice. "I find he is usually spot on with his assessment of most situations."

"What the hell does that mean?" Roy took a step forward.

"It just means that I trust my dog's judgment when it comes to people I don't know," JD replied.

"I think you're full of shit! That goes for your mutt, too!"

"Opinions vary," JD replied.

Roy was not sure how to respond to that, but JD could tell he was working himself up toward a fight. Finally, Roy spat.

"If it weren't for your damn dog, I'd kick your ass. I think you're a coward hiding behind that fucking dog."

JD didn't hesitate. "Ajax, Zit." Stepping away from his dog, he grinned at Roy. "Ajax doesn't mind if I clean up the trash. He won't move. Give it your best shot."

In the circles these men traveled in, a challenge like that could not go unanswered. These contractors would need to respect the men of SEAL Team 5, especially if they were to be trusted to work with them on a mission such as this. Trust and respect among warriors had to be earned, but once acquired, it was a precious commodity.

Suddenly unsure, Roy glanced over at Slim, who merely shrugged. Roy had started this quarrel; he needed to end it. Slim wasn't getting involved. Besides, it was just getting exciting, and anyway, from what Slim could see, the Chief didn't look particularly worried.

Roy unbuckled his tactical vest and shrugged it off, handing it to the former SAS operator, Milt, who now was grinning instead of scowling. By now, the contractors had formed into a circle of men, with JD and Roy standing near its center. Chief Whitley, standing near Slim just outside the ring, just shook his head.

"Get this over with quickly, JD. We still have a lot of shit to do today."

"Sure thing, Chief."

Roy had taken a boxer's fighting stance. Bouncing lightly from one foot to the other, he started to circle JD. JD, however, just stood there, relaxed, arms hanging loosely at his sides, waiting. Roy threw a tentative left jab, which JD ignored, only shifting slightly to his right. Encouraged by the fact JD hadn't moved and still had his hands at his side, Roy threw another left jab, but this time going fast, followed it in with a hard right cross aimed at JD's chin. JD's right palm effortlessly deflected the right cross to the outside. Reversing the direction of his right hand and closing it into a fist, the back knuckles of his right fist slammed into the bicep of Roy's left arm, instantly shutting down the left hook Roy intended to follow the right cross. The pain that shot up Roy's left arm was intense and caused him to stumble. Roy stepped back to recover his balance. JD stepped through with his left foot and hit Roy squarely in the chest with the two big knuckles of his right fist. It was a perfectly timed and focused punch that had all of JD's momentum and body weight behind it. Roy dropped like a sack of potatoes to the dirt and lay still.

"Sonofabitch!" someone exclaimed. All these men were experienced warriors, but none had seen anything quite like that before.

"What the fuck!" It was Milt this time, who had a look of sheer disbelief on his face. Ajax was still sitting where JD had left him, quietly taking it all in. JD walked over to where Ajax was sitting and knelt to scratch his head. Slim came over to join him and Chief Whitley.

"Are we good now?" Slim asked.

"We're good," Whitley replied.

"Roy can be a bit of an asshole. But believe it or not, he's a good man in a pinch. This lesson will settle him down a bit, and he'll be good to go." Slim glanced over at Roy, who still hadn't moved. "That is if he lives."

JD chuckled. "He'll live. Just got a bit of the wind knocked out of his sails."

"I'll say," Slim agreed. "What the hell was that punch? I've never seen anything like that before. It was fucking perfect!"

"It is just a little something my instructor picked up from a good friend of his. That guy called it his 'fencepost' punch."

Slim laughed again. "Fencepost, my ass! More like a battering ram! Anyway, we will be ready to roll when you are. Roy, too, if he wakes up in time." The three men glanced over at Roy, who was now sitting up with a very dazed expression on his face. Nobody was saying much, many still unsure of exactly what had just happened.

"Be ready to roll at 0300. We want to be at that old hotel before the locals are out and about. We will roll out of the base and quietly circle to approach from the desert. With any luck, we can get in there without being noticed."

"Got it," Slim replied. "We'll be ready."

CHAPTER 12
VIETNAM

The old French colonial plantation house served Colonel Trần's needs quite well. The location provided easy access to Highway 13, the main route south to Ho Chi Minh City, about sixty kilometers away. The secluded house sat well back from the road, surrounded by the Long Nguyen Secret Zone, a heavily forested area located between Highway 13 and the former Michelin Rubber Plantation. Michelin established the plantation in 1925, and at 31,000 acres, it was the largest rubber plantation in Vietnam. After the war, both the plantation and the Michelin factory in Saigon, now Ho Chi Minh City, were nationalized by the new communist government.

The Long Nguyen Secret Zone once served as a strategic base and staging area for the Viet Cong and NVA. The plantation provided significant revenue for the South Vietnamese government and therefore was of vital importance during the war. Michelin paid the Viet Cong to keep the enterprise running. At the same time, the U.S. reimbursed Michelin for any damages to the rubber trees inflicted during military operations. Despite these "arrangements," the plantation saw many bloody battles fought by U.S. and South Vietnamese forces during search and destroy missions in attempts to dislodge the Viet Cong and NVA. It was also the site of intense fighting during the Tet Offensive.

Now, the house served as a base of operations for the former Viet Cong colonel-turned-drug warlord. In addition to the house itself, several outbuildings provided quarters for his private army, as well as storage and processing facilities for the opium he brought in from Thailand. It was a short trip to An Loc, which sat near the border with Cambodia. From there, his men utilized the remote mountain trails to travel where the boundaries between Vietnam, Cambodia, and Laos met. From that point, it was a relatively short trip west into Laos and his opium supplier.

Trần distributed his product among the pimps, prostitutes, and general drug addicts in red-light districts of Ho Chi Minh City, Hanoi, Ha Long, and Hoi An. His reputation as a brutal Viet Cong colonel during the war, combined with his ready willingness to inflict harsh punishment for any infraction of his rules, kept his organization running smoothly with little fear of betrayal. It helped that the communist government maintained the official position that neither prostitution nor a drug trade existed within the Socialist Republic of Vietnam. Colonel Trần was exceptionally well connected within that government.

Trần sat at his desk in a dark, wood-paneled room, once the private library for those living in the house during happier years. Going over the ledgers was not something he particularly enjoyed, but it needed doing. He trusted no one, especially when it came to his money. And, there was much he needed to track: payments for shipments of opium coming in from Laos, which he processed into heroin; distribution through his network of drug dealers; the collection of income from the sale of heroin; the many brothels he controlled; and the protection money collected from many other red-light district businesses. There were also bribes to various government officials, to keep them happy and out of his business.

There was the expense of the secret war Trần was waging against his competition. His men regularly ambushed mules working for other drug lords on the trail and seized their opium shipments. Occasionally, the bodies made their way to the police morgue in Ho Chi Minh City, and an article describing a significant border drug bust would appear in the news as evidence of the success of the communists at keeping the corruption and drugs of the western world out of Vietnam.

Yes, Trần thought with satisfaction. *The bribes I pay these government officials are a nuisance, but worth every penny.*

He'd just finished checking the previous week's numbers when there was a knock at the heavy wooden double doors.

Closing the ledger and sliding it into the top right drawer of the massive wooden desk, he turned the key in the drawer's lock. Then, withdrawing the key, he slipped it into his pocket.

"Enter." Trần's voice sounded impatient. He did not like being disturbed. The door opened, and two members of his security team entered, escorting a third. The third man, while Trần had not seen him before, was one of his mules.

"Yes, what is it?" Trần inquired.

"This is Phan," the man to the left replied, indicating the frightened-looking one. "He has brought news we think you should hear."

"Well, what is it?" Trần demanded.

Hesitantly, the man relayed his tale of the events that had transpired on the trail between Sisaket and Dak To, beginning with their leader, Chung's, demand for food, and his attempt to use Colonel Trần's name to scare the other men into complying with his order. The other men's leader, a man named Dish, had promptly shot Chung and Tống, who'd made an ill-fated try for the AK-47 slung over his shoulder.

"And yet, you survived?" Trần's voice was not angry or menacing. If anything, it sounded slightly curious.

"Yes, Sir! It all happened so fast, and my rifle was a few feet away, leaning against my pack. Their leader, the man named Dish, spared me to deliver this message. I came as quickly as I could, knowing you would want to hear what happened." Phan paused, a slight tone of hope in his voice.

Trần's old leather chair squeaked as he leaned back and pressed his fingertips together in front of his chest, contemplating Phan for a few seconds. Then, leaning forward, he placed the palms of both hands firmly on his desk.

"I do appreciate your bringing me this news. You are correct that it is important."

Phan felt a powerful sense of relief build, and his stomach began to ease for the first time.

"However," Trần went on, "Chung made a grave mistake in using my name to impress this man, Dish. That was foolish and stupid." Reaching down with his right hand, Trần opened the second drawer in the desk. "I generously reward those who work hard and serve me well, as my men know and understand."

Phan nodded in agreement.

"However, stupidity, treachery, and cowardliness are dealt with severely."

The colonel's hand came up from the desk drawer, a Makarov pistol in its grasp. Trần fired twice, both 9 mm rounds striking Phan in the chest. The dead man collapsed to the floor.

"Get this piece of dung out of here," Trần ordered, dropping the Makarov back into the desk drawer. He would reload the pistol later. "Put out the word; anyone who mentions my name to anybody, not in our organization, will be dealt with accordingly."

"Yes, Sir." The two bodyguards nodded. Moving quickly, one took the dead man's ankles while the other grabbed his wrists. Together they lifted the corpse and carried it from the office.

"And get someone in here to clean up this mess!"

Colonel Trần leaned back into his chair. The leather was old and shaped to him, quite comfortable. Trần loved the smell and how the chair squeaked when he shifted in it. It was a comforting sound. So much better than squatting in the damp, smelly tunnels beneath the jungles.

At first, Trần was surprised to hear the name Dish from his now-deceased lackey. It had been many years since he had heard that name mentioned, but he remembered it well. Dish and his father, Mund, were both well-known to the Viet Cong, a real thorn in their sides. Many VC fighters died at the hands of those two Montagnard savages, who seemed to make it their life's mission to rid the jungles of his men as well as any other Viet Cong units.

The Montagnard dogs and their American friends got what they deserved, Trần thought to himself, shaking his head with a smile at the irony of the situation. Trần was no communist, more of an opportunist. Communism turned people into sheep. *Sheep ready and waiting to be fleeced,* he thought.

Then, the colonel's mind returned to the Montagnard. So, this killer of VC was still alive and operating along the border. Thinking about it, Trần decided it was not such a surprise. Trần knew the man Dish was tough to kill. So many had died trying. *But what was this Dish up to now? Not smuggling drugs,* Trần decided. *I would know. Guns, maybe? Perhaps he is supplying the anti-communist bandits in the central highlands. That would make sense.*

A twisted grin made its way onto Trần's face. At one time, there had been a substantial reward posted, first by the North Vietnamese

Army and later by the communist government, for the Montagnard named Dish. The fact that Dish was still alive meant the prize was never collected. And capturing or killing a Montagnard gunrunner would buy a lot of goodwill with the communist regime. Trần's thoughts were interrupted when a quiet knock sounded at the door.

"Enter!" He was now in a much better mood. The prospect of adding to his fortune always made him feel better. The door opened, and a young woman entered carrying a bucket of water and some rags. She knelt and began wiping the pool of blood from the hardwood flooring. Trần watched as the young woman went quietly about her task. She kept her face down, eyes averted as she worked, but it was clear to the colonel that the woman was quite attractive. Finishing her task and dropping the now bloody rags into the bucket, the woman stood. Keeping her eyes down, she made a quick bow toward Colonel Trần and turned to leave.

"Stop," Trần ordered. "Put the bucket down and come over here." Placing the bucket on the floor, she approached within a few feet of Trần and stopped. Hands trembling, her gaze remained glued to the carpet. All the women knew about the colonel.

"Such a lovely young woman," Trần murmured, his voice sounding gentle, but with an icy tone beneath.

"What is your name, child?"

"Hoa," the young woman answered. Her voice was almost a whisper. Keeping her eyes on the floor, she fought the urge to turn and run. It would only make things worse.

Suddenly, Trần's right hand shot out, slapping the young woman hard across her face. Crying out, she staggered back a step but did not fall. A drop of blood collected at the corner of her mouth. Tenderly, Trần reached up and, using his index finger, captured the drop of blood from her lip and tasted it.

The colonel decided he now felt much better.

CHAPTER 13
NIGER

Khalid was sitting at a table in the building he used as his headquarters in the Oungouai-Bayi quarter of Agadez. He could not shake the feeling that something was wrong.

What have I missed?

He could think of nothing, and yet the nagging feeling that he should do something would not go away.

Complacency, he thought. *That is the real enemy to plans such as this.*

"Mustapha," he called.

"Yes, Khalid," Mustapha replied as he entered from another room. He had been checking an assortment of Kalashnikov rifles recently procured on the local arms market.

"Mustapha, I want you to take some of your men and move the doctor tomorrow morning. It is just a feeling, but move her to our building in the Ager-garin-saka Quarter. Take some of your most trusted men and be ready for trouble. We should not make the mistake of underestimating the Americans."

"I will take care of it," Mustapha replied. Mustapha had grown to respect Khalid as a leader. The man was as ruthless as he was fearless. If he had a feeling, there must be some reason for it, even if he could not put his finger on it yet.

Returning to the room where he and a few other men had been inspecting the new weapons, he called out to one of them. Tuarek was one of Mustapha's most trusted fighters. Not merely a soldier for pay or bandit for hire, Tuarek was a true jihadist, a genuine believer and follower of the Prophet Muhammad.

"Tuarek." The man looked up from the AK-47 rifle he was disassembling to clean.

"Yes, Mustapha?"

"Gather our most loyal fighters. I want them here before tomorrow morning. Khalid has given us an important task. Go now."

Tuarek put the Kalashnikov down. "Yes, Mustapha, of course." Tuarek left right away.

The next morning, thirty-three men waited near five beat-up trucks parked at al Qaeda's headquarters in the Ager-garin-saka Quarter of Agadez. The two-story building, deep in an al Qaeda-controlled section of the city, was in relatively good condition for the area. Amazingly, the building still had some windows in walls pitted from small arms fire and general neglect. There was neither electricity nor running water, and kerosene lanterns provided lighting. But the building did have a sound basement complex. It was here that Khalid had set up his headquarters.

Because of his strict rules for maintaining hygiene in the building, the smell was not too bad. Khalid did not like filth and squalor. At first, a few men ignored his standards. After he shot the last man for not cleaning up after himself because he had decided it was somehow beneath his station in life to do so, the rest of the men seemed to fall into line.

Four Toyota trucks had Soviet-made heavy machine guns mounted in the back. The machine guns were left behind when the Soviet army fled Afghanistan in 1988 and found their way into Niger as al Qaeda retreated into North Africa to escape the advancing surge of U.S. forces. All thirty-three men were fierce fighters, many having seen action in Afghanistan, Iraq, or Syria. A few were involved in the genocide in the Darfur region of Western Sudan.

Most of the men carried Russian or Chinese AK-47 rifles. Bandoleers of ammunition crisscrossed their chests. A few had Russian F1 hand grenades in the pockets of their jackets, and many carried knives on their belts.

Mustapha appeared through a rear door in the building and walked briskly toward the men waiting at the trucks. Tuarek followed close behind. Seeing Khalid's lieutenant approach, the men began climbing up into the vehicles, preparing to move out. There was no need for orders, so there was little talking. Tuarek had briefed them on what they were going to do.

"Let's go," Mustapha said to Tuarek as he climbed into the passenger seat of his Hilux. Tuarek climbed in behind the wheel and started the engine.

CHAPTER 14
NIGER

At 0245 hours, four Humvees quietly drove through the back gate of Base 201 with their lights turned off and engines barely above an idle. They headed due north into the desert. Three kilometers from the base, the drivers switched their vehicles' lights on, and the engines roared to life, continuing another ten kilometers in the same direction before swinging off to the east to start their circle back to Agadez.

Rick Hahn drove the lead Humvee with Chief Whitely riding shotgun. Slim drove the second Humvee with Roy Manning taking the .50 Cal turret gun position. Before they'd loaded up, Whitely had joked a bit with Roy to make sure the air was clear, smiling in a friendly manner when he asked Roy if he felt he was still up to it.

"I'm alright," Roy replied. "Just a little sore, but don't worry about me. If the shit hits the fan, I'll be in the middle of it."

Whitely nodded. "I know you will be."

After Roy walked off to load up, Slim, who'd been standing close by, chuckled.

"Shit, Chief! Roy has the dandiest purple-colored, fist-shaped bruise in the center of his chest. I've never seen anything like it. That boy of yours sure can hit!"

Whitley laughed. "You don't know the half of it." Both men headed off and climbed into their respective vehicles. JD and Ajax settled into Slim's Humvee. Roy followed but paused before climbing up into the turret. He looked down at JD and Ajax.

"I guess I owe you an apology, man. You ain't no coward. Nobody's

77

ever hit me like that. And, if that dog is half as tough as you are, he's got my respect as well." Roy reached down to pet Ajax on the head. Ajax did not object.

"It's cool, man. No hard feelings! We just got off on the wrong foot," JD replied with a friendly grin. JD held out his hand. Roy, somewhat surprised, took it and they shook. Roy turned and climbed up into the turret. Vivas had climbed into the vehicle with Ajax and JD and was busily sharpening his combat knife.

"What was that all about?" Vivas asked.

"Nothing," JD replied. "Just a little misunderstanding."

Pallie, Washington, and Sweeney climbed into the Humvee that Milt, the former SAS guy, would be driving. Jackson and Maddux jumped into the last vehicle with the two former SEALs turned private security contractors. As the Humvees roared along through the desert night, JD looked over at Vivas, who somehow, despite the somewhat rocky ride, was still working on the blade of his knife. JD was intrigued by the shape, having never seen one quite like it.

"Interesting blade," JD commented.

"Yeah. My dad's instructor designed it. It's called a flesheater."

"Flesheater! Now that's an appropriate name for a knife."

"Yep, since that is pretty much what it does. Guru Advincula designed it to replace that crappy knife that the Marine Corp tried to make standard issue. He worked with a master knifemaker named Jim Hammond to develop it. It's a hell of a weapon when you know how to use it."

"You'll have to show me sometime," JD replied. He was familiar with AJ Advincula and had once seen the man perform a knife fighting demo that included a free-fighting session with dull training knives. Advincula had destroyed the other fighter. That man could move. His own Isshin-ryu Karate instructor, Sensei Tokumura, was good friends with another respected karate instructor, a former Marine from Iowa, who'd served on Okinawa with Advincula in the late 1950s. JD was interested in learning more about this knife and talking to Vivas about AJ Advincula, but that would have to wait. Right now, it was time to focus on the mission at hand.

Sometime later, the Humvee's engines again slowed to just over an idle, and the headlights went dark. The vehicles quietly worked their way through the outskirts of Agadez, pulling up out of sight behind the old hotel designated by Hahn. So far, the plan seemed to be working fine. As far as Whitley could tell, they'd made it this far undetected, and it was still sometime before sunrise.

Pallie, Washington, and Milt set up security while the remaining men settled in to get a little rest. The local driver and his delivery truck would show up shortly after daylight, so they had a little more than an hour to kill. Hahn and Whitley made their way carefully to the front of the ruined hotel, to a point where they could see the main road. The Chief verified that the road provided a straight shot to their target a bit less than a kilometer away.

Nothing stirred on the streets. It was still quiet as the sun began to creep above the eastern horizon. The two made their way back to the Humvees where the rest of the men performed last-minute weapons checks. Moments later, the sound of a vehicle, its engine coughing and sputtering, drew closer. The truck circled behind the hotel and came to a smoking and wheezing stop. Abaeze climbed out of the cab, leaving the engine running. Making his way around to the front of the truck, he relieved himself. Once that business was taken care of, he approached the group of men gathered near the crumbling back wall of the hotel.

Roy whistled softly. "You guys are riding down the street in that? It'd be safer and faster to walk!"

Pallie grinned. "Yes, but not nearly as stylish."

Hahn approached the men. He had been talking to Abaeze. "We better load up. Abaeze says he often stops here to take a leak, so nobody will think anything of him pulling back here momentarily, but we need to get moving while things are still quiet. He passed many of the laborers headed to the base on the road. Most will already be on the base and ready to start working. We are as ready as we are going to be."

Whitley agreed. "Let's go."

The men of Golf Platoon climbed up into the bed of the old delivery truck and found room to sit among some old crates, sacks of rice, and empty boxes.

"At least the driver could have cleaned some of this crap out of here," Sweeney muttered.

Pallie chuckled. "Quit your bitching! Would you rather fight your way down the street?"

"Better than breathing this freaking blue smoke," Washington observed with a grin. Even Ajax wrinkled his nose and whined a bit when he jumped up into the back of the smelly old truck. JD jumped up right behind Ajax.

Maddux climbed up after JD. "Hey JD, even Ajax doesn't like this shitty ride!" The last SEAL to climb up into the back of the truck was Chief Whitley, who sat on a crate beside Jackson. Hahn moved to the front of the truck bed and signaled to Abaeze in the cab that they were ready. He then jumped up into the back. Abaeze ground the transmission into first gear, and with a big puff of blue exhaust, the truck lurched forward, making its way around the hotel and down the street toward their objective, the building where al Qaeda held Dr. Ellen Chang.

Ellen Chang lay on a dirty rug in the corner of the small room. She no longer noticed the acrid smell that emanated from the carpet. There was no light in the room, other than what little filtered through the cracks around the door. Sometimes Ellen thought she could hear rats scurrying around, but she couldn't see them. So far, they hadn't come near her. At least as far as she could tell.

Sleep fitfully came when it came at all. Ellen was scared.

What is going to happen to me?

She knew she was in the hands of some radical Islamic group, but she wasn't sure which one. Ellen knew that al Qaeda was active in the region, and there had been rumors of ISIS operatives moving into the area as they fled U.S. forces to the north. Ellen's thoughts went back to Bram Alderik, who had died trying to help her and Norman escape. She felt suddenly angry with Doctors Without Borders. While they performed valuable humanitarian work around the globe, their naive belief in the innate goodness of all men combined with their perpetual budget issues, causing them to skimp on security measures. She and Norman had needed a bigger escort. One like that team of contractors she'd met at the base. Alderik might still be alive, and she and Norman might not be in this Godforsaken rat hole. Many questions flashed through Ellen's brain.

Have they asked for ransom? Is someone coming for me? Or, are they going to kill me?

Ellen did not want to die, but lying there in the darkened room, dirty, hungry, and afraid, she decided that she would not give these assholes any satisfaction. She was determined to meet whatever came game-on, head held high. Dignity might be the only thing she had left, and she would not let these terrorists take that from her.

Three times each day, the locked door opened, and she was led out into the hall, then out through a barred exterior door and into a small courtyard. The courtyard opened onto a back alleyway where she could relieve herself in a small pit in one corner. Once finished, Ellen returned to her dark room with its dirty rug and old folding metal chair. They would hand her a bottle of water and a bowl of plain rice. This routine hadn't changed for several days. At other random intervals, a guard would open the door, glance in to check on her, then close the door and go away.

At least she was no longer strapped to the metal chair. They had strapped her to the chair for the first day or so. She'd lost track of time. Had she been here a week, two? There was no window in the room; only faint streams of light through the cracks in the door, or when the door opened for whatever reason.

Ellen had no idea where they'd taken Norman or what had happened to him. They had come and taken him from the room shortly after bringing them here. She knew they'd beaten and tortured him. Ellen heard it through the walls. Norman's screams had stopped after a while. Ellen did not know if he was alive or dead. She suspected they had killed him.

Footsteps approached the door. Ellen heard the old barrel lock slide back. The door opened, and one of her guards poked his head in and glanced around the room. Satisfied, the guard again closed and locked the door. She heard his footfalls fade as he went back down the hall. The faces of the guards changed, but the routine stayed the same. They checked on her and went back to whatever they were doing. Thankfully, other than that, they'd left her alone.

The two guards sat on folding metal chairs in the front room. Between them sat an old crate on which was a checkerboard. Just returned from checking on the woman, the guard made sure none of the pieces had miraculously moved in his brief absence.

"Abba, it is your move. What are you doing?"

"I am checking to see if you moved any checkers around while I was gone," Abba replied. "Give me a minute."

The second guard frowned. "Are you saying I would cheat?"

"Certainly not," replied Abba, laughing. "I am merely making sure

Allah did not allow the temptation to get the better of you, momentarily."

The familiar coughing sound of a truck coming down the deserted street ended the quiet morning.

Sayyed looked up at the sound. "Ahh! Our good friend Abaeze is coming, and right on time. We need both rice and bottled water." Abba scowled at that.

" I am getting sick of rice. Perhaps he brings more of those stolen American MREs. Even they would be good for a change." Abba stood and moved over to one of the remaining crud-covered windows to peer out. He recognized the truck's belching and backfiring, but it was always better to check.

"Yes, it's Abaeze." Abba turned back to the checkerboard. "It is my move, correct?"

As planned, Abaeze slowed the truck to a stop, parking it where he always parked. Everything needed to appear normal. Abaeze killed the engine and clambered out of the cab. Slamming the cab door, he walked up to the entrance of the building and knocked loudly.

"It is Abaeze! Open, I say. Let me tell you what I have for you." Abba opened the door.

"Do you have any American MREs?" he inquired.

"Do I have any MREs?" Abaeze wiped the sweat from his brow with the sleeve of his shirt. "It's already damnably hot out here! Let me in out of this heat, and I will tell you everything I have."

Abba moved aside, and Abaeze entered the dark, shaded interior of the building. With a quick look around, Abba decided everything looked quiet. He followed Abaeze into the building and closed the door.

In the back of the truck, Whitley nodded. Silently, one by one, the team members dropped from the bed of the vehicle. Jackson and Pallie moved quickly down the alley to the right. Their job was to cover the back courtyard Abaeze had mapped out for them. Maddux and Vivas took up positions to the right of the door, with Vivas watching the door and Maddux facing the street, alert for trouble.

Washington and Sweeney took the left of the door, where Washington turned to cover any approach from the street. JD, with Ajax beside him on his leash, knelt by the back corner of the truck from which JD had an excellent field of fire, covering the full street down which they had just come. Hahn moved to the other end of the

82

vehicle to cover the other end of the road. Whitley knelt beside JD. In about five seconds, Abaeze would open the door to retrieve some merchandise from the truck. When the door opened, the team would strike.

The convoy of five al Qaeda trucks was now just a few blocks from the building Abaeze had just entered. While it was still early morning, it was already getting hot. Mustapha sat in the passenger seat of the lead vehicle. There was little chance the Americans knew where the doctor was, and he expected no trouble. It would be a simple matter of moving the woman to the new location. Still, Mustapha had learned to trust Khalid's instincts. Therefore, the four other vehicles carried some of his best warriors, all of them well-armed.

Yes! It is an excellent precaution to move the doctor, he thought.

Khalid's instincts were often correct. Mustapha shifted in his seat. His back was troubling him again. A relic of his days in Darfur, his back was very tricky now. Sometimes, if he moved just so, he could not stand straight for a week. The opium helped.

His driver, Tuarek, looked over at Mustapha. "We are almost there. Seems quiet enough."

Mustapha acknowledged Tuarek's comment with a grunt. He did not want to talk. Tuarek was right, though. It all seemed quiet so far. What could go wrong? There would be no trouble.

CHAPTER 15
VIETNAM

Colonel Trần had no one he considered a second-in-command. He ran his operation alone. There were "bosses" running certain areas of the enterprise; the opium smugglers and those who later distributed the refined heroin to dealers in the major cities. Some men ran the brothels he controlled. But they all answered to him. It was a simple matter of trust, and Trần trusted no one.

Seventeen "bosses" stood in the old library. There was only one chair, and that belonged to the colonel. They had already gone over the regular business of the monthly meeting the colonel required his bosses to attend. Each took their turn reporting on whatever operation they oversaw, covering gross revenues, expenses, and net profit as well as any other items they felt the colonel needed to know. Aside from the location and the outward appearance of the bosses, it could have been a business meeting in any boardroom on Wall Street.

There was little to fear from the authorities. Generous cash bribes to key government and law enforcement officials ensured privacy. The colonel had little to worry about as far as government interference, but his secretive nature—born of many years as a VC commander during the Vietnam War—would not allow him to become too bold.

Finally, all the topics on the meeting's agenda were covered. Few ever tried to sneak anything past Colonel Trần. Those who attempted were made an example of, and it was an example few would ever forget. Satisfied, Trần leaned back in his leather chair. His gaze wandered over the men standing in his office. Then, he addressed his underlings on one last topic.

"There is one more thing," he paused. "If someone so much as whispers about a man named 'Dish' in a conversation anywhere, I want to know about it immediately." Each of the seventeen heads nodded and murmured their agreement. Each had heard about the incident on the trail, resulting in the death of three of his smugglers. All agreed that the man named Phan deserved to be shot for his stupidity and lack of courage. None of those present wanted to be the next man determined to be stupid or a coward. "I want to capture this Montagnard savage alive if at all possible, but dead will do if unavoidable. Am I clear on this?"

Again, all seventeen heads nodded. There were murmurs of agreement.

"Good! That is all, then. You may go. Send Huỳnh in as you leave." As one, the bosses turned and filed out through the heavy double door. Seconds later, the colonel's chief bodyguard stepped into the room.

"Yes, sir?"

Trần turned to the man. "Find that girl, Hao, who cleaned the blood from the floor last week and send her to me. I need her."

Huỳnh paused before responding. "Sir, I believe she has gone home to Lai Khe, to care for her sick mother. The other women have said she would be back in a few days."

Trần grunted his disappointment.

No matter, he thought. He would enjoy Hao another time. Anyway, it would be better when he had more time to spend. That one was special.

"Very well, send Tuyet to me."

CHAPTER 16
NIGER

Abaeze watched the game of checkers as he and the two guards haggled over the price of the rice and bottled water. Finally, agreeing on a price, Abaeze portrayed the aggrieved merchant perfectly.

"I lose money every time I do business with you. Life is unfair. My children will starve."

"Your children are both fat and healthy," Sayyed observed. "You do very well between working on the American base and selling us your stolen goods."

Abaeze chuckled at that. "Allah is most kind to his loyal followers."

"And do you have MREs?" Abba inquired again. "I am getting sick of rice for every meal."

Abaeze laughed. "Yes. I have some American MREs; the same price as last time. Finish your game, Abba. I will get them and bring them in. Also, the rice and bottled water, as we have discussed." Abaeze walked back over to the door and opened it.

Using the door for concealment as it swung inward, Maddux, followed closely by Vivas, entered the room. According to plan, Abaeze yelled a warning to provide himself cover if needed later.

"Abba, Sayyed, look out! Americans!" Abaeze dove for the floor.

Abba never had time to react. A burst from Maddux's MP-4 hit him squarely in the chest. Vivas took out the second man as he grabbed the AK-47 leaning against the wall near his chair. The man collapsed, knocking the checkerboard and its pieces to the floor. A few checkers rolled across the ground, and then everything was quiet again.

"Clear," came Vivas' voice across the comm unit. Sweeney and Washington moved into the cleared room. Maddux and Vivas started down the hall, clearing each room as they went.

Maddux's voice came over the comm unit. "Found a body... male... looks like it must be Holley."

Lying on the dirty rug in the darkened room, Ellen heard sudden noises coming from the front. She couldn't understand what the guards were saying and had given up trying days ago, but the sudden metallic clattering made her sit up. It took only a second to realize the sound was gunfire. Ellen had seen enough movies to know what silencers did to the sound of an automatic weapon.

Oh, my God! What next?!

Ellen heard movements coming down the hall. From the noises, it sounded like someone was moving carefully from room to room. Then the sounds were at her door. She heard the lock slide back, and the door opened. A man's silhouette filled the space previously occupied by the door.

"Are you Ellen Chang?" a voice asked.

"I am," Ellen replied, her voice quivering a bit, still not sure what was happening. The man had spoken English.

"I'm Petty Officer Vivas, Ma'am. U.S. Navy. We're here to get you out." Ellen couldn't help it; she started to cry.

"Dr. Chang, we have to move. Can you walk?" Ellen nodded. Vivas offered the woman his hand and helped her to her feet. "I've got you. Stay right behind me. Extraction vehicles are on the way." Together, they started down the hall.

Maddux had moved the other body into the front room. Ellen gasped when she saw Norman. Being a doctor, she had seen some ugly sights, but nothing compared to what they had done to Norman. Ellen started to pull away from Vivas, to go to him.

"Ma'am, don't. There is nothing you can do, and it's pretty bad." It was Maddux. "He is dead, and we need to be ready to move in a few seconds."

Vivas gently steered Ellen to a position near the door, covered by the thick mud walls of the building.

"Sit here, Dr. Chang. We'll be leaving momentarily. Don't worry. We will bring your friend with us." Ellen sat and leaned her back against the cool, dry mud of the wall and waited.

When Maddux and Vivas entered the building, Hahn signaled the contractors who were standing by with the engines of the Humvees idling. At Hahn's signal, the drivers hit the accelerators, and the Humvee's 6.2L diesel engines roared to life as they circled the old hotel and started down the main drag toward the building the SEALs had just entered. The turret gunners kept a sharp eye out for any signs of trouble.

As Mustapha's convoy approached the building, he spotted the familiar truck parked near the building.

Abaeze was peddling his ill-gotten goods!

Mustapha chuckled. He had availed himself of Abaeze's merchandise several times in the past. Abaeze managed to come up with some interesting items from time to time. Not too long ago, Mustapha bought several stolen cell phones from Abaeze. He hadn't needed to use them yet, but they would undoubtedly come in handy at some point.

As they drew closer to the building, Mustapha frowned. Something didn't seem quite right. At first, he'd not been able to put his finger on it, but now he knew what was bothering him. It was too quiet. He expected to see Abba, Sayyed, or even Abaeze come out to carry purchased rice and water into the building, perhaps other purchases as well. Mustapha grabbed the radio sitting beside him on the seat.

"Be ready. We may have trouble." The men in the accompanying trucks checked their weapons.

Ajax let out a low, throaty growl. JD spotted the approaching convoy of what appeared to be five rather beat-up Toyota Hilux trucks. The dust cloud formed by the approaching vehicles swirled up the broad street toward where the SEAL waited, as yet unseen.

"We've got company!" JD warned as he brought up his MP-4, sighting in on the closest truck. Chief Whitley rolled to a better firing position, taking cover near the truck's rear tires and sighted down his weapon at the approaching vehicles.

"The Humvees are thirty-seconds out." It was Hahn. He'd taken up a firing position near the front of the truck and checked with Slim on the convoy's arrival time. "They're coming in hot!"

Inside the building, Vivas grabbed Ellen. "Get down, Ma'am. Lay down at the base of that wall. It's thickest there. It looks like we've got trouble, but don't worry. We'll handle it." Ellen took cover where Vivas had pointed. Vivas took a position at one window, Maddux, at the other. Sweeney was kneeling at the door.

"Washington, you've got the hall. Make sure nobody sneaks up behind us."

"Got it," Washington replied. He moved to a position to cover the hall and back entrance.

Chief Whitley's voice came over the comms system. "Pallie, you and Jackson cover that alley. Nobody gets through! Got it?"

"Got you covered, Chief!" Pallie replied, settling into his chosen firing position. It was already hot. Pallie could feel the sweat trickle down his back.

This spot will do nicely, Pallie decided. He'd located a good firing position from which he could cover the alley with the M-27 Infantry Automatic Rifle he carried as the platoon's heavy weapons expert. Commonly called an IAR, it was a handy weapon in a fight with its cyclic firing rate of 700 to 900 rounds per minute. Jackson found a position to Pallie's left, behind a section of the wall. His MP-4 was locked and loaded. The two SEALs were ready. Anyone coming down that alley was dead meat.

Two of the approaching Hilux trucks suddenly turned off left, down another alley.

"Jackson, Pallie, looks like you have company headed your way. Two pickups just turned left down an alley a bit farther up the street. It looks like they're trying to circle the building. Maybe seven or eight men in each truck."

"They'll wish to hell they hadn't," Pallie replied.

After ordering two of his vehicles around behind the building, Mustapha saw that the door to the building was open. Then he spotted the figure kneeling near the right rear wheel of the truck.

"Slow down, Tuarek, the infidel Americans are here," he growled. Barking some additional orders into the radio, he waived the two remaining trucks around him. The pickups had Soviet-made DShk 12.7x108 mm heavy machine guns mounted in the back along with their cargo of jihadist fighters. The two beat-up old Hilux trucks roared past, the gunners struggling to maintain their balance in the speeding vehicles.

"Here they come," JD spoke into the comm unit. It was now scorching. He wiped the sweat from his forehead to keep it from running into his eyes. "Maybe twenty-five or thirty men and heavily armed. I'm engaging."

JD opened fire with his MP-4, firing on the closest truck. The truck's windshield shattered, but it continued to come toward them. Wild shots began spraying from the heavy machine gun mounted in the back of the vehicle. For some reason, al Qaeda fighters seemed to rely on the "spray and pray" method of shooting and never really took the time to get the hang of accurate, aimed fire.

Just as well for us, JD thought. Of course, accurate shooting would be problematic from the back of a fast-moving pickup truck anyway. Ajax let out an excited whine as the bullets began to fly but stayed put, crouching at JD's side. Firing again at the oncoming truck, JD aimed a burst at the machine gunner in the back of the truck and saw him slump over, then topple from its bed.

Pallie crouched in his position, waiting. He could see Jackson to his left, also ready. They could hear the sound of trucks approaching the back of the alley between the scattered gunfire. The lane was too narrow to drive into, even for a small vehicle like a Hilux. Therefore, the jihadists would have to park and continue down the alleyway to the courtyard on foot.

That's good, Jackson thought. *These trucks often carry heavy machine guns mounted in the back. These would have to be left behind.* Jackson's whispering voice came over the SEAL comms unit.

"Pallie, you cover the entrance to the alley with the IAR. I'll cover that lower stretch of the wall. They might try to climb over it if you shut them down at the entrance."

"Roger that," Pallie replied softly.

A few minutes later, two trucks stopped near the alley entrance.

"I've got an idea. Let these guys get into the alley," Pallie whispered into his comms unit. "There can't be too many of them, seven or eight per truck, the Chief said. We'll have them boxed in and can take them all out at once."

"Good idea. Roger that!" Jackson whispered back.

A few minutes later, a head peered around the corner of the alley and quickly withdrew. Pallie and Jackson both held their fire. The head reappeared, followed slowly by a body. Again, the two SEALs held their fire. Slowly the man crept into the alley, moving in about twenty feet, taking up a position behind a badly rusted old dumpster. The man paused, staring intently toward the SEAL's position. He saw nothing move. A few minutes later, Pallie saw him signal. Seconds later, five more men started into the alley. Leaving the questionable cover of the rusted dumpster, the first man moved forward, followed by the other five.

"That's it! Come to papa!" Pallie whispered to himself. He and Jackson still held their fire, waiting.

More men entered the alley. Fifteen terrorists were now slowly making their way down the alleyway toward the courtyard.

"You say go," Jackson whispered into the comms unit. "You've got the big gun."

"Roger that," Pallie replied. He waited until the group's point man was only a few yards from the gate, and the rest of the terrorists were well into the alleyway. His finger slowly tightened on the trigger of the IAR. Suddenly, the machine gun came to life, sending a hail of 5.56 mm rounds down the alley. Jackson, on his left, opened fire with his MP-4, firing with deadly accuracy, each burst knocking a man to the ground. It was over quickly. Eight dead terrorists now lay in the dust of the alleyway.

A voice came across the comms unit. "You guys okay back there?" It was Chief Whitley.

"We're good," Jackson replied. "Scratch fifteen bad guys."

"Hang there for a few, in the case any more show up. We've got this covered in front."

"Will do," Jackson replied. Pallie changed magazines in his IAR.

Seconds later, four Humvees roared onto the scene, their .50 caliber machine guns firing steadily. Mustapha's remaining fighters, caught between the crossfire of the .50 caliber turret guns on the Humvees and the SEAL team on the ground, had no chance. The turret gunners concentrated their fire on the trucks, while the SEALs took out those who'd bailed out. Mustapha, still seated in the passenger seat of his Hilux, was dead. Tuarek lay on the ground beside the driver's side of the truck, not moving.

"Ceasefire!" Whitley commanded through the comm unit. The firing stopped. "Secure the perimeter. Keep your eyes open. Anybody down or injured?" Nobody on the SEAL team got a scratch. JD unsnapped Ajax's leash. Ajax would let them know if anyone was moving or playing dead.

"Vivas. Maddux. Get the doctor and her assistant out here. We're leaving in three minutes. Pallie, Jackson. Up front. Move."

"Roger that, Chief!" Pallie responded. He and Jackson made their way carefully into the alleyway and around to the front of the building. Inside, Maddux moved to where Ellen Chang still crouched on the floor.

"Let's go, Doc. Let's get you out of here." Ellen looked up, nodded, and got shakily to her feet. Maddux slipped an arm under her shoulder. "I've got you. Let's go."

Vivas stooped and gently lifted Norman Holley's body over his shoulder, then followed Maddux and the doctor out the door.

JD saw Maddux leading Ellen Chang through the doorway and out into the street. Vivas followed closely behind, carrying the body over his shoulder. JD started toward the three of them to see if he could help. Ajax dutifully followed at JD's side, keeping a wary canine eye out for any trouble.

Several yards away, Tuarek slowly regained consciousness. His head throbbed sharply from the .50 caliber bullet that had grazed his skull. He lay still. With a slight but painful turn of his head, Tuarek could make out the American soldiers moving about. They were getting ready to load up into their Humvees. The dead bodies of his fellow fighters lay scattered around him. Rage and hatred flared within him, desperate to kill these Americans. His eyes shifted, looking around for a weapon. An AK-47 lay in the street several feet away, but it looked like it had taken several hits from the American machine guns. There was no other weapon in sight.

It cannot be! How could this be the will of Allah?

It was then Tuarek remembered the hand grenade in the pocket of his fatigue pants. Moving slowly, trying not to be seen, Tuarek began inching his hand down toward the large pocket on his right pant leg. After what seemed like an eternity, Tuarek felt his hand close around the hand grenade. He withdrew it from the pocket.

Maddux had Ellen Chang at the back of the closest Humvee, so JD moved to help Vivas with the body of Norman Holley. Gently, the two SEALs laid Holley's body in the back of a second Humvee.

Ajax let out a ferocious growl. JD turned to see him springing toward an al Qaeda fighter just getting to his feet. The man was pulling the pin from a grenade. Several rifles sighted in on the lone jihadist, but before anyone squeezed a trigger, Ajax barreled into the man, his powerful jaws clamping down on the forearm of the hand holding the grenade. Ajax dropped his weight, dragging the man to the ground. The al Qaeda fighter landed hard on his side with Ajax chomping up to get a better grip on the man's arm. The terrorist screamed as the bones in his forearm snapped from the pressure in the Malinois' jaws. There was a loud explosion. Even with the noise of the detonating grenade, JD heard Ajax let out a single yelp.

JD and Maddux reached the spot where the al Qaeda fighter and Ajax both lay still. While the turret gunners kept an eye on the area, JD gently checked his dog. Ajax was breathing and alive, but JD could tell he was severely injured. There was a lot of blood covering his side and right rear leg.

Maddux quickly checked on the man. "This asshole's dead. Is Ajax okay?"

JD looked up. The look on his face gave Maddux his answer. Lifting Ajax gently into his arms, JD headed quickly toward the Humvees. At the closest Humvee, JD laid Ajax down gently in the back. He looked up to see Ellen hurrying toward them. She knelt at the dog's side and started to examine his wounds.

She looked at JD. "This is your dog?" JD nodded. "Get me a medical kit." JD started for the medical kit each Humvee carried. Maddux had beaten him to it and thrust a medical bag toward Ellen.

Chief Whitley yelled. "Load up! We're getting the hell out of here. Hahn, get on the radio. Tell them we are coming in. We have the doctor, one dead assistant, and we have one wounded team member."

Hahn started toward his Humvee.

JD and Maddux both jumped into the Humvee with Ellen and Ajax. Ellen looked over at Maddux.

"Open the kit for me, please!"

Maddux quickly opened the medical kit. JD sat, holding Ajax's head in his lap, gently stroking the fur of his neck. The Humvee's engines roared to life, and the convoy started back to the hotel. Maddux held a flashlight for Dr. Chang, who, after glancing over at JD, began to probe the dog's wounds gently.

CHAPTER 17
NIGER

JD nodded as Chief Whitley sat down next to him at the base mess hall. After helping himself to a forkful of scrambled egg followed by a swig of hot black coffee, Whitley turned to JD.

"How is Ajax this morning?"

"He's doing okay. Dr. Chang checks on him every day."

"I've noticed that. Ellen is one hell of a doctor. Handy, especially since there's no veterinarian on this base."

"Yep. The doc saved Ajax's life," JD acknowledged.

JD had already thanked Ellen Chang several times. In the back of the speeding Humvee, Dr. Chang had managed to stop some severe bleeding from Ajax's right side and rear leg. After the rescue team reassembled at the old hotel, the convoy of Humvees gunned their engines and headed straight back to Base 201. Radioing ahead, Chief Whitley learned that there was no veterinarian on the base. Hearing this discussion, Ellen told JD to get her somewhere she could operate.

Once on base, the Humvee carrying Ajax, Ellen, JD, and Maddux sped directly to the SEAL team's quarters. Pulling up to the front entrance, Slim slammed on the breaks. Before the Humvee came to a full stop, Roy was out, running around to open the back hatch. JD gently lifted Ajax from the back of the vehicle and carried him into the Quonset hut, setting him down on a table. Maddux followed with the medical kit, with Dr. Chang right behind him. Slim and Roy brought up the rear.

Slim, who'd spent some time as a Special Forces team medic, assisted Dr. Chang as she operated on the dog. Ajax was too out of it to object as she explored the damage. Ellen carefully searched for signs of internal injuries or bleeding while digging several pieces of shrapnel from the dog's wounds. Finally satisfied that she had all the metal fragments removed and everything looked as good as it could, Ellen began to clean him up.

"I'd like to shave around these gashes before closing them. Do we have anything to use?"

Maddux snapped his fingers. "Yes. Sweeney is nuts about his beard. He keeps a small battery-powered hair trimmer in his gear bag." Maddux sped off. A few seconds later, he was back with Sweeney's battery-powered Wahl beard trimmer in his hand.

With Slim's help, Ellen carefully trimmed away the hair around Ajax's cuts and lacerations. Then, cleaning them a second time, she sutured each wound closed and coated them with a strong antibiotic ointment from the SEAL medical kit. When she finished, Ellen stood back as Chief Whitley entered the Quonset hut and came up to the table.

"Well, that's all we can do for now. The bleeding has stopped. The shrapnel is removed. We need to get fluids into the dog and keep him still. I will see if I can get some IV units of normal saline solution from the aid station, and figure out the right painkiller dosage for a dog to keep him still."

"You worry about the painkiller, Doc," Chief Whitley broke in. "I'll have the saline solution over here quick." He turned and went back out through the Quonset hut door.

Once Ajax was hooked up to an IV and receiving fluids, things began to return to a less chaotic state. Dr. Chang had somehow "requisitioned" a painkiller called Tramadol from an Air Force medic in the aid station. It was safe for dogs, and Ajax was now resting comfortably.

The SEAL team turned their focus to the mission debriefing and taking care of other remaining tasks. They turned the body of Norman Holley over to the Air Force, and preparations were now underway to return his remains to the U.S. for burial. Hahn volunteered to escort the body back, planning to make a stop at Langley before spending a few weeks relaxing in Thailand.

Dr. Chang grudgingly submitted to a thorough check-up by the base physician at the aid station before being allowed to shower and grab a quick meal. She next attended a debriefing session that included a group of military brass, state department officials, and senior staff from Doctors Without Borders. They'd even brought along a trauma counselor. Ellen assured Dr. Clemmons that she was okay and just needed a good night's rest.

During the meeting, Ellen described the events leading up to the kidnapping as best she remembered them, including Bram Alderik's death, and her and Norman's kidnapping. There wasn't much she could tell them about her confinement, having spent most of it in a small darkened room. Ellen could only describe a couple of her captors, and anyway, they were probably all dead now at the hands of her rescue team. Finally, with all the questions answered, Ellen was allowed to slip off to her quarters for some much-needed sleep.

While Ellen was exhausted, sleep did not come easily. She lay on her bunk, thinking through the events of the day. So many thoughts and emotions coursed through her brain. Suddenly, she found herself laughing and crying at the same time. She had never experienced such a release of pent-up emotion in her life. There were feelings of gratitude for her rescue, guilt for Norman and Bram's deaths, and wonderment at the men who had risked their lives to save her. Just a few short hours ago, she'd been sure she was going to die. Now she was here, in her bunk, safely back on the base.

That is one hell of a dog, Ellen thought. *Several of us would be dead now if Ajax hadn't taken down that man with the grenade.*

Ellen knew the dog would be okay. While not trained to operate on animals, she was good at what she did and prided herself on being a skilled doctor. The dog had lost a lot of blood, but Ajax was healthy and had a strong will to live.

Yes. Ajax will be just fine. I'll see to that.

The last thing Ellen remembered as she finally started to doze was seeing JD, sitting there gently stroking his dog's head as she worked to stem the blood loss. *A man and his dog*, she thought, and then Ellen was asleep.

Across the base, JD settled down on his cot. He'd moved it over to where Ajax still lay resting on one of the tables in the team's Quonset hut. Not one man on the team objected. If Ajax needed the table, he got the table. It was as simple as that.

JD closed his eyes and lay quietly for a few minutes, listening to the dog's steady breathing. It sounded much better, that is when he could hear it through the loud snores of the other team members sharing the quarters. JD was deeply thankful that Dr. Chang had been able to save Ajax. He knew from his training that dogs don't have nearly the reserve blood supply that humans do. Ajax surely would have bled out in a matter of minutes, way before they'd made it back to the base. Ajax owed Dr. Ellen Chang his life.

Ellen had kept her cool through the rescue and ensuing firefight. And, despite clearly being exhausted and scared, she'd treated Ajax in the Humvee and performed surgery just a short time later, right here on this table.

She's quite a lady, JD thought. *Smart and nerves of steel. At the very least, I owe her a cup of coffee.*

JD reached up to scratch the dog's back, where it was near the edge of the table. He heard Ajax's tail gently thump on the tabletop.

Yes. Ajax will be okay.

He'd see if he could catch up with Ellen Chang sometime tomorrow. Right now, it was time to sleep. JD rolled over and, in a few seconds, was sound asleep, snoring gently.

CHAPTER 18
WASHINGTON, DC

President Steele was pacing back and forth on the blue carpet in front of his desk in the Oval Office. General Clay Ellerson, appointed to replace the recently retired General Dunning as Chairman of the Joint Chiefs, sat alone on one sofa. Rear Admiral Robert Spence, Commander, Naval Special Warfare Command, and CIA Director Mike Connors sat across from Ellerson on a second sofa. The president's Chief of Staff, Martin Sansby, sat in a chair near the end of the sofa occupied by General Ellerson. Admiral Spence had just finished briefing those present on the successful rescue of Dr. Ellen Chang by members of SEAL Team 5 from a group of al Qaeda terrorists the previous day.

"And, Dr. Chang is still in Niger?" the president inquired.

"That is correct, sir," Admiral Spence replied. "She wanted to stay and complete her rotation. The doc checked out okay. A little hungry and tired, but other than that, she's in good health. The shrink seems to think she is fine as well."

"Tough lady," General Ellerson observed. Director Connors nodded his head in agreement.

'That she is," agreed President Steele. The president circled behind his desk and sat back in his chair. "Go on, Bob."

"Dr. Chang is also treating the SEAL team's K9. The dog got injured in the firefight. The K9 took down a terrorist who was about to toss a grenade at a small group of SEALs and Dr. Chang. The grenade still went off; the terrorist caught most of the blast as he fell.

However, the dog caught some shrapnel. That dog saved the doc and several members of the team." Spence paused to check his notes, then continued. "Since there is no veterinarian on Base 201, the doc took over treatment of the dog, and according to the Chief, saved the dog's life. The dog's handler is JD Cordell. He and the dog are the same two who got sucked into that Iranian terrorist plot a few years back."

"Really?" Ellerson interjected. "I knew Cordell's father. He served under me in Vietnam. Damn good officer."

The president looked up. "Small world, isn't it." Looking over at Admiral Spence, he went on. "Bob, can we give the dog a medal? That dog is a hero, and I think the American people would love that."

"That is a great idea," Sansby agreed. "The press would eat that up."

The Admiral glanced over at General Ellerson. "Mr. President, there currently is no official military medal for dogs. I believe there is a civilian version that the American Humane Society awards to military dogs."

"That is correct, Admiral," the general replied.

The president shifted in his chair and leaned forward, placing his elbows on the desk. He addressed General Ellerson and Admiral Spence directly. "Clay, Bob, that dog is a highly trained U.S. Navy SEAL. It saved the lives of Dr. Chang and several members of one of my damn SEAL teams. I am going to give that dog a military medal, and you are going to make it happen."

"Yes, Sir," General Ellerson replied.

Admiral Spence grinned. "I think that is an excellent idea, Mr. President. We will be pleased to make that happen."

President Steele nodded. "Thank you, gentleman. Is there anything else?"

"Sir," Mike Connors leaned forward. "One of my agents posted in Niger, Rick Hahn, assisted with the operation and provided a team of private contractors who volunteered as vehicle drivers and turret gunners for the Humvees the SEAL team used in the rescue. Rick is escorting the body of Norman Holly back to the U.S. The contractors volunteered for the mission because they know and like Dr. Chang. However, let's show them some gratitude for what they did. They are all former Spec Ops or civilian SWAT team members."

"Contractors..." the president paused. "Well, they are helpful at times. Whatever you think is appropriate, Mike. If you need any help, talk to Martin. My chief of staff can certainly light a fire under someone's ass if necessary."

Sansby nodded. "Sure thing, Mike. Just call me if you need anything at all."

"That's great. Thanks." replied the CIA director. "We need to keep it out of the news to protect the identity of both the SEALs and the contractors, but we'll let the public know as much as we can."

The president stood. "Okay. I must make an appearance at a damned party fundraiser this afternoon. So, unless there is anything else, the meeting is over. Keep me in the loop on the medal for the dog. I want that to happen as soon as possible."

The remaining attendees got to their feet.

"Yes, Sir, Mr. President," General Ellerson and Admiral Spence both answered in the affirmative. Mike Connors, followed by the general and the admiral, headed through the open door, leaving President Steele to discuss the rest of the day's activities with his chief of staff.

CHAPTER 19
NIGER

JD caught up with Ellen Chang as she made her way toward Base 201's mess hall.

"Hey, Doc. Ajax seems to be doing great. I wanted to thank you again for everything you've done for him."

"You're welcome. And please, call me Ellen."

JD grinned. "Okay, Ellen... on the condition that you call me JD."

"Fair enough. I'm going to the mess hall for some lunch. Care to join me?"

"How can I refuse?" JD laughed. "The least I can do is buy you lunch." Ellen smiled at that. She'd not seen anyone pay for a meal since being on the base. Lunch would be compliments of the U.S. Air Force. Ellen figured it was little enough compensation for being on a hardship tour in Niger.

Together, the two made their way through the chow line, opting for the short-order line. Both came away with a cheeseburger, french fries, and iced tea. Finding an empty table in a corner, they sat down and started their lunch. After sampling a fry, Ellen looked up at JD.

"You are quite attached to your dog. I could tell when we were in the Humvee."

JD looked up. "We've been through a lot together. So yes, I guess I am. He's not just my partner. He's part of my family."

"Family?"

JD nodded. "Ajax is quite an amazing dog." He paused to take a bite of his cheeseburger. "He probably saved the lives of both my Mom and Dad."

"Really, how so?"

JD hesitated. "It's a long story."

"That's okay. We have time, and I'd like to hear it," Ellen replied.

JD proceeded to give her a somewhat shortened version of the story beginning with the raid in Afghanistan and uncovering the terrorist plot and ending with the attack on his family's home in Knoxville, Tennessee. Ellen listened attentively. As JD got to the part where Ajax's growling had awakened his Dad and allowed him to stop several of the terrorist assassins from getting in the house, she stopped eating. JD went on to describe Ajax's breaking out of his crate and taking down one killer that was about to enter the bedroom where his mother was. When he finally explained how his mother had killed the leader of the assassination team, a female Syrian killer named Fatima, Ellen was astounded.

The doctor sat back in her chair. "Holy shit!" she exclaimed. "I heard about some of that on the news. There was something about an Iranian terrorist plot too."

JD nodded and took another bite from his cheeseburger before reaching for his unsweetened tea. Swallowing some tea, he replied, "It's hard to believe, I know. But it's all true."

Ellen shook her head. "So that was you and Ajax." She paused. "And what about Julie?"

JD looked up, meeting Ellen's eyes. "I liked her. We had a thing for a short time, but we didn't have much in common. I think it was all the danger and excitement that drew us together. Once that was over, we drifted apart."

"Sorry to intrude..." JD and Ellen both looked up. It was Chief Whitely. JD could tell by the look on his face that something was very wrong.

Whitley handed JD a folded paper. "You'd better read this, JD."

JD took the paper and started to read. Ellen watched as the expression on his face changed. Suddenly, he looked up.

"I am sorry, Ellen. I have to go. I've enjoyed talking to you." JD stood and turned to Whitley. "Chief?" Whitley nodded. JD turned and, after one more glance at Ellen, headed toward the mess hall door. Ellen watched him go.

Turning back, Ellen reached up and took hold of Whitley's arm. "What's the matter, Chief Whitley? What happened?"

Whitley turned and looked down, seeing the concerned look on Ellen's face. "It's bad news from home. JD's father just died from liver cancer. Something he picked up in Vietnam."

"Oh no," replied Ellen, her gaze turning back just in time to see JD exit through the dining facility door.

Chief Whitley arranged JD's flight back to the U.S. through the Air Force and Base 201's commander. That flight was taking off in about thirty minutes. The Chief stood on the tarmac with JD, waiting for departure time.

"Don't worry, JD. Take the time you need. We've got you covered as far as leave time, and Maddux has volunteered to take care of Ajax until you get back."

JD grinned at that. Ajax would be in great hands. Maddux and the dog had gotten off to a rough start but were now best buddies. Maddux was second only to JD in Ajax's pecking order. Whitley turned and spotted Roy and Ellen coming toward them across the tarmac.

"You've got company." The Chief moved off a few steps as Roy approached first, extending his hand.

"Sorry to hear about your dad, man. If there is anything our guys or I can do, just let me know."

JD took Roy's extended hand and shook it firmly. "Thanks, Roy. I appreciate that. Thanks a lot." Roy nodded and turned to head back the way he'd come. JD turned and found Ellen standing beside him.

"JD, I am so sorry to hear about your father." Ellen paused, looking for the right words with which to continue. "I'm not sure what to say, other than thank you, and I have enjoyed meeting you and Ajax. I wish we had more time to get to know each other. I will take good care of Ajax." She laughed. "That is if I can pry your friend, Maddux, away from him."

JD smiled. "I guess Ajax will be in two excellent sets of hands while I'm gone."

Ellen nodded. "He will be." She paused again, searching for something to say. JD beat her to it.

"Look, Ellen... I hope I'll see you again sometime."

Impulsively, Ellen reached out and hugged him, kissing his cheek. "I would like that very much," she whispered in his ear. Releasing him, Ellen turned and headed back across the tarmac.

Back in her quarters, Ellen sat on her bunk and kicked her feet up on the footlocker that contained most of what she had in Niger. So much had happened in the past week; it was hard to sort it all out. She assumed it would take some time to work through everything she had just endured. It isn't every day you are kidnapped by terrorists, rescued by a SEAL team, survive a deadly firefight, and then operate on a military dog.

Ajax's shrapnel wounds were healing, and the dog was recovering nicely. He was up and moving around, but she'd suggested to Maddux that he keep Ajax confined to his crate for a few more days. Ajax made no effort to chew at his stitches, but Ellen didn't want to risk him re-opening any of his lacerations or getting an infection. Maddux was taking great care of Ajax, keeping him fed and watered, and taking him out for walks so the dog could regain his strength.

The SEAL team had received orders to stay in Agadez a few more days, in case there were any reprisals by al Qaeda for Ellen's rescue. There had been none so far, and the team would soon be loading up to return to Coronado. Besides, Rick Hahn's group of contractors were quite capable, and teamed with the Marines on the base, made quite a deterrent.

Ellen had learned from her talks with JD that he was getting out of the Navy soon and taking Ajax home with him. The plan was to process out from Coronado as soon as Ajax was ready and the paperwork stamped.

"Time to let the younger guys have it. Ajax and I have done our share."

Ellen guessed JD was about forty. She knew he'd been in over twenty years, so that would be close. She'd also learned he'd extended his enlistment long enough to be able to take Ajax home with him when Ajax had finished his term of service, and her rescue was going to be the dog's last mission. At first, Ellen had been amazed by the bond between JD and Ajax. After her rescue, Ellen felt she could understand the relationships combat can forge between men who fight beside each other. Having been raised in a family that did not keep pets, seeing that same strong bond between a man and his dog was astounding to her. Ellen had witnessed first-hand the fact that Ajax would sacrifice his life to protect JD. As crazy as it seemed, she could almost see JD doing the same for Ajax.

What kind of a man does that, she wondered? Some might say a foolish man, but Ellen thought she could see beyond that. JD was no fool. He was simply a strong man who did what he felt was right, no matter the situation. *That man has a strong sense of family and loyalty.*

She thought about what he'd told her about the terrorist plot his team had uncovered and the resulting attack on his friends and family. It all seemed so incredible. Now he was heading back to Knoxville, to bury his father. Ellen wished she had been able to spend more time with JD before he left. He was an interesting man, a good man.

Suddenly, she sat up straight. A thought had just solidified in her mind. It was crazy! But it was what she was going to do.

CHAPTER 20
KNOXVILLE, TN

The Boeing-built C-17 Globemaster III touched down at McGhee Tyson Airport in Knoxville at 3:00 a.m. The flight had been uneventful. Except for several large crates, JD had the cargo hold to himself. There was a brief stopover at Charleston Air Force Base to refuel and to load up three brand new Humvees destined for Elmendorf Air Force base in Alaska.

JD had spent the seventeen-hour flight alternating between sleep, worrying about Ajax, and running through the Isshin-ryu katas. It helped to pass the time and kept him from getting too stiff from sitting in the barely adequate nylon-webbed seating.

Knoxville's public terminal had recently undergone significant renovations, but the military side looked pretty much the same as it always had. Modernizing a few hangars servicing Blackhawk helicopters was not very high on the Pentagon's priority list.

JD hefted his duffle bag over his shoulder and strode down the lowered cargo ramp, making his way toward the hangar. A warrant officer overseeing the service work on one of the Blackhawks looked up and saw the Navy SEAL walking toward him. Having been around service members of all the military branches for many years, he recognized the Senior Chief rank as well as the SEAL trident on the approaching man's uniform.

"Afternoon, Senior Chief. I'm Chief Hadley. Can I help you?"

"Hey, Chief. I'm fine, just headed over to the gates. Home on leave for personal business."

"They don't want us cutting across the runways, so it's a pretty good hike. My jeep's right here. I'd be happy to give you a lift over to the civilian side of the airport if you'd like."

"That'd be great. Thanks."

A few minutes later, Hadley dropped JD off at a gate-side entrance to the terminal. The security officer waved him through after a brief couple of questions. Once inside, he made his way through security and into the main lobby, where his younger sister, Annie, promptly greeted him. Her husband, Robert, had stayed at the house to help Mai with the two boys. JD greeted his sister with a hug.

"How's mom?" he asked.

"You know mom," Annie replied. "She's a rock on the outside."

JD nodded. That she was. However, he also knew how much his mom and dad had loved each other. They'd shared an extraordinary life since meeting in the central highlands of Vietnam. He worried that their father's death would be nearly impossible for her.

The siblings made their way out to the short-term parking area, and JD slung his duffle bag into the back seat of Annie's Audi A4. A few minutes later, they were on Alcoa Highway, headed toward Knoxville and home, about a forty-minute drive.

"The boys are excited to meet their uncle, finally," Annie commented after a few minutes. "Especially since Robert told them you're a SEAL." Annie laughed. "They were a bit disappointed when he explained that you don't have flippers and can't balance a beachball on your nose."

JD chuckled at that. "Well, actually, I do have flippers in my gear bag, but I didn't bring it along on this trip. I could work on the beachball thing, though. Who knows? How are you doing?" JD asked.

"I'm fine. You know me. Nothing rattles me." That was true. Annie had always been able to take even the most upsetting events in stride. "I'm a bit worried about mom, though," she went on. "She's talking about taking a trip back to Vietnam, to look for Uncle Dish and see if she can bring him back here to Knoxville. She and Dad talked about doing that at one time, but then Dad got sick. Now, mom wants to go by herself."

"You know Mom," JD observed. "It will be impossible to stop her if she decides to do it."

"I know. That's what worries me. Vietnam has changed a lot since she left. There is no way to know where Uncle Dish might be, or even if he's still alive."

JD nodded. "That is a problem. Let's get the funeral over. Then we can sit down with Mom and have a family discussion. I understand her wanting to go back. I can go with her if she waits for a few months. Ajax and I will be retiring soon."

"That'd be great. If mom is with you, I'll know she's safe."

The funeral took place three days later. Curtis and Mai had prearranged everything. They were both meticulous about things like that, and there was little for JD or Annie to do. Mai bustled about, making sure everything was perfect. JD tried to catch his mother alone for a few minutes, to see how she was holding up, but Mai never slowed down enough to give him a chance.

JD was shocked when the day before the funeral, Carlos Vivas, Joe Palazzolo, and Jim Maddux showed up and knocked on the Cordell family home's front door. Annie greeted them at the door and led them into the living room. When JD saw his three teammates, his jaw dropped in surprise.

"What the f...?" he stopped himself just in time, glancing over at his mother, who seemed not to have noticed. He knew, reminding himself to be more careful, that Mai saw everything. "What the heck are you guys doing here?"

Pallie spoke up first. "The Chief sent us. Told us to make sure you arrived safely."

Maddux slapped Pallie on the back. "Yep. Told us to make sure you didn't get lost on the way home."

Carlos just nodded at JD.

"The team's earned some downtime, and the Chief called some general at the Pentagon... Ellerson, I think, and requested that a few members of the team be present at the funeral. The general agreed that it was a good idea and made it happen. We're here to give your father a three-gun salute. He deserves it."

JD was stunned. He looked over at his mother, who had gotten to her feet and walked over. Much to their embarrassment, she gave each one of them a big hug. Finally, JD remembered his manners and properly introduced his colleagues to Annie, Robert, and Mai.

Just then, two little boys rounded the corner into the living room at full speed. Suddenly, they screeched to a halt and stood there, staring wide-eyed at the three men.

Robert bailed his sons out. "Jimmy, Allen, these are friends of your Uncle JD."

"Are you guys SEALs too?" Allen blurted out.

Pallie and Maddux said nothing. Vivas just smiled. "I reckon so."

The military ceremony was beautiful. The funeral procession up Lyons View Pike approached the East Tennessee State Veterans Cemetery. They drove to the chapel overlooking the neat rows of graves dating as far back as World War I. The old cemetery was full now; all the plots sold. Curtis and Mai had purchased one of the few remaining spots many years ago. Curtis had always loved the beautiful cemetery and wanted his final resting place to be there. When the time came, Mai would join him.

The casket team—volunteers from the 278th Armored Cavalry Regiment of the Tennessee National Guard—secured the casket and followed the Chaplain to the gravesite. They were followed by Mai and her family, with friends bringing up the rear. With coffin ready, the military funeral team had the Stars and Stripes stretched out, level, and centered over the casket. Mai and the family took their seats.

Mai was flanked on either side by JD and Annie. Annie's two boys, Jimmy and Allen, sat between her and her husband, Robert. Friends surrounded them. Father Joe Patterson, who'd performed a short service at the funeral home, was there along with Sensei Tokumura, Joe Trenton, and Bill and Nancy Peterson. Julie Spencer had driven down from Washington, D.C. Though she and JD no longer saw each other, their shared experience had created a strong bond of friendship between them. General Ellerson had taken time out of his busy schedule to attend the burial.

When everything was ready, the NCO in charge of the casket team backed away, and a U.S. Army chaplain who had served with Curtis in Vietnam stepped up and performed the service, after which the NCO again stepped forward and asked those seated to rise for honors.

"Present, Arms!" rang out clearly in the quiet mid-morning air. Vivas, Palazzolo, and Maddux fired the M-14 rifles three times at the command of the NCO. The salute completed, the bugler played TAPS, the traditional military call's notes drifting along on a slight breeze.

Once the last haunting note receded into the distance, the NCO asked everyone to be seated. The casket team began folding the flag, which, when properly folded, was presented to the NCO, who, in turn, gave it to General Ellerson, who had stepped forward.

General Ellerson turned and stepped up to Mai, to present her the folded flag. "On behalf of a grateful nation."

Mai took the flag and then, not worried too much about military protocol, stood and gave the General a big hug. There were tears in her eyes.

"Thank you, General Ellerson," Mai replied before sitting back down.

Their task completed, the casket team, with NCO leading them, left the gravesite.

After the burial, most of the attendees paid their respects and left. General Ellerson spoke to JD a few minutes and greeted the three other SEALs before making his way over to where Mai was standing with Annie and her husband. Mai spotted Ellerson approaching and stepped forward, a brave smile on her face.

"It was so nice of you to come, General Ellerson."

"It was my honor, Mai. Your husband was one of my best officers and a good man. Today is a sad day, but I am so happy you two had a good life together."

"Thank you, General." Mai always prided herself on her inscrutability, but Ellerson could tell she was struggling to hold back tears. He reached up and gently placed his hand on her shoulder.

"Mai, if there is ever anything I can do, you only have to ask." Mai nodded.

"I appreciate that. Really. Thank you again," Mai leaned forward and gave the General another hug. Ellerson gently returned the embrace, then stepped back, turned away, and started toward the parking lot. His driver was waiting to take him to the airport to catch his flight back to Washington.

Father Joe and Joe Trenton also made sure Mai knew that if she needed anything at all, she only needed to call, and then they headed back to the church, to take care of several tasks related to the next morning's service. Bill and Nancy Peterson both hugged Mai and promised to stop by for a chat in a few days when things had slowed down a bit. Tokumura Sensei paid his respects to Mai and elicited a promise from JD to stop by the dojo for a visit. JD promised he would. Julie came up and gave both JD and Mai a hug.

"Your father was a good man, JD," Julie whispered. "I will never forget what your family did for me."

JD hugged her back. "Thank you, Julie. It's nice to see you again." Julie smiled and moved off to let others pay their respects.

Mai had JD invite Pallie, Vivas, and Maddux over for lunch and a visit before they left for Coronado. Things had remained quiet in Agadez since Dr. Chang's rescue. The team, along with Ajax, would be deploying back to Coronado at the end of the month. Chief Whitley had called to pay his respects and extend condolences from the rest of the team. He'd given Maddux, Pallie, and Vivas orders to report to Coronado and prepare for the rest of the team's arrival. JD had two more days of leave before he would return, and shortly after that, he would begin the retirement process for himself and Ajax.

Once at the house, JD and the guys retired to the back yard where at Vivas' suggestion, he and JD spent some time exchanging Isshin-ryu and Escrima techniques. Jimmy and Allen both sat on the back porch, looking on with wide-eyed admiration. The boys felt lucky to be seeing two world-class experts practice their craft right in front of them. Maddux and Pallie watched as well but seemed to be more interested in drinking the cold Heineken provided by Robert.

"Hey Pallie, you big lummox! Put down the beer and come out here and give this a try," Vivas chided.

"What for?" Pallie called back laughing, then holding up both his hands. "If I can get these meat hooks on somebody, I won't need any fancy knife tricks to take care of business."

Maddux, for his part, had become intrigued. He joined JD and Vivas.

Pallie put down his beer and looked up when he heard Maddux let out a grunt. "Sonofabitch, JD, how the hell do you hit so damn hard?"

JD laughed. "It's easy, Jim. It's just timing, patience, and focus."

"Focus, my ass," Maddux grumbled, still rubbing his chest. "That felt like a baseball bat."

"Well, I guess there's also the many hours spent with a makiwara."

"A maki-what?" Vivas asked.

"A punching post," JD answered.

"Oh, that clears it up," Maddux chuckled.

"Oh, come on!" Pallie interjected. He'd heard about JD's fighting skills, but never really seen them in action. "There's no way some little guy JD's size is going to knock me off my feet."

Vivas grinned. That sounded a lot like a challenge. "Well, here's your chance to prove it, Pallie. Step right up!"

"By God, I will!" Pallie got to his feet and strode out to where the other three men stood. "What do I need to do?"

"You don't have to do anything," JD responded. "However, if you feel you need the experience, take your best shot."

Pallie grinned. For a big guy, he moved fast. Dropping into a fighter's crouch, he shifted forward and launched a powerful right cross.

No need to hurt the little guy, Pallie thought, throwing the punch toward JD's chest rather than his chin, which would have been Pallie's preferred target.

But JD was no longer in front of him. He'd shifted to Pallie's left.

Damn, JD is quick flashed through Pallie's brain, just as his left shoulder was struck by something that felt like a freight train.

"Damn, JD! You've killed Pallie!" Vivas observed with a wry grin.

"Holy crap! He hit him in the damn shoulder," Maddux added, shaking his head. Pallie lay on the grass, not moving.

"Is he breathing?" JD asked.

"I think so," Vivas said.

Just then, Annie appeared, coming out to announce that lunch was ready.

"What's wrong with him?" she exclaimed, seeing Pallie lying motionless on the ground.

"Your brother hit Pallie in the shoulder," Maddux answered, in a mildly worried tone.

"Oh! Well, okay. Lunch is ready if you want to come in and eat."

Just then, a soft groan rose from Pallie. Almost in slow motion, he rolled over to see Annie and his three friends standing there, looking down at him.

"What the hell happened?" he asked.

"I'd say you just had a genuine religious experience," Vivas laughed. "We're going in to eat. Join us when you can."

There was a lot of food. Many friends had stopped by to deliver an assortment of covered dishes: fried chicken, baked beans, both a tuna and a green bean casserole, sweet cornbread, a ham, macaroni and cheese, and a giant pineapple upside-down cake. Mai had added steamed dumplings and fried rice to this already bountiful selection. Lunch was buffet-style, and people were free to sit where they chose.

A few minutes later, Pallie appeared at the table. He was favoring his left arm just a bit. Maddux walked up and stood next to him.

"Want me to fix you a plate?" Maddux asked, only half-joking.

"No, but thanks. What happened?" Pallie asked again.

"JD punched you in the shoulder. Knocked you out cold."

"No fucking way," Pallie whispered.

"It was a hell of a punch," Maddux laughed.

Still not sure what to believe, Pallie began scooping food with his right hand onto the plate he held gingerly in his left. Maddux grinned, noticing this. Pallie was left-handed.

After lunch, the entire group retired to the living room to let their food digest. The emotional strain of the day had everyone feeling a little tired. It was a pleasure to sit and relax and watch the two boys, Jimmy and Allen, entertaining themselves. They were old enough to understand that their grandfather was gone but young enough to not dwell on the fact. Eventually, though, Jimmy stopped playing and looked up at his grandmother. "Grandma, will you tell us something about Grandpa?"

Mai smiled. "Sure." She then relayed a few tales from the time she and Curtis spent together in Vietnam. Vivas, Pallie, and Maddux enjoyed the story of the night at the old Buddhist temple and their subsequent detour to warn the Marines of the trap the NVA and VC had set for them.

"That Captain Sparks seemed like a decent enough sort, for a jarhead," Pallie observed.

"Seems like," Maddux agreed.

"I've read those Montagnard were tough fighters. The Special Forces and LRRP teams liked having them along," Vivas commented.

"What? Vivas! I didn't know you could read," Pallie exclaimed with a laugh. "You never cease to amaze me."

"You know, JD," Maddux cut in. "I was talking to one of those contractors in Niger, and he told me his uncle served with your dad in Vietnam. I can't remember what his name was, but he was telling me a story about a guy named Steve and an orangutan. I didn't believe it, though. Sounded like bull.... to me." Maddux had caught sight of the two young boys, listening with rapt attention. He shifted gears mid-sentence.

"Nope, it's a true story," JD replied, laughing.

"An orangutan, Uncle JD? What story?" Jimmy asked excitedly.

Pallie laughed. "Yeah, Uncle JD. What story?"

"It has a sad ending," JD commented thoughtfully, looking over at Annie, who nodded her head.

"Tell us!" Allen pleaded.

"Okay," JD relented. "There was a guy named Steven Taylor in the same unit as your grandfather. Same company, but a different platoon. Anyway, Steve was this short, wiry little guy, but with a reputation for being tough and a good fighter." JD paused.

"Go on, Uncle JD," Vivas urged with a big grin.

"Well, his platoon had been out on a long patrol, and they were resting in a Montagnard village for a few days. It was blazing hot, so they had a few cases of beer and some blocks of ice flown in by helicopter. What they would do is take a block of ice and roll the beer back and forth on it until it got cold. Then they'd drink that one while rolling the next beer on the ice, and so on."

"That would work," Maddux observed, winking at Pallie.

"Anyway, some members of the platoon had consumed a little too much beer and were getting drunk. According to your grandfather, the chief of the village had a pet orangutan he'd raised from a baby. I don't think orangutans are native to Vietnam, but Malaysia and Sumatra are close. Anyway, he'd probably traded for it in some market somewhere." JD paused, taking a sip from his beer. "The orangutan used to like to sit in the shade of this big old tree and eat the fruit the chief fed him."

"I know where this is going," Vivas observed. Annie nodded and looked over at Robert, who was enjoying the story, never having heard it before.

"Some of the members of Steve's platoon started teasing him, daring him to go over and slap the chief's orangutan in the face. Well, Steve, who'd already had a few beers, finished the one he was drinking, stood up, and marched right up to that orangutan and slapped it in the face." Again, JD paused.

"No, shit?" It was Robert. Annie glanced over at her husband, giving him a shushing noise, and pointing at their two sons.

"Sorry," Robert mouthed back with a grin. Jimmy giggled. Allen had missed his father's transgression.

"Then what happened?" Allen urged excitedly.

"Well, you have to understand, orangutans are very strong," JD continued.

"Comes from swinging around in trees all day," Pallie observed, winking at Allen.

"Exactly," JD agreed. "So anyway, this orangutan just stretched out one long arm, grabbed Steve by one of his ankles, and started swinging him around like a dish towel, bouncing him off the ground."

"Like the Hulk did to Loki in the Avengers?" Jimmy asked.

"Just like that."

"Wow," Allen commented rather thoughtfully. "Then what happened?"

"Well, that's the sad part. They had to shoot the orangutan to keep it from killing Steve."

"Oh, no!" Robert exclaimed.

"They shot it?" Jimmy asked, not believing what he'd heard.

"They had no choice," JD replied. "Steve was beaten up pretty bad as it was. A few more seconds, and he'd have been dead."

"And, that's a true story?" Vivas inquired.

"The orangutan's name was Chu," Mai responded. "My father knew the Montagnard chief who kept the animal as a pet. The chief's name was Glun. The Montagnards in that village were very angry with the Americans for a long time. It took a lot of gifts and apologies to appease Glun and keep those villagers from trying to kill Steve."

Maddux sat back and whistled. "Now, that's a story."

Robert nodded, catching the eyes of his two sons. "I guess the moral of that story is, don't start a fight unless it is over something worth it."

"Especially with an orangutan," Pallie added, getting up for a good stretch.

"That's a sad story," Allen commented. Jimmy nodded.

"Yes, it is, boys. And there certainly is a lesson to be learned from it," JD added.

Jimmy grinned, looking up at Pallie. "Right! Never slap an orangutan in the face."

"Something like that," JD agreed.

Eventually, the afternoon ended. Robert offered to drive Pallie, Vivas, and Maddux to the airport to catch their flight to San Diego. He knew Annie and JD wanted some time alone with their mother. The two boys, exhausted from the day, passed out on the couch. It would be a while before they stirred.

JD thanked his mates for their part in his father's burial ceremony. Maddux placed a hand on JD's shoulder and stated, "It was a real honor, JD. We all enjoyed meeting your mother. She's quite a lady."

JD grinned. "That she is."

After they drove off with Robert in Annie's Nissan Xterra, JD found his sister and their mother in the kitchen, cleaning up a bit. He looked over at Annie, who, catching his eye, nodded.

"Mom, Annie tells me you're planning a trip to Vietnam, to try and find Uncle Dish."

"Well, yes, JD, I am. I didn't know Annie told you."

"I didn't know it was a secret, Mom."

"Well, I guess it isn't." Mai hung the dishtowel on the oven handle and turned around. "I would like to find Dish and bring him back with me to America if I can."

"I think that's a great idea, Mom. Both Annie and I would love to meet him and have him here with us." JD paused. "Vietnam has probably changed a great bit since you were there. It's been a long time. If you can wait a couple of months, I would be happy to go with you. I want to help. I just need to get my retirement process completed first."

"That's very kind of you, JD. But you have your own new life to establish here at home. You will need to find a job and a place to live. I am sure I'll be fine. I am perfectly capable of taking care of myself."

JD and Annie both laughed at that. "You certainly are, Mom," Annie replied. "But I admit, I would feel much better if JD went with you. He's pretty capable too."

It was their mother's turn to laugh. "That is certainly true. Okay, you two. Let me think about it. You go back to Coronado, JD, and do what you must do. I will make my plans and let both of you know before I go anywhere. Okay?"

"Sounds good," JD replied. Annie agreed.

CHAPTER 21
CORONADO NAVAL BASE

It was Sunday. JD loaded Ajax into the jeep and took I-5 for the short run from Shelltown up to Coronado. Crossing the bridge, he merged onto 4th Street. With the top off the jeep, it was a pleasant drive. Ajax, his nose in the wind, checked out the many smells along the way. JD turned left onto Orange Ave and continued on Silver Strand Boulevard, finally turning left down Tulagi Road. He parked at the Turner Field Recreational Area.

Already dressed to workout, JD grabbed a gym bag containing a towel, a bottle of water, and a few other items from the passenger seat.

"Ajax, Komen!" Ajax jumped down out of the jeep and fell in at JD's left side. Once inside the gym, JD pointed to a corner out of the way. "Ajax, Plaats." Ajax trotted over to the spot JD had indicated and settled in for a nap. Setting the gym bag down near the dog, JD moved out onto the gym floor to loosen up and stretch out. A few minutes later, he was working through the Isshin-Ryu katas. Just as he finished working through the last kata, Ajax sat up excitedly.

"Hey, JD! What's going on, man?!" It was Vivas. "Is that some of your Isshin-Ryu? Interesting! Those looked like elbow strikes."

"You could say that. Technically, many of those are not elbow strikes. I guess some might argue it's not Isshin-Ryu," he laughed. "But it's all Isshin-Ryu technique."

Vivas looked puzzled. "I'm not sure I get that."

"The name of this kata is Seishin no Tomodachi, or My Spiritual Friends... something like that. It is Sensei Sherman Harrill's kata. My

Sensei, Tokumura, learned it from Sherman Harrill before he died. They were good friends."

"That's pretty cool. They still look like elbow strikes to me."

JD ran through one of the techniques consisting of an open hand block with the right arm followed by an 'elbow strike' with the left, immediately followed by a rising 'elbow strike' and a back-fist strike with the right. He laughed. "I guess they do look like elbow strikes after all."

"If they're not elbow strikes, what are they?" Vivas wanted to see what else they could be.

"I can demonstrate if you like. That is if you can take a shot."

Vivas snorted. "I'm a frogman, dude! If you can dish it out, I can take it."

"Okay! Keep your teeth closed," JD warned with a grin. The two warriors squared off. Vivas shifted into a fighter's crouch while JD stood with his hands at his sides, calmly waiting.

Shit! If he's going to stand there like that, I'm going to deck him. Vivas moved in fast, launching a quick right at JD's midsection. JD stepped forward, deftly blocking the punch with a right open-handed parry. That surprised Vivas, but he recovered and, withdrawing his right, fired his left at JD. JD's rising left-arm met the punch and traveling across, deflected Vivas' blow to the right and downward. This action caused Vivas' head to move forward where his chin was met by the two knuckles of JD's rising right fist, snapping his jaw up and back. Immediately, JD's back fist was poised at the carotid area of Vivas' throat. Vivas was glad when JD stopped the strike.

"Sonofabitch," Vivas exclaimed, grinning. "That was freakin' awesome. I am glad you warned me to keep my teeth together."

JD laughed. "Are you okay?"

"Hell yeah!" Vivas rubbed the spot where JD's fist had connected with his chin. "I'm just glad you weren't seriously pissed at me."

"There are a few variations if you'd like to see them."

"Absolutely. But if you don't mind, let's walk through them a bit slower. I want to go home in one piece tonight."

Thirty minutes later, they took a break and grabbed a drink from their water bottles.

"Man, that is some intense shit! There's no sport karate there. That is some serious life and death stuff."

JD nodded. "A lot of people seem to like sport karate. That's okay,

I guess. I just never had any interest in that side of things. There aren't too many people who train like this anymore."

"I know why," Vivas chuckled. "It hurts too damn much."

"Probably so. So, tell me about this Escrima you do. I know about it, but I've never really seen much of it. I know your instructor, Sensei Advincula, also did Isshin-ryu. He and Sherman Harrill were both stationed in Okinawa at the same time. From what I understand, your instructor, Sensei Tokumura, and Sensei Harrill were pretty good friends."

"That's right," Vivas agreed.

Walking over to his gym bag, Vivas retrieved a knife. It was the same knife JD had seen him sharpening on their flight to Djibouti.

"Meet my Flesheater. This one is the FE9… since it has a nine-inch blade. Like I told you on the way to Niger, this knife is the result of a collaboration between Sensei Advincula and Jim Hammond. For a while, you could get these, and its smaller variant, the FE7, from Columbia River, but not anymore. I got this one from Jim Hammond."

Vivas withdrew the knife from its sheath and handed it to JD, butt first.

The knife felt great in JD's hand. He examined it with a professional eye; it was well-balanced and heavy enough. He gripped the Flesheater and performed a few thrusts and slashes. All SEALs are familiar with basic knife fighting skills. The handle seemed to lock the knife into his grip nicely in both the fencer and icepick grips. The angle of the blade was perfect for thrusting, while the weight and curve made it ideal for chopping and slicing. JD handed the knife back to Vivas.

"Very nice."

Vivas took the knife from JD and stepped out onto the floor for a little room.

"Sensei Advincula created a form, or what you would call a kata, for his Escrima. It's called Ascension. Would you like to see it?"

"Sure." JD was certainly interested in seeing the form.

Vivas started into Ascension and moved through the increasingly complicated patterns of parries, cuts, and thrusts. JD spotted the influence of Isshin-ryu, at least in the layout of the form, but the techniques were purely Escrima. When Vivas had finished, he walked back over to where JD was standing.

"That was impressive."

"Would you like to play with some of the techniques?"

"With that?" JD laughed, indicating the Flesheater still in Vivas' hand. "I don't want to lose an arm."

Vivas grinned. "No, I have a couple of hard rubber training knives in my bag. They might leave a bruise, but they don't remove body parts."

"Sounds great. I have another thirty minutes or so before Ajax will begin to get bored. When we're done here, I'm taking him down to the beach. He loves playing in the surf."

"Alright, let's get started. We certainly don't want to cut into Ajax's surfing time."

Vivas moved off to stow the Flesheater in his gym bag, returning with the hard two rubber practice knives, handed one to JD.

JD received his clearing papers Tuesday morning and was ready to begin the retirement process, but he soon found it quite involved. There was a great deal of equipment to turn in and paperwork to sign. He presented his clearance papers at each station in turn for approval signatures. He had to clear the medical facility, finance, and quartermaster, among other stations. JD then repeated some of this same process for Ajax.

A week later, early Friday morning, in full dress uniform and surrounded by fellow members of SEAL Team 5, JD completed his retirement ceremony. Ajax was present, looking particularly regal after his trip to the groomer and sporting a brand new collar and leash. Several members of Golf Platoon went to the podium and spoke eloquently, recounting some of JD's accomplishments as a Special Warfare Operator. Commander Richard Murphy, JD's guest speaker, then stepped up to the podium, giving a short discussion of JD's role as a K9 handler and how the entire team had come to respect and appreciate the abilities of both JD and Ajax. His comments struck home. Many of the men attending the ceremony were alive or in one piece because of Ajax.

Commander Murphy said that JD was not just a great sailor; he was also a fine man and would leave behind an excellent example for young frogmen of the future to follow.

There was a somewhat lengthy pause. JD, still standing at attention, let his eyes wander over the crowd. Many were looking around as if expecting something to happen. JD's gaze suddenly landed on Doctor Ellen Chang.

What? No way, he thought. *What is the doc doing here?*

Ellen was seated in a folding metal chair in the back row. She was wearing a floral print dress and a wide-brimmed summer hat for protection from the California sun. She looks remarkably pretty, JD decided. He noticed several other men giving Ellen appreciative looks.

JD's eyes snapped to the front when Commander Murphy called out, "Attention! Commander in Chief on the deck!" All present leaped to their feet as President Benjamin Steele, flanked by his Chief of Staff, Martin Sansby, and Chairman of the Joint Chiefs, General Ellerson, stepped up to the platform. Steele walked to the center of the stage, where Commander Murphy saluted him. Steele returned the salute.

"Have your men stand at ease, Commander," Steele requested. Murphy gave the order, and the men of Golf platoon relaxed just a bit.

The president took the podium. "Commander Murphy, men, and women," he added, spotting Dr. Chang in the last row. "It is a real honor for me to be here today. It isn't very often, as president, that I get to stop and talk to a small group of soldiers or sailors. I did not want this to turn into a big affair. I remember not liking big 'to-dos' when I was in uniform."

There was an appreciative nod from the group at that.

"But today is a special day for me. I wanted to come here personally, to join your team member's retirement ceremony, because this nation and some of you, from what I understand, owe Senior Chief Cordell and his K9, Ajax, a great deal, maybe even your lives."

JD was beginning to feel a bit uncomfortable.

"I am here to make two presentations. The first presentation is a new award. When my staff briefed me on the successful rescue operation in Niger, I was very pleased. I also learned that we still have several Navy SEALs as well as an outstanding doctor because of the courageous action of the Trident dog standing behind me. I wanted to give this K9 hero a medal, but I learned that there was no military award for our service dogs, only a civilian award. I decided I needed to change that. As a result, we now have the K-9 Medal of Courage, and the first recipient of this prestigious award is Ajax, of Golf Platoon, SEAL Team 5."

President Steele paused, and the men in attendance let out a loud HOO-YAH!

The president continued. "Commander Murphy, if you please."

The commander called the team to attention as General Ellerson handed the president a polished wooden box. Opening it, the president removed a red, white, and blue ribbon with a gold medal hanging from it. The president turned to JD and Ajax.

May I approach your dog, Senior Chief?"

"Yes, sir, Mr. President. Ajax, Zit." Ajax sat.

"Dutch, huh..." the president winked at the Senior Chief as he approached Ajax, who was sitting proudly, almost like he knew what was happening. As General Ellerson began to read the citation, the president took a knee and hung the medal around Ajax's neck. He gently patted the big dog's head.

"Thank you for your courage and your service, Ajax."

The president stood and returned to the podium where the general was again standing, holding a second polished wooden box. President Steele reached out to adjust the microphone.

"Now, for the second presentation. As many of you probably know, members of SEAL Team 5 were instrumental in uncovering a terror plot a few years ago, in which radical Islamic terrorists planned to detonate several nuclear devices in major cities across our country. Thanks to intelligence seized in Afghanistan, this plan was discovered and disrupted. Many of the organizers and perpetrators of that plot are now deceased or at Guantanamo." Steele paused for a second. "What many of you don't know is that Senior Chief Cordell managed to get himself mixed up in this while temporarily assigned to Ft. Bragg to train with his new K9 partner, Ajax. During the events that followed, the Senior Chief and his new partner rescued a young lady who worked for the CIA from three assassins, disabling all three. He then provided this country's intelligence services with additional critical data essential to uncovering additional components of this deadly terror plot. After that, the Senior Chief and his family, and Ajax, battled a team of six assassins sent to kill them in their home, killing five and capturing one. Your Senior Chief is the kind of man the U.S. Navy Special Warfare Group needs. He is the kind of warrior I know all of you are."

President Steele took the wooden box from General Ellerson. Opened it and removed the medal it contained.

"I am here to present Senior Chief JD Cordell with the Navy Cross for valor in combat and for his service in defense of our nation. General Ellerson, if you will..."

As the general began to read the medal's citation, President Steele walked over and stood behind JD, to hang the ribbon around his neck.

When he'd finished, he moved in front of JD to shake his hand.

"Senior Chief, I know you didn't do any of this for a medal. Just consider it a small token of thanks from a nation and its people, grateful for your courage and extraordinary service, and for your dedication to keeping our country safe."

"Thank you, Mr. President. It is an honor," JD replied, saluting the president.

President Steele returned JD's salute, then turned and saluted the assembled men of SEAL Team 5. The presentation over, Steele and his entourage turned and walked off the stage. He had a flight to catch back to Washington for a meeting that evening at Camp David with the Israeli Prime Minister.

Next, the audience listened as JD made his farewell remarks. Keeping it short, he spoke of his family and his career, and what it meant to have served alongside so many brothers in arms. Finally, his platoon presented JD with a hand-made display case containing several mementos. These included JD's BUDS helmet, Ajax's old collar, and one of Maddux's old jungle boots that Ajax had destroyed before he and the dog became friends.

Following a Benediction, JD's retirement ceremony closed with a reading of The Watch, after which the U.S. Navy piped JD ashore.

At 1300 hours, both JD and Ajax were civilians. After a few minutes of general back-slapping, handshaking, and head petting, JD spotted Ellen standing to one side. Excusing himself, JD, with Ajax at his side, made his way over to her.

"Ellen... hi! What on earth are you doing here?" He began to offer his hand, but thinking better of it, greeted her with a hug instead. Ellen returned the hug.

"Well," she laughed. "Chief Whitley told me about your retirement ceremony and medal presentation, and I decided I wanted to come. So, I flew out yesterday."

"You flew out yesterday to see my retirement ceremony?" JD asked, slightly stunned by that.

"Well, not exactly." Ellen paused. "I flew out to see Ajax's retirement."

JD frowned.

"I'm kidding ... I'm kidding," Ellen laughed. "To be honest, I guess I flew out here because I didn't want things to end as they did in Niger.

Something more needed to be said."

JD slowly nodded his head. He had felt that way too. Before he could say anything, Ellen went on.

"Chief Whitley told me you were planning to move to Knoxville. He says your family lives there."

"That's true. I grew up there. My mother lives there. My sister Annie and her husband live in Nashville about three hours away. I figure it's a good place to try and start my new civilian life."

Ellen stooped down to pet Ajax, giving the dog a big hug and receiving a canine slurp to her cheek in return. Laughing, Ellen straightened back up.

"I have taken a position at UT Medical Center, JD. I want to be in Knoxville if you are going to be there."

"Really? That's great!"

Ellen paused, gently stroking Ajax on the head again. "I felt something with you, JD. Something I think could be great. I want to see where it goes."

"I want the same thing, Ellen," JD replied.

Ellen smiled. "Good."

A moment of awkward silence began, neither knowing what to say next. Finally, JD broke the silence.

"When do you fly back to Knoxville?"

"I am flying to Chicago tonight. My position starts in three weeks. I've leased an apartment temporarily, but all my worldly possessions are in Chicago, with my parents. I'll get stuff moved down over the next few weeks and get settled."

"Tonight," JD repeated. He'd hoped to have more time to talk, but there was that retirement party looming ahead.

Ellen handed JD a business card. He looked down at the cardboard rectangle that read, Dr. Ellen Chang.

"My cell phone number is written on the back. Now, go! Be with your friends tonight. It's where you should be. When you get settled in Knoxville, give me a call."

Ellen hesitated just a second before reaching up to place her palm on JD's cheek. Then, without another word, she turned and walked off.

JD stood there, shocked by what had just happened. He'd wanted to say so much more to Ellen when he left Niger the first time, the day he'd gotten the news of his father's passing. But everything since then had happened so fast, and it seemed awkward. Now, here was Ellen again. She'd flown to San Diego to see him. JD smiled, suddenly feeling slightly lightheaded. "Son of a gun!" he exclaimed to no one in particular. "Come on, Ajax. Let's go."

The team had put together an incredible retirement bash for JD, which both he and Ajax felt obligated to attend. It turned out to be a great time. One of the better local barbecue establishments catered the party, and there were many cases of ice-cold Corona and Heineken. There was even a meal specially prepared for Ajax, consisting of a carefully chopped up sirloin steak mixed with a raw egg. Ajax wolfed it down appreciatively. Maddux also made sure there was a constant supply of cold water for Ajax to quench his thirst.

There was a lot of good-natured harassment about the medal. It seems that Ajax's medal was larger than JD's, which led to a lot of other humorous comments and comparisons.

The team had chipped in and gotten JD an Omega "James Bond" Limited Edition diver's watch. They had also gotten Ajax a pair of stainless steel food and water bowls. Each bowl had the Navy SEAL Trident engraved in its bottom. The dog bowls almost brought a tear to JD's eyes.

"The bowls were Maddux's idea," Pallie explained as he handed JD another frosty Corona. "Chief Whitley suggested the watch."

"It's great, Pallie," JD replied. "How's the shoulder?"

"It's fine. I still swear you hit me with a sledgehammer, but Vivas and Maddux both attest that you didn't. Guess I gotta believe them." Pallie took a swig from his Heineken, then laughed. "I've still got the fucking bruise! It's gone from black to dark purple, then to green and light purple, and now it's a lovely shade of yellow and green."

JD laughed. "I've been there. We used to call them seminar tattoos." Pallie laughed and then wandered off in search of another cold beer.

Shortly after Pallie walked away, Vivas took his place. "Man, it's been great. Stay in touch. It'd be good to train together some more. If you get back out here, let me know. We'll take a day and go down to visit with Sensei Advincula. If you're lucky, he might give you a few pointers."

"That'd be great," JD replied, clapping Vivas on the back. Vivas turned as if to go, then stopped. "Oh, I almost forgot. I have something for you. Wait here."

Vivas returned a few seconds later with something wrapped in cloth. He handed it to JD, who took it. It was heavy.

"What the hell is this?" JD asked. Vivas shrugged. "Look and see."

JD unwrapped the cloth and discovered it contained a leather sheath holding a Jim Hammond custom nine-inch Flesheater knife. JD looked over at Vivas.

"Don't sweat it. I have several. This one is now yours. Keep practicing. I'll keep working on the karate you shared with me."

JD extended his hand. "Thanks, Vivas. This blade is awesome. I appreciate it."

They shook hands.

"Been a pleasure serving with you, JD. I learned a lot from you, man. Well, I have to go. Got a date with this Filipina chick I met yesterday." With that, Vivas turned and headed toward the door.

"Heading out, JD?" It was Chief Whitley. "I know parties aren't your thing."

"Yeah. But it's been a blast. I enjoyed myself, and I sincerely appreciate it, Chief."

"Did the doc catch up with you today?" Whitley asked with a sly twinkle in his eye.

JD almost blushed. "Yes, she did. She's moving to Knoxville."

Whitley laughed. "Better run, JD. That gal has her cap set for you. That is, unless you want her to catch you."

It was JD's turn to laugh. "Hypothetically speaking, if I wanted someone to catch me, I think Ellen Chang might be the one I'd want to do the chasing. We shall see."

"Well, shove off, Senior Chief. It's been great having you in my command. You're one hell of a frogman. If you ever need anything, give me a yell."

"I will, Chief! And, thanks. It's been an honor serving with you."

JD turned and whistled for Ajax, who appeared at his side. Together, they walked through the crowd and toward the door.

CHAPTER 22
KNOXVILLE, TN

The more Mai thought about it, the more it seemed silly to wait. Never one to put things off once she'd made up her mind, Mai decided not to wait for JD to accompany her to Vietnam.

There's no need for that. JD will have enough to do getting settled into civilian life without having to worry about taking me to Vietnam for a few weeks.

She had no idea how long her trip would take. It could take a little time. Not having seen or heard from Dish since she and Curtis left the Montagnard village where she'd lived, she didn't even know if Dish was still alive. Somehow, she felt that he was. Dish was a survivor.

Mai knew life was extremely harsh for any Montagnard people who remained in Vietnam. They had three strikes against them as far as the communist government was concerned. They'd sided with the Americans in the war and dared to protest for the right to keep their lands. Many had converted to Christianity. As a result, the Vietnamese government imposed severe restrictions on the few Montagnard people who still lived there, restricting their ability to practice their culture, speak their native language, obtain an education, or secure a reasonable job.

Dish could be dead, in prison or a re-education camp, or even hiding somewhere, Mai thought. But she also knew that, if it weren't for her adopted brother, she would not be here in the United States today. She felt it was her duty to try.

Mai still had sixteen of the old gold coins her father had left to her. It was more than enough to pay for such a trip and bring Dish to

America if she could find him. Even those old coins were hers because of Dish. They were all that remained of a proud family legacy, a time when her great grandfather was a retainer at the court of Thieu Tri, the last emperor of Vietnam. Because his sons were too young, Mai's father shared his secret with Dish, showing him the old leather pouch containing the gold coins that he kept hidden away.

Her father told Dish, "Should anything happen to me, please see my family is safe. These will help."

Dish had gone back and retrieved the coins after the Viet Cong murdered the rest of Mai's family. He'd kept them safe and presented them to her the day she and Curtis left the village.

Yes, Mai thought. *I owe my brother a considerable debt.* She would do what she could to repay that debt.

Mai already had her passport. She applied for a visa for entry into Vietnam, which was approved; the official notification came via email five days later.

Deciding to give herself three weeks in Vietnam to find Dish, Mai chose the dates and booked a round-trip flight on Delta Airlines, from McGhee-Tyson Airport to Ho Chi Minh City. The flight would have layovers in Atlanta and Dallas before flying on to Incheon, South Korea. In South Korea, Mai would switch to Korean Airlines for the final five-and-a-half-hour leg to Tan Son Nhat International Airport in Vietnam.

The previous week, Mai had driven to Atlanta and met with the coin collector, who had appraised the gold coins she inherited from her father years ago. A kindly gentleman, Tom Skeller, had helped her sell a few coins some years ago, to pay for her education as a registered nurse. Her dream as a child growing up in Vietnam was to become a doctor. However, her lack of formal western education made that extremely difficult. In the end, she'd decided to become a registered nurse, a more realistic goal, and equally satisfying.

Tom found a buyer for ten of the gold coins, and when hearing what she was using the money for, he waived his usual fee. Mai returned to Knoxville with $110,000 in cash. She decided to carry $10,000 with her in cash. Amounts exceeding $5,000 needed to be declared, but even that much cash was not unusual and would raise no eyebrows. The rest she deposited into her checking account. She could access that with her debit Mastercard or by wire if needed. While they had planned well, Curtis's estate was still in probate, and Mai had no access to many of their joint holdings until that process completed. She knew that it could take up to a year.

As final preparations ended, Mai decided to do one more thing before she left, and placed a call to General Ellerson, who answered on the third ring.

"General Ellerson speaking."

"Hello, General Ellerson, this is Mai Cordell. How are you?"

"Mai! What a pleasant surprise. I'm fine. How are you doing?"

"I'm fine, general. Thank you for asking. Your wife is doing well too?"

"Jean is fine. She's visiting the grandkids this week. Probably spoiling the hell out of them."

"That's what grandmothers do," Mai laughed.

"So, to what do I owe this call?"

"General, I have a small favor to ask..."

"Anything I can do, Mai. You know that."

"I am traveling to Vietnam on Friday, and I should be there for about three weeks. I'm going to try and find my brother, Dish."

Ellerson's voice took on a concerned tone. "That could be difficult, Mai. It's been a long time, and Vietnam has changed a lot over the past forty years. It's been tough for the Montagnard people, as you well know."

"I understand that, General. But I must try. I'm not asking for any help with that. I'll be fine. I just want someone who knows me, a friend, to know where I am. And, I was hoping that maybe you could give me the name of someone you trust at the U.S. Embassy in Vietnam. Someone you know that I can trust."

Ellerson thought for a minute. "I am sorry, Mai. I don't know anyone at the embassy in Vietnam. But here is what I will do. I will call a friend of mine, Bill Powell. He works for the State Department. I'll let Bill know you are a friend visiting Vietnam, and I will have him tell someone at the embassy there to keep an eye out for you. You'll want to check-in at the U.S. Embassy in Ho Chi Minh City after you arrive, and make contact. Okay?"

"That will be fine. Thank you, General. I will do that, and I appreciate it so much."

"No problem, Mai. And, you know, you can call me Clay if you want to. We're friends."

"I know that, General," Mai laughed. "And thank you again. Give my best to Jean." Mai ended the call.

On the way to the airport, Mai called Annie, who answered on the fourth ring. "Hi, Annie."

"Hi, Mom. What's up?"

"I'm on my way to the airport. "

"The airport? Where are you going?"

"I am going to Vietnam, to try and find Dish. I'll be gone for three weeks. Everything is taken care of at the house, so you don't have to worry about anything. Okay?"

"Mom!" Annie sounded resigned rather than surprised. "I thought you were going to wait and let JD go with you. That was the plan."

"I know, but that seems silly to me. Your brother will have so much to do, trying to get settled here in Knoxville. And, he is talking to that wonderful doctor, Ellen. I am not going to ask him to stop in the middle of that to traipse off to Vietnam with his mother. I can take care of myself. I speak the language and know the customs. I'll be fine."

Annie was not giving up that easily. "I don't know, Mom. Maybe we should call JD."

"Annie, don't you go bothering JD with this. I will be back before he even notices I'm gone. And I might even have good news about your uncle."

Annie thought about this for a few seconds before answering. "Okay, Mom. But you keep me posted. If I go three days without hearing from you, I am calling JD."

"It's a deal. Got to go. Love you, Annie."

"Love you, Mom."

Well, I should have seen that coming, Annie thought to herself. Stubbornness ran in the family.

Despite her mother's request not to say anything to JD about her trip, Annie decided she needed to let her brother know. Keeping secrets like that did not sit well with her. Annie chalked it up to her mother's attempt to process her grief at losing her husband and attempting to re-establish some balance in her life.

Annie called JD that evening. "Hey, JD."

"Annie. How're things with you?"

"We're all fine. Robert's at the hospital, checking on a football player who got his knee crunched in last Saturday's game against South Carolina."

"Ouch. Dangerous line of work ... playing football."

"Look who's talking," Annie responded with a short laugh. "The boys are in bed."

"What's up?" JD sensed Annie wanted to talk about something important.

"Mom left for Vietnam this morning."

"What? She was going to wait until I could go with her in a couple of weeks."

"I know, but she decided that was silly and said she'd be back before you even got moved to Knoxville."

"Finding Dish may take longer than she thinks. Vietnam has changed a lot since she left. It's a communist country with some appalling human rights problems that have only been getting worse." JD shook his head. "Damn."

"I know. I tried to talk her out of it, but you know Mom. I think she misses Dad a lot and can't stand to sit still. It gives her too much time to think about things."

"I guess you're right about that, Annie. But Mom is a Vietnamese American alone in Vietnam, looking for a man who, if half of what we've heard is true, is probably still on the communist government's Most Wanted list if he is even still alive. Those people don't play around, Annie. They control everything and brutally enforce their laws. If Mom were to get arrested for poking her nose where they don't think it belongs, it could be dangerous for her. I'm not sure what, if anything, the State Department could do. The communist party controls the courts and tells them how to rule in criminal cases. They seem to have a lot of brutal prison sentences for people convicted on bogus charges."

"I didn't realize it was that bad. People vacation in Vietnam now."

"That's true, Annie. But tourists only go where and see what the government allows them to. Stray off the beaten path, and it's a different world. I know this because it was part of my job to know such things."

"So, what do we do now?"

"There's not much at this point we can do. And knowing Mom, she could be back with Uncle Dish in tow in a few weeks. I hope so. Are you in contact with her?"

"I made her promise to call me every three days. She should call the day after tomorrow."

"Okay. Keep me posted, and let me know right away if mom doesn't call."

"I'll do that, JD. Goodnight."

"Goodnight, Annie."

JD frowned, shaking his head. He didn't know why, but he had a bad feeling about this.

CHAPTER 23
VIETNAM

Mai's flight landed at Tan Son Nhat International Airport in Vietnam at 5:45 p.m. Gathering her two checked bags, she cleared customs and went directly to the Mai Linh taxi company's counter. There she arranged for a taxi to the Park Hyatt Saigon Hotel where she'd reserved a room for two weeks.

After paying the 300,000 VDN, a friendly staff member secured her luggage and led Mai out of the terminal building to her cab. Fortunately, the charge included all tolls and the airport surcharge, only leaving a tip to deal with once she reached the hotel.

The Park Hyatt was one of Ho Chi Minh City's 5-star hotels and occupied a prime spot in central District 1. It was pricey, but Mai felt it would be a safe place for her to stay. Her taxi ride to District 1 confirmed without any doubt that Vietnam had changed a lot since she left with Curtis over forty years ago. Mai looked forward to exploring the many boutiques, restaurants, and parks. There would probably be a good deal of time spent waiting for any developments as her planned search for Dish unfolded.

The fourth-floor room had a balcony overlooking the pool and was pleasing with French provincial decor. Mai spent a few minutes unpacking, put her toiletries in the large bathroom, and stowed her clothing in dresser drawers. Taking a thick envelope of cash from her carry-on bag, she counted out enough money to get her through a few days and locked the remaining cash in the room's safe. Satisfied for the time being, she stepped out on the balcony. The evening was hot, but a pleasant breeze stirred four floors up, and it felt good.

What next? Mai thought to herself. She planned first to take a taxi to her old village—provided it still existed—to see if there was anyone she knew and could question; anyone who might have seen or heard about Dish over the years. The odds were slim at best.

At least it's a place to start, she thought.

Tired after the long flight, Mai decided to take a shower, get something to eat in the hotel restaurant, and get a good night's sleep. Tomorrow, she could choose how to get to Đăk No. Her original plan was to take a taxi for the thirteen-hour trip, but now, the idea of taking a bus seemed more intriguing. She could see so much more along the way. It would be a longer ride, of course, making more stops. But that was okay with Mai. It would be fun to see the countryside and the many sights and villages they would pass through. Maybe a bus would be better.

After a quick shower, Mai took the elevator down to the lobby and entered the restaurant, where she was quickly seated. At the waiter's recommendation, she ordered the roast chicken with couscous and a small fruit salad with yogurt dressing. Mai was quite hungry, and the food was excellent. Charging the dinner to her room, she took an after-dinner stroll around the block to help settle her meal before turning in for the night. A little over an hour later, she fell instantly asleep when her head hit the pillow.

Rising early the next morning, Mai dressed and walked around until she found a small café. She ate a quick breakfast, then crossed the street to a shop where she purchased a small backpack and a few other odds and ends. Returning to the hotel, Mai placed a change of clothes, a few toiletries, her travel papers, and some cash into the backpack. Calling the desk, she arranged for a cab to take her to the bus station, where she purchased a ticket for 287,231 Vietnamese dongs, or $12.38.

Since the bus didn't leave until 10:00 a.m., Mai had a little more than an hour to kill. Wandering around the shops near the station, she purchased a few magazines for the long ride. Since it was an express bus, it was only a nine-hour trip. According to the helpful lady at the ticket counter, Mai would be riding in one of the new VIP Sleeper buses, which carried forty-one people on two levels and offered reclining seats, an on-board toilet, and TV.

Boarding the bus, Mai selected a second level seat near the front for a better view of the countryside. She wanted to see as much as possible. Not having visited her home country in over four decades, it was quite an exciting adventure. Mai found she relished the risk and thrill of being on her own. She missed Curtis dearly and wished he had been able to accompany her on this trip as they had initially planned. The two of them had shared a beautiful life, raised two great children, and now had two grandchildren.

I have so much to be thankful for, Mai thought. *And Curtis will always be with me in my heart.*

Her thoughts turned to Dish next. It was a lifetime ago when she and Curtis said goodbye and left the Montagnard village. So much time has passed.

Is Dish even still alive? Can I find him? Mai had followed the plight of the Montagnard people since the end of the war. It shamed her that her people had mistreated them.

Well, not my people, the communists ... Mai corrected herself. Most Vietnamese people did look down on the Montagnard tribes, considering them savages. There were some exceptions, of course. Her father, Ang Dung, had been one of those exceptions. While alive, he'd had many good friends among the Montagnard, including Dish's father, Mund, the old warrior who took her in as his daughter after the Viet Cong butchered her family.

If my brother is alive, I will find him and bring him back to America with me. Resolute in her decision, Mai sat back and waited for the bus to leave.

It pulled out of the station at precisely 10:00 a.m.

Mai was unprepared for how much the village of Dak No had changed. When Dish had led her away that dreadful night, there was a single dirt road and a few simple structures of mud or wood, mostly with thatched roofs. There had been rice paddies and livestock pens.

The bus dropped her off on the main road through the village, now paved. Many of the buildings seemed constructed of concrete blocks, some with metal roofs. She quickly spotted a market, a noodle house, and several small shops. Mai also spotted what appeared to be a police station with a Vietnamese flag, which in the intense heat and lack of a breeze, hung listlessly from its pole.

There was no sign of her father's house or the village houses she remembered from her childhood. Mai was unsure of what her next steps should be. There were still a few hours of daylight left. Perhaps she should try to find a place to stay the night.

Then Mai remembered her Aunt Binh, her father's sister. Binh had a little house to the west, just outside the main village. She had raised chickens and pigs and had several children who'd been Mai's age. Aunt Binh would have died years ago, but it was possible one of her children still lived there.

Mai shouldered her backpack and looked around to get her bearings. Satisfied, she headed into an alleyway that led between two buildings, toward the trees beyond a large field. After going several yards, it dawned on her that this was the same field she had crossed to tend to her father's water buffalo on that terrible, foggy day when the Viet Cong had descended on their village. That realization placed her father's house approximately where the police station now stood. Mai could see active rice patties to her left, and a small factory off in the distance to her right.

Reaching the tree line, Mai followed the edge of the field, looking for a track that led into the woods and past her aunt's little house. Suddenly, she stopped. She was standing where Dish had led her into the trees and away from the VC. Mai ducked down and pushed her way into the brush.

This spot is the place where Dish hid me. She remembered the location like it was yesterday. There was the same tree she had sat and leaned against, crying until she fell asleep. She would not know until she later awakened that the Viet Cong had brutally killed her father, her pregnant mother, and her younger brothers and sister, while Dish hid her right here. Then, while she was sleeping, he'd gone back into the village to get the leather pouch of gold coins her father had shown him.

It's almost like he knew, Mai thought, looking back on her father's actions. Dish kept those coins a secret for years, giving them to her just before she and Curtis left the village. He had refused to take even one for himself.

"You will need them in America," he'd said to her. "Make a good life."

She and Curtis had certainly done that. It had been a good life. And now, Mai was going to try and do the same for her brother. She closed her eyes, just for a second, and prayed for everything to turn out as she hoped it would. Then, turning, she made her way back out to the field and continued along until she found the track.

Montagnard

Mai didn't remember it being too far from her aunt's house. After walking about half-a-mile, a little clearing opened to the left, and there sat Aunt Binh's small house. It was just as she remembered it. Everything was neat; the house itself in good repair. Mai smiled, seeing a flock of chickens strutting about, squawking and pecking at the ground.

Mai spotted about a dozen pigs in a pen to the right of the house and thought wistfully about the pet pigs she left behind years ago. Spotting no one about, Mai called out, "Hello!" Then, laughing to herself, she tried again in Vietnamese, "Xin chào." This time there was an answer from within the house, and a young Vietnamese woman stepped into the doorway.

"May I help you?" The young woman spoke pleasantly. Mai found she had no trouble with the language. She had always worked at keeping up her Vietnamese and served as a translator for the medical center whenever needed.

"This house once belonged to my Aunt Binh," Mai replied.

"Aunt Binh," the young woman repeated, then frowned. "Aunt Binh died some years ago."

"She was my father's sister, my aunt. I was hoping to find some of her family."

"Your aunt," the young woman repeated, somewhat suspiciously. "What is your name?"

"It is Mai. Ang Dung was my father. The Viet Cong killed my father and the rest of my family during the war."

The young woman stepped out of the doorway and into the sunlight. She was quite pretty.

"Your aunt Binh was my great grandmother. Her son, Danh, was my grandfather."

Mai recognized the name of one of her cousins from when she was a young girl.

"He too is dead, I think," the young woman continued. "I have not seen him in many years. He fled into the mountains when the communists took over. He'd been smuggling food to Montagnards hiding in the border region, and a friend warned him to run. Someone from our village betrayed him, but nobody knows who."

Mai nodded. "I am sorry."

The young woman shrugged. "It was some time ago." She paused, eyeing Mai. "So, I guess you are my cousin?"

Mai laughed. "I guess that is so. We are related somehow. But please, call me Mai if you will."

"My father works in a factory. They cut big rocks into slabs and send them to the cities. I tend the chickens and pigs. Father won't be home until dark if you would like to talk to him. That is still a few hours. Would you like some tea while you wait?"

"That sounds nice. What is your name?"

"Xuan. Please, come in and sit. I will get the tea." Mai followed Xuan into the house, finding it neat and well-kept. The shade provided by the thatched roof was a welcome relief to the heat outside. Spotting a small table with three chairs in the corner, Mai set her backpack down on the floor and sat on one of the chairs. Moments later, Xuan set a teapot and two teacups on the table and took a chair. The green tea was slightly bitter, not having all the extra flavors Americans tend to add to it.

"How old are you, Xuan?" Mai set the teacup down after a second sip.

"I'm seventeen. You have been in America, I think."

"How do you know?"

"I know you are Vietnamese, but your speaking is strange. Not like others in our village. And your clothes. I have seen pictures of Americans in the magazines we sometimes get in the store."

Mai smiled. "Yes. I have lived in America for over forty years. I married an American officer during the war, and went to America with him."

"Do you have children?"

"I have a son named JD and a daughter named Annie. And, two young grandsons named Jimmy and Allen. They are my daughter's boys." Mai took another sip of the tea. "My son just retired from the American military."

"Why would you come back here?" Xuan asked. "If I got to America, I would never come back."

"I am here to find someone. I want to find the man who saved my life when the Viet Cong came that night. He is my adopted brother, a Montagnard. His name is Dish."

Xuan caught her breath, looking sharply at Mai, who noticed the change.

"Do you know anything about Dish?" Mai asked.

"You will need to talk to my father," Xuan replied and took another sip of her tea.

Shortly after dark, the sound of footsteps outside the doorway alerted Xuan and Mai to someone's approach. A few seconds later, a man entered and set a small sack down on a shelf near the door. The man hadn't yet noticed Mai sitting at the table in the corner.

"Father, we have company," Xuan announced as the man turned back toward the center of the small house, his eyes falling on Mai.

"Who are you?" The man's voice was business-like, with a suspicious edge to it.

"This is Mai," Xuan replied. "Ang Dung's daughter. Mai is your cousin. We are related!" Xuan continued excitedly.

"Mai is dead," the man stated flatly. "Who are you?"

Mai laughed. "No, I am not dead. On the night my family was killed, I was out early, tending our water buffalo, which had broken through the fence. I was there when the Viet Cong came. A student of my father hid me in the trees while the VC butchered my family." Mai's face turned serious. "Ang Dung was my father. My mother's name was Hue. She was pregnant at the time. My brothers were Anh and Bao, and my little sister was Tien. After the VC had finished their slaughter, my father's student, a few years older than me, led me away to his father's village. It was a walk of two days. My father's student was Montagnard, of the Jarai tribe. His father, Mund, took me in and protected me, and I lived with the Montagnard for many years."

"This is not possible." The man shook his head. "How can this be true?"

Mai continued. "Your grandmother was my father's sister. She raised chickens and pigs. I used to come here to help her feed the pigs." Mai remembered something else. "Aunt Binh played the Đàn Bao very well. As children, we used to sit and listen to her play." Mai pointed to the door. "She would sit in the doorway, and we would sit on the ground around her." Mai looked directly at the man who had suddenly sat down in the last chair, a look of disbelief painted on his face. "Your father always hoped to learn to play the Đàn Bao. He loved to listen to her play."

The man slowly looked up. He'd been looking down at his hands. "My father was very good at playing the Đàn Bao. I too play, but not as well." He paused, looking into Mai's face. He could see no hint of falsehood.

He spoke. "I do not understand how this is possible. But you are Mai. I know that now. My name is Chinh. But why are you here? Where have you been?"

"She has been in America," Xuan interjected excitedly, pleased with how things were going.

Chinh looked toward his daughter. "Xuan, make supper for us." He turned back to Mai. "You have been in America?"

"Yes," Mai replied, telling the story of the American officer her Montagnard brother had rescued in the jungle, how she had nursed him back to health, and later guided him back to an American military base. She described how they had grown to love each other over the weeks spent together and how he had asked her to marry him.

"But I do not understand why you are here now. Why are you back in Vietnam?"

A sad look flickered across Mai's face. "My husband died several weeks ago. We had a wonderful life together, and I am happy. I have two grown children and two grandchildren in America. But none of this would have happened if it were not for my adopted brother. I am here to try and find him, to help him if I can. I owe him a great debt."

Chinh brushed the hair back on his head, thinking. "There are not many Montagnard around here anymore. Many are dead or hiding in the mountains, or perhaps in prisons. Many Vietnamese will not hire them. What is the name of this Montagnard brother of yours?"

"His name is Dish."

Chinh nervously glanced over at Xuan, who was bending over a big pot of rice. He knew his daughter had heard the name. His gaze returned to Mai. "Your adopted brother is Dish?"

"Yes." Mai could tell from the look on Chinh's face that he knew the name. "Do know him or where I can find him?"

"Many know of Dish. You will not find him unless he wants you to ... or Dish might find you if he wants to see you." Chinh paused. "Dish is an outlaw, a gun smuggler. It is rumored he sells guns he gets from Thailand to anti-government rebels hiding in the mountains."

"He is a patriot, a hero," Xuan interjected.

Chinh scowled at her. "In some eyes, yes. But it is best not to say that too loudly." He turned back to Mai. "My daughter has the star-filled eyes common among those of her age. This country will soon cure that. She is much like her mother." Seeing the curious look on Mai's face, he added. "She took sick and died when Xuan was still very young."

"I am sorry," Mai replied.

"Thank you; it was some time ago."

"How do you know this; about Dish, I mean?"

"There is talk among the villagers. And, there is a big reward for your brother's head offered by the communists. I saw Dish once, several years ago, but I have not seen him in a long time. He is a dangerous man, and I do not know how you would find him. You cannot simply wander around in the mountains looking for him. There are many bad people—drug smugglers and other bandits, in the mountain region. You might find him, but I think the odds are much better that bad people would find you first."

Mai nodded, accepting this information. "And yet, I must try."

Chinh thought about that for a few minutes. "If I were trying to find Dish, I would go back to Ho Chi Minh City. I have heard that many Montagnard find work in the bars and brothels there. It is also a great place to hide from the government."

Again, Mai nodded her understanding. Chinh noticed the firm set to her jaw and decided it would be useless to try and talk her out of what she planned to do.

"Your brother is... a hero to these Montagnard people, but be careful with whom you talk. It will be dangerous. It will be hard to gain the trust of any Montagnards, especially being Vietnamese. There are many bad people there as well. However, I think you will be safer there than in the mountains. If you can convince one of them who you are and get them to help you, you may be able to get a message to Dish or one of his spies. They may even try to protect you. I do not know. Like the communists, your brother has many eyes. I am sure if Dish learns you are here and your reason for coming, he will find you."

Both sat back in their chairs as Xuan placed three plates on the table, followed by a plate of steamed fish and a massive bowl of steaming rice. Mai suddenly realized she was starving.

Chinh helped himself to a large piece of fish and a scoop of rice before going on. "Xuan will fix a pallet for you next to hers. You should stay here tonight. Tomorrow you can take the bus back to Ho Chi Minh City and continue your search for your brother. I wish I could do more, but I am afraid that is the extent of what I know."

Mai smiled. "Thank you, cousin Chinh. You have been very gracious and helpful. I appreciate it; sincerely." She then helped herself to a small piece of fish and some of the rice. Xuan, grinning happily, was already into her second serving of fish.

CHAPTER 24
KNOXVILLE, TN

After looking at several options, JD leased a beautiful, dog-friendly, two-bedroom condo with an attached garage at Cherokee Bluff, overlooking the Tennessee River. He began the process of setting up housekeeping as a civilian. He and Ajax made the trip from San Diego in the jeep, but the moving van traveled at a much slower pace, with a scheduled stop in Arkansas to load another home's furnishings.

JD didn't have much. A bed, a dresser, a recliner and sofa, a washer and dryer, and his weight set made up the most significant portion of his furniture. The van could carry three houses worth of stuff when carefully loaded, and the moving company had to make the trip as profitable as possible.

Man and dog spent two nights at his mother's house while waiting for the moving truck with his stuff to arrive. JD had a key, and it gave him a chance to make sure all was well there while Mai was in Vietnam. She had called Annie on schedule and filled her in on the trip to her childhood village, including locating a cousin, Chinh, and his daughter, Xuan. JD was happy that his mom had been able to do that. It must have been exciting to find her cousin and meet some family, as well as learn that Dish was still alive. Mai had said nothing to Annie about their uncle being an anti-communist gun smuggler; perhaps she felt that information could wait.

I should have gone with Mom, JD thought. But Annie was right. Their mother was not one to sit around and wait to do anything. Anyway, she was pretty good at taking care of herself. There was little reason to worry.

On the evening of the second night, the driver of the van called and confirmed they would be at the condo the next morning, about 9:30 a.m. JD and Ajax arrived at 8:30 a.m. to open the apartment. Once the van arrived, the movers had his stuff unloaded and set in place in less than an hour. JD spent the rest of the day assembling the bed, hooking up the washer and dryer, and opening boxes to distribute pots, pans, linens, clothes, toiletries, and other assorted items where they needed to go.

By 6:00 p.m., they were both quite hungry. JD fed Ajax and dug out the leash.

"Come on, old boy. I don't feel much like cooking now."

They drove downtown and parked in the State Street Garage, then walked up to Gay Street, deciding to eat at the Downtown Grill & Brewery. Taking an outside table, Ajax settled down to relax while JD ordered buffalo shrimp tacos, french fries, and decided to try the Downtown blonde ale. Waiting for the food to come, JD dug into his wallet and found the card Ellen had given him in San Diego. Neatly written on the back was her cell number. JD hesitated just a moment before punching the number into his phone. Ellen answered on the second ring.

"Hello?"

"Hi, Ellen... it's JD."

"JD! Oh wow. I am so glad you called. Where are you?"

"Here... in Knoxville. I've leased a condo over at Cherokee Bluff until I figure out something more permanent. Right now, Ajax and I are sitting at the Downtown Grill & Brewery, getting some supper. Well, I am, at least. He had his dinner before we left the condo."

Ellen laughed. "No way! I'm right above you. I have a loft on the fourth floor. Give me a second, and I'll come down."

"Okay. That's pretty funny. We'll be here."

Ten minutes later, Ellen slid into the seat across from JD and reached down to pat Ajax on the head. "Hello there, stranger," she stated with a smile. "How're things?"

"Looking better by the minute," JD responded with a grin. He'd forgotten how pretty Ellen was, and she looked more rested and much healthier than she had after her captivity in Niger. "You look great."

"Thank you. You don't look so bad yourself."

"Are you hungry? Do you want to order something?"

Ellen shook her head. "Thanks, but no. I just finished eating, right before you called."

Just then, the waitress arrived with JD's dinner.

"You got the buffalo shrimp tacos?" She laughed.

JD decided he loved the sound of her laugh.

"They're one of my favorites. I seem to eat here more often than I should."

"It's handy. Since you live here, I mean. Did you buy it?"

"No, I'm just leasing. I plan to wait a bit. You know, look around, see what opportunities might arise."

JD laughed. "That is exactly what I'm doing. So, anything promising in the wind?"

Ellen sat back in her chair, folding her arms across her chest. "Well, there's this guy I met in Niger. I think he's amazing. And, I am very interested in seeing where we might take things; that is, if he is interested as well."

JD took a sip from his beer as he looked directly into Ellen's eyes. He liked what he saw there. Her eyes shone with honesty and happiness. He'd not seen that before with the other women he'd dated.

"This guy has a pretty cool dog as well," she added, looking down at Ajax.

JD set his beer down on the table and leaned toward Ellen. "Well, the guy sitting at this table thinks the woman sitting across from him is the most amazing woman he has ever met and is very interested in exploring the potential he sees in this future relationship."

Ajax chose that precise moment to loudly thump his tail twice on one of the table's legs.

"And, the dog agrees with him," JD added without breaking stride.

Both laughed at that. "Well, finish your supper, JD. Then I'll give you and Ajax the grand tour of my loft if you'd like to see it."

"Sure. We'd love to see it. Isn't that right, Ajax?" Ajax looked up at JD, tilting his head to one side, indicating that he thought that would be just fine.

After eating, JD paid for his meal and, with Ajax trotting alongside, followed Ellen. The entryway to the apartments on the floors above the Downtown Grill & Brewery was just a few yards down Gay Street. In the elevator, Ellen knelt and ruffled the thick hair around Ajax's neck. Ajax didn't mind that a bit and leaned into Ellen, almost pushing her over.

JD laughed. "I think he likes you."

Ellen looked up at JD. "Well, I think it's a good thing he approves of me. Makes things easier, don't you think?"

"Certainly does."

The elevator stopped on the fourth floor, and Ellen, JD, and Ajax exited, turned left, and walked to the door at the end of the hall. Opening the door, Ellen let JD and Ajax in and gave them the grand tour. The loft had a nice open feel to it. Most of the walls were brick. There was a large modern kitchen with stainless steel appliances and a spacious dining area with a good-sized pantry. The expansive living area had high cathedral ceilings. In the living area sat a huge sofa and two recliners around a large coffee table. A giant window had a great view of the city lights and Gay Street below.

There was a nice-sized balcony accessible via a door to the left of the window, and a cute little half bath just off the kitchen. JD spotted the staircase to the right of the entry door.

"That stairway leads to the bedroom and full bath. They are over the kitchen, pantry, and dining area."

"Wow. This is pretty nice."

"Thanks. Would you like a beer? I think I'll have a glass of wine."

"Sure. That sounds great." JD took a seat on the sofa. Ajax had already stretched out on the carpet and seemed quite content for the moment.

A few seconds later, Ellen returned and handed JD a cold Samuel Adams. Her other hand carried a glass of red wine. Sitting on the sofa next to JD, she leaned back into the cushion. "I was so happy to get your call today. It was funny, you being right downstairs."

JD laughed. "I think the word is serendipitous."

It was Ellen's turn to laugh. "Wow! Good word choice!"

"Not bad for a dumb grunt."

Ellen looked across her wine glass at JD. "You are so much more than that, JD. I haven't met too many men like you."

"What do you mean?"

"Well, you're a gentleman, and yet I know you're capable of extreme violence, if necessary. I see the way Ajax responds to you, and it is evident that your dog loves you. Chief Whitley told me you're quite an amazing martial artist as well."

JD shrugged. "I'm just a long-time student. I guess the longer you do it, the better you get."

"If you say so." She took a sip of her wine. "I think a lot of people, if they knew what you are capable of, would be afraid of you."

"There's no reason to be. I'm a nice guy."

"I know that. And I am not afraid of you at all. You make me feel— I'm not sure this is exactly the right word to use, but it's the best I can come up with right now—you make me feel safe." She paused. "But it's much more than just safe."

"I think I know what you mean, but there's a different word for how I feel."

"What is it?"

"Sitting here, right now, the feeling I have... it feels like I am home."

Ellen didn't say anything for a few minutes. She just sat there, looking at JD. She took another sip of her wine before saying, "I like how that sounds, JD."

They both sat there quietly, neither speaking, neither sure what to say.

The silence was broken by the deep sigh of a contented dog on the rug a few feet away. Suddenly, Ellen laughed. "Wow. That was deep, JD."

"Yes, it was," JD agreed, smiling. "And so was the conversation."

"So, what do we talk about next?"

"Well, can I ask you something personal?" JD set his beer down on a coaster on the coffee table.

"I think that would be appropriate at this point."

"Can I kiss you?"

Ellen smiled. "I would like that very much."

JD slid closer on the sofa as Ellen sat her wine glass down. He could feel his heart beat faster as he drew close to Ellen. He reached up, almost timidly with his right hand, gently touching her cheek, guiding her forward. As she moved close, JD could smell the fruity fragrance of the red wine she'd been sipping. Their lips met, hesitantly at first, then more urgently, the intensity growing. JD tasted the wine on her soft lips, which parted. As Ellen returned his kiss, he felt pulled into a swirling whirlwind of sensations unlike anything he had experienced before, a feeling of total joy - and then it was gone. Ellen had pulled away.

"Would you like to see the bedroom, JD?" Ellen asked softly.

"Very much so." JD's voice was barely a hoarse whisper.

"Good, but Ajax stays down here. He can use that older chair over there." Ellen indicated a comfortable old overstuffed chair sitting in the corner.

JD pointed at the chair and, regaining his voice, called out, "Ajax. Plaats." Ajax trotted over to the chair and jumped up into it, circled once, and settled himself comfortably. He seemed quite happy.

Catching the look on Ellen's face, JD shrugged. "My dog speaks Dutch." Ellen smiled at that, then reaching out to take JD's hand, led him up the stairs to her bedroom.

CHAPTER 25
VIETNAM

The return bus trip from Dak No to Ho Chi Minh City gave Mai plenty of time to consider her options going forward. Before falling asleep the night before, Xuan had been full of questions about Mai's life in America, her marriage to Curtis, and how they'd met. She asked about JD and Annie, and was most intrigued by JD's military service and his dog, Ajax. While Mai didn't mind answering her seemingly endless questions, she was relieved when Xuan finally yawned and, a few minutes later, fell asleep. The pallet Xuan had prepared for her was quite comfortable, and being very tired herself, Mai was not far behind.

The next morning's breakfast of rice and vegetables with hot tea brought back memories of her life in the Montagnard village and fixing breakfast for Curtis while he stayed there. Though it saddened her just a bit, they were good memories. After breakfast, Xuan walked with Mai back to the village and its small bus station, where Mai purchased a ticket back to Ho Chi Minh City. It was warm, but a breeze stirred the air as the two sat outside on a bench, waiting for the bus. It was clear Xuan liked her newly found cousin and was sad to see her leaving so soon.

The bus soon arrived, and, after discharging its passengers, began to board the new passengers for the return trip. Mai stood and gave Xuan a warm hug.

"I will try to come back for a visit before I return to America," Mai promised.

Xuan smiled happily. "That would be wonderful. I hope you can."

A few minutes later, the bus left the station and began its nine-hour run back to Ho Chi Minh City. Mai sat back in her seat, thinking about what she'd learned and what her next steps needed to be. Venturing into a red-light district was not something she would have imagined herself doing, but Chinh's suggestion made sense. Then Mai remembered her phone call with General Ellerson and decided it would be wise to check-in at the American embassy before heading into what could potentially be a dangerous situation. The odds were good she'd be just fine. She knew from her research that many tourists looking for a little excitement went into these areas for the bars, go go dancers, and massage parlors.

Tomorrow morning, I will check-in at the embassy and then, in the evening, take a taxi to the red-light district, she thought to herself. She would stay out of the terrible-looking places and see if she could spot a friendly-looking Montagnard face, then take it from there. Mai decided to make sure she dressed like a tourist.

I think it would be bad to stand out, but she chuckled softly, *I certainly don't want to look like I belong there.*

The next morning, Mai showered, dressed, and called the front desk to arrange a taxi to the U.S. Consulate, which was in the same district as the hotel where she was staying. The cab pulled up at the Consulate at 8:10 a.m. Asking the driver to wait, Mai approached the door, where she was surprised to find there was no line. The concierge at the hotel had warned her that the lines could sometimes be very long. Mai was greeted just inside the door by a uniformed Marine. Showing her passport and mentioning that General Ellerson had called on her behalf got an immediate reaction from the Marine guard.

"Ma'am, did you say General Ellerson? General Clay Ellerson, Chairman of the Joint Chiefs?"

"Yes, young man," Mai replied graciously. "The general is an old friend of the family. My late husband served with him in Vietnam."

"Just one moment, Ma'am." The Marine quickly made his way to a phone on a nearby desk and dialed a number. A few moments later, a young man in a suit stepped from a small office and walked quickly over to where Mai waited, chatting quietly with the Marine guard. Approaching, the young embassy staffer offered his hand.

"I'm Bill Cunningham. It's a real honor to meet you, Mrs. Cordell. General Ellerson explained the circumstances of your visit to the

Consul General and me. Why don't we step into my office for a chat and see what we can do for you?"

"Why, thank you, Mr. Cunningham." Mai turned to the Marine guard and smiled. "And, thank you, Sergeant Jefferson. It has been delightful talking to you."

Turning, she followed Bill Cunningham into his office, where he offered her a seat before going around his desk and sinking into the chair.

"Mrs. Cordell, I am not going to beat around the bush with you. What you are trying to do is risky, and you could find yourself crosswise with the Vietnamese government very quickly. The communists do not look kindly on the Montagnard tribes. Most are dead, in prison, in hiding, or living hand-to-mouth."

"Thank you, Mr. Cunningham, for being upfront with me. I know what you are saying is true, and I am not here to cause trouble. If I can find my brother, I will try to take him to America." Mai smiled. "Maybe the communists would be happy to see him go?"

"Maybe," Cunningham replied. "But the communists have long memories and are not particularly noted for any sense of humor."

"I suppose that is true. I have given myself three weeks. If, after that time, I have not located my brother, I will go home." She smiled at Bill. "And, I promise to do all I can to stay out of trouble. But this is something I have to do. I owe my brother a great deal."

It was Bill Cunningham's turn to nod. "I understand. Unfortunately, there is not very much we can do to help officially. If you manage to get yourself arrested, we will do everything we can to help. Hopefully, it won't come to that."

Mai laughed. "Hopefully not."

"Look," Cunningham continued. "I know who your son is and what he did. I know the sacrifices your family has made for our country. And I also know the general recently attended your husband's funeral, that they served together in Vietnam. Off the record, Mrs. Cordell, I will help if I can. Let's keep in touch." He handed her his card. "Where are you staying?"

"I am at the Park Hyatt," Mai answered.

"That's a good choice. Why don't we meet for lunch the day after tomorrow, say 1:30? We can compare notes and see where things stand." Cunningham paused, giving Mai a reassuring look. "I promised General Ellerson I'd keep an eye on you, and if, God forbid, anything happened to you, he'd have my ass."

"Well, we certainly don't want that," Mai replied. "Okay. 1:30. Day after tomorrow at the Park Hyatt. Should we meet in the lobby? I am in room 417 if you need to call me."

"Sounds good."

"Thank you for your understanding and your help, Mr. Cunningham. I appreciate it." Mai stood. "I guess I should be going. I know you're busy, and I have a cab waiting."

"You are very welcome, Mrs. Cordell. I have a brother who is Army Special Forces. I understand how you feel. Here, let me walk you back to your cab."

After returning to the hotel, Mai called Annie to check in and let her know all was well. Then she lay down for a short nap. Not yet fully recovered from the jet lag caused by her long flight, Mai had continuously been on the go since arriving in Vietnam. Two hours later, she showered and dressed like an American tourist, in jeans, a yellow printed peplum top, and comfortable shoes. Stuffing several hundred thousand Vietnamese dongs into her purse, she took the elevator to the lobby and walked to the hotel restaurant for a late lunch.

Feeling much better, Mai took a cab to Bui Vien Street and wandered around, looking in shops offering everything from paintings and statues to clothing and bags. Most of the popular bars and pubs wouldn't begin to get busy until at least 6:00 p.m., so she had some time to kill. As the evening wore on, the streets started to fill with a mix of local Vietnamese and foreign tourists. Loud pop, dance, country/western, and rock music filled the air.

As she walked through the crowd, slowly making her way in and out of several drinking establishments, Mai began to wonder if she was wasting her time. Noticing a club just up the street named Apocalypse Now, Mai decided to check out this last club and then call it a night. Entering the bar, she found an empty table to the left of the small stage and sat. The DJ was spinning a fun mix, and many young people were out on the dance floor, having a great time.

A waitress quickly approached, and Mai began to decline politely, but then decided she was a bit thirsty. Deciding to play it safe, she ordered a bottle of Saigon beer. The waitress shortly returned with the beer. Taking a sip, Mai watched as a fair number of working girls wandered through the crowd in hopes of plying their trade. *Such a sad way to live*, Mai thought to herself. *What causes a young girl to choose such a life?* Then it dawned on Mai that many had no choice, and she shuddered. Vietnam, during her childhood, was a war-torn country offering little in the way of hope for a good life. Mai's father had been a good man, and so too was her adopted Montagnard family. *It is sheer luck I didn't end up like one of these girls*, she observed.

One of the working girls caught Mai's eye as she walked toward the table where Mai was seated. Lost in her thoughts, she didn't realize why the young woman stood out at first. Then it dawned on her. The girl was a Montagnard. While generally about the same size as the Vietnamese people, the Montagnards are typically darker-skinned and do not have the epicanthic folds around their eyes.

As the young woman began to walk past, Mai—speaking in Jarai dialect—touched her arm. "Please, wait ..."

The young woman stopped and turned toward Mai, an amused look on her face. She spoke in Vietnamese. "You want to have a good time with a young woman?" She laughed. "Are you a crazy lady?" The young woman turned as if to walk away, then stopped and turned back, changing her mind. "No problem. I can do that. You are a very pretty lady. But it will cost much more."

Realizing what the young woman was saying, Mai was instantly embarrassed. Switching to Vietnamese, she responded, "No! Please. I just want to talk to you for a minute."

The young woman seemed to consider this, then turned to walk away. Again, she stopped and turned back to Mai, a surprised look on her face. "You spoke Jarai! You speak Jarai?"

Mai nodded. Again in Jarai, she spoke quickly. "As a young girl, I lived with the Montagnard for many years. I have a brother who is Montagnard. Please, will you sit and talk with me. I will buy you a drink."

"Just talk?" the young woman repeated.

"Just talk," Mai assured in Jarai. "I will pay for your time if it helps, but I want to talk to you. It is important to me."

"Okay. It is your money. We will talk." The young woman sat down at Mai's table, and almost instantly, a waitress arrived with a cocktail. The girl took a sip from the drink. "What do you want to talk about?"

"What is your name if I may ask?"

The young woman shrugged. "My name is Jum Y." She paused. "You lived with the Montagnard when you were young?"

"Yes," Mai replied. "My father was the village elder in Dak No, before the Vietnam War. He had a good friend who was the chief of a Montagnard village about a two-day walk to the west of our village. My father's Montagnard friend had a son a few years older than me. We, ah, became friends. During the war, the Viet Cong came to our village. They killed my father, my mother, and my brothers and sister because our village helped the Americans. The Montagnard boy hid me in the trees and later took me to his village where his father took me in as his daughter, and the boy became my brother."

Jum Y shifted uncomfortably. "I am sorry to hear that, but why are you telling me this? Yes. I am Montagnard. I am Jarai. But I know nothing of these things."

"Please," Mai pleaded. "Bear with me. Some years later, my brother rescued an injured American officer he found in the jungle. He brought the American to our village, where I cared for him. He stayed in our village for several weeks until he could travel. Then, because all the men were out fighting, I led him back to an American military base. I ended up marrying him and going to live with him in America."

"This American was a good man? He was good for you?" Jum Y asked, now intrigued.

"Yes," Mai replied. "We were very happy for many years and had two children. They're both grown now."

"I still don't understand why you are telling me all this." Jum Y took another sip from her cocktail. "But it is your money; I will listen."

Mai continued. "My husband and I planned to come to Vietnam, to try and find my brother, to bring him to America. But my husband got very sick and died several weeks ago. So, I am here alone, to try and find him, and bring my Montagnard brother back home with me." She paused. "And I need a little help."

Jum Y frowned. "I do not see how I can help you."

"I have been told that my brother is well-known. He is an outlaw to the communists, but a hero to the Montagnard. I do not know why. A cousin I spoke to told me that he has friends in many places. I want to get a message to him - to tell him that I am here and want to speak with him. That is all."

Jum Y stared at her empty cocktail glass for several long minutes before speaking. "I wish someone would come looking for me." She looked up at Mai. "I have an uncle living in America, near someplace called Fort Bragg. I have never seen him. My mother is dead. My father is no good, but he owes a lot of money to a drug dealer, so I work like this to pay." She paused as the waitress appeared with another cocktail.

"Maybe you shouldn't drink another one of those. That drink looks strong," Mai commented.

Jum Y laughed at that. "These are special cocktails. No alcohol. A drunk whore is no good for anyone." She paused to take a sip before looking up at Mai again. "I will help you if I can. What is your brother's name? If he is, as you say, a known man, it shouldn't be too hard for certain people to get a message to him."

Mai didn't know what to say. She was still trying to wrap her head around the last few comments Jum Y had made. Finally, getting her thoughts together, she said, "Thank you! And, in return, I will help you if I can. My brother's name is Dish."

The name caught Jum Y mid-sip, causing her to snort some of her drink and almost drop the glass. "Did you say Dish? Your brother's name is Dish?"

"Yes," Mai affirmed. "His name is Dish. Do you know him?"

"No, I don't know him. But all Montagnards know of him. He is the outlaw who sells guns to enemies of the communist government. Your brother is the Montagnard who never surrendered, who has helped many people, both Montagnard and Vietnamese. That Dish is your brother?? Holy shit! No fucking way!"

If Mai was offended by the language, she did not show it. "Will you help me?"

Jum Y considered before replying. "Yes, I will help you. But if I do, and if everything works out okay, will you ask Dish to help me?"

"I will do whatever I can. I promise that. But right now, I am hungry. Would you like to get something to eat? Do you know a good place?"

Jum Y smiled. "Well, it is your money. Yes, I know a good place." Mai paid for their drinks. Leaving the club, the two women headed toward Ben Thanh Night Market and Jum Y's favorite seafood stall.

Pham was an exceedingly dirty little man with red-rimmed eyes and seven teeth, compliments of his extensive use of the product he pedaled. At this moment, he was sitting at the next table, trying to convince one of the working girls to give him a free short time. The young woman, repulsed by Pham's manner as well as his lack of hygiene, wanted none of it, and Pham was getting angry.

The stupid little bitch doesn't know just who I am, or who I work for, he thought.

He drew his right hand back to slap the offending whore when something managed to penetrate his drug-muddled brain. He'd noticed the attractive older woman ask another whore to sit down at her table.

What the hell, he'd thought. *That's pretty crazy! Older or not, a woman that damn good looking shouldn't be paying - and with a younger lady. Why I'd show her...*

That was when he heard the name! The name about which Colonel Trần wanted information. If anyone asked about a man named Dish, the colonel wanted to know immediately.

Dish! The woman was looking for a Montagnard named Dish. This name could not be a coincidence. Surely, there would be a reward for this information. The colonel was generous to those who deserved it. Today was his lucky day.

Pham shoved the young Vietnamese working girl away from his table. Later, he'd come back and teach her better manners. Right now, lady luck had dropped a gold mine into his lap. Relieved, the working girl quickly vanished into the crowd on the dance floor. Pham stood and followed Jum Y and Mai out of the club. Staying back a short distance to keep from being spotted, he followed them. Pham needed to know where this woman was staying.

CHAPTER 26
VIETNAM

Hai approached the small pavilion that served as a gathering point for the group that lived in Dish's remote little village. Dish sat in the shade, relaxing. It was quite pleasant today. Warm, but not overly humid. The sun's warmth soothed his aches and pains, a result of several decades fighting with his enemies.

"Excuse me, Dish. I do not wish to intrude, but I've received a message I'm sure you will want to hear."

"You are not intruding, old friend," Dish replied. "What have you heard?"

"We have heard from one of our sources in Ho Chi Minh City that your sister, Mai, is in Vietnam and trying to find you. Your sister is staying at the Park Hyatt hotel in District 1."

Dish sat up. "Are you sure? Is this true?"

"This source, you know of her, the old cleaning lady, Haub, in District 1. She has proven consistently reliable in the past. According to her, a Jarai girl named Jum Y contacted her for Mai. This girl met Mai in one of the bars. Your sister spotted her as a Montagnard and befriended her, hoping to get word to you."

"Do we know this girl, Jum Y?" Dish asked.

"The cleaning woman met her a few months back, and they have become friends," Hai replied. "It is the same old story. The girl's father owes money to the drug dealers and sold his daughter into prostitution to pay off his debt."

Dish spat. "What kind of a man does that to his daughter?"

"The old woman also said Mai told Jum Y if she helped her get a message to you, she would ask you to intercede on the girl's behalf. It seems the girl told Mai you could help her if you wanted to."

Dish stood and placed his right hand on Hai's shoulder. "If my sister is asking about me in Ho Chi Minh City and the wrong people hear of it, she will be in danger. Have our people watch over her. I will figure out how to get her out of the city and to our village." Hai nodded. "And find this Jum Y, bring her here... I will help her. I do not like to see our young people treated this way. I think we must also talk with her father."

Hai nodded. "I will take care of this right away."

Turning, he walked to his longhouse where, in the corner, sat an old PRC-77 military radio left over from the Vietnam War. There was one just like it in a small apartment in Dak To, which someone monitored continuously. From Dak To, communications could be forwarded by phone and other means, to trusted friends as far away as Hanoi or Ho Chi Minh City.

CHAPTER 27
VIETNAM

Colonel Trần had just finished his dinner when there was a short knock on the door to his office. He was dining alone tonight while going over his accounting books.

"Enter," the colonel spoke as he placed his napkin, neatly folded, over his now empty plate. The door opened, and Huỳnh, his chief of security, stepped in.

"What is it, Huỳnh?"

"We have news from Ho Chi Minh City. One of our dealers, a man named Pham, called in. He claims to have followed a Vietnamese woman to her hotel, and that he overheard her talking to a Jarai whore. According to Pham, this woman was asking about a Montagnard named Dish. She is looking for him."

Trần settled back into his chair. "Pham, you say. I know that name ... a little weasel, I believe. But, if he heard the women correctly, I want her brought here to me."

Huỳnh nodded. "I will see to it, Colonel, personally."

"Good. Take the men you need; bring this woman to me." He paused. "On second thought, have our friends in the police department pick her up. There will be less trouble that way, and we don't want to create a scene. Once they arrest her, they can turn her over to you."

Again, Huỳnh nodded. "Good idea, Colonel. Anyone seeing her arrested will not want to get involved."

"Wait a moment more, Huỳnh. I want to check something. The name Pham rings a bell."

Opening the ledger he'd been poring over before dinner, Colonel Trần scanned a few pages before looking back up at Huỳnh.

"Bring Pham along too. I have a few questions I need to ask him regarding his account with us."

"Yes, Colonel," Huỳnh replied as he backed from the office and hurried down the hall. Exiting the main house, Huỳnh made his way to the quarters the colonel's men shared while on the plantation. He had a couple of men in mind who would be perfect for this job. Brutal and loyal, but not stupid. It did not pay to fail the colonel.

Huỳnh's thoughts turned to Pham, the dealer who'd followed the woman to her hotel. If the colonel wanted him brought here as well - Huỳnh grinned at the thought. He did not want to be in Pham's shoes if something was not adding up in the colonel's ledger.

Mai woke early and decided she was in the mood for pastry and coffee for breakfast. Deciding to explore a bit more around the hotel, she would see if she could find someplace that looked good. Other than lunch with Bill Cunningham from the embassy, she had no real plans for the day.

Jum Y had promised Mai she would get word to someone she knew that would be able to get a message to Dish. For some reason, Jum Y was sure Dish would be able to get her out of her life as a prostitute, and Mai was undoubtedly willing to ask him to help on her behalf.

Mai was not surprised, either, to hear that her brother was an outlaw, a gun smuggler. She understood what fueled the hatred in his heart for the communists, and Mai knew that he would never have surrendered or submitted to their rule. This hatred was the reason she'd been afraid she would find out her brother was dead. *He must be quite powerful*, she thought, *to have that kind of a reputation as an outlaw.*

The fact that Jum Y knew so much about Dish and believed he would be able to help her, certainly supported the idea. The girl said she would get back to Mai as soon as she succeeded in getting the message off, and Mai had given her the number to the hotel with her room number. She had not heard back from Jum Y yet.

Mai showered and dressed in casual American attire, and took the elevator to the lobby. Exiting the elevator, she headed toward the hotel's main entrance.

"Excuse me, Ma'am." A man dressed in a suit and tie approached, speaking in Vietnamese. Two uniformed police officers from the mobile police force accompanied him.

"My name is Lieutenant Colonel Fong. May I see your papers, please."

"Why, certainly. Is there a problem?" Mai was caught a bit off guard.

"No, Ma'am. Just a minor issue we would like your help with."

Mai handed the officer a copy of her passport, which she kept in her purse. The officer looked the passport over quickly.

"Ahh! Mrs. Mai Cordell. Yes. Please come with us. We have a minor misunderstanding at the station and would appreciate your help in clearing it up. We will have you back here within the hour."

Mai did not like the sound of that. "What is the problem, Officer? You know I am an American citizen. Should I contact the Consulate?"

The two uniformed officers closed in on either side of Mai. There was nowhere to go, and there might not be a problem; however, Mai could not silence the warning bells going off in her head.

"That is not necessary, Mrs. Cordell. As I said, we will have you back here shortly. We need your help with clearing something up. Shall we go?"

Mai could see the police car parked out in front of the hotel entrance. On the surface, everything looked official. But, she still had a bad feeling. Glancing around the hotel lobby, Mai could see no one who might be able to help her. Then Mai spotted Jum Y, standing near the door to the hotel gift shop. She wanted to call out to her, but the young woman seemed to be signaling Mai to say nothing. Jum Y was out of the line of sight of both Lieutenant Colonel Fong and the two uniformed officers.

Turning directly toward Mai, Jum Y mouthed the words, "I tell Dish."

The young woman silently repeated the phrase and then quickly turned into the gift shop to escape the lobby and possibly being spotted by the policemen.

Mai felt the fear in the pit of her stomach quell ever so slightly. *Jum Y knows what happened, and she will tell Dish.* For now, she would have to trust the young woman. It wasn't much, but it was all Mai had.

Jum Y had been successful in getting Mai's message to the right people. Any time a group of people is brutally oppressed, underground communication networks form, purely in the interests of mutual survival. The Montagnard people were no different. A message dropped with the right person would find its way to the intended recipient quickly enough.

Jum Y had spoken to an older Montagnard woman she'd come to trust, who managed to earn a living by cleaning toilets in several District 1 go-go bars. The old woman had promised to send the message along, telling Jum Y that she knew people who could get the news to the right ears.

Rather than call Mai, Jum Y had decided to stop at the hotel. Mai had been so kind to her, and for some reason, Jum Y believed she could trust Mai. It felt good to talk to her, and it gave the young woman real hope. If Mai could help her get out of her current existence, she would help Mai all she could. A realist, Jum Y, recognized that it was only a matter of time before she became lost for good. So far, she'd managed to keep clear of drugs and other destructive habits that went with life in the red-light districts of Ho Chi Minh City. Somehow, she'd managed to hold on to a shred of dignity and self-respect, but this life would wear her down before long. Jum Y wanted out before that happened, and Mai was her ticket out. She knew she was using Mai, but justified it to herself. *I am helping her too.*

When Jum Y entered the lobby of the hotel through the side entrance, she'd seen the two uniformed mobile police force officers first. That seemed odd. She knew they typically dealt with organized crime or terrorists, or kidnappings of government officials. They did not make routine arrests, and everything around the hotel seemed quiet. Then, she spotted Lieutenant Colonel Fong. You couldn't survive long in the red-light area of District 1 without learning who Lieutenant Colonel Fong was.

Everyone knew Fong had sold out—a dirty cop who collected protection money and made trouble disappear for his real boss. While nobody knew for sure, many believed Fong worked for Colonel Trần Nam Tin, one of the most brutal drug lords in Vietnam. There were rumors that Colonel Trần had been a Viet Cong commander during the Vietnam War, before the communists took over.

Jum Y ducked into the lobby gift shop out of habit. It was always best to avoid being seen by Fong. He probably would never have recognized her, but she was taking no chances. She didn't want to be on his radar at all. She peered out through the door just as Mai stepped out of the elevator. Then Jum Y saw Fong begin to walk toward her.

Oh shit, Jum Y thought. *What am I going to do now?*

Starting to panic, she forced herself to remain calm.

Talk to the old woman; she will know what to do.

After managing to get Mai's attention, Jum Y hoped Mai had understood her message. If anyone could help her new friend now, it would be Dish. She needed to get the news to Dish right away. Jum Y exited the gift shop through a side door that opened onto the street. She watched as Fong and the two uniformed officers led Mai to their car. One of the officers got in front to drive. Fong and the second officer got in back, one on either side of Mai. Jum Y watched as the car drove off.

Turning quickly, Jum Y walked as fast as she could to the bus station. The old woman did not have a cell phone. She would have to return to the cleaning lady's apartment to get a new message sent to Dish.

Getting off the bus at Bui Vien, Jum Y walked quickly along the river for several blocks. Just past Cafe Minh Phuang, she turned left, crossed the street, and headed down an alleyway. A short while later, she made another left turn into a narrower and darker alley. A short distance on, she opened a rusty metal gate into a small, damp courtyard surrounded by several rundown single-room apartments. Prostitutes often rented these apartments, as well as go-go dancers and low-level employees from the many bars and nightclubs in the area.

Crossing the courtyard to one of the doors, Jum Y knocked. There were sounds from within the apartment, and a few seconds later, the door was opened by the old woman who cleaned the toilets.

"Grandmother ..." Jum Y blurted out. "They took her."

"Come in, child. Come in. What is wrong? They took who?"

It was then that Jum Y noticed the man sitting on a stool by the stove. The man was older, maybe sixty or so. He looked clean but slightly unkempt, like he lived in the country or even the highland mountains. He was holding a steaming cup of tea in his hand.

"Who is he?" Jum Y asked nervously. "Who is that man?"

"Do not worry, child. He is here to help. Dish has sent him to us."

When the man spoke, his voice was firm and commanding, but not unkind. "You are Jum Y." It was a statement of fact. She nodded. "Tell me what has happened, quickly, girl."

"Fong took Mai. He arrested her at the Park Hyatt hotel. I was scared and ducked into the lobby store. He had men from the mobile police force with him. I tried to let her know I would get help. I think she saw me. They put her in their car and drove away."

The man shook his head. "She was not arrested. If that pig Fong took her, they are taking her to Trần. Fong works for him, the lousy bastard."

The man stood and set the empty teacup down, then turned toward the older woman. "Can Jum Y stay here for a few hours? I will check to make sure they didn't go to the police station; then, I must get word back to Dish about what has happened. After that, I will come back and get her." He turned to Jum Y. "Do not be frightened. You have helped Dish's sister, Mai. He said he would do what he can to help you. For now, we will get you out of the city to a safe place. Then we will see what Dish can do. There is much happening. You must trust me and be patient. Okay?"

Jum Y decided she had little choice at this point, and this was what she had hoped for from the beginning. "Okay."

CHAPTER 28
VIETNAM

Dish was sitting down for tea when Hai came bursting through the door, startling Chanmali so that she almost poured the hot tea into Dish's lap instead of the mug. The cup was a gift from a second lieutenant, a platoon leader he had met during the war. Though now old and stained, it had the screaming eagle logo of the 101st Air Mobile Division on it. It was the cup from which Dish always drank his tea.

"What is it, Hai?" Dish asked.

"Dish, I am afraid there is bad news. It's about your sister."

"What is it?" Dish quickly got to his feet.

"I just heard back from Phuoc in Ho Chi Minh City. He contacted the old woman, Haub, and was talking to her about meeting with Jum Y, when the girl came to the woman's apartment. She had gone to the Park Hyatt to tell Mai she'd sent the message off to you, and she saw that pig, Lieutenant Colonel Fong, arresting Mai. They drove off in a mobile police car, but Phuoc checked, and the car never arrived at the station for District 1."

"That means Trần must have her."

Dish walked to the door and gazed out at nothing for a few minutes, thinking.

"Since we killed his men on the trail and I sent that smuggler to tell him I am going to kill him, he will try to use Mai to get to me. That means we have some time. If Trần knows she is my sister, he will use her as a bait to try and trap me. He knows I will come for her. I don't believe he will harm her until he has me where he wants me. She will be his leverage, which means he will keep her alive."

"I agree," said Hai. "She will be safe for some time... at least until he no longer thinks you will come for her."

"Yes. But Trần knows I will come for her ... Hai, get the word out to all of our people. I want to know where he is holding Mai, as soon as possible. Trần will probably let that information leak out. It is what I would do if I were setting a trap. Once we know where Mai is, we will send a message of our own to Trần."

Hai was immediately out the door and running toward his longhouse. Chanmali approached Dish and handed him the tea, then placed her hand on his chest gently.

"Phua khong khony." It was Laotian for "my husband," and the first time Chanmali had used this expression. It did not go unnoticed by Dish. "Your sister will be okay. You will get her back safely. I know it. I know the man you are. I know your heart."

Dish turned to Chanmali. "She should not have come here. It isn't safe for her here. She should have stayed in America."

"She came to find her brother, a brother she loves and hasn't seen in many years. She is a good woman, and you will get her back."

Dish nodded but said nothing. Taking the tea, he stepped out onto the veranda, feeling sick inside. He stood still, ignoring the mug in his hand. Slowly, the sick feeling went away, replaced by something he hadn't felt in some time—rage, fury. That same fury that made him the implacable, relentless fighter he'd been during the war. It was the same feeling he felt when the Viet Cong had attacked Mai's village and slaughtered her family. He'd felt that same fury again when his father died, killed by the VC while fighting with the Americans, and then he'd felt it again upon learning that Colonel Trần and his men had massacred his village.

I will get her back, and I will kill that bastard Trần if it is the last thing I do. It is a score too long unsettled. Dish tilted the mug over and dumped the cold tea onto the ground. Turning, he went back in.

"Chanmali, sa nya, please make me some more tea. I let it get cold." Chanmali gave a quick start and nodded, heading toward the kitchen to heat more water. She smiled. He'd used the Laotian word for wife.

Dish walked to the old trunk he kept in the corner near their shared sleeping area. Opening it, he removed the old Belgian Browning pistol and an M-1 Carbine. They could stand a good cleaning. He spotted the Buck General, the bowie-style knife the American soldier had presented him before leaving the village with Mai. Lifting it, still sheathed in its black leather scabbard, he turned the knife over in his hand. That was long ago. The knife had served him well during the war. While scarred and slightly worn from years of use and sharpening, it was still an excellent blade.

A good knife, Dish thought. *I should check the edge. I am sure it could use a little sharpening.*

Finishing the supper Chanmali had prepared, Dish set the bowl and chopsticks down on the table in front of him. Chanmali quickly cleared the setting away and set a mug of steaming coffee in its place.

"Thank you."

He leaned over to pick up the Buck General and his whetstone from the bench beside him, and carefully went to work on the knife's edge. Soon, it was sharp enough to shave. Satisfied, Dish sheathed the blade and set it and the whetstone down on the table. Reaching for the coffee, he took a sip of the strong, black beverage he had come to appreciate while working with the Americans during the war.

Moments later, Hai appeared in the doorway. "I have more news. I just received a message from a very reliable contact in Ho Chi Minh City. Trần is staying at the house on the old Michelin rubber plantation, about sixty kilometers north of the city. Many of his men are with him there. It varies, but sometimes there are thirty or forty men at the house. They stay in outbuildings converted into sleeping quarters. Trần stays alone in the house, except for his bodyguards and a few housekeepers."

"Who is this contact? Are we sure of this?"

Hai nodded. "Yes. The information comes from a woman who worked as a housekeeper in the plantation house. She fled the house, telling the staff she had to see her sick mother." Hai paused. "Our contact reported that the woman is his cousin, Hoa. Trần abused her badly. It seems he often abuses the prettier female employees, taking pleasure in beating and raping them. This time Trần chose the cousin of one of our most loyal people in Ho Chi Minh City."

Dish, thinking about this turn of events, did not immediately respond. Hai waited.

"We need to know if Trần brings Mai there. I will not ask her to go back and endanger herself, but if she knew of a place from which one of our people could closely watch the plantation house, that would be most helpful."

Hai nodded in agreement. "Yes, that should be possible. I will radio our contact and have him talk to his cousin."

CHAPTER 29
VIETNAM

The four traveled in silence. Mai, pressed between the two police officers, had little room to move. It was when she realized they were heading out of the city that she started to become truly frightened.

"Excuse me, but where are you taking me? You know I am an American citizen. I want to call the American Consulate."

Fong laughed. "Be still, woman! We have orders not to harm you, but we can tie you up and throw you in the trunk. We have a one-hour ride ahead of us, and I will not put up with any nonsense. Do you understand me?"

Mai did understand and did not want to be locked in the trunk. Reluctantly, she settled into her seat.

I saw Jum Y mouth the words, 'I will tell Dish.' I know that's what she said. So, I have to trust her, and that Dish can help me.

It was then that Mai remembered her lunch meeting with the man from the Consulate. At least, Mai knew her disappearance would not go unnoticed. That was another slightly comforting thought.

At precisely 1:25 p.m., Bill Cunningham entered the lobby of the Park Hyatt. Glancing around, he noticed that Mai Cordell was not yet down from her room, so he took a seat in one of the lobby chairs and waited. At 1:40, when Mai still hadn't shown, Bill walked over to the lobby phone and dialed her room number. After ringing seven times, there was still no answer. He hung up the phone and walked over to the front desk.

"Can I help you, Sir?" The attendant greeted Cunningham with a smile.

"Yes. My name is Bill Cunningham. I had a lunch meeting with Mai Cordell at 1:30, and it is now 1:40. I called her room, and there is no answer. She is in room 417. Did she leave any message for me at the desk?"

"Ms. Cordell, you said?" The attendant had a funny expression on her face.

"Yes. Mai Cordell."

"I am so sorry," the attendant replied. "But Ms. Cordell was picked up this morning by officers of the Mobile Police Force. They took her away in their car."

"What? What time did this happen?"

"It was early, maybe 8:00 a.m., I think."

"Listen. I am with the U.S. Consulate, and as you know, Mai Cordell is an American citizen. I received no notification of an American citizen being placed under arrest, and Mrs. Cordell would have certainly called the Consulate. Did the police officers identify themselves?"

"I was not on the desk at that time." The attendant sounded a little worried. "Let me check. I'll be right back with the manager." The attendant disappeared into an office at the far end of the reception desk. A few seconds later, she reappeared, followed by a younger man with a manager's badge over his shirt pocket.

"Mr. Cunningham? I am Cao." the younger man looked more nervous than the reception desk attendant. "There were three officers. Two in uniform and a detective who identified himself as Lieutenant Colonel Fong."

"Sonofabitch!" Cunningham exploded. "Listen! I am with the U.S. Consulate. Mia Cordell is an American citizen and a friend of important people in the U.S. government, including the President of the United States." (He may have been exaggerating just a bit here, but he needed the edge.) Showing his diplomatic credentials to the manager, Bill continued, "We know Lieutenant Colonel Fong, and he is a crooked cop. Unless you want serious trouble, I want to see all the security footage for that time frame, and I want to see it now. I also want Mai Cordell's room sealed immediately. You may open it to the proper Vietnamese authorities, but nobody else. Do you understand?"

"Yes. Yes." Cao replied. "I understand. I will speak to the security department and get you access to the video right away. Please, wait right here, sir!"

Cunningham pulled his cell phone out of his pocket and dialed the number for the Consulate security office.

"Ted, this is Bill. We have a big problem. Someone kidnapped Mai Cordell. Yes, she was kidnapped. She was picked up this morning at the Park Hyatt by that crooked cop, Fong. Yes... I know what that means."

The embassy staff knew of Fong and suspected that he worked for the known drug smuggler, Colonel Trần.

"Listen, Ted. I need you to call the Vietnamese police and verify that they did not pick up Mrs. Cordell. Okay? Then call General Ellerson. Yes, that Ellerson, the Chairman of the Joint Chiefs of Staff. Mai is a good friend of his. Yeah! Shit is right! I am getting copies of the security tapes here at the hotel. I'll be back to the Consulate as quickly as I can." Bill paused to collect his thoughts. "Listen, can you also send a couple of Marines over to watch her room here? I need them to help make sure only the Vietnamese police are allowed in ...! What? I know that, Ted. Fuck the protocols. You know who Mai is, and you know who her son is. He's a hero, for Christ's sake. If anything happens to her, there will be hell to pay. Okay. Thanks, Ted. Just do whatever you can. See you in a little while."

Cunningham ended the call.

Shit!

Two hours later, Cunningham was back at the Consulate, viewing the security footage from hotel security cameras. Ted Baines, from the security department, and Stan Woodson, the resident CIA station chief, stood hunched over behind him, to better see the computer display.

"Yep, that's Fong alright," Baines observed. "A real slimeball. The man's a pimp, protection money collector, and general enforcer who uses his office to protect Trần and perhaps a few other drug dealers. But," Baines continued, "there's something wrong with those uniformed officers. Look at the uniforms. The mobile police are sticklers, and those uniforms are too big for the men wearing them. And, look at the patches on their shoulders. They belong to the Mobile Police Force in Hanoi, not Ho Chi Minh City. I'd say those uniforms are stolen, and those two men belong to Trần."

"I'd say so." Woodson agreed. "Looks that way to me."

"Did you get a hold of General Ellerson?" Cunningham looked over his shoulder at Ted.

"Yes, I did. And I never want to make a call like that again. Ellerson is furious. I don't think he blames us, but damn, he was pissed. He wants an update asap." Baines paused. "I checked, and the Mobile Police have no record of any Mai Cordell being picked up or arrested. Other than that, not much help will come from that end, not unless the top brass gets involved."

Cunningham nodded, then sighed. "Shit. I better give Ellerson a call. The general personally asked me to keep an eye on Mrs. Cordell. Damn it; she is such a nice lady. If she is really in Trần's hands, it will take a miracle to get her back."

Both Woodson and Baines nodded at Cunningham in sympathy. He was right. It was not Cunningham's fault, but the two men were both happy they weren't in his shoes.

CHAPTER 30
WASHINGTON, DC

Clay Ellerson hung up the phone. He did not like what he'd just heard in the update from Bill Cunningham. At least they had identified this Fong character. That was great. But the question now was, what the hell could they do with the information? He decided to call Bill Powell at the State Department, but that second call did little to relieve his concerns.

Essentially, Powell told Ellerson that if a Vietnamese drug smuggler was holding Mai, there was little the U.S. government could do about it. Relations with Vietnam were just starting to improve, even though the war had been over for more than forty years. There was still not a lot of cooperation between the two countries. The communist government would not even acknowledge that there was any drug usage or prostitution in Vietnam, so official help in dealing with drug smugglers was undoubtedly out of the question. Powell assured the general he would talk to his counterpart in the Vietnamese government, but warned Ellerson against getting his hopes up.

Damn it, Ellerson thought. *There must be something I can do.* People can't just go around kidnapping American citizens, especially the mother of a U.S. Navy SEAL and a bonafide American hero.

Ellerson picked up his phone and punched in his secretary's extension.

"Yes, General?"

"Maddie, I need an appointment to see the president, and I need it just as fast as you can make it happen. See if you can get Admiral

Spence and the CIA Director there as well."

"I'll get right on it, sir."

"Thank you, Maddie." The general hung up the phone.

Three hours later, General Ellerson, Mike Connors, and President Steele were sitting in the Oval Office. At the insistence of General Ellerson, the president asked his chief of staff to take a short walk or get some coffee. Admiral Spence was not currently available, so Ellerson would fill him in later if the meeting went as he hoped.

"What's up, Clay?" the president asked. He was sitting in his shirt and tie; the suit coat slung over the back of his chair. "It must be damn important. Maddie wouldn't get off the phone with Sansby until I chiseled this meeting in granite."

Ellerson shifted in his seat. "Mai Cordell has gone missing in Vietnam. We are pretty sure she was kidnapped from her hotel by a Vietnamese drug lord named Trần. We have video footage showing her being picked up by a Lieutenant Colonel Fong with the Mobile Police Force and two fake uniformed officers. Fong is known to be a crooked cop and in the employment of this Trần."

"Shit," Connors stated. 'How do we know this?"

"Mai was scheduled to have lunch with Bill Cunningham, an official at the U.S. Consulate in Vietnam. She was a no show. When Bill checked at the desk for a message, they notified him that their Mobile Police Force had arrested her. Bill was alarmed by that because they are Vietnam's elite anti-terrorist and VIP protection unit, and it made no sense for them to be arresting Mai at her hotel."

Connors nodded. "That would be highly unusual."

"Bill wrangled copies of the hotel's security videos," Ellerson continued, "and they quickly identified Lieutenant Colonel Fong. The two uniformed men were wearing stolen uniforms. The shoulder patches indicated units in Hanoi, not Ho Chi Minh City. And, they were quite clearly not sized for the men wearing them."

The president leaned back in his chair and said nothing for a few seconds, then asked, "What was Mrs. Cordell doing in Vietnam?"

"She was there to try and locate her brother—adopted brother. She hasn't seen him since she and the late Captain Cordell left during the war. If you remember, Mr. President, Captain Cordell served under my command during the war in Vietnam. This brother of Mai's was a Montagnard soldier who worked with U.S. Special Forces units for years."

"How do we know this connects to this Trần?" Connors asked.

"While nobody has proven anything yet, Fong is strongly believed to be in the employ of this Trần, rumored to be an especially brutal Viet Cong leader now turned drug lord operating in the central highlands. He and Mrs. Cordell's brother may have a history. We aren't sure at this point, but it seems likely that there could be a connection." Ellerson paused, shifting in his seat. "If you remember, Mr. President, Mai Cordell is also the mother of JD Cordell, the SEAL you pinned the Navy Cross on a few months ago."

"I certainly do remember."

"Does her son know about this yet?" Connor's asked.

"Not yet, but he will soon enough. I plan to call him this afternoon," Ellerson replied. "The family needs to be told, and I'd much rather JD hears this from me than someone else."

"That falls to the State Department, Clay," the president observed. "They will have to call him."

"State can call him as well," Ellerson replied. "As a friend of the family, I'd like them to hear it from me first. I'll let them know to expect an official contact from the State Department."

"What can we do about getting her out of Vietnam?" the president asked.

Connors answered. "That is the real problem. The communist government still remembers the war. They let American tourists in because they want the revenue, but they are hardly a friendly regime. Also, they follow the standard communist propaganda playbook, and officially claim that there is no drug problem in Vietnam, so they can hardly admit to there being drug smugglers. You could threaten economic sanctions, I suppose, but to be honest, I doubt we'd get very far." Connors paused, letting out a worried sigh. "If some drug lord has her, she could be anywhere by now—in Ho Chi Minh City, Hanoi, or some little village in the middle of a rice paddy. Hell, they could also have her stashed in China, Cambodia, or Laos, anywhere in that damned Golden Triangle region.

If we push too hard, it might end up getting Mrs. Cordell killed, especially if this Trần sees her as more of a liability than an opportunity. Mrs. Cordell could easily disappear. The government would appear to be very helpful, but would claim to know nothing and blame it on outlaw elements."

"Shit!" This time it was the president's turn. "What do you think JD will do when he finds out?"

Ellerson cleared his throat. "Sir, I know this family. I believe JD will get on a plane and fly to Thailand, sneak into Vietnam through either Laos or Cambodia, and try to rescue his mother."

"I was afraid you'd say that." Connors shook his head slowly.

"We could stop him," President Steele commented.

"Mr. President, I think that would be a mistake. If you let me explain, I have an idea I think you should consider."

"Go ahead, Clay."

"Yes, sir. First, the entire family are all heroes. People still talk about the Iranian terrorist plot and the Brookstone fiasco. If word got out in the press that the U.S. government did nothing and let that Navy SEAL's mother die in Vietnam... there'd be hell to pay. So, in my opinion, we have to try something." Ellerson paused. "JD Cordell, while retired now, was a top hand in the teams. If anyone can pull off a covert rescue mission like this, it would be him. After all, we're talking about his mother."

"That's crazy," Connors interjected. "We let him try?"

"Exactly," Ellerson replied. "And we help him. If he succeeds and nobody is the wiser, no harm done. If he fails, he is simply a loyal son sneaking into a dangerous country to try and rescue his mother. Anyone would understand that. The fact that he is a retired Navy SEAL is what made him think he could get away with it. The U.S. government could disavow any participation and be understanding of his actions, but still disapproving of his attempt."

"So," President Steele observed, "we are sending a lion to the slaughter?"

"Perhaps," Ellerson conceded. "It might look that way. Except, I think if anyone can do it, JD can. Especially with some unofficial logistical support. If his mother is alive, he will get her out of there."

"And if she is dead?" Connors asked.

"He'll kill the son of a bitch who did this," Ellerson stated calmly.

The president let that go by without comment.

"So, how do you propose we help him?" Steele asked.

"We get a couple of volunteers. I'd recommend members of his former platoon. They know him and have fought with him. We give them the straight story. Strictly covert and off-the-books. This mission will be an ultra-top-secret black op. That means no U.S. military equipment, uniforms, or support. The rescue team will be completely on their own as far as they know and will be disavowed if they are caught or killed. But behind the scenes, we can have the CIA keep an eye on them and quietly help where we can."

"It might work," Connors agreed. "I can trust Rick Hahn. Rick knows JD and likes him. They worked together in Niger when Cordell's team rescued Doctor Chang from al Qaeda. Hahn has spent a lot of time in Thailand and the Golden Triangle area for the CIA, so he'll have connections there. He'd want to help, I think." Connors paused. "We could also steer Cordell toward using one of our charter airlines to fly in and out of Thailand. That would help us keep tabs on them."

"Sounds pretty damned risky to me," President Steele observed.

"That's because it is," Ellerson agreed. "But I think it is the best chance we have of getting Mrs. Cordell out of there alive. And, I'll be damned if I am going to sit here and do nothing." He paused, then added. "We can have the State Department pursue its normal diplomatic channels to help Mrs. Cordell, and we will make sure the press knows we are doing all we can through proper protocols. We will need to keep very tight operational security on our Plan B."

"Will any of Cordell's former platoon members volunteer to help? Sounds a lot like suicide to me," Connors asked.

"Of course," Ellerson stated. "They're Navy SEALs. The bond between these guys is beyond the average man's comprehension. And, if the whole thing goes to hell in a handbasket, the only three who know anything are sitting right here in this room. Any others involved will just be following orders and won't know the who, how, or why."

"What about your operator, this Rick Hahn character?" Steele asked, looking at Connors.

Connors thought about that for a second. "Mr. President, Rick Hahn is one of only a handful of people on this planet I'd trust with my life."

Benjamin Steele swiveled around in his chair and stared at the wall for nearly two full minutes. It was a tough call, one any president doesn't want to make. Steele had been a soldier too. He swiveled back around to face Ellerson and Connors. He'd made his decision.

"Gentlemen, we will not discuss this again. This conversation never even took place." He looked at Ellerson and then at Connors. "Make it happen."

The president stood.

"Now, if you will excuse me, I have a dinner date with my wife, and she gets quite annoyed if I'm late."

Both Ellerson and Connors took their cue and stood. After wishing the president a pleasant evening, Connors followed the general out of the Oval Office.

"Mike, let's keep in close contact on this one... I guess we might as well call it Operation Plan B. I will need to talk to Admiral Spence before I can approach Cordell's former commander for volunteers. Spence is an old warhorse; he can keep a secret." Mike nodded.

"I agree," Mike replied. "There will be less chance of any snafus if the three of us stay in close communication on this. I also think it will be better to stay outside regular channels for this one. Hahn has made a lot of contacts over his years as an operator. I think he can handle anything these guys will need on the outside. Less chance of any leaks that way."

"That sounds smart." Ellerson extended his hand. "Let's do our best to get Mrs. Cordell out of there. We go back a long way."

"Understood," Mike replied. The two men shook hands and went their separate ways. Both had a lot to do in a short time. General Ellerson first faced the unpleasant task of calling JD Cordell to let him know his mother was missing.

JD parked his jeep in the State Street Garage and opened the back gate to let Ajax out. The pair made their way toward Ellen's loft in the old Woodruff building. Ajax trotted happily along at JD's side, seemingly unaware of the knot in his handler's stomach. As a trained SEAL, very little frightened JD, but today he was feeling unnervingly apprehensive. The fingers of his right hand absentmindedly toyed with the small box in the right pocket of the light jacket he wore. It was a chilly October evening, and this was a huge step, one for which he was confident he was ready. He knew Ellen loved him, but there was still a nameless cloud of uncertainty hovering overhead.

Ellen was fixing a dinner of steamed dumplings, fried rice, and bok choy. JD had come to appreciate her cooking. While he was a decent cook himself, Ellen was excellent. Truthfully, he had to admit that just being in her company made any meal taste better.

His mind went back to the small box in his pocket, containing a .9 carat round-cut diamond in a thin white gold band. The stone was color F and slightly imperfect. JD didn't know much about diamonds, but he knew he wanted it to sparkle. The woman in the store said this ring was the best value for the money. JD liked the simple elegance of the setting. It reflected, he thought, the uncomplicated honesty of his feelings for Ellen.

Man and dog entered the building foyer and took the elevator up to Ellen's floor. JD knocked on the door. When it opened, and JD saw the happiness shining in Ellen's eyes, he knew everything would be just fine. Ajax made straight for his chair, making himself comfortable.

"Can I help with anything?" JD asked.

"Nope. You're right on time, and dinner is on the table. Let's eat. I'm starving," Ellen replied with a laugh. JD loved to hear her laugh.

Dinner was delicious, the conversation light. Ellen was interested in hearing about the new position he had with National Strategic Security. The company specialized in designing and testing security at the nation's nuclear facilities. They also provided state-of-the-art security forces and testing services—probing secured sites to identify weaknesses and test the readiness of each facility's security teams. While there would occasionally be travel involved, JD would be primarily concerned with the Department of Energy complex in Oak Ridge, Tennessee.

"I haven't done much yet," JD laughed. "It's taken several weeks to get through the paperwork, security clearances, and orientations. I might get to start doing something in the next week or so." He was anxious to get started, never being one to sit around and wait.

"It sounds exciting. Not too dangerous, I hope?"

JD smiled. "A lot less dangerous than taking out terrorists, Somalian pirates, or rescuing doctors from al Qaeda. It's just enough of a real mission to keep me on my toes."

"Now that's a low blow," Ellen replied, laughing. "But then, I guess not too many girls can claim they met their boyfriend in a gun battle in Agadez."

"Speaking of that, Ellen, I have something for you." Getting to his feet, JD walked to his jacket hanging by the door. He retrieved the small box from his pocket and returned to the table.

"What is it, JD?"

"Ellen, I want you to know that meeting you, even if it was in the middle of a firefight," JD grinned, "has been the most wonderful thing that has ever happened to me. I feel like the luckiest man in the world.

But more than that, I feel like my life is now filled with something I never knew was missing until I met you. I don't want that ever to change."

"JD," Ellen began...

"Please, Ellen, let me finish this... I would be the happiest and luckiest man alive if..." JD dropped to his knee next to Ellen's chair."... if you would be my wife." He presented Ellen with the little box he held in his hand.

Ellen took the box and looked at JD, who suddenly could not read anything in the expression on her face. She opened the box and looked at the ring.

"It's beautiful, JD. It is." Ellen seemed to be rooted in thought, and there was no change in her expression. JD began to fear the worst. Suddenly, she grinned.

"Oh, my God! Are you going to put this ring on my finger or what?" Ellen handed JD the box and held out her left hand with the ring finger extended. JD laughed, his heart soaring.

"Absolutely!"

JD lay still, holding Ellen in his arms, enjoying the clean fragrance of her dark hair. He'd dozed off for a bit. It sounded like, from her breathing, she was also sleeping.

Glancing at the clock on Ellen's nightstand, he saw that it was 8:15 p.m. Ajax would have to go out. JD started to slide his arm out from under Ellen, who stirred.

"Where are you going?"

"To take Ajax out for a short walk. You don't need to get up. I'll be back in a few minutes."

"No, I'll get up and do the dishes." Ellen rolled over, looking up at JD. She smiled. "Then, maybe I'll pour us both a glass of wine, and when you get back, maybe you'll be up for round two," she teased.

"You're on," JD laughed as he leaned over to kiss her. He got up and walked over to the chair where he'd tossed his clothes a short while ago.

Downstairs, JD grabbed his jacket and the leash, making sure he had a couple of dog poop bags in his pocket. Ajax was ready to go for a walk. Leaving the Woodruff Building, the two crossed Gay Street and headed toward the small park at the end of Market Square, where Ajax did his business. After JD bagged it and dropped it into a trash can, they circled Market Square, where Ajax enjoyed the attention of several children who asked JD if they could pet his dog. Finally, about twenty minutes later, they were back on the elevator heading toward the fourth floor.

Ellen, having cleaned up the dishes, poured two glasses of Chardonnay, and was sitting on the couch in a beautiful Chinese silk robe. JD had never seen anything so stunning.

"Your phone rang twice while you were out, JD. You left it on the chair. I didn't answer it, but I think someone left you a message."

"It can wait," JD replied. He had other things on his mind.

"You should check. It might be something important. I set it on the table." Ellen pointed toward the kitchen area.

"Okay then, let me check." JD walked over to the kitchen table and picked up the phone. Not recognizing the number which had a 703 area code, he thought, that's odd. JD played the voicemail message.

"JD, this is General Clay Ellerson. I need you to call me as soon as you receive this message. This message is vitally important. I repeat, please call me as soon as you get this." The general gave the number JD had already seen on the missed call notification.

"What the hell?" JD muttered.

"Is something wrong?" Ellen asked.

"I'm not sure. It's General Ellerson. He says I need to call him back right away."

"Then I think you should call him now, JD. He would not be calling you if it weren't important."

JD was already pressing the dial button.

"General Ellerson."

"Sir, this is JD Cordell. I got your message. What's up, General?"

"JD, I am afraid I have some bad news. I'm going to be straight. Your mother has gone missing in Vietnam."

"What? Missing? How?" Ellen looked over at JD, the tone in his voice catching her attention.

"I can tell you what we know at this point. Your mother scheduled lunch with Bill Cunningham, one of the Consulate staff, at her hotel today. She was a no show. When Bill went to the desk to see if your mother had left a message for him, the staff informed him that the Mobile Police Force had arrested her."

"What the hell for?" JD interrupted.

"Well, JD. There are two problems. First, the Mobile Police only deal with active anti-terrorism operations and government VIP protection. They don't arrest tourists in their hotels." Ellerson cleared his throat.

"Second, Bill got hold of the hotel security footage, and we've identified one of the police as a Lieutenant Colonel Fong. Fong is a crooked cop and heavily suspected of working for a major Vietnamese drug lord named Trần. The two uniformed officers with Fong were identified as impostors wearing stolen uniforms."

"What the hell would a drug lord want with my mother?" JD was trying to make sense of the situation. Ellen, alarmed at the direction the conversation had taken, walked over to JD and placed her hand on his arm.

"We aren't sure yet, but we suspect this Trần has a history with your mother's Montagnard brother. If she was looking for him and asking questions, he might have gotten wind of it and decided to grab her, maybe to get at her brother somehow. It's only a theory, but at this point, it's the only thing that makes any sense."

JD accepted that for the moment. "What are we doing?"

General Ellerson paused. "JD, Vietnam is a communist country. We don't have the best relations with their government, but we are doing everything we can through diplomatic channels. The Secretary of State has already been in contact with the Vietnamese government, and President Steele is supporting us one hundred percent." There was a pause. "JD, listen to me. Don't say anything. Do you understand?"

"Yes."

"If a dangerous drug lord has your mother, there is not much we can do. She could be anywhere—Vietnam, Laos, Cambodia, Thailand, even China, for Christ's sake. If this is a vendetta between a Vietnamese drug lord and your uncle, the communist government will stay out of it. It is simply too lucrative for them to do nothing."

"I understand." JD had seen that kind of situation before.

Ellerson continued. "I knew your father, and I know you almost as well. I know you are already planning to go to Vietnam yourself. I would if I were in your shoes. I can't do anything officially. Do you understand that?"

"I do."

"I would suggest that if you plan to go to Vietnam, you will want to talk to ICS Aviation in San Diego. In the meantime, I will do everything I can to help."

"Yes, sir. I appreciate that."

"JD, I know you understand what I'm saying here. If your mother is, as we believe, a pawn in some game, as bait for your uncle, we should have some time. If he kills your mother, she is no longer bait for a trap. Instead, she is a reason for revenge, and from what I know of your uncle, that would be counter-productive. Give me a day to make whatever informal arrangements I can. I will do all I can to help."

"I know, sir. Thank you. Besides, it will take me a day to get my stuff together on this end. I have to talk to my new employer, and I'll call ICS Aviation tomorrow morning."

"Okay, then. I will call you again tomorrow, same time, and give you any additional information I have then." Ellerson ended the call.

"What's happened?" Ellen asked. "That sounded serious."

"It's my mother. A Vietnamese drug lord has kidnapped my mother."

"What?! But how? Why? What would a drug lord want with your mother?"

"Colonel Ellerson thinks this drug lord has a feud of some kind with my mother's brother, from the days of the war. They think when she showed up asking about him, this Colonel Trần, who may have been a VC commander during the Vietnam war, got wind of it. He has most likely snatched her to use as bait to get to her brother." He paused. "Ellen, I have to go to Vietnam. I'm not sure ..."

Ellen cut him off. "Of course you have to go. I know. It's okay." She stepped closer and reached for his hands, taking them in hers. "I will admit... it scares me a little. No," she shook her head, "it scares me a lot. But I am not going to try and stop you." She reached up and wrapped her arms around her new fiancé in a hug. "I will be here when you get back. Please make sure you come back to me..."

JD hugged her back, words failing him for a moment. Finally, he spoke. "I promise, Ellen. I will be back."

Back at his Cherokee Bluff condo, JD climbed the stairs to the second-floor bedroom and opened the door to the walk-in closet. Kneeling beside an olive drab wooden footlocker that had once belonged to his father, he spun the combination lock to open it, and removing the lock from the hasp; he lifted the lid. Reaching in, he pulled out a Kydex holster made by R&R Holsters. It contained a

Glock 19 Gen 5 9 mm semi-automatic pistol. Next, he pulled out a cardboard box containing several 15-round magazines for the gun. There were also two ammo cans, each containing 500 rounds of 9 mm ball ammunition. He set one of those on the floor beside him.

Finally, JD reached into the footlocker and removed a cloth-wrapped object. Removing the cloth revealed a Jim Hammond-made Flesheater 9 combat knife. Sliding the blade from its leather sheath, JD carefully checked the edge. It was razor-sharp.

Ajax quietly came into the closet and sat next to JD. Setting the knife down, JD shifted to a sitting position on the floor. He ruffled the dog's neck, and Ajax let out a soft whine.

"You know, don't you buddy," JD spoke quietly, scratching Ajax behind his ears. "I think we have to wait just a bit to begin our retirement."

Suddenly, JD gave Ajax a playful shove on his shoulder. "What do you say, boy? Have we got one more mission left in us? You're getting pretty old there, buddy." Ajax responded by whining and giving JD a quick lick on the left ear.

"I knew I could count on you, partner. Come on ... let's go rescue your grandmother." JD closed the lid on the footlocker and replaced the lock. Getting to his feet, he sheathed the FE9, shoving the knife into his belt. Picking up the holstered Glock, the box of magazines, and one 500-round box of ammunition, he left the closet and started down the stairs to the first floor. Ajax followed close behind.

CHAPTER 31
CORONADO NAVAL BASE

"You wanted to see us, Chief?" Pallie and Vivas stood in the doorway to Chief Whitley's small office at Coronado Naval Base in San Diego. Space was made even smaller by the presence of a four-star general seated on a metal folding chair in the corner. Seeing the general, the two sailors stood at attention and saluted.

"Vivas. Pallie. At ease. Yes, come in and shut the door," Whitley urged.

The two men entered and closed the door. There was no place to sit, so they stood waiting to discover why the chief had asked them to report.

Whitley sat back in his chair. "Pallie. Vivas. You've met General Clay Ellerson, Chairman of the Joint Chiefs. Nothing discussed here leaves this room. Do you both understand that?"

"Yes, Chief. Absolutely."

Whitley turned to Ellerson. "They're all yours, General." Chief Whitley then turned his attention to a stack of paperwork on his well-organized desk.

Ellerson stood. "Gentlemen. Yesterday morning an American citizen was kidnapped in Ho Chi Minh City by a Vietnamese drug lord. As you know, we don't have the best diplomatic relationship with Vietnam or its communist government. We are pursuing everything we can through diplomatic channels, but there is little hope of a successful outcome. The American is not in the hands of the Vietnamese government, or there might be more positive expectations.

She is in the hands of a known criminal who is also a former Viet Cong colonel."

"She?" Vivas asked.

"Mai Cordell," the general replied.

"Oh shit," Vivas muttered, looking over at Pallie.

"Does JD know?" Pallie asked.

"I told JD last night on the phone. He is planning to leave for Vietnam in two days."

"Will you try to stop him?" Vivas asked.

"That was the initial reaction the president had." Ellerson paused. "But I talked him out of it. I believe JD is the best chance his mother has of getting out of there alive." The general paused again, then continued. "I know you two know JD pretty well, and I know you've met his mother."

Pallie and Vivas nodded. They knew Mai and liked her.

"I'm looking for two men willing to go in with JD to help him succeed in getting her safely back home. Mai, JD's father, Curtis, and I have a long history. Mai is a close friend of my wife. I will never hear the end of it if we don't bring her back alive."

There was no hesitation. "We'll go," Vivas stated.

Pallie nodded his agreement.

"Before you raise your hands, understand this. This mission is completely off the books — no U.S. military equipment or support. If anything goes wrong, our government will deny any knowledge of the mission."

Ellerson paused to let that sink in.

"I can help you get in and out of Thailand, strictly behind the scenes, but while you are in Vietnam, you are totally on your own."

Vivas shrugged. "Same answer. We'll go."

Again, Pallie nodded, then added. "What about Maddux? He'd want to go to."

Whitley looked up from his stack of paperwork. "Maddux would most definitely want to go. Unfortunately, he is currently tasked for another mission and cannot volunteer."

"I do have a few things already in place," Ellerson continued. "Mike Connors, the CIA Director, is involved... strictly off the books. The only ones in the loop are you two, the president, Admiral Spence, Connors, your chief here, and me. Connors is using a contractor, one he trusts implicitly, to help with any needed operational support. This guy spent years in Thailand and has many contacts there."

"Who is he?" Vivas asked. "Are you sure we can trust this guy?"

"I think so. You know the man. His name is Rick Hahn. You met him in Niger."

"Rick Hahn?" Vivas looked over at Pallie, who nodded. "Okay, he seems solid enough."

"What's the plan?" Pallie asked.

"You link up with JD at ICS Aviation in San Diego tomorrow. You get to Thailand. Once in Thailand, according to Rick, you go to a nightclub called Obsession in Bangkok and find his contact there, someone named Hana. Rick will let this Hana person know you're coming. Hana can get whatever you need and take you wherever you need to go." He paused. "Rick says you can trust Hana completely. He's done so on several occasions. After that, it's all on you guys. There is no more plan. Simple enough?"

"Simple enough," Vivas agreed.

"Okay. I was never here." General Ellerson turned to go but paused, turned, and looked back at Pallie and Vivas.

"Thank you, gentleman, for volunteering. I knew you would, after all, JD is your brother. If I were younger, by God, I'd volunteer myself to help the Cordell family. Good luck, gentlemen. Please get Mai out of there safely."

With that, the general turned, opened the door, and left the room.

Whitley looked up from his desk. "You two got work to do?"

"Yes, Chief," Pallie replied.

"Well then, get on with it."

Vivas and Pallie both nodded, and turned to leave the Chief's tiny office. As they reached the door, the Chief called out, "If you two miscreants let anything happen to Cordell or his mother, I'll have you both busted back to Seaman, and you'll spend the rest of your miserable lives on KP!"

"Yes, Chief," both Vivas and Pallie responded.

"Good luck," the Chief added, before returning to the paperwork on his desk.

CHAPTER 32
THAILAND

His copilot having completed the preflight checklist for their McDonnell Douglas KC-10A, Aircraft Commander Bob Holiday requested permission from ground control to proceed to the runway for takeoff. They were on a scheduled training flight from McGhee Tyson Air National Guard Base to Oakland Air Force Base and back. The flight engineer and boom operator—both new to the crew—needed a shakedown flight. The tanker's fuel tanks were currently empty, but they would pick up fuel upon arrival in Oakland and refuel a flight of F18 Hornets, somewhere over the Texas desert on the way back.

"Ground control, kilo four seven lima, ready for taxi to runway two three left."

"Kilo four seven lima, this is ground control. Please hold your position. You are taking on two passengers ready to board now."

"Passengers?" Holiday queried the tower, looking over at his copilot, Gerry, who just shrugged.

"One man, one dog, with gear. Orders from the Pentagon. Your flight plan now includes an additional stop at ICS Aviation in San Diego. You will drop off your passengers there."

What the fuck?! A dog? Holiday thought. *This isn't a commercial passenger flight!*

"Tom!" A disgruntled Bob Holiday called back to the new boom operator. "Open the back hatch. We're taking on passengers."

"Passengers?" Tom replied.

"Just open the damn door, Tom," the aircraft commander repeated, getting up from his pilot's seat to move to the rear of the tanker.

The man, carrying a duffle bag, climbed the crew maintenance air stairs at the tanker's rear hatch. A large dog resembling a smaller version of a German Shepherd accompanied him. Holiday recognized the dog as a Belgian Malinois.

"Where do you want me to stow my gear?" the man asked. "Sorry about the short notice."

He had an air of quiet authority about him, and Holiday immediately saw the passenger for what he was. Suddenly, he was no longer disgruntled.

"No problem. Just not something we see very often. Welcome aboard." Holiday turned to his boom operator, who was standing there with his jaw hanging open.

"Tom, stow the man's gear and make him and his K9 as comfortable as you can."

"Yes, sir," Tom replied, taking the duffle bag from their passenger.

"We have an eight-hour flight to Oakland Air Force Base, but I understand we are dropping you in San Diego. That's about six hours." Holiday shrugged. "We're not set up for passengers, but there is an extra seat near the flight engineer's station. It's just a fold-down seat. And your dog is welcome to a spot on the floor. Tom will show you where. Eric, my flight engineer, is busy checking aircraft systems."

"We'll be fine, and we'll both try to stay out of your crew's way. We appreciate the lift," JD replied.

Holiday nodded. "Okay. Let's get this bird in the air."

Six hours later, JD, followed by Ajax, disembarked the fuel tanker near the ICS Aviation hangar at San Diego International Airport. Holiday handed his duffle bag down to him from the hatch.

"Thanks again for transport." JD extended his hand.

Holiday shook it. "No problem. I don't know what you're up to and don't want to know. It must be important to require a last-second change like this from so high up. Whatever it is, I wish you luck."

"Thanks," JD replied and continued down the airstairs after Ajax, who, he was shocked to find, was being greeted and petted by two men he knew who were waiting.

"What the hell?" JD exclaimed. "What are you two doing here?

"We're going with you," Vivas replied with a shrug. "Orders."

"The chief said, and I quote, 'if you two miscreants let anything happen to Cordell or his mother, I'll bust you both back to Seaman, and you'll spend the rest of your miserable fucking lives on KP." Pallie laughed. "So... here we are."

"But how? You can't do this. I appreciate the thought, guys, really, but there's no way you're going with me. The Navy will put you under the stockade if they ever find out about this."

"It's cool, JD. The chief had a little help from somebody at the Pentagon. It seems your mother has some powerful friends. We volunteered. It's a top-secret, need-to-know mission, and nobody needs to know," Pallie explained.

"So, either we're going with you, or we're going in addition to you. The way I see it, it would be better if we work together," added Vivas.

"Sonofabitch!" JD shook his head. He knew these guys understood what they could be getting into. It was one thing when it was for the job, but this was for him and his mother. He was moved that they showed no hesitation in taking such risks on his behalf. "What about your equipment?"

"Hell, JD! We can't take stuff with 'Property of the U.S. Government' stamped all over it into Vietnam. We have a few personal items, and we have a contact in Thailand, a friend of the CIA, who can get us whatever else we need when we get there," Vivas replied.

That was true enough, JD decided. He wasn't carrying much either. Just his Glock 19, the Flesheater knife Vivas had given him a few months ago, and all the cash he could gather. Flying a private charter into Thailand, combined with a few well-placed calls by General Ellerson, would eliminate any problems of getting his weapons into the country.

JD knew they'd still need additional firepower to pull off this impromptu search and rescue mission. He planned to talk to a few expatriate former Deltas he knew living in Bangkok, seeing what he could find.

"The CIA?" JD asked, baffled.

"Yeah," Vivas replied. "Our old friend from Niger, Rick Hahn."

"Ain't it great to have friends in low places," Pallie added with a wink. "Get your shit and let's get a move on. Glad Ajax is coming."

"He should have some stuff I ordered here somewhere... just dog food, treats... stuff like that."

"It's already on the jet," Vivas replied.

Pallie squatted down to give Ajax a good scratching. "He's looking fit for a damn civilian! Good to have you along, old boy."

Ajax whined in response.

"Couldn't leave him behind. Ajax was quite upset when he heard someone snatched his grandmother." JD's face suddenly took on a very hard look. "If they've hurt her, I'll kill every fucking one of them."

Vivas placed his hand on JD's shoulder. "We're with you, man. Let's go."

Ajax bounded up the airstairs, followed by the three men. Boarding the Bombardier Global 7500C, JD set his baggage down at the rear of the cabin with the rest of the jet's cargo. There was a box marked for Ajax and gear belonging to Vivas and Pallie as well. The men relaxed into seats nearer the front as the four-man flight crew prepared for takeoff. Total flight time to Bangkok would be about nineteen hours, with short stops in Honolulu and Seoul.

It was about eight hours to their first stopover in Hawaii. JD made sure Ajax took care of business before they boarded the jet, so he'd be okay for the first leg duration. Ajax found a comfortable spot on the floor not too far from JD to lie down.

Typically configured to carry up to nineteen passengers, this model carried eleven. The rear of the jet was modified to haul smaller shipments of cargo, accessible through a drop-down hatch at the back of the cabin. JD leaned his seat back and closed his eyes, half-listening as Pallie and Vivas discussed the finer points of nightlife in Bangkok. Neither of them had been to Thailand before but had undoubtedly heard stories from those who had.

JD smiled when he heard Vivas comment, "I don't know about that, Pallie. You might do better to keep it in your pants. You might bring back something you can't get rid of."

Pallie just laughed. "I know that, Vivas! I'm just shooting the shit with you, man."

JD sat quietly, thinking about his mother. She was a strong woman, and if anyone could come through this, she would.

Must have been something to do with looking for her brother, he thought — *something she said or did caught the wrong person's attention*. JD knew about the treatment of the Montagnards by the Vietnamese government. If his uncle were still alive and in Vietnam, he would at least be an outcast, possibly even an outlaw. Could the two somehow be connected? It was possible. It was the only connection he could draw that would explain his mother's disappearance. There had been no ransom demand, and visitors to the country getting kidnapped would be bad for the growing Vietnamese tourist trade and economy. There had to be a link. The only thing that might draw unwanted attention would be his mother's interest in finding a former Montagnard fighter who had helped the American forces during the war.

At least I have a name, JD thought. It was all General Ellerson had been able to give him. Once they were in Vietnam, he would have to find this Lieutenant Colonel Fong of the Ho Chi Minh City Mobile Police Force.

Vivas got up and moved over to sit near JD. "She'll be alright, JD. We'll find her."

JD opened his eyes and looked over at Vivas. "Thanks, Vivas. I certainly hope so." Vivas just nodded. The two warriors sat quietly, lost in their thoughts as Pallie began to snore softly across the aisle. Soon Ajax joined in the snoring.

JD's mind turned to Ellen. *God, she was something*, he thought. He knew the decision to propose had been sort of fast, but he also knew that he didn't want to waste any time. Since he'd gotten to Knoxville, they'd gone to the movies and had dinner several times. They'd enjoyed picnic lunches in several of the local parks, coffee at Starbucks and Barnes and Noble, and had even gone ice skating once. She was a great skater. For JD, it was a first and humbling experience.

He had come to his conclusion and bought the ring because he enjoyed Ellen's company, admired her character, and both were discovering a great deal in common. Ellen was also a fantastic cook and had fixed them a quiet dinner for two on several occasions. They'd spent a few beautiful nights together at her condo, and now, she had said YES. It was hard to process the thought of getting married on this flight to save his mother from a brutal drug lord in Thailand … but JD couldn't help thinking, *once this crap is over and mom is safely home, I am going to settle into a normal life—whatever the hell it takes.*

The journey was uneventful. Pallie and Ajax snored most of the time. Vivas and JD dozed off and on, occasionally discussing Isshin-ryu or Escrima, or the task before them.

"So, who is this contact in Thailand Hahn gave us, and how do we get in touch with him?" JD asked Vivas after a lull in the conversation.

"Simple enough. But, I'm not sure it's a guy with a name like Hana. All I know is that we are to go to a bar in Nana Plaza called Obsession and ask for someone named Hana. We give this Hana Rick Hahn's name, and he or she will tell us how to get in touch with some major who is now an arms dealer. I understand his base is in Sisaket, which is the closest decent-sized city to the Laotian border. We'll have to travel about 600 kilometers through Laos to get to Vietnam. We'll need to arrange some transportation to the Vietnamese border. After that, I think we'd be better off on foot. Less chance of being noticed or arousing suspicion."

"Sounds about right. It tracks right along with what I saw checking Google Maps earlier."

Vivas stifled a yawn. "Shouldn't be too bad. I understand a lot of westerners are vacationing in the area these days. It's become quite popular. Good cover for us."

"Great," JD acknowledged.

"I wonder why the detour through Bangkok and this Hana?" Vivas added. "Seems a bit Hollywood to me."

"I am sure she's a cut-out. If this major knows his business, he'll have protection, security of some kind. He may know Rick Hahn, but he doesn't know us. This Hana must be part of his organization, a front line of his security."

"That makes sense. This major's in a pretty dangerous line of work. I guess he might want more than Hahn's 'say-so' before doing business with us."

The short layovers in Honolulu and Inchon provided a much-needed stretch of the legs for both man and dog. Approximately twenty-three hours after leaving San Diego, the weary travelers disembarked the Bombardier 7500 near the small private hangars of Suvarnabhumi Airport in Bangkok, Thailand. One of the flight crew escorted the three men and Ajax to the small terminal where the lone attendant, after a short conversation with the crew member, waved them on through.

"What the hell," Pallie observed. "He didn't even ask to see our passports."

"Compliments of the CIA," the flight crewman replied with a wink. "The attendant will call an honest taxi company for you guys. It shouldn't be more than ten or fifteen minutes. However, you are on your own from here. We will be ready to get you out when you are ready to leave. Just give us a shout." The crewman handed JD a business card. JD looked at it, reading East Asia Imports. "Use the mobile number on the card. You will reach one of my staff or me. There's not much we can do for you while you're in Vietnam. Officially, this is not happening."

"Damn, does everyone know what we're up to?" Vivas asked.

"Only what we need to know," the flight crew member replied reassuringly. "Good luck and good hunting."

JD nodded. "Thanks." With that, JD turned and, with Ajax trotting beside him, followed Pallie and Vivas out through the terminal door to wait for the taxi.

"That guy must be CIA," Pallie observed. "Wonder if he knows Hahn."

"Maybe," JD commented. "But it's a big world and a large organization. Who knows?"

Several minutes later, a taxi from the Thai Happy Taxi company pulled up. An elderly Thai gentleman jumped out, surprisingly agile for his age.

"You called for a taxi?"

JD nodded. "Yes, sir, we did." The older man ran around to the back and opened the trunk. The men stowed their gear while the taxi driver eyed Ajax warily.

"Nice dog?"

"The best," Vivas assured him. The driver seemed to relax a little. Pallie claimed the front seat and JD, Vivas, and Ajax clambered into the back.

"Where you go?"

JD looked over at Vivas. "I have a room at the Ambassador Hotel."

"We do, too," Vivas nodded. "The general told us where you'd be staying."

"Should have known," JD laughed.

The Ambassador Hotel was about nineteen kilometers from Bangkok Airport. The ride in the taxi took just over twenty minutes. Arriving, the driver jumped out and opened the trunk. Bellhops were immediately there to assist with the luggage, but the new guests waved them off politely. JD paid the cab fare and gave the driver a good tip.

"Can you pick us up at 8:00 p.m. here at the hotel?" He handed the driver 600 Baht.

The driver nodded enthusiastically. "Yes. Yes. 8:00 p.m. I will pick you up right here."

"Great." Grabbing his gear bag, JD crossed the entryway and followed the other two men to check-in. JD had booked a room with a single king-sized bed on the seventh floor. He'd paid a pretty serious pet fee to have Ajax stay at the hotel with him, but there was little choice.

They had several hours to kill before they could head down to Nana Plaza and meet their contact. Agreeing to meet in the bar at 7:30 p.m. — Pallie, who had slept most of the flight, headed to the bar for a cold beer. Vivas decided a nap was in order, especially since he had the room to himself for a while. JD took Ajax for a long walk around the hotel block; then, making the dog comfortable in the room, went for a swim in the pool.

Forty minutes later, feeling refreshed, JD returned to his room. Ajax merely lifted his head and looked when JD opened the door and entered. Then, after a welcoming thump of his tail, he quickly went back to sleep.

Connecting his phone to the hotel's Wi-Fi network, JD checked on the location of Obsession in Nana Plaza. He chuckled when he discovered that it was the most popular ladyboy bar in Bangkok. He saw that it was located at the far end of the plaza, away from the main entrance.

Tonight could be interesting. Pallie and Vivas will be in for quite a shock if they don't take the time to check for themselves.

At 7:00 p.m., JD took Ajax for another walk. Then, digging into the dog's travel bag, he dug out a pre-measured dinner, left some water in the bowl, and after a quick scratch behind the dog's ears, took the elevator down to the lobby and found the bar.

It was now 7:25 p.m. Vivas and Pallie were already there. JD noticed they were not drinking. It was time to get serious. JD purchased a bottle of water and walked over to where Pallie and Vivas sat waiting. Vivas was also drinking bottled water. Pallie had a cup of black Starbucks coffee. None of the men carried their weapons. They weren't expecting any trouble, and even unarmed, any one but certainly all three of them, would be a tough proposition to handle.

"Guess we're all set," JD stated. "So, the plan is we take the cab to the Nana Plaza, find this person, Hana, at the club called Obsession, and then find out how to meet with this major."

"Piece of cake," Pallie replied before draining the last swallow of his coffee.

"Should be," Vivas agreed.

JD checked his watch. It was the Omega, a retirement gift from his team. "Time to go."

The taxi driver was waiting for them, standing there leaning against his cab. "Okay! I am here. Where do you want to go?"

"Nana Plaza," JD replied.

"Yes. Yes. Great place. Short ride!" The driver hurried around the taxi and opened all three passenger doors.

Pallie grinned at Vivas as he climbed in. "Now, that's service for you." Vivas laughed.

A few minutes later, the taxi pulled to a stop near the entrance to Nana Plaza.

"Damn," Pallie laughed. "We could have walked."

"We can walk back if you want, Pallie," Vivas kidded.

"No, I am beginning to like this taxi driver, and he looks like he needs our business."

The old taxi driver perked up at this. "You want I wait?" the driver asked as JD handed him 100 Baht.

JD looked at the other two. "What do you think? We shouldn't be too long. And, I want to get an early start in the morning, to wherever it is we need to go."

Pallie and Vivas looked at each other. They knew JD was thinking about his mother. He couldn't get to her fast enough.

"Sounds like a plan," Vivas agreed.

JD turned to the driver. "Please wait. We are on business and won't be gone long. We are not here to party."

The driver nodded happily. "I will park over there." He pointed to a line of taxis across the street. "I will watch for you."

JD nodded his thanks, and the three men turned and headed into the plaza.

JD led as they made their way through the crowds of tourists, patrons, and those trying to entice the three men into various business establishments. All three were somewhat used to such sights, having spent many years in different countries and on different military installations. As the men approached the end of the plaza, JD spotted the sign for Obsession glowing brightly. They headed that way.

"Welcome to the world-famous go-go bar," Pallie read aloud as they entered the club. "This should be fun," he went on, winking at Vivas, who just smiled.

The place was busy, but large enough to handle a good-sized crowd easily. The bar boasted a spacious square dance floor with good music that was not too loud. Perhaps a dozen or so dancers were performing, some doing a pretty good job while more than a few seemed to be eyeing the three men who had just walked in with great interest.

A few minutes later, a cute hostess approached, smiling. "Would you gentlemen like something to drink, or some company?"

"Just drinks right now," JD replied politely, smiling at the hostess. "I'll have a whiskey... neat."

"The same for me," Vivas added.

"Do you have a cold beer, honey?" Pallie asked with a grin.

The hostess smiled. "We have the best beer in all of Thailand. Chang, Leo, or Singha. I prefer the Singha," the hostess added, smiling brightly at Pallie.

"Sounds good to me," Pallie replied.

"I'll be right back," the hostess smiled again and wandered off with maybe just a bit too much wiggle in her walk.

"Damn," Pallie exclaimed. "She was something. A man could learn to like it here in Thailand."

JD and Vivas simultaneously burst out laughing.

"What?" Pallie demanded.

JD grinned at Pallie. "That's a guy, Pallie. This club is a ladyboy bar."

Pallie looked over at Vivas, who nodded, grinning as well.

"That was a guy?" Pallie repeated incredulously. "No fucking way!"

"Pay attention to her voice when she comes back," JD commented. "She's pretty good, but you can tell."

"Very pretty for a guy though, Pallie," Vivas teased.

"No way," Pallie repeated.

A few minutes later, the hostess returned, and nonchalantly leaning closer to Pallie, placed their drinks on the table. "Here you are, gentleman. Let me know if I can get you anything else," she offered, beaming at Pallie before again wandering off.

"Sonofabitch," Pallie muttered. "I don't believe it. She, uh, he, uh, whatever - even had great tits."

JD and Vivas just laughed.

"It's okay, Pallie," JD replied. "I only knew because I checked the place out online. If you didn't know, it would be damn hard to tell."

"I guess you checked too?" Pallie growled at Vivas. Vivas just grinned.

A quiet voice interrupted their banter. "Would you gentleman like some company? My name is Hana." All three men looked up.

The person standing before them was stunning. Dressed in a simple red cocktail dress with elbow-length swath sleeves and a slit part of the way up the left thigh, Hana wore her hair up in a neat bun. She wore simple gold hoop earrings, and just a touch of makeup. The effect was stunning. If not for their present location, you could not possibly have convinced JD, Vivas, or Pallie that the person standing before them was not a gorgeous young woman.

JD was the first to react. "Hi ... uh ... Hana. Yes, please, have a seat."

"Yes, join us," Vivas added. Pallie nodded, his mind still trying to wrap itself around the present situation.

"Would you like a drink?" JD asked. Hana raised her hand, and a hostess appeared, setting a drink down in front of her.

"What brings you three gentlemen to Obsession?" She ignored the ladyboy drink in front of her. "Are you looking for ladyboy entertainment?" She spoke nearly flawless English.

"Uh... no," Vivas replied. "But, thank you anyway!"

Hana just smiled.

JD shifted in his seat to face Hana directly. "A friend of ours, Rick Hahn, recommended we check this bar out. He said it has the best whiskey in town."

"And the coldest beer," Pallie added, trying hard not to stare.

"Ahh, I see," Hana smiled at Pallie. "And how is Rick? Still playing at saving the world?"

The three SEALs looked at each other. "You could say that," JD finally responded.

"Is Rick a friend of yours?" JD asked after taking a sip of his whiskey. It was pretty good.

"You could say that," Hana replied with a twinkle in her eye. "So, you must be JD. I assume the darker one is Vivas, and the one who can't take his eyes off me is Pallie."

Pallie blushed. "Sorry, ma'am ... uh ... Hana. This scene is just a bit new to me."

Hana laughed. "It is okay. You should relax. We don't bite ... too hard."

"You seem to know a lot about us," Vivas observed.

"Rick told me you were coming, and I was watching for you. He asked me to help you in any way I can." She winked playfully at Pallie. "I know who you are and why you are here. And I have decided I want to help."

"Is Rick a good friend of yours?" Pallie asked.

Hana laughed. "Oh, he is much more than that." Then, her face turned serious. "You can ask your cab driver to arrange transportation to Sisaket. We will leave tomorrow morning, and I will go with you."

JD started to object.

"It is the only way you will get to meet the major. He has strict rules. It is about a twelve-hour drive to Sisaket. I would recommend a van, especially since you have a dog with you." Hana smiled. "I can't wait to meet Ajax."

Now the three men recognized that Rick had given Hana a full briefing.

Hana saw the looks on the men's faces. "Do not worry. Your secret is safe. Rick trusts me, and you can too. I will get you to who you need to see. Shall we meet at your hotel? Say… 8:00 a.m.?"

"I guess you already know where we're staying?" JD asked.

Hana smiled. "Of course, don't be silly. You are in my city."

The taxi was parked exactly where the old driver said he would be. As the men approached, they could see their driver sitting in the back seat, reading what looked like a newspaper. He spotted them as they walked up and hopped out of the cab.

"Ah," he exclaimed. "My number one American friends. Is everything okay? No trouble?" The driver held open the door he had just exited. "We go now?"

"Yes," JD replied. "We go now."

Once they were in the cab, this time with JD claiming the front seat, Pallie, who was sitting behind JD, tapped him on the shoulder. "So, how the hell do we get to Sisaket?"

JD shrugged. "We will have to come up with something and quickly."

"You go to Sisaket?" the driver interjected excitedly. "I take you to Sisaket. No problem. Okay?"

JD turned to the driver. "What is your name?"

"My name is Hung."

"Well, Hung, I appreciate it, but we need a van. We will have a dog and one other traveler."

"Van? No problem. I bring a van." Hung pulled the taxi up to the entrance of the Ambassador Hotel. "I bring number one van, cost maybe 4,000 Baht... everything. What time we leave?"

JD looked at Pallie and Vivas in the back seat. Pallie shrugged as if to say, "why not." Vivas nodded.

JD turned back to Hung. "There could be trouble in Sisaket, Hung," he warned. "We don't want to cause any problems for you."

Hung grinned widely. "No problem. No Trouble. My name, Hung. It means brave."

JD laughed. "Okay, Hung! We'll see you at 8:00 a.m."

"Okay. 8:00 a.m. I will be here."

CHAPTER 33
VIETNAM

The clouds lay heavily over the remote village on its lonely rock shelf, holding the promise of a rainy day. Several men were busy preparing for a three-day trip into the jungle. Some were busy cleaning and checking weapons, several loaded bullets into the magazines of an assortment of rifles, while still others put together traveling rations for three days. Nobody was sure exactly what Dish had planned, but they'd be setting out later that afternoon.

Everyone in their village now knew about Dish's adopted sister, Mai, and that she was in the hands of one of Vietnam's most brutal and dangerous drug lords, Colonel Trần. From the team he had chosen for the upcoming mission, it was apparent that Dish had something serious on his mind. He'd chosen specific men, those who'd been with Dish during the war and seen combat.

The previous night, a Hmong tribesman named Kaus had returned to their village with the young woman named Jum Y. Like the Jarai, the Hmong were another Montagnard tribe who'd sided with the Americans during the war. Kaus took Jum Y directly to Dish's longhouse where, after Chanmali placed a bowl of hot soup and some tea in front of her; the girl reported the events of the previous days. Dish listened quietly as the young woman explained how she'd met Mai in the nightclub and how Mai had befriended her, even buying her supper at the night market. Jum Y continued her story between spoonfuls of the delicious soup.

"Mai asked me if I could get word to her brother, Dish, to tell him she was staying at the hotel and wanted to see him. I thought of my friend, the older woman who cleans the clubs. She seems to know everyone and told me stories of ..."

Jum Y paused, looking up at Dish. There was a look of both uncertainty and pride on her young face. She continued.

"... our people during the war. I was sure she could help." Jum Y took another spoonful of the soup and continued. "Mai said if I helped her, she would ask her brother to try and help me. I don't want to be a business girl, but my father owes money to bad people..."

Dish cut her off. "I know your situation. Do not worry, child; you're finished with that. My people will take care of it. I thank you for helping my sister and getting word to Kaus and Haub when Fong took her. You must have been frightened, and many would have kept quiet. You are brave."

Dish waved Chanmali over. "For now, you can stay here. Chanmali will fix you a place to sleep, and you can help her while you are here in our village." Chanmali nodded, giving Jum Y a friendly smile. Dish continued, "You are safe here. Once I attend to this business with Trần and my sister, we will see what we can do to help you make a new life."

Jum Y set the wooden spoon down in what little remained of the hot soup. She looked from Dish to Chanmali with tears in her eyes.

"Thank you. Oh my God, thank you so much." Her voice quivered, and her hands shook just a bit, from the sudden release after prolonged, pent-up emotional stress and fears. The nightmare she had thought might never end, was ending. "I don't know what else to say. Just thank you."

Dish looked at Jum Y, and his typically stern gaze softened just a touch.

"No, child... I thank you."

Dish sat hunched under his poncho, forcing himself to be patient. He and twelve of his most trusted men lay waiting, hidden in the brush just above the dirt track that ran along a ridge just west of Dak To. They were all heavily armed and, to a man, understood the importance of their task. The plan was first and foremost to make sure Dish's sister, Mai, remained alive and unharmed. Dish planned to send a message to Colonel Trần that would ensure the drug lord would keep Mai alive, at least for the time being. Dish knew that he was Trần's real target. Mai was simply the bait.

Trần wants me dead, not an all-out war. That would be bad for his business. If he wants me, he will have to keep Mai alive.

Looking for an opportunity such as this, he'd directed all his contacts to notify him of any movements through the Dak To area by known drug smugglers. Just one day later, he received word that a small group of opium smugglers had worked their way down through Laos and had just turned east toward Vietnam. Tracking their movements, his scouts reported that the smugglers would soon be traveling along the trail just below them. The rain made judging the drug smuggler's speed of travel difficult; however, on the positive side, it also helped to conceal the ambush Dish had planned. The rain had been coming down in buckets, rendering the poncho he was wearing virtually useless. The ground was becoming treacherous and slippery, the few flat areas having taken on the consistency of a soaked sponge.

The twelve men huddled in the wet, seeking shelter under whatever cover they could find. Each knew his job and would do as expected. The deluge of rain reduced visibility and muffled any sounds made by the approaching drug smugglers. Preparing to send a man out to scout for them, Dish heard the sound of a man laughing carried over the rain. He knew it was not one of his men; they were not so foolish.

Twelve men readied their weapons, waiting for Dish, who worked his way down close to the trail.

A few minutes later, five men came into sight. It was clear that the leading man, as well as the man bringing up the rear, were well-armed. The three in the center of the group carried bamboo pack baskets in which they transported their cargo.

Opium, Dish thought.

The five men were not disciplined; he noted with disgust. The three with the baskets laughed and joked. Dish quickly knew it was the second cargo bearer's laugh they had heard over the rain, warning his men of their approach. The two armed guards were not much better. The lead man kept his eyes on the trail directly in front and did not once look up to scout the way ahead. The last man was too busy trying to keep his cigarette burning in the steady downpour to notice much going on around him. Dish stepped out onto the trail about ten yards ahead of the smugglers, pleasantly greeting the five in Vietnamese.

"Hello friends, damned lousy day to be traveling, isn't it?"

The five men stopped dead in their tracks, shocked at the sudden appearance of the lone man on the trail. The smuggler in the lead recovered enough to respond, suspicion apparent in his voice.

"Yes, stranger. It is. Now, if you want no trouble, move aside quickly and let us pass."

Dish laughed. "No need to be quarrelsome, friends. But you should know, your day just got much worse."

Twelve men rose like ghosts along the trail, just a few yards back from its edge — the metallic clicks of the safeties disengaging on several weapons were audible to the smugglers, even over the rain.

"If you move, you die." Dish's voice had lost its previous pleasant tone, and was now icy cold, leaving no doubt that he meant what he said. "I would happily kill you, but today that is not in my plan. Drop your weapons and your packs, and you will live."

The five men looked over at the twelve ghosts along the edge of the trail, then turned their attention back to the man who'd greeted them.

"Do you know who we work for?" the lead smuggler asked, astonishment replacing the suspicion in his voice. "We work for a powerful warlord. You are making a grave mistake. You will all die for this!"

"Perhaps," Dish acknowledged. "But that is my concern. I will not ask again. Drop your weapons and the pack baskets, or you will die right here today. Decide now."

The lead smuggler turned to look back at his companions and shrugged. Then, returning to face the stranger in front of him, dropped his AK-47 into the mud at his feet. The three carrying the packs dropped them carefully from their shoulders and did the same. The fourth smuggler, for whatever reason, perhaps fearing they were going to die anyway, decided to bring his rifle around to fire on the ghostly figures to his left. It was the wrong decision. Several shots rang out, and the smuggler dropped like a heavy sack of rice into the mud of the trail. He did not move again.

"That was too bad," Dish observed. "That man need not have died today."

Focusing his attention on their leader, Dish continued. "You will take a message to your Colonel Trần. You will tell him that Dish stopped you on the trail today. You will tell him I have taken the poison he sells, and that I spared your lives." He glanced at the dead body lying in the mud. "Your comrade died because he was stupid. It need not have happened." Dish again focused his gaze on the lead smuggler. "You will tell Trần that I will trade his shipment for my sister, who he is holding. I will meet with him in Ho Chi Minh City to make the exchange."

Dish's voice took on an even colder, more dispassionate tone. "You tell Trần that if he harms one hair on my sister's head, all deals are off. I will bring a war to him that he has not seen since the war with the Americans. I will end his loathsome business and his life. You tell your boss that."

Dish paused to let the words sink in. Then, raising his arm, he pointed up the trail in the direction the smugglers were traveling. "Go, before I change my mind and kill you now."

The four smugglers wasted no time in hurrying up the trail. They did not bother to look back.

Hai approached Dish and stood beside him, speaking quietly. "Trần will not trade Mai back to you for the opium. He wants you dead. There is too much history. And, there are too many deaths for him to account for among our people."

"I know that," Dish replied. "But I think Trần does not know that I know that. He is arrogant, and that will be his downfall. He will believe he can use this idea of trading the opium for my sister to trap me."

Hai thought about this for a second. "Why can't he do exactly that?"

Dish turned his gaze on Hai. "Because I am the one setting the trap."

Hai nodded, accepting that. "Just be sure you are not the one being arrogant, my old friend."

Dish smiled at that. "You have known me many years, Hai. You, for one, should know that, while I may be many things, I am never arrogant."

"That is true enough. What now?"

Dish considered this for a moment. "Break apart the opium bundles and scatter them in the jungle. This rain will last several days and will make short work of them. Once that is done, we will return to the village."

Hai nodded and headed off to give the orders.

CHAPTER 34
THAILAND

At precisely 8:00 am, Hung pulled up to the hotel entrance in an older, but decent-looking Toyota van. He stopped in front of three men and a dog who stood waiting with their gear. Pallie circled the vehicle, kicking the tires. A few seconds later, he declared it would do. The van was new enough to be reliable but looked beat up enough not to attract any attention.

"Perfect," JD stated.

As the men loaded their gear into the back, a Hyundai sedan pulled up near the van. The driver-side door opened, and a tough-looking Thai man in mirrored sunglasses got out. JD and the others watched as the man's eyes carefully surveyed the surrounding area, resting momentarily on the three men and the dog standing together near the van. Satisfied, he went around and opened the passenger door. Hana got out. She was dressed like a model for REI ladies hiking apparel, in khaki shorts and a short-sleeved Patagonia shirt, wearing Merrell hiking boots. There was a small shoulder bag slung over her right shoulder.

Pallie glanced at JD, who was standing close by and muttered, "That's a serious-looking bodyguard."

JD just nodded.

The man went to the back of the sedan and extracted a backpack. Carrying it to the van, he stowed it with the rest of the gear. The man then stepped back so he could observe the goings-on without being in the way.

"Thanks, Quan."

Hana turned toward the three men and smiled brightly at Pallie, who was again trying not to stare. She walked up to JD.

"I see we are ready to go."

Looking down at the dog sitting patiently at his left side, she bent over to pet Ajax's head, then paused.

"This must be Ajax. Is it okay if I pet your dog?"

"Sure," JD nodded. "Ajax will let you know if he doesn't want the attention."

Ajax didn't seem to mind at all, going so far as to lick Hana's fingers when she stopped.

Hana turned back to her bodyguard. "Quan, I will be fine now. I have these three brave men and Ajax to protect me from here on. You can go." Quan nodded and walked back to the Hyundai. Getting in, he started the car and drove off.

Turning back to JD, Hana asked, "Shall we?"

Hana walked to the van and greeted Hung, waving at him. Hung grinned and returned the wave.

"You to know each other?" JD asked.

"Oh, yes. Hung and I go back a long way." Hana replied. JD did not know what to make of that but decided not to say anything more at the moment. He would wait until they were on the road.

Pallie called shotgun and climbed into the front passenger seat. Hana, JD, and Vivas each made themselves comfortable in one of the van's four rear swiveling seats. There was plenty of floor space for Ajax to stretch out. Hung fired up the engine and, pulling out of the hotel parking lot, headed toward Route 24 and Sisaket.

The group traveled along in silence until the van was out of city traffic. Taking Route 1, Hung headed for the main highway. Finally, JD spoke.

"Okay, we have about eight hours in this van together before we reach Sisaket. I think it's time for some questions and answers."

Vivas raised his eyebrows, and Pallie swiveled around in his seat, looking from JD to Hana and back. Ajax pricked his ears up at the change in JD's voice.

Hana looked directly at JD. "Sure, JD, what's going on in that suspicious mind of yours?"

"Who the hell are you, Hana?" JD asked bluntly. "Do you work for the CIA?"

Vivas sat up at that. JD noticed that Pallie shifted so he could watch Hung with one eye. The other eye was still glued on Hana.

Hana laughed. "No, I don't work for the CIA."

"You seem to know an awful lot about us, too much for just a cut-out between Hahn and this retired Thai army major we're going to meet. You also speak exceedingly good English for a native Thai."

"You sound serious, JD," Hana replied, steadily returning his gaze.

"I am serious," JD went on. "I'm am American civilian heading into Vietnam with two buddies on a dangerous mission to rescue my mother from some damn ex-VC colonel turned drug warlord. Vivas and Pallie are here because they volunteered for this shit, and I care a lot more about them than I do some ladyboy from a go-go bar in Bangkok."

"Easy, JD," Vivas started.

JD cut him off. "Stay out of it, Vivas. This discussion is between Hana and me."

Both Pallie and Vivas had survived many dangerous missions with JD. Neither had seen this side of him before. There was now a lethal look on his face.

Hana turned to Vivas. "It's alright. After all, it's what makes JD so good at his job, isn't it?" She turned back to JD, a funny smile on her face. "So, this is what you think of me? After I offer to help you?"

JD nodded. "You could be helping us," he admitted, "but you could also be setting us up." He turned to Pallie. "If Hung tries to pull that Tokarev pistol from the small of his back, stop him."

Pallie's face was suddenly serious. "Got it, boss."

JD looked back to Hana. "Once more, Hana. Who the hell are you? I can shoot you and Hung and drop you both in a ditch somewhere if I must. This mission is personal for me, which I assume you already understand. Right this minute, I think that's what I should do. Would you like to change my mind?"

Hana laughed, unconcerned. "No wonder Rick likes you so much, JD." She shifted slightly in her seat. "Okay. Ask away." Vivas had turned around to face Hana squarely as well.

"In the club, I asked you if Rick Hahn was a friend of yours. You said he was much more than that. Is he your boss? If you don't work for the CIA, who do you work for?"

"Well, JD. I work for myself. I own Obsession. It is my club."

"What the hell...?" Pallie interjected, looking at Hana. JD looked sharply at Pallie, who quickly turned back to keep his eyes on Hung. The driver made no effort to do anything other than keeping the van on the road.

"You own the club," Vivas repeated.

"How does someone like you come to own a club like that?" JD continued.

"Simple," Hana replied. "Rick bought it for me."

This time it was Vivas' turn. "Hahn bought you that bar? What the fuck for?"

Hana shrugged. "Rick is a black ops contractor for the CIA. He doesn't have any government retirement plan. If he dies on some covert mission somewhere, the CIA will deny any knowledge of what he was doing or even who he is." She paused. "Sometimes, on these missions, there is a great deal of money seized. Sometimes the money gets turned in," Hana stopped again. "And, sometimes, it gets invested."

"Invested in what?" JD asked.

"In Rick's retirement fund," Hana replied.

"So, Rick Hahn bought Obsession in Bangkok as an investment for his retirement?" JD asked.

Hana nodded, "Yes, exactly."

"Then why do you own it?" Vivas asked.

"Oh, that's easy," Hana laughed. "My name is Hana Hahn. Rick Hahn is my father."

For a few seconds, the only sound to be heard was the hum of the Toyota's engine.

Finally, JD broke the silence. "You're not a ladyboy, are you?"

"Nope. I am one hundred percent female. And I can prove it if I need to. A little show and tell would certainly beat getting shot and dropped in a ditch."

JD had to smile at that. "That won't be necessary."

"Good. I'm relieved to hear that. I also don't entertain customers. But how did you know?"

"Well, I wasn't completely sure, but your voice sounded different from the others I heard, and you don't have an adam's apple."

Hana winked at Vivas. "I knew your friend was smart."

Vivas was astounded by the turn of events. "But why the charade?" he asked.

"I am the daughter of a contracted covert operator for the CIA, half

American and half Thai. I work with gun smugglers, and my club is a gathering place for some pretty important, wealthy, and sometimes dangerous men who, shall we say, like to live on the edge. They also often like to brag to their favorite ladyboys about who they are and what they've done. It's a gold mine of information for Rick and a few others I trust. Running the club for Rick helps keep me safe, and frankly, it's fun. I get a kick out of it."

"But what if one of the customers decides to get a little rough with you," Pallie asked from the front seat.

Hana just smiled. "You met Quan. He is very good at what he does. Just like you guys." She paused, then added, "Hung works for me too. He's a bit old, but he's like an uncle to me and pretty good with that Tokarev you spotted."

"I'll be damned," Pallie muttered.

"I get a lot of great information from my club. You'd be amazed by the number of seriously rich businessmen and politicians who frequent my establishment. I get all kinds of information, tidbits that have helped my father and the man you are on your way to meet, and yes, probably the CIA as well."

"I can see that. We have a similar problem with rich elitists in the U.S.," JD muttered. "But what about the ladyboys in your club? It sounds like a rough life for them."

A sad look flashed across Hana's face for just an instant, then disappeared. "It is a rough life. But this is Thailand." She paused for a moment before going on. "If they didn't work for me, these ladyboys would be doing what they do now, just someplace else. Or, still worse, out on the streets. I hire them as go-go dancers. If they choose to get more, uh, intimate with a client, that is up to them. But I keep them safe. I pay them well and don't allow drug use by anyone working for me. They trust me."

She looked up at JD, her eyes searching his face for something that showed he understood. "It's the best I can do."

JD nodded. He understood.

Hung stopped at a gas station in Takut, a small village in the Saraburi province, for gas and cold drinks, and a welcome chance to stretch their legs. Hana asked if she could walk Ajax. Ajax didn't seem to object, so JD handed her the leash, but followed along.

When they had moved off a bit, JD spoke. "Sorry about all that,

Hana. I just needed to be sure."

"It's okay, JD. I would have been more worried and disappointed if you hadn't done what you did."

JD laughed at that. "I guess so."

"So, Hana, how did you ..." he paused, looking for the right words.

"End up where I am," she finished for him.

"Well, yes."

"Before working for the CIA, Rick spent a good deal of time in Thailand, combating drug smugglers as a consultant to the Thai government. You know the region they call the Golden Triangle?"

"Yes."

"He met my mother in Phuket. Her name was Mekhalaa, and she was the daughter of a Thai police commissioner. She was beautiful. Rick says I look just like her."

"She must have been beautiful then." Hana glanced up at JD but quickly looked away and went on.

"I know he loved her very much. They were never married. Her father forbade it. Unfortunately, she was pregnant, and I was the result. While Rick was off working in the triangle, my mother's father found out she was pregnant and threw her out. She was able to move in with Rick and shared his apartment. Seven months later, I was born. I know they were going to get married. He told me that. But before they got around to it, my mother was killed by one of the drug warlords Rick was pursuing. He thinks he was the target, but the gunman missed and killed her instead."

"I am sorry." JD didn't know what else to say.

Hana shrugged. "It was long ago." She watched as Ajax's nose worked overtime, exploring all the intriguing scents on the breeze. "If we had more time, I would show you around Saraburi. There are many beautiful Buddhist temples in this province. Some are quite old."

"That would be interesting," JD replied, relieved to have the subject changed.

"How about you, JD? I know you are a retired U.S. Navy SEAL and that you are half American and half Vietnamese. Your friends respect you. I know Rick likes you a lot." Hana paused, reaching down to scratch Ajax behind the ears. "Do you have a girlfriend? Is there someone special? Or, am I too bold?"

JD looked at Hana. "No, you're not too bold. Yes, there is someone. Her name is Ellen Chang."

"Ahh, yes! The doctor you helped rescue in Niger. She must be quite a woman." There was a slightly disappointed tone in Hana's voice, and she looked away momentarily. She was smiling when she turned back to face JD. "Rick said she saved Ajax after a firefight."

"Yes, she is, and she did," JD replied. He stopped walking and turned to face Hana. "I want to thank you for what you are doing. You are quite a woman too, Hana. I owe you a great deal."

"You owe me nothing, JD. I think we are friends now." Hana paused. "Are we friends?"

JD nodded. "Yes, Hana. We're friends."

"Good," she replied. "Friends don't owe friends." They stood there for a minute as Ajax watered a shrub near the end of the parking lot. "I think your mother must be quite a woman too. Let's go. We need to get you to Vietnam so you can get her home." They turned and, with Ajax happily trotting alongside Hana, walked back to the van.

The city of Sisaket is the capital of Sisaket Province, which sits near the borders of Cambodia and Laos. The region had a long history with strong cultural roots going back to the Khmer period over one thousand years ago. Much smaller than Bangkok or Phuket, Sisaket was best known for its silk and cotton products.

"You won't find any taxis or tuk-tuks here," Hana had explained. "But there are motorbike taxis and samlors."

"What's a samlor?" Vivas asked.

"It's a three-wheeled bicycle taxi," Hana explained.

Hung guided the van through the busy streets, which were full of pedestrians, bicycles, and the occasional samlor. Hana pulled a mobile phone from her shoulder bag and, shortly after punching in a number, began speaking rapidly in Thai. A few seconds later, she ended the call. She looked up at JD.

"We will go to Leo's," she announced.

"Leo's?" JD queried.

"Leo's is an excellent restaurant. Good Thai food. Good farang food. We will be met there."

"Farang?" Pallie asked.

"Round eyes," Vivas replied with a grin.

Hana nodded. "Anyone who is white." She turned to Pallie and Vivas. "Only JD and I will go in. Don't worry. He will be safe with me," she added, seeing the look on their faces. "There are several small food stands very close if you are hungry. Hung can show you. You should try the Ma kuear soup. It is excellent."

"Ma kuear?" Vivas asked.

"It is a fish soup with eggplant and chili," Hana explained as she started to make a second call, again speaking rapidly in Thai. JD wondered how Asians talked as fast as they did. It was amazing to him.

"I suppose a steak is out of the question?" Pallie laughed.

"I'm afraid so," Hana replied as she ended the second call. "You could get one at Leos, but the major was most specific. Maybe later?"

"Don't fret, Pallie. I'll eat one for you," JD joked.

"Thanks a bunch," Pallie grumbled.

Ten minutes later, JD and Hana were seated at a corner table in Leo's. A waitress had just set the tea Hana ordered down when three men walked in. One took a table near the entrance while the second took a table at the back of the restaurant. The third man, clearly older, made his way directly toward the table where JD and Hana were seated. To the casual observer, it would appear the three were not together. JD knew they were. The men at the front and rear of the restaurant were security. The third had to be the retired Thai major he was here to meet.

The man sat down at their table without being invited and began to speak to Hana, who responded. The two spoke for several seconds. JD waited calmly, sipping his tea, which was quite good.

Finally, Hana turned to JD. "This is Major Anurat Detphong. He agreed, as a favor to Rick, to meet with you. But he wants to know why he should help a farang like you. Sorry, his words, not mine," she added after a quick pause.

JD nodded. "How much does he know?" he asked Hana.

"That I do not know, and he wouldn't tell me anyway," Hana replied. "Tell him what you want and be honest. He is a tough man, but also a good man in his way. I've worked with him many times."

JD frowned.

"I will translate what you say exactly," Hana added.

JD considered this for a few seconds, then leaned forward and rested both hands firmly on the table.

"Let's cut the bullshit. Any Thai major worth his salt, especially one who helped the Americans in Vietnam, would speak English well enough, so I know you will understand most of what I say. Hana can jump in if anything is unclear."

Hana nodded.

"I am only here because some former Viet Cong colonel turned drug smuggler kidnapped my mother, who was traveling in Vietnam. My mother is Vietnamese, and she was there to find her adopted brother who happens to be Montagnard, Jarai, to be precise, and who she hadn't seen since she left Vietnam with my father, an American officer. I don't know what caused her to run afoul of this drug smuggler, and I don't care. I am here to find her and take her home. Two friends of mine have come to help, and Hana here has been most helpful." JD paused.

The major had not yet said a word, just sitting there listening, his face a blank mask.

He'd make a good poker player, JD thought.

"I don't care about you or your business. My only business is to rescue my mother and get her out of Vietnam."

Major Anurat sat there a few seconds as if weighing what he had just heard. Then he asked, "Who is this Montagnard she was seeking? What is his name?"

"His name is Dish. He is my uncle, that is, if he is still alive. My mother named me after him. I go by JD, but my full name is Jacob Dish Cordell."

The major's face betrayed no surprise. "And what is your mother's name?"

"Her name is Mai."

Anurat sat back in his chair, remaining silent for several more seconds. Finally, he leaned forward slightly. "And what do you want of me?"

"Just some equipment. Weapons and ammunition suitable for a rescue mission. We have sidearms, but need something heavier should we encounter serious trouble. I have cash in American dollars."

The major considered this for a moment before turning to Hana. Their exchange seemed to be fast and furious. JD could not tell if they were arguing or discussing the weather. After Hana completed her last response, the man turned back to JD.

"I can provide what you seek. I will send a few of my men to get you tomorrow morning in front of your hotel — just you and Hana. Your men will wait at the hotel with some of my men. When we conclude our business, my men will take you back to your hotel. We will arrange a place to make the exchange after we have spoken tomorrow. Where are you staying?"

"They will be staying at the Kessiri Hotel," Hana cut in. She glanced at JD. "I called them, or you would have had trouble getting a room with Ajax."

"Good." The major paused. "You should drive to the village of Xayden in Laos. From there, you can hike into Vietnam."

"That is precisely what I planned on doing," JD replied. "We will need a vehicle to get to Xayden. It's just over five hundred kilometers from here."

"You have one," Hana offered. "Hung will drive you to Xayden."

Turning to Hana, JD nodded. "Thank you, Hana. We could use the van. Hung does not need to go with us."

"Hung can be helpful in many other ways. You are Americans in an unfamiliar area. Hung can make things much easier for you."

JD thought about that for a few minutes and agreed.

With that, Major Anurat stood and turned to go. Pausing, he looked down at JD. "Two more things." He smiled. "First, I know Rick and Hana very well. If I didn't know them and I did not believe you, you would not leave here alive."

JD nodded. "Perhaps ..."

Anurat accepted that. "My men will be at the hotel at 8:30 a.m." He started toward the door, then paused and turned back to add, "Your uncle is alive." Then, the major left the restaurant, followed by his men.

Seated in the passenger seat of his Land Rover, Anurat considered his talk with the American as his driver navigated the busy Sisaket streets, heading toward the small but comfortable home he owned a few kilometers north of the city.

That was very interesting, the retired major thought. *The American's story fits much of what I already know to be true.*

Anurat did not want to think about a member of his family in the hands of any drug warlord, especially one suspected of being a particularly savage former VC colonel. In the past, he and Dish had occasionally shared war stories over a bottle of good Thai whiskey. Their long business relationship had built up genuine trust and friendship. Anurat knew of Dish's adopted sister, Mai, and what had happened to her family. He also knew that Dish believed Mai was living in America, married to a soldier they'd met during the war.

And now, here was this American, a retired U.S. Navy SEAL. While Hahn was not a close friend like Dish, Anurat had many dealings with the man over the years, and Hahn had always been straight with him. Plus, he'd worked with Hana several times over the years. He trusted her as much as he trusted anyone.

The major could see in the man's face that this retired SEAL was half Vietnamese, and while strong and solid, his build was small and wiry. While sitting at the table in the restaurant, Anurat had decided he believed the man. He'd looked into the American's eyes, and there was no dishonesty in his gaze. This man was here to rescue his mother, and his mother's name was Mai. Dish would have to be the brother. The major suddenly came to another realization. That meant the former Viet Cong colonel was almost certainly the drug warlord known as Colonel Trần.

With that conclusion, Anurat had no trouble making his decision. Dish was a long-time business partner and a loyal friend. Anurat knew that if the situation were reversed, Dish would do the same thing.

Unfortunately, his friend had no cell phone. In his remote little village, there would be no signal. There was no tower in range. However, Dish had several loyal friends in Xayden who would be willing to get a message to him. The two had communicated in this manner a few times in the past. Anurat slid his cell phone out of his jacket pocket and, selecting the correct number, pressed the call button.

People living in the tri-border region were often fluent in several languages. It was a basic necessity. The retired major not only spoke his native Thai but was also fluent in Laotian and Vietnamese. He could even manage some passable Cambodian. The call was answered on the fifth ring, and Anurat began speaking in Laotian to the man on the other end.

JD, Vivas, and Pallie quickly checked into their rooms at the Kessiri Hotel. Thoughtfully, Hana had booked each man their own room as well as one for herself. And, she'd cleared the way for Ajax to share JD's room. After stowing his gear, JD made sure Ajax was fed and comfortable. The three men decided to walk back to Leo's for supper so that Pallie could get his steak. They invited Hana to join them. She and JD were both quite hungry. While the other men had gotten to eat lunch, their meeting with Major Anurat at Leo's had never made it to

216

the eating part.

Hana gave Hung the night off, to visit with members of his family living in Sisaket, and he took off in the van to do just that.

"After all, if I am not safe in the company of you three, I am not sure what Hung could do," she quipped with a wink at Pallie, who blushed.

It felt good to walk after spending the previous eight hours cooped up in the van.

"Did you try the Ma kuear soup?" Hana asked as they worked their way along the busy street.

"I did," Vivas replied. "Pallie got some meat on a stick."

"Oh no," Hana exclaimed, glancing at Pallie with a concerned look on her face.

"What's wrong with that," Pallie asked, now looking alarmed.

"Oh, nothing," Hana replied. "I hope..." she added a second later. Pallie did not see the conspiratorial grin she gave Vivas. "It's just that... well, you never know what kind of meat is on those sticks. It could be cat, or dog, or even rat. Might be chicken, though, if you were lucky."

Pallie's face suddenly paled. "Rat...?"

Hana laughed. She liked these men. Tough as nails, but still slightly boyish at heart. Vivas seemed to be the strong silent type, but with a great sense of humor. Pallie was fun-loving and a bit boisterous, with a huge heart. JD, being older, was calm and stern, but with a sentimental side. Hana looked back at Pallie.

"I am teasing you," she grinned. "I'm sure it was fine."

Vivas laughed. "Well, both Hung and I had the soup. It was delicious."

"I told you it was," Hana replied.

The waiter brought them glasses of water. Hana assured them it was safe to drink. "It's bottled water," she explained. Thus reassured, all three men ordered steaks with fried potatoes and the Thai version of a Caesar salad. Hana ordered a red curry noodle soup that even Pallie had to admit, looked delicious on the menu. After the waiter left to enter their order, JD glanced at Hana, who was seated to his left.

"Can I ask you something, Hana? It's personal. I'll understand if you don't want to talk about it."

Hana smiled. "Why do I do what I do? Why do I own and run a ladyboy go-go bar and hang out with gun smugglers, and..." she laughed, "now, with U.S. Navy SEALS?"

'Well, yes," JD replied, a bit surprised by her openness. "Something like that." Pallie and Vivas shifted a little uncomfortably in their chairs.

"It's okay. I have seen and heard a great deal in my twenty-six years. I am not easily embarrassed. Don't you be."

She seemed to take a minute to think, deciding what to say.

"I can answer your second two questions first. I am my father's daughter. I hate communists and drug smugglers. You already know, JD, that drug smugglers killed my mother."

Vivas and Pallie looked up. This was the first they'd heard of this.

"Major Anurat, whom you just met, is a patriot. He loves Thailand and does not want to see the communists come here, so he sells guns to those fighting the communists. It is that simple." She paused and took a sip of water. "He also hates drug smugglers. So, I help him. Rick worked with him on several occasions, and I just sort of got involved. My ladyboys hear a lot in my club from their clients. They hear whispers about drug shipments, payments, where this or that warlord is currently hiding. This information is beneficial to both Rick and Major Anurat." Hana paused.

"The first question is a bit more complicated. It was my idea to buy the club. It makes a lot of money and has been a good investment. Rick and Major Anurat both provide excellent protection if I need it. Anurat recommended Quan to me, and Rick recommended Hung. Hung often went with Rick on trips into the Golden Triangle region, but was getting a bit old for that." Hana looked up at JD and frowned slightly before continuing. "Thailand is very open to the transgender community. That is becoming a well-known fact. Some ladyboys, if they are lucky, can become quite famous, celebrities even. It can mean big money here. There are ladyboy beauty pageants and modeling companies in Thailand. They can gain fame, wealth, and acceptance, even travel the world."

Hana took a sip of water. "I think it is like your American football. Many players but only a few make it to the professional level. For every ladyboy who becomes a famous model, thousands become performers in clubs like mine, or worse, sex workers, often out on the streets. It is quite sad."

Vivas nodded in agreement, not sure what to say.

Pallie sat back in his chair. "I guess it would be at that," he observed.

Hana continued. "Most of them are not bad people. Yes, there are drug addicts, pickpockets, con artists, thieves, and gold-diggers. But many are just sad kids trying to get by." Hana took another sip of her water. "Let me try to explain why they do what they do. Can you imagine being so poor that you can't even afford a meal? Now add to that the feeling that you're trapped inside the wrong body with no way out. These kids are all mixed up and can't even afford their lipstick. I don't know why there are so many in Thailand, but there are. So, what do they do when they are desperate and have no hope? They do what Thailand has become famous for." Hana's voice took a different tone. "It isn't fair. Look at Amsterdam, Prague, or Las Vegas. They are just as bad."

JD slowly shook his head. "I had no idea. I guess I never thought about it like that before. It is quite sad."

"At least in my club, they are safe. I tolerate no drug use and no pickpockets or thieves, either. That keeps my clients happy, and any client who tries to hurt one of my ladyboys answers to Quan. He is a former Thai Special Forces member and very good. He might even give you a run for your money, JD."

JD laughed. "I hope we don't have to find out."

A few seconds later, the waiter arrived with their dinners. Suddenly, the mood was much lighter. The steaks were first-rate, and the red curry noodle soup smelled delicious.

Hana coaxed Pallie to try a spoonful, after which he announced, "Not bad at all... for soup." All four laughed at that.

Dinner passed pleasantly with casual topics of conversation, including sights to see in Thailand. They spent a few minutes going over the drive from Laos to Xayden, as well as the trek from Xayden into Vietnam. JD did not have much of a plan after that point. A lot depended on how things played out. But he had an idea that if his uncle was half the man he understood him to be, when Dish heard that three Americans were tramping around in his backyard—one claiming to be his adopted nephew—he might arrange the meeting himself. And, JD was damn sure the Thai major would give Dish a heads up that some Americans were headed his way. They had to hope his uncle would talk first, shoot second.

After dinner, the guys allowed themselves a couple of Singha beers. Once they arrived in Xayden, alcohol would be off the menu until after the mission. Hana joined in with a glass of red wine. It was beginning to get late when the four made their way back to the hotel and retired for the night. JD took Ajax out for a short walk to stretch his legs and empty his bladder on a few nearby shrubs, then returned to his room and it was lights out. Everyone needed to get a good night's sleep. Tomorrow morning, things would start to get serious.

The plan discussed at Leo's was to meet in the lobby at 8:15 a.m. and wait for the major's men to arrive. After that, they would have to see how things unfolded. JD would have liked to have a better plan, but it was the best they could do under the circumstances.

After all, he mused, *even the best-laid battle plans rarely survived first contact with the enemy.*

JD was up at 6:30 in the morning and took Ajax for a run. It felt good to stretch the muscles. There had been too much time cooped up in jets and taxis lately. Ajax needed the exercise as well and seemed to enjoy working the kinks out. Figuring they'd gone about two miles, JD headed back toward the hotel for a four-mile roundtrip loop. Once back in the room, JD fed Ajax his breakfast and took a hot shower.

Getting dressed, he slid the CrossBreed holster out of his travel bag and into position just behind his right hip, then tightened his belt. He thought about carrying an extra magazine but decided against it. Where he was going, if he couldn't get out of trouble with sixteen rounds, he probably wasn't going to get out of it. Unloading and reloading the fifteen-round mag, he slapped it into the grip of his Glock 19 and racked it, seating one round in the chamber. Dropping the magazine, JD replaced the missing cartridge and re-seated the magazine.

Slipping the gun into its holster, he pulled on a loose-fitting, gray cotton t-shirt. The CrossBreed was a great in-the-waistband holster, and it would be hard for anyone except a professional to notice he was armed. Satisfied, JD put the leash on Ajax, and the two headed toward the elevator and the lobby. They spotted Pallie and Vivas in the restaurant, putting away platefuls of scrambled eggs, fried potatoes, and sausage accompanied by toast and jam. JD was amazed when the host waved them on into the restaurant. He'd not expected them to allow Ajax in the dining area. However, Ajax took it all in stride and lay quietly at JD's feet while he ordered breakfast.

"Morning," Vivas grunted as JD sat down.

"Morning," JD replied. "I see you two found something to your liking."

Pallie grinned. "Almost as good as back home."

"That's his third plate," Vivas observed dryly.

"Second," Pallie corrected. "The pancakes were a side item and didn't count. And besides, it's always better to face danger on a full stomach."

Vivas laughed at that. "Absolutely! That way, you have something in place should you need to shit your pants!" JD grinned while Pallie just scowled at Vivas.

Hana arrived a few minutes after 8:00 a.m., fending off offers of breakfast from both Pallie and Vivas. I'm not much of a breakfast person," she explained. "But I will take some coffee." Being a bit faster on his feet, Vivas was soon back at the table with a cup of black coffee in hand.

"Cream or sugar?"

"Just black... and thank you, Carlos." JD grinned. He was pretty sure Vivas had just blushed.

A few minutes later, the four of them were comfortably seated around a coffee table in a semi-private area of the hotel lobby, sipping their drinks. Ajax was happily getting his back scratched by Hana, who seemed to be enjoying it almost as much as the dog was.

At 8:30 on the dot, four capable-looking Thai men walked into the lobby and, spotting the four at the table, approached. Ajax stiffened a bit and let out a low growl. "Stil," JD commanded quietly. Ajax settled only a bit and remained focused on the approaching strangers. JD noticed that while they seemed to be all business, there was nothing aggressive or hostile in their mannerism.

So far, so good, JD thought as he stood. One man stepped forward, clearly the leader of the group. He spoke excellent English. "Good morning."

"Good morning," JD replied. Vivas and Pallie nodded and shifted in their chairs. All three were carrying concealed personal sidearms. "Better to have them and not need them, than need them and not have them," JD had advised the night before. "But for God's sake, be discreet."

The man continued speaking to JD, his tone of voice friendly. "You and Hana will come with Kiet and me, indicating the man on his immediate left. We will take you to see the major. These two," he indicated the men to his right, "will wait with your friends and drink coffee. Everything is okay?"

JD nodded. "Okay. How long will we be gone?"

"Maybe two hours," the man replied.

JD glanced over at Hana, who smiled and nodded. Then he turned to Pallie and Vivas. "You two okay with this?"

Pallie shrugged. "We got this, JD. No worries."

Vivas turned his gaze on the leader of the group of Thai men. "Make sure our friends arrive back here safely. If anything bad were to happen to them, we would be greatly displeased."

The man smiled. "Do not worry. Everything is okay — the boss and his uncle," indicating JD, "long time good friends. No lies. No trouble."

JD laughed at that. "Okay. We're good then. Let's go!" Hana stood, and she and JD walked with the leader toward the door. Suddenly, JD paused. "Ajax, Komen." The dog was immediately on his feet and at JD's side. He turned to the Thai leader. "Is this a problem?"

"No problem," the man smiled. "We have a big van. The boss also has dogs."

It was then that JD realized they had never even frisked him for a weapon.

The ride took about forty minutes. JD and Hana sat in the second row of seats with the two Thais in front. Ajax made himself comfortable in the back. They had not gone too far when JD had a thought. He turned to Hana. "You know," he began. "I was amazed they let Ajax into the restaurant at the hotel. I wonder why they didn't raise a fuss over that."

Hana smiled. "That's because I told them Ajax was a heroic war dog, that he has killed many communists and terrorists, and that if they raised any fuss, he might kill them as well."

"You told them that?" JD asked incredulously.

"No. Don't be silly," Hana laughed. "I just paid them lots of money to let the dog have the run of the hotel."

"Oh!" JD laughed. "Is that all?"

"Don't worry about it. I like Ajax. He is my friend, too, I think."

They were several kilometers outside Sisaket city limits when the van turned off onto a hard-packed dirt road. The road followed a creek winding randomly through the trees before ending in front of a traditional Thai house of wooden construction. The stream continued to the left and beyond the place, which JD noticed had the elegantly tapered roof of many such dwellings he had seen since landing in Thailand.

This house was a raised structure, sitting up on wooden posts. JD assumed correctly that this was to prevent flooding during the monsoon season. There was a wide veranda on the front of the house with an ornate staircase leading up to it. *Very nice*, JD thought.

Getting out of the van after Hana, JD had Ajax on his leash. He spotted Major Anurat coming down the stairs, followed by two good-sized dogs.

"Ajax, Zit," JD commanded. Ajax let out a little snort as he sat at JD's left side. JD's hand slid down and unsnapped the leash from Ajax's collar. If things got out of control, he didn't want Ajax hampered by the leash. Anurat stopped a few paces away, and the two dogs sat.

"Is your dog friendly?" he asked.

"Yes," JD replied. "To those who are friendly."

"Fair enough." Major Anurat smiled and gave a command. His two dogs relaxed and began to approach Ajax in a cautious but friendly manner with tails wagging.

"Ajax, Breken," JD commanded. Ajax was now free to do as he pleased, given the 'break' command. He approached the two strange dogs cautiously, but without fear. After a minute or two of canine sniffing and greeting, the tension seemed to ease; all three dogs being satisfied that nobody presented a threat.

"Good," the major observed. "That went well. I have two rules. One, I never trust people my dogs do not trust, and two, I don't like people who don't like dogs."

JD laughed. "I have the same two rules."

"Good," Anurat replied. He turned to Hana. "And how are you this morning, Hana? Your father is well, I trust."

"He is well. But he is still in North Africa. I am not sure when he will get back to Thailand."

"When he returns, we must get together. I have done business with your father several times, but we have never really talked. If he is friends with men like this," indicating JD, "I think I would like to get to know him better."

Hana smiled. "He is a good man. A hard man, but a good man, like others we know. I will let you know when he is back in Thailand."

"Good," the major responded. "Now, let us walk." Anurat led the way down a path that followed the creek behind the house and into the woods beyond. Ajax and the other two dogs joined the procession, never straying too far from their respective owners.

"What kind of dogs are these?" JD asked as they headed into the trees behind the house. "They look almost like Rhodesian Ridgebacks with that raised ridge of hair on their backs."

"They are Thai Ridgebacks," the major answered. "Or Mah Thai Lan Ahn. They are good dogs. Smart, loyal, and brave; like your Belgian Malinois, I think. Yes?"

The path ended in a clearing where a small pickup truck with a tarp over the bed was parked. When the two men walked over to the pickup, the major pulled the tarp aside.

"This is what I have on hand. I think you will find everything you may need. Pick out what you wish to have." With that, Anurat stepped back and let JD look through the contents of the truck bed.

The first thing JD spotted was the M-27 Infantry Automatic Rifle. He glanced over at the major. "I won't even ask." Anurat just smiled.

Pallie will love that, he thought.

Sticking with 5.56 mm so they could share ammo if needed, JD selected two MP-4 rifles that looked to be in great shape except for a little needed cleaning. There was a box of ten M67 fragmentation grenades, two LAW rockets, several cases of ten and thirty round magazines, and several thousand rounds of 5.56 mm ammunition. JD would have liked to have had a bolt-action rifle for long-distance shooting, but there was nothing suitable in the truck bed.

"Grab a rifle for Hung, as well," Hana commented. "He might be useful if things go south."

"What would you suggest," JD asked, glancing over at Hana.

"Another MP-4 would be fine. The Thai army uses M-16s. He would be familiar with its operation."

"Okay," JD agreed. He stood back and turned toward Major Anurat.

"I'll take three of the MP-4s, the M-27, forty thirty-round magazines, the box of grenades, the two LAW rockets, and two thousand rounds of 5.56 mm... I guess that's about it."

Anurat nodded. "Good."

Glancing down at Ajax, who happened to be standing close, the major reached down to scratch him behind the ears. JD noticed the dog didn't move away.

"That is good. I will have my men deliver everything just before you plan to leave. You can meet at the old warehouse north of Sisaket. Hana knows where it is. It is safe, my men patrol it regularly, and the police keep away. When do you go?"

JD thought about that for a few seconds. "I'd like a chance to clean the weapons and get our gear in order. Can we meet at the warehouse tomorrow morning, say at 0900? Then we could move on a bit and find a spot to do an equipment check."

"You can stay at the warehouse a day, no problem. Check weapons, equipment, and prepare, then go. It is no problem. My men will make sure you are not bothered."

JD met the major's gaze. "This is very kind of you. We haven't even settled on a price yet. Why are you doing this for me?"

Major Anurat stopped scratching Ajax behind his ears, and looked up, turning to face JD.

"My dogs... they like you," he stated, pointing at JD's feet. JD hadn't noticed, but the major's two Thai Ridgebacks were calmly lying near his feet. Anurat went on.

"Dish and I have been friends many, many years. He is like a brother to me. We fight the damned communists together, even after the war ended. Many of these powerful drug lords were Viet Cong during the war. We fight them when we must." He paused as if searching for the right words. "If my mother, or my sister, or my child were in the hands of one such as these, Dish would leave no stone unturned to help me find those responsible and kill them. I will do the same for him. His sister, Mai, is your mother, so I help you too. You take what you need, no problem. After you have rescued your mother, you must come back through Thailand, yes?"

JD nodded, "Yes."

"Then we see when you get back. You bring guns back, it is good." The major laughed. "Maybe pay a small rental fee and for used bullets, yes?"

JD didn't know what else to say, so he said, "Yes. Thank you."

"Good," Anurat grinned as he approached JD, slapping him on the back. "Now, you come with me, yes?"

The major took off back down the path with his two dogs close behind. JD, Hana, and Ajax had to hurry to keep up. When they got back to the house, Anurat's two men were still leaning against the van, waiting. The major headed straight up the stairs to the veranda and into the house. JD and Ajax stopped near the vehicle, and Hana joined them. A few minutes later, Anurat came back down the stairs carrying a package which he presented to JD.

"I have two of these for my dogs," he announced, a bit out of breath. "But they don't need. I thought they are very, what is the word, cool?" Anurat again reached down to ruffle Ajax's head. "But, your dog. I think he needs this."

JD looked down at the package, an unopened box containing a K9 Storm Intruder harness. The harness offered excellent protection for Ajax.

"Very cool," JD replied. He extended his hand to the major, who swept it aside and grabbed JD in a mighty hug.

"Now, you go meet Dish. I sent word you are coming, and Dish will be watching for you on the trail. You meet Dish, you rescue Mai, and you kill that no good fucking communist drug lord! Yes?"

"Yes," JD replied. He was in full agreement with that plan.

Back in the van, the major's two men were laughing up in front as JD examined the K9 Storm harness still in its packaging.

"What are they laughing about?" he asked Hana.

She smiled. "The driver said the boss must like you. The other man said... either that, or he likes the dog. Then the driver said, it must be the dog, because, after all, you are only a farang."

JD laughed. "The joke is on them."

"Why is that?"

"I am only half farang."

Hana laughed at that, and then asked, "What will we, I mean you, carry all this gear in?"

"We have rucksacks and other gear with us. We just needed more firepower."

Hana nodded at that.

One hour and fifty-six minutes after leaving Pallie and Vivas in the lobby, the van dropped JD, Hana, and Ajax back at the hotel. The four men were waiting in the lobby near the entrance and saw the van pull up. The major's two men nodded to Pallie and Vivas and headed outside to meet the vehicle. JD grabbed the package Anurat had given him, and he, Hana, and Ajax climbed out from the back seat. JD immediately started toward the lobby with Ajax, but Hana hesitated.

"Something wrong?" JD asked.

"No, not at all. I have some shopping to do. I'll meet you here at the hotel for dinner."

"Okay. About 6:00, then?"

Hana smiled. "Sounds good." With that, she took off toward the taxi line in front of the hotel.

JD walked over to greet Vivas and Pallie near the door, and the three of them moved into a quiet corner of the lobby.

"How did it go?" Vivas asked.

"Great," JD replied. "Even got Pallie an M-27."

Pallie grinned at that. "No shit?"

"No shit," JD laughed. "I also got four MP-4s and about ten 30-round magazines each. We have a couple of thousand rounds of 5.56 mm ammo. He also had ten M67 fragmentation grenades and two LAW rockets, which I grabbed."

"That should do the trick," Vivas commented.

Then JD remembered the package. "The major gave this to Ajax. It's a K9 Storm Harness he'd ordered for one of his dogs but never used. We won't have the secret squirrel stuff we normally have, of course, but it will still be good body armor for Ajax."

"Nice," Vivas replied. "Why four MP-4s?"

"Hana suggested I get one for Hung, just in case... said he carried an M-16 while in the Thai Army and would be familiar with its operation. It made sense to me. I wanted a sniper rifle, but the major didn't have anything suitable."

"Too bad," Pallie observed. "But the other carbine won't hurt. What's the plan?"

"We will meet Anurat's men at an old warehouse just north of the city. Hana knows the place. He will have the hardware there and says we can stay there long enough to clean and zero the weapons and check our gear. Then we will load up in the van with Hung and get underway."

"Sounds good," Vivas commented. "What happened to Hana?"

"She wanted to do some shopping; said she'll meet us in the restaurant at 6:00 p.m. for dinner. We've got a few hours to kill. I think I will take Ajax for a run and then go over my gear. I may call Annie after dinner and let her know what I can. I need to call Ellen, too."

"Pallie and I will run with you," Vivas suggested. "That is if you can keep up."

JD laughed. "If you get too far ahead, I'll have Ajax bite you in the ass. That'll slow you down." JD looked at his watch. "Okay, I'm going to go change. Meet back here in twenty minutes?"

Pallie grinned. "Shit, man, I'm going to grab a skateboard and let

Ajax tow me along. See you here in twenty."

At 6:00 p.m., JD stepped out of the elevator to find Hana in the lobby, arms full of packages, waiting to take the elevator up.

"Just in time," JD grinned. "Do you need some help?"

"No, thanks. I've got it. I'll take these up to my room and meet you in the restaurant in a few minutes." Hana looked around. "Where're your two sidekicks?"

"If I know them, they're already in the restaurant going over the menu. We'll hold you a seat." JD walked across the lobby toward the restaurant as Hana stepped into the elevator. Finding Vivas and Pallie already seated at a table, he joined them.

"Hana will be just a few minutes. I met her in the lobby. She's taking some packages up to her room."

"And you didn't offer to help?" Vivas asked with a grin.

"I did, actually, but she said she could handle it. Besides, I think Pallie has a thing for her."

Pallie looked up from the menu he'd been reading. "What? Who... me?"

Vivas laughed. "Yes, you, Pallie!"

Pallie looked puzzled. "Why would you say that, Vivas?"

"Shit, Pallie! You can't keep your eyes off her."

"Well, damn!" It was Pallie's turn to laugh. "Vivas ... are you blind? Hana is one beautiful lady, especially since we found out that she is a she, and not a he pretending to be a she."

JD had to laugh at that. These guys were easy company, and he knew when the operation came to unfold, he could count on them to have his back.

Other men might have mentioned that he'd proposed to Ellen, and she'd accepted. After all, these guys had been there when they rescued Dr. Chang in the first place. But to say that JD was a private person would be an understatement. His engagement to Ellen had happened fast, and now he was focused on getting his mother home safely. There would be plenty of time for jokes about his engagement to Ellen later.

"Besides, Vivas, I'm Sicilian. She's not my type," Pallie offered.

"What the hell is that supposed to mean?" Vivas asked. "You're Sicilian, and she's not your type?"

"Well," Pallie replied with a grin, "I am Sicilian, and I prefer a tall Swedish blond." JD laughed all over again as Vivas shook his head in wonderment.

Pallie is right, though, Vivas thought to himself. *She sure is pretty, and funny too ...*

"Can I join you, gentleman?" It was Hana.

CHAPTER 35
VIETNAM

Lieutenant Colonel Fong and his two lackeys delivered Mai to the old Michelin plantation house, where Trần's head of security met them.

"I am Huỳnh, the colonel's head of security. Do not try to escape, or you will die," he warned. Mai searched his face, but couldn't detect any hint of human compassion. *His eyes are dead*, she thought. They reminded Mai of the eyes of the men she had seen in the news, men who were terrorists or killers.

Huỳnh quickly escorted her to a second-floor bedroom with an adjoining bathroom.

"You will stay here. A guard will bring food and drink to you at mealtimes."

Mai said nothing as she glanced around the room. It looked comfortable enough. A bed sat against the far wall. There was an old wingback chair with a small table near a large window on the left. Mai noticed the wrought iron bars over each of the bedroom's two large windows. A chest of drawers stood against another wall. There was an old radio sitting on the chest.

If that works, at least I can get some news or listen to music, Mai thought. She turned back toward the man with the dead eyes and watched as he left the room and shut the door. Mai heard a key turning in the lock, waited a few seconds, and walked over to examine it. The door was solid wood and heavy. The bedroom was a prison.

A lone figure, hidden by densely overgrown brush about three hundred yards from the house, carefully put the M19 binoculars back in their leather case and returned them to the worn canvas rucksack on the ground. Retrieving a bottle of water, the watcher took a drink and settled down to wait in an old stone foundation. The slightly elevated position of the small abandoned building, once used to store tools for harvesting rubber, had a great view of the front of the house. The structure had long since rotted away.

The binoculars brought the police car into perfect focus as it approached, following the dirt drive from the main road to the plantation house. The observer watched as Lt. Col. Fong got out of the car, followed by an attractive older woman who refused Fong's offer of help. Huỳnh stepped from the house and immediately took custody of the woman, who, from the description provided, had to be Mai. Huỳnh led her up onto the house's wide veranda and into the darkened interior. Less than a minute later, a light showed through the two second-story windows of a room at the front of the house. Keeping a focus on those two windows, the observer saw Mai pass in front of the one on the right.

Adjusting to a more comfortable position while taking care not to disturb any of the concealing brush, the watcher waited. Once it was dark, it would be safe to sneak out to the main road where a bicycle lay carefully hidden among the trees. It was a short ride to the tiny village where descendants of the men and women who once worked on the rubber plantation still lived. It was also where the contact waited each day for any news about a woman imprisoned at the plantation house.

Today, that news would shortly make its way to a village on a remote rock shelf in the mountains close to the Laotian border.

Mai sat in the wingback chair, trying to figure a way out of the mess she had gotten herself into, but she found no answers. The fact that Jum Y had signaled that she'd get word to Dish and that Bill Cunningham from the U.S. Consulate would, by now, certainly know she was missing, gave her a little hope. *But how could they know where I am?*

Mai knew her situation was desperate. For now, there was little she could do except learn all she could and try to figure out a way to escape. Her thoughts turned to the man with the dead eyes, and she shuddered. That would be difficult.

The sound of a key turning in the door lock caught Mai's attention. The door opened, and a man stepped into the room. Mai guessed he was in his early seventies. He wore traditional clothing—a gray jacket with white pankou, the traditional Chinese knotted buttons, black pants, and sandals. His face showed his age. He wore his gray hair combed back. A thin mustache hung down from the corners of his thin lips, almost reaching the small goatee. The man looked at her and smiled. Mai noticed that the smile did not make it to his eyes.

"Hello, I am Colonel Trần Nam Tin. And you," he paused, "are Mai Cordell?"

Mai said nothing, waiting.

"An interesting last name for a Vietnamese woman, I think."

Mai decided she would not play his game. She was not ashamed of who she was and had nothing to hide.

"It is the name of my late husband, an American officer I met during the war," Mai stated, meeting Trần's gaze evenly.

"Ah! I see. And, what is your relationship to the Montagnard bandit you were looking for, the Jarai named Dish?"

"He is my adopted brother."

Trần appeared to be shocked by this revelation. "A Vietnamese woman with an adopted Jarai brother? Very interesting. And, how did this travesty come about?"

"My father was Ang Dung, the mayor of Dak No. He taught Dish the family martial art as a favor to Dish's father, an old friend, and leader of a nearby Montagnard village. When the Viet Cong murdered my family, Dish took me to his father's village, where he welcomed me as a daughter."

Trần smiled. "That was some time ago, but I remember that village. I have a great memory for such things, an essential element in my current business. I sent my men on that mission to punish traitors helping the American soldiers." He paused, thinking. "They reported they'd killed the entire family."

Mai fought to contain the rage struggling to break free on hearing this revelation. Now was not the time. Getting her emotions under control, she kept her response simple.

"They missed one."

Trần laughed. "So it seems." He looked directly at Mai. "You know, your Montagnard brother and I have quite a long history. He killed many of my men during the war, a fierce adversary, even for a traitor.

Because of this, I eventually ordered Dish's entire village wiped out." Trần smiled. "I believe he has recently been made aware of this fact."

Mai was not quick enough to stop the horrified look that flashed briefly across her face. She had not known this. Had Trần noticed? Mai was determined not to give this man any victory, no matter how small.

"So, you have taken me as bait to trap my brother." It was a statement, not a question.

"Exactly."

"He will kill you," Mai stated this as a forgone conclusion.

"Perhaps," Trần acknowledged. "Or, perhaps, I will kill him. The question is, where will that leave you if I succeed?"

Mai shrugged, not replying.

Trần grinned. It was not a pleasant grin. "You are still beautiful for a woman of your age. I find that my passing years have not diminished my appetite for attractive women."

Mai looked steadily into Trần's eyes. "If you try to touch me, one of us will die."

Trần chuckled. "Good. Good. I like the challenge." He turned to go out the door but paused, looking back at Mai. "It will have to wait a bit, however. I must keep you safe for our meeting with your brother. Then, once we've completed our business, we shall see."

He pulled the door closed behind him, and Mai heard the key turn in the lock again, shutting her in.

Sitting back down in the old wingback chair, she took a deep breath, a bit surprised at her feelings. She did not feel afraid. She felt only anger and determination. This man, a former Viet Cong leader, had ordered her family and everyone in her adopted Montagnard village, killed. No matter what else transpired, Mai's mind was made up. This man would die.

CHAPTER 36
THAILAND

As planned, the three SEALs had all their gear in the lobby at 7:00 a.m. Ajax chose a spot near the stacked equipment and promptly fell asleep.

"Rough night?" Pallie asked, indicating Ajax, now snoring away. JD shrugged. He hadn't slept well the night before, either. He'd had something on his mind.

"What's up, JD?" Vivas asked.

"Well, it's you and Pallie, to be honest. It is not too late. You can back out now if you want to. I don't want you guys to get hurt. This whole mess is really on me."

It was Pallie who answered. "Belay that shit, JD. We have orders, you know. Our mission is to rescue your mom. Now, it would be much better for all of us to work together on this. I mean, you've got the experience and all that crap, but this is our mission, too, either way."

"Besides, if you think we're going to let you try this on your own, you're an idiot," Vivas added. "This is the team. You're family. So, don't give us any more of that bullshit, or old man or not, I'll kick your ass!"

JD laughed. "Okay, guys. Sorry. You know I had to say that." He paused. "The truth is, I'm grateful you're both here." JD turned and walked toward the lobby entrance, to see if Hung was here with the van yet.

"Belay that shit?" Vivas asked Pallie with a grin.

Pallie shrugged. "Think I heard it in a movie once."

Vivas laughed and headed toward the door after JD.

The van pulled up to the entrance, and the driver door opened. JD and Vivas were both surprised when Hana, not Hung, got out from the driver's side.

"What's up, Hana? Where's Hung?"

"I'm sorry," Hana replied. "I just found out yesterday that Hung can't drive. It's stupid. He was playing with one of his granddaughters and threw his back out. He can't sit or stand. I guess he's getting too old for this stuff. I may have to give him a desk job."

Vivas glanced at JD, "Now what the hell are we going to do?"

"That's easy," Hana replied. "I'm going with you."

"No way," JD stated. "That's not happening."

"Don't be silly, JD. You need someone who speaks the languages, and I am fluent in Thai, Laotian, and Vietnamese. I've traveled with Rick all through where you're going, and I can handle that MP-4 if needed. You need my help. The three of you won't make it through Laos and into Vietnam without running into serious trouble with soldiers, gun runners, or drug smugglers."

JD looked at Vivas, who shrugged. "She may have a point."

Just then, Pallie came up from behind. "What's up?"

"Hung can't drive. He was playing with a grandkid, and now he's down with a bad back. Hana says she's taking his place," Vivas answered.

"Okay," Pallie replied.

"Okay?" JD almost yelled. "Did you say, okay?"

"Well, yeah. JD, we need a local guide. None of us speak Vietnamese or Laotian. We'd stick out like a sore thumb and are sure to get into trouble before we ever got near your mom."

"You can't be serious!" JD was dumbstruck.

"Look, JD." It was Vivas this time. "I'm sure Hana knows what she's getting into. She's Rick Hahn's daughter, for God's sake."

"That's part of the problem." JD shook his head. "If we get her killed, I'd say Rick just might be seriously pissed at us."

Vivas ignored that. "She does business with that Major Anurat. He's no pushover, and that says a lot. I don't see as we have any real choice." He turned to Hana. "Can you shoot?"

"Better than most," Hana replied seriously. "JD, I know you guys are the experts, and you're good at your jobs. Don't worry. I can follow orders, and I won't be a problem. If you run into a group of soldiers or gun smugglers, you'll be glad I am there."

"And, we just don't let her get killed," Vivas added. "Hell, JD, she's got Ajax and the three of us as her escorts."

"Sonofabitch," JD muttered. "What about drug smugglers?"

"Well, you'll probably have to kill them," Hana said with a shrug.

"What about your gear?" JD asked, still unconvinced. "We're not going on a picnic, you know."

"I have everything I need. That's what I went shopping for yesterday. Hung called me while you were talking to Major Anurat. I didn't say anything at the time because I was pretty sure you'd object."

"Well, you were right about that." JD walked off for a few minutes to think. He didn't like this one bit. But, was he being objective? Sure, he liked Hana and didn't want to see her hurt. He didn't want to see Vivas or Pallie get hurt either. And to make matters worse, Hana was right; they did need her help. Any way he looked at it, there was no reasonable alternative.

Well, shit, JD thought.

"Okay! I don't see that we have much choice. But Hana, if one of us yells jump, you jump, okay?"

"Yes, sir!" Hana flashed JD a big smile. "And don't worry. We'll make a great team!"

"Can we load up now?" Pallie inquired. "We ought to get on the road."

"Yes," JD replied. "Let's get the gear loaded. I'll give Ajax a chance to relieve himself, and we'll go."

Ajax, who'd been dutifully standing guard over the pile of gear in the corner of the hotel lobby, was ready to get going as well.

It was an eight-and-a-half-hour drive to Xayden, not counting the stopover at the abandoned warehouse. They saw no reason not to share the driving. Pallie volunteered to start at the wheel, and Hana took the passenger seat to give directions to the old warehouse. JD, Vivas, and Ajax piled into the back of the van.

With all the gear loaded up and Ajax settled comfortably on the floor near JD's seat, they left the hotel parking lot. Pallie had driven a limousine in New York City before joining the Navy and liked to drive. His previous experience served him well, as he had no trouble with the narrow streets and heavy Sisaket traffic. Once he'd cleared the city following Hana's directions and they were headed north, Hana reached into her shoulder bag and pulled out a medium-sized envelope.

"Might as well give these to you guys."

Removing three smaller envelopes from the bigger one, Hana handed one to each man. Each packet had a neatly handwritten name on it. Pallie glanced at the papers he'd been given and handed it to Vivas. There was still a fair amount of traffic, and he needed to focus on driving.

"Rick had these made for you by an old business acquaintance of his. I don't know what documentation you are traveling with, but these papers identify you as three expatriates living in Thailand. You'll find passports and work permits, plus documentation showing all three of you employed as security for my club, Obsession." She paused when JD looked up at her. "It seemed to be the best choice. You don't look like three guys who'd work in the garment industry. And, both the club and I are known where we are going. It may help."

JD nodded. "Makes sense to me."

Hana laughed. "So, if we are dealing with border guards, soldiers, or gun smugglers, if I tell you to jump, you jump. Okay?"

Vivas laughed and punched JD in the arm. "Paybacks are hell, aren't they."

JD grinned at that. "I guess so."

"And, if they're drug smugglers, we just kill them," Pallie added in a more serious tone.

Hana looked up. "We will try to avoid them. But they are a very nasty bunch. If we run into them, you may have little choice if you want to live to rescue JD's mother."

All three men correctly understood what Hana was saying.

"These forgeries are excellent," Hana went on. "They will be adequate for any border guards or soldiers we meet, and for any common identification purposes. You need to avoid a search in any Thai government computer systems. So, you will need to stay out of trouble."

"Trouble?" Pallie raised an eyebrow.

"No bar fights or traffic tickets along the way," Hana replied.

"Pallie will be on his best behavior," JD commented.

After twenty minutes of driving through the Thai countryside, Hana directed Pallie to turn left onto an old paved road that was in desperate need of repair.

"Somebody should scrape out the holes and fill in the bumps,"

Pallie observed wryly.

About fifty yards later, they approached a closed gate.

"Just wait," Hana advised.

A few seconds later, a man stepped out from the trees and approached the van. He was carrying an older M16 rifle slung over his shoulder. Both Pallie and Vivas recognized him as one of the men they'd sat within the hotel lobby while waiting for JD and Hana to return from their meeting with the retired major.

Recognizing the van's passengers, the man lifted his hand in greeting and walked over to open the gate. Pallie drove through, and it closed behind them. Continuing along the bumpy road, surrounded by tall brush and thickets for another hundred yards, they rounded a curve and pulled into a clearing, which revealed a good-sized warehouse. Few of its windows were intact, and the bay doors were either open or missing.

Two more Thai men were sitting on a bench near one of the open bays. The same truck JD and Hana had seen at the major's home was parked inside. Pallie pulled the van over and turned the ignition off. JD opened the sliding back door and got out, followed closely by Ajax, then Vivas. Ajax moved forward a few steps and sat between JD and the two men sitting on the bench. The dog focused on the two men.

Hana got out of the van and came around to stand near JD, calling out to the two men in Thai. JD had immediately recognized them as the two who had driven him and Hana to the meeting with Major Anurat. The men stood and approached, one of them answering Hana.

Hana turned to JD. "They said the equipment you requested is in the truck, and we are free to stay as long as needed, but he asks that we leave by tomorrow morning. He has men patrolling the fence, and they will stay until we leave."

"Thank him and tell him we will be gone later this afternoon. Oh, and ask him if it would be a problem for us to test-fire the rifles here, to zero them."

Hana again spoke rapidly in Thai, and the man responded. "It should not be a problem. We are welcome to test the weapons here, but he recommends doing that just before leaving. He said they sometimes practice shooting here, but then, they are Thai, and you are not. It is better to be safe."

JD nodded. "Makes sense to me."

The man spoke once more, and then he and his companion turned and headed toward the truck. A few minutes later, the weapons unloaded, the major's men headed out the way they'd come in.

"What else did he say?" JD asked.

Hana looked at JD. There was a somber look on her face.

"He said, 'Good hunting.'"

Within minutes everyone was busy. Vivas and Pallie set to work on the rifles. All three of the MP-4s and the M-27 needed to be disassembled and thoroughly cleaned. JD unpacked the grenades from their crate and inspected them. After he finished, he carefully packed them back into their container for traveling before moving on to check the condition of the LAW rockets.

Hana asked what she could do to help. JD pointed to the box of forty 30-round magazines and the metal ammo boxes.

"Can you load those magazines?"

Without a word, Hana headed over to the box of magazines and the ammo. Opening the ammo cans, she discovered the containers were full of loose ball ammunition.

Stripper clips would have been a help, she thought.

Undeterred, Hana began thumbing rounds into one of the 30-round magazines. JD watched long enough to see that she knew what she was doing before returning to his inspection of the LAWs.

Satisfied with the LAW rockets, he next turned his attention to the K9 Storm vest Major Anurat had given him for Ajax. JD let out a low whistle in appreciation. It was the top of the line Intruder vest, the same model Ajax had sported in Afghanistan, Iraq, and Niger. The harness was bulletproof and could stop a bullet from a 9mm or .45 caliber handgun. It was also waterproof and provided excellent protection from knives, thorns, briers, and other assorted hazards military dogs often encountered. Even without the high-definition camera, which allowed the handler to see whatever the dog saw, the vest would have cost about $20,000. It was an incredibly generous gesture on the part of the major.

JD called for Ajax, who, left to his own devices, had explored every square foot of the old warehouse before settling down in the shade near Hana, dozing while she continued to load magazines. Jumping up when he heard JD call him, Ajax trotted over, and they began the process of fitting the vest to the dog's size.

Hana, by now, had thirty-two magazines loaded, and her thumb was getting a bit tired. She looked up as Vivas squatted down next to her.

"Let me give you a break. You've got most of the magazines loaded already. That's great."

Hana smiled appreciatively. "Sure. I'll admit my thumb could use a few minutes rest."

Vivas grabbed a magazine from the box and began thumbing rounds into it quickly. It was clear to Hana that Vivas had probably done this a few more times than she had. She watched him work for a few minutes before saying, "I want to thank you for speaking up for me at the hotel. I figured JD would be pretty set against me tagging along."

Vivas shrugged. "To be honest, I have my concerns. But I don't see how we would have much chance for success without your help. We don't speak Thai, Laotian, or Vietnamese." He laughed. "Spanish wouldn't do us much good here."

"No, I guess not. I have a lot of connections along this route as well. You'll see. You will be happy I'm here when we get to the Laotian border. Besides, I can take care of myself."

Vivas looked up from the magazine he was loading and smiled. "I don't doubt that for a second. Hand me another magazine, will you please?"

Once the weapons were zeroed and cleaned, and the other equipment checked out, the five gathered near the front of the van. Hana proved herself to not only be an excellent shot but also very familiar with the MP-4's operation. All three SEALs were impressed.

Ajax now stood by JD, sporting his new Intruder vest. Pallie laughed. "Ajax looks proud of his new vest."

"He certainly does... and he looks very handsome in it too," Hana added.

As if on cue, Ajax sat and gave an appreciative whine.

"Okay, JD. What's the plan now?" Vivas asked.

JD knelt and gave Ajax a scratch. "Well, the way I see it, we load up and start for Xayden. We'll have to figure some way to hide the weapons in the van, and hope we don't get caught with them. I think we'll be fine once we start the hump into Vietnam. That's pretty remote terrain we will travel through; lots of armed smugglers running around from what we've heard. Being employed as security for Hana's club may offer us some cover there."

Hana nodded. "It will help."

"We have to figure something out for these border crossings. A close inspection of our van would be bad," JD continued.

"That's for damn sure," Pallie laughed.

"You can leave that to me," Hana interjected. "When we're ready, I will contact the right people. I have connections that will ensure we cross the border with no problem."

"Really?" Vivas asked, surprised.

"Really. Remember, I grew up in this world, and I've known Major Anurat since I was a very young girl. Many of these gun smugglers are like family to me. Most of them are just plain folks who, like you, love their country. They hate the communists. I've helped get many shipments of guns into Vietnam for Major Anurat in the past." Hana laughed. "It helps that I have a lot of money. Obsession does very well."

"Now I am impressed," Vivas commented softly to Pallie, who nodded. If Hana heard his comment, she gave no sign of it.

"Do you know my uncle, Dish?" JD asked.

Hana looked up. "I have met him several times. He is a longtime good friend of Major Anurat."

"You never told me that," JD observed.

"You never asked."

"Fair enough. Okay. Here is how I see it. If my uncle is the man my parents described to us growing up, and the major sent word to him that we're coming, Dish will be on the lookout for us. Once we cross into Vietnam, we'll almost certainly make contact."

"Sounds reasonable," Vivas commented.

"Agreed," Pallie added.

"Once we connect with my uncle, I imagine he'll have valuable information that can aid any rescue attempt. I am betting he's already working on finding out where this drug lord is holding my mother."

CHAPTER 37
VIETNAM

Things were coming together. Hai brought word that morning that their spy had spotted Mai at the old Michelin plantation house north of Ho Chi Minh City. The person watching the house saw Lt. Col. Fong delivering her just yesterday afternoon. The observer also relayed that Mai was in the second-story room on the left front corner of the old house. Coincidentally, it was the only room, at least on the front side, with wrought iron bars on its two windows.

Not too difficult to spot, Dish thought. His mind turned to the next problem. *How do I get Mai out of there without getting her killed?*

Dish told Hai to see if the former housekeeper could draw a layout of the house. Even though he knew which room Mai was being held in, knowing the floorplan would be extremely helpful in planning a rescue attempt.

"Also, have our people spread the story that I am coming to Ho Chi Minh City in two days, on a trip of some importance."

"Are you?" Hai asked.

"No," Dish replied. "When we leave here, we will go directly to the old Michelin plantation to get Mai. But if Trần thinks we are getting ready for an exchange, he will think his plan is working. Or, Trần may even think we are coming to the city to be closer to his base of operations for a rescue attempt. Either way, it should buy us a few days."

Hai nodded. "It might work. It will be better if he believes you want to trade the opium for your sister." Hai paused. "However, he'd have to scrape the opium from the jungle floor."

"He doesn't know that," Dish commented.

The next morning, Dish relaxed on his bench. His muscles were a bit stiff from yesterday's hike back to the village, and he was enjoying the slightly cooler morning temperature. Hai made his way over with a younger man in tow. The two men stepped up on the veranda.

Hai introduced the younger man, who looked to be in his late twenties. "This is Khai, from the village of Xayden. He has a message for you from his father."

Dish nodded. "Greetings, Khai. What news do you bring?"

Khai stepped forward, clearly nervous about speaking to Dish. "We have never met, but my father sends his regards. He would have come himself, but he is quite ill. My father owns the building in Xayden in which you store your vehicles, and you have been very kind to him over the years."

"Ah, yes! I know your father—a good man and a loyal friend. I am sorry to hear he has taken ill. I hope it isn't too serious. Tell me, what message does he send?"

"My father received a call from Major Anurat in Thailand. Anurat says three Americans should be arriving in Xayden sometime today. He believes one is the son of your sister, Mai."

Dish sat up and leaned forward. "How is that possible? Why does Anurat believe this nonsense?"

Khai continued.

"Major Anurat is convinced this is your sister's son. The American's name is JD Cordell, and two American Navy SEALS travel with him. This JD was also once a SEAL, but no longer. He is now a civilian. They have a guide, the woman named Hana, who often works with Anurat. You know her. She is the daughter of Rick Hahn, the American who sometimes works for the CIA.

Dish sat back on the bench and leaned against the wall of the longhouse. Rarely caught off-guard, he was now astounded.

"The American says he is here to rescue his mother from Trần," Khai added.

Dish shook his head in disbelief. "How can this be true?"

"The American," the young man continued, "this JD Cordell... his middle name is Dish."

Dish invited Khai to stay the night in his village.

"I appreciate your delivering this message for your father. It is a long walk. Rest today. We can make you comfortable. You can return to Xayden in the morning."

Khai shook his head. "Thank you, but I must start back. My father is very ill and will not live long. I will be fine." Khai paused. "I wanted to thank you personally for all you have done for our family over the years. We owe you much."

Dish shook his head. "You owe me nothing. I pay a fair price to rent your father's building in Xayden. If there ever was any debt, your family repaid it with your friendship and loyalty. It is I who am grateful to you for this information about the Americans." Dish paused, remembering something he'd thought about the night before. "There is one thing. I would like to have a map of the old Michelin plantation north of Ho Chi Minh City. Do you think there is one in Xayden?"

Khai considered this. "There is a man in Xayden, a scholar who collects books and maps. I am sure he would have such a map. When I get back, I will see what he has."

Is there anything I can do for your father?" Dish asked.

Khai shook his head.

Dish accepted that. "I have been deeply honored by our years of friendship. Tell your father I will come to see him tomorrow night. If such a map is available, perhaps I could get it at that time?"

Khai bowed. "If a map is available, I will have it when you come. If we can be of any other assistance, ask."

"You have done enough," Dish replied. "Be safe on your journey." He paused. " Wait, Khai. If you do meet these Americans, tell them I will find them on the trail. If my sister's son is coming here, it would be better to work together."

Once Khai had left, Dish turned to Hai. "Gather five of our men. We will go to meet this JD Cordell on the trail. If this is true, if he is Mai's son, they will need to come here."

Dish had never worked with U.S. Navy SEALS, but almost nearly everyone on the planet knew of them. However, he'd worked with many Special Forces teams in years past, and these men would be a significant asset on any rescue mission. It would be much better to join forces and work together to rescue Mai from Trần.

And, thought Dish, *if this is indeed true, it will be interesting to meet this man.*

Trần sat alone at the long table in the dining room. He was enjoying the meal the cook had prepared for him. The roast duck was one of his favorites. Good food was one of the colonel's chief pleasures in life.

Suddenly, he frowned, hearing a knock at the door. He hated being disturbed at dinner.

It'd better be important.

"Enter," Trần

Huỳnh stepped into the dining room. "We have word from Fong. Our spies report there is some talk among the Jarai that this Montagnard, Dish, is coming to Ho Chi Minh City in the next few days. They have heard some talking about getting a chance to see him, others are speculating about why he is coming."

Trần sat back in his chair. "He has my opium. I suspect he thinks he can trade it for the Vietnamese woman upstairs; his adopted sister." Dish almost spat those last words out. "He will try to contact us. I will not make the trade. I have plans for the woman. But he cannot know that." Trần paused to take a sip of tea. "You will set up a meeting, and we will collect our opium. But, Huỳnh, I want this Dish taken alive. The woman will watch him die slowly. See to it."

Huỳnh nodded.

Trần stood, a wicked smile on his face. "This is an excellent new development. I must inform our guest upstairs about this news."

CHAPTER 38
VIETNAM

The drive to Xayden was uneventful. Pallie drove with Hana riding shotgun, giving directions where needed. JD and Vivas sat in back while Ajax settled himself comfortably on the pile of gear, now covered with blankets in the back of the van.

Most of the eight-hour drive passed by with good-natured joking and the swapping of increasingly outrageous war stories. Hana enjoyed listening to the interactions between the three Americans. She'd grown to be quite fond of each of them.

"Carlos told me you are an excellent martial artist," Hana offered during a lull in the conversation. "He said, and I quote, 'There's no bullshit in what JD does, it's some serious shit.'"

JD glanced over at Vivas, who suddenly was very concerned with what was transpiring in the empty rice paddy he could see from the van window.

"Oh, he did, did he?" JD responded, laughing. "Did he also tell you how much he likes to play with knives?"

Hana glanced at Vivas, who merely shrugged.

"No, somehow he failed to mention that. But tell me, JD, what is the difference? I have done Muay Thai for several years. It's pretty good, I think."

JD nodded. "Yep. It's damn brutal. You've got to be tough to practice Muay Thai, that's for sure. The difference is really in your focus."

"How so?" Hana asked.

"As brutal as it is, you step into a ring, you have rules. It's a sport. There are certain things you are not allowed to do."

"I see," Hana responded. "And you have no rules?"

JD smiled. "I have lots of rules." He paused. "But, when it comes to life and death combat, there are no rules, especially when the lives of others depend on you."

"I understand that," Hana agreed. "But I am not sure I understand the focus difference you're talking about."

JD thought for a few seconds before continuing. "When I was training in the dojo, one evening, we had visitors. I think I was about seventeen at the time. Anyway, one of the visitors was a mixed martial arts fighter, clearly tough as nails. Somehow, he'd heard about my Sensei, Tokumura, and wanted to find out what was so special compared to most of the karate he'd seen. The guy had a poor opinion of karate."

JD paused, remembering the incident. He went on.

"Tokumura Sensei remained polite and answered the man's questions, but it quickly became clear that he wasn't after answers; he was making a challenge. I guess having his buddies with him made him want to show off a bit. After a while, even Sensei had enough, and asked this jerk if he wanted a lesson."

Pallie, Vivas, and Hana were all interested now. "So, what the fuck happened?" Pallie inquired.

"Well, the guy goes to the changing room and comes back in a couple of minutes wearing his shorts and gloves and walks out to where Sensei is waiting in the center of the dojo floor, just in his gi... no gloves.

The guy asked him, 'What next?' Sensei answered, 'You choose.' So, this fighter begins to circle a bit and throws a few punches and kicks, which Sensei easily deflected or ignored. Then the guy dove for Sensei's left front leg, I guess, in an attempt at a single leg take-down."

"And? What happened?" Hana asked.

"Sensei shifted his leg back and dropped into what we call Shiko-dachi—a horse stance—and dropped his right forearm across the back of the guy's neck. The guy dropped to the floor."

"That's it?" Hana's eyes were open wide.

"That's it," JD replied. "But you have to understand, Sensei's forearm was like a baseball bat. I've seen him work the makiwara, and, I am pretty familiar with what his forearm can do."

"And the dumbass?" Pallie asked, remembering his bruised shoulder.

"Out cold," JD replied. "It was several minutes after his pals dragged him off the floor before he woke up. He was eventually able to leave. I don't remember him coming around again."

"Lucky he wasn't killed," Vivas commented.

"That was not Sensei's focus," JD replied.

Hana looked confused. "I am still not sure I understand."

JD smiled. "The point is that, as big and strong and skilled as that guy might have been, he fought according to certain rules. What Sensei did would have gotten him disqualified in the ring. It would've been against the rules."

"But in life and death, there are no rules," Hana added. "Ah! I think I understand."

There was only minor excitement when they crossed the border into Laos. About thirty minutes from the checkpoint, Hana pulled out her phone. She was soon chattering rapidly in what JD took to be Laotian. Ending the call, she turned back to look at him.

"Everything is set. When we get to the border, relax, and follow my lead. Oh, and be ready to hand me your papers when I ask for them."

JD nodded, deciding to trust Hana.

As they approached the border crossing, Hana gave her three new friends a reassuring smile. "Act natural. Leave this to me. Remember, I employ you three; security at Obsession."

Vivas grinned. "Better tell Pallie not to act naturally then! We'd be screwed, for sure."

"Screw you, goombah," Pallie retorted.

"There you go again, mano. I'm Puerto Rican, not Italian."

JD laughed. "Cool it, guys. Just follow Hana's lead and try to look like muscle for hire. Shouldn't be too hard."

Approaching the barrier, Pallie rolled the window down. The border guard approached and rattled off a string of questions in Laotian. Pallie merely shrugged and looked over at Hana, who leaned toward the driver-side window and let forth with a blistering barrage of what sounded like angry Thai.

Undeterred, the border guard repeated his requests. Hana turned to the men with her and, speaking in authoritative English, said: "hand me your papers now, please."

The three dug into their jacket pockets and produced the papers she'd provided them earlier. Hana collected the documents from JD and Vivas, handing them to Pallie with hers and indicated he should present them to the border guard.

Taking the papers from Pallie, the border guard gave each set a cursory look and handed them back to Pallie. Directing his attention to Hana, he issued what sounded like a series of questions. Hana testily responded as if annoyed by the unnecessary waste of time. Finally satisfied, the man turned toward the guardhouse and gave a command. The barrier began to rise. The guard grunted at Pallie and waved him on. They were now in Laos.

"What just happened?" Pallie asked as soon as the border crossing was safely behind them.

"Yes! That went well," JD added with a smile.

Hana shrugged her shoulders. "The commander of the border guard is a regular customer at Obsession. The call I made before we got to the border was to him."

Vivas looked at Hana, an amazed expression on his face. "What if he hadn't taken the call?"

Hana laughed. "He always takes my calls. He'd be foolish not to. At worst, we would have had to pull over a few minutes until he could return my call."

"It looked to me like the border guard was fairly curious about us," JD interjected. "What did you tell him?"

"I told him that I was tired of hiring pussies as security guards and that American mercenaries were much, much better. I also told him that if he didn't want to find out why he should get the damned barrier up."

Pallie laughed. "I'll be damned."

"Well, it sure worked," Vivas observed. "I wouldn't have tried that."

Hana smiled. "That's because you don't understand Asian culture like I do, Carlos."

JD smiled. That was the second time he'd heard Hana use Vivas' given name. *What's that all about?*

The remainder of the drive passed quietly, with one short stop to stretch their legs and let Ajax water a few shrubs. Pallie seemed to enjoy driving and refused to share the wheel with anyone else. JD slept off and on, occasionally waking to find Hana and Vivas chatting away about nothing in particular, just having a good time. It seemed like no time at all before Hana announced they were approaching Xayden.

Hana directed Pallie. "Turn left up here at the next alley. We will pass through a gate into a courtyard. The guard knows me and will open the gate. Across the courtyard will be a larger building. We'll stop there." She turned to JD in the back seat. "This is where Dish stores his vehicles for his trips to Sisaket. He has several old Land Rovers, among other things in this old warehouse. We are in friendly territory here."

JD nodded. Pallie pulled the van up to the gate. A guard, armed with what looked to Pallie like an old Mossberg 12-gauge pump shotgun, approached the driver's side from an open doorway. Hana leaned over and called out through the driver's side window to the guard. Recognizing Hana, the guard nodded and opened the gate, waiving the van through. Pallie guided the vehicle to a spot near a large wooden garage-style door with a smaller access door next to it and killed the engine. Hana jumped out of the van.

JD got out a bit more cautiously, scanning the courtyard for signs of trouble. Pallie, Vivas, and Ajax soon followed suit. It had been a long ride, and it felt good to walk around and limber up the muscles. The smaller door opened, and a man approached slowly. He smiled when he recognized Hana, but there was something odd, almost sad, about his smile.

"Saibaidee." The man greeted Hana.

Hana returned the greeting and turned to JD. "This is Khai. His father owns this building and has worked with Dish for many years. Give me a few minutes to explain the situation to him."

JD nodded. He, Vivas, and Pallie began to dig through the cargo in the back of the van. JD planned to move out toward the border region as soon as they could get ready. Ajax explored the courtyard, never straying too far from his teammates.

Hana and Khai conversed quietly for several minutes. As the SEALs approached, they were surprised to see Hana give Khai a heartfelt hug. When she turned back to the three men, there were tears in her eyes.

"What's wrong?" Vivas inquired, moving closer to Hana. He stopped short of putting his arm around her, but his concern did not go unnoticed by JD or Pallie.

"Khai's father is very sick. The doctor says he may not last the night, a day or two at most. It is stomach cancer."

"Tell Khai we are very sorry to hear that," JD responded. "Please extend our condolences." Hana nodded and spoke again to Khai, who nodded to the three Americans.

"Khai just returned from Dish's village a little while ago. Dish knows we are coming and told Khai to tell us he will meet us on the trail. Khai said he would drive us as far as he can in the van, and then bring it back here to store until we return."

"Tell Khai that's not necessary. We can leave the van and hump it from here. He should be here for his father."

Hana shook her head. "He will not do that. It is only a few kilometers outside the city to the trail we will follow." Hana smiled at JD. "And, it will get us out of Xayden more discretely than marching through town in full combat gear. Besides, he feels it is a matter of honor. You should understand that."

JD nodded. "I understand that. I figured we could wait until after dark, but you are right about it being much more discreet. Tell Khai we thank him, and we will leave as soon as everything is ready."

"I will tell him." Hana walked over to where Khai stood waiting.

Vivas approached JD. "I've been thinking. Maybe we should leave the LAW rockets and grenades behind. They'd sure be nice to have, but I can't see too many other travelers running around with them, even if they are bandits or outlaws. I don't think our cover as security for Hana would explain them either. It could make us a target."

JD considered this for a minute. "I agree. We can leave them with the van if Khai has no objection. And, I am sure Major Anurat will be happy to get them back. Good thinking, Vivas."

CHAPTER 39
VIETNAM

Three men, a young woman, and a dog climbed steadily upward into the mountains. JD figured they were not too far from the border between Laos and Vietnam. The trail, now used by very few, mostly smugglers and perhaps a few gutsy old-timers, was rugged. Despite the elevation, it was hot.

While the days spent in Bangkok and traveling to Xayden had helped the men get acclimated, the climb into the mountains soon had JD sweating. Hana seemed relatively unaffected. Aside from the weapons they carried, and maybe Ajax's K9 Storm Intruder harness, they could easily have been mistaken for a group of hikers.

JD led the way with Ajax. Hana followed, then Vivas. Pallie brought up the rear, keeping a watchful eye on their back trail. Taking quick stops every hour or so, mostly to replenish lost fluids, they were making good time. JD knew it was about twenty kilometers to the area in which Dish was known to operate. Hana had never actually been to the little village on the rock shelf but knew it existed. JD lifted his left hand, bringing the small group to a halt.

"Let's take ten."

They moved into a small clearing just off the trail. Pallie shifted the sling for his M-27 IAR and reached for his canteen. Mopping his brow with the back of his hand, Vivas then reached for his. Hana squatted in the shade of a tree, scratching Ajax behind the ears. All four traveled lightly, mostly carrying water, power bars, and of course, ammunition. JD had also packed what was left of Ajax's dog food, enough for four days if they were careful. After that, he'd have to find something else to feed the dog. He doubted the local Vietnamese village stores would carry Ajax's favorite brand.

"I estimate we are very close to the border if we haven't already crossed it," JD spoke softly.

Hana nodded. There were no border markers where they were traveling.

"If my uncle is going to meet us on the trail, I figure it should be any time now," JD added. "I suspect he'll have some of his men with him, but we have no way of knowing for sure."

Vivas nodded and took a swallow from his canteen before he spoke. "We could also run into some folks we don't want to meet. How will we know?"

"We won't until we meet. It's going to be tricky. I think it'd be better to avoid trouble if we can, even if it is with drug smugglers."

Hana spoke up. "I will know the drug smugglers."

Vivas looked over at Hana. "How?"

She wrinkled her nose. "They stink. That's how."

Pallie chuckled softly at that. "Great. Hana can be our early warning system."

"We still have to be close enough to smell them," JD added. "We'll move out in five more minutes."

A moment later, Ajax stood abruptly, focusing his eyes and nose up the trail in the direction they were traveling. His low warning growl caught everyone's attention.

"Someone's coming down the trail," JD whispered. "Ajax, zit!" Ajax sat, but remained focused on the trail. JD shifted to cover the path. "Pallie, watch our back."

Pallie nodded and disappeared into the dense foliage. Vivas shifted to a better position, to cover the trail. Hana stood, placing her hand on Ajax's back, reassuring the dog while her right hand rested on the MP-4 slung from her right shoulder.

"Don't shoot unless I do," JD ordered. Neither Vivas or Hana questioned that; they just nodded their understanding. Quietly, they waited.

A moment later, they could hear voices approaching from up the trail, speaking Vietnamese.

Hana whispered. "Drug smugglers."

Vivas sniffed the air, and to his surprise, found that he could smell something. It was unpleasant, dirty, clammy, and there was something else.

Maybe the opium? Vivas thought.

A few seconds later, a group of seven men came into view on the trail. The men were dirty and ill-kept. They were also heavily armed.

Drug smugglers, JD agreed. Hana had been right. Vivas stood and nonchalantly brought his MP-4, still slung over his shoulder, around to bear on the approaching men. His thumb flicked the selector switch to burst mode, and his forefinger moved to register, near the trigger.

Finally, spotting JD and his team in the clearing, the approaching men moved closer, spreading themselves out along the trail. One particularly nasty looking man stepped forward and stopped about six paces from JD, then started yelling in angry Vietnamese.

"He says we're trespassing and wants to know what we're doing here," Hana translated.

Hearing Hana's voice, the man looked over, spotting her standing next to Ajax. He shifted his eyes to the dog for a second, then back to Hana. His red eyes grew wide, and a lascivious grin spread across his dirt-smeared face. The man turned back to his six companions and spoke rapidly. Some of the men laughed. One reached down to scratch at his groin.

"He told his friends that they should kill the two men, take your guns, and eat your dog." She paused. "I won't repeat what he said they should do to me."

Without taking his eyes off the smugglers, Vivas whispered to JD. "Looks like we just stepped in it."

JD nodded. "Sometimes you have to dance in the minefield, and it looks like this is one of them." He paused. "Okay, then. Hana, tell this asshole he and his pals have five seconds to drop their guns before I kill him. His six friends will die, as well."

Hana repeated this loudly so all could hear it. The man in front of JD looked shocked, while some of the other men laughed.

JD spoke sharply. "Ajax, Blijven!"

He strode purposefully toward the Vietnamese drug smuggler who, eyes widening in fear, moved to bring his rifle up. He never completed the movement. JD swung down with his left arm brushing the rifle barrel aside as the two knuckles of his right fist slammed into the smuggler's solar plexus. There was an audible gasp as the man's air left his lungs. Instantly, JD's right hand shot upward, striking the carotid sinus on the left side of the man's throat with the edge of his thumb and index finger. The force of the blow sent the blood stored there rushing up into the drug smuggler's brain, causing him to pass out. Reaching up with his left, he grabbed the hair on the back of the man's head and, stepping back quickly with his left foot, slammed his right palm into the unconscious man's chin, violently snapping his neck around. There was an audible crack as the man dropped to the ground.

The man's six comrades stood there, frozen, shocked by what they had just witnessed. Instantly, Vivas brought his MP-4 to his shoulder and opened fire—controlled three-round bursts at each smuggler. Hana quickly followed, firing her MP-4 as well. In a matter of seconds, all six drug smugglers were down. Ajax, obeying JD's command to 'stay,' had not moved from his spot near Hana.

Vivas moved forward to ensure that each man was no longer a threat, verifying that all six were deceased. JD turned back toward where Hana stood with Ajax and spotted Pallie stepping out of the foliage with a grin on his face.

"Holy shit, JD. What the hell was that? You snapped that man's neck like a freaking twig." He paused. "Oh, and I found some friends of yours in the jungle."

As Pallie stepped forward, six more men followed him out of the jungle and moved to stand on Pallie's right.

Vivas grunted at Pallie. "Did you even fire that thing?" He indicated the M-27 still slung from Pallie's right shoulder.

"Hell," Pallie retorted. "Never got the chance. They were already dead. Besides, you three were directly between them and me."

JD turned his attention to the six men now standing to the right of Pallie. Two were Vietnamese. Four others had a slightly different look to them.

Montagnard, JD thought. *Probably Jarai.* JD knew the Degar people comprised several different tribes. Better kept and cleaner than the drug smugglers, they wore an assortment of light, plain-colored jackets and pants. Five of the six were heavily armed and stood together quietly. One stood to the front. While still an imposing figure, he was much older. The older man wore a holstered Browning semi-automatic pistol at his right hip, and JD spotted a Buck General, still in its original, but well-used black leather sheath, at his left hip. JD walked forward and stopped a few feet in front of the older man.

"You must be my Uncle Dish," he stated calmly.

Dish nodded. "You look like Mai," he replied in a matter-of-fact voice, then added. "You are JD."

JD nodded. Dish stepped forward and, to JD's surprise, hugged him warmly. JD hesitated only an instant before returning the embrace. Stepping back, Dish spoke again.

"It is good to meet. You are a great warrior, like me." Dish indicated the man with the broken neck and his now-deceased companions.

JD shrugged, a bit embarrassed by this statement. Dish glanced down at Ajax, who now sat quietly at JD's left side; his attention focused on the old Montagnard. Ajax was alert but did not seem concerned.

Dish smiled at Ajax. "Number one dog." Dish extended his hand, which Ajax gave a tentative sniff before tolerating a quick pat on the head. "Good dog."

Dish turned and greeted Hana warmly in Vietnamese. Hana responded in kind. Then Dish stepped up to Vivas and then Pallie, offering his hand. Surprised by this, both men shook hands with the old Montagnard warrior.

JD shifted over closer to Hana. "I didn't think Montagnards shook hands," he whispered.

"They typically don't," Hana replied. She spoke to Dish for a moment in Vietnamese. Dish chuckled before replying to Hana, who, with a grin on her face, turned back to JD.

"He said that he learned that from your father."

Introductions completed, Dish made his way back over to where JD was waiting with Hana. He introduced one of his men.

"This is Hai. He will take you to my village." Dish turned to Hana and spoke at length to her before turning and disappearing down the trail.

Hana turned to JD. "Your uncle said that Hai would guide us to their village and make sure we have what we need. He says we should eat and rest. He is going to Xayden to pay his respects to Khai's father and will bring back something to help in Mai's rescue. They will be back before morning." Hana paused. She could see the impatience on JD's face. Seeking to head it off, she continued. "Be patient, JD. Your uncle knows what he's doing. He has survived a long time. Many here have not. He said that tomorrow morning he would listen to what you have to say and lay out his plan to rescue your mother."

Hana could tell JD was not entirely convinced.

"JD," she continued, "he knows the situation better than we do and has already been working on this. Several things are already in motion. You should hear him out."

JD nodded. *Hana is right*, he thought. *Dish knows the layout and this Colonel Trần.*

His instinct was to take charge, but JD realized that their chances for success were much better if he let Dish take the lead. He, Vivas, and Pallie could fill whatever holes might need filling. His gaze swung over to where Pallie and Vivas were helping Hai collect the weapons and ammunition from the dead bodies. After a second, he returned his gaze to Hana.

"You're right, Hana. Please tell Hai we are ready to move out whenever he is."

Before they left, they helped Hai drag the six bodies of the drug smugglers off the trail, tossing them into a narrow but deep ravine that ran down the slope from the track. The bodies were not visible from where they stood.

"They'll get pretty ripe in this heat," Vivas observed.

"Yep! It will stink bad here for a few days," Pallie commented. "Unless tigers eat them."

Hana grunted. "It'd have to be one sick tiger to eat those filthy bodies." JD had to agree.

Gathering up the weapons and ammunition they'd collected, the team followed Hai up the trail with Ajax trotting along at JD's side.

It took about two hours to reach the rock crack that hid access to Dish's little village. Now the hole Dish had stumbled into so many years ago was visible. It had been cleared out and widened to allow easier access when carrying stores and purchases of firearms through it. Of course, now it was guarded around the clock. JD's sharp eyes noticed that the tunnel was wired with explosives and could be sealed if the need were to arise. He was pleased to see that both Pallie and Vivas had noted this as well. Dish's men had cleared the wash, and stairs were cut into the rock, making the climb up to the ledge less difficult.

Hai made sure the three guests were comfortable in the longhouse he shared with his wife. Chanmali ushered Hana over to the longhouse she shared with Dish and introduced her to Jum Y. It was easy enough to prepare one more sleeping mat, and there was plenty of room.

Once everyone settled, the group gathered on the veranda of Dish's longhouse where, with the help of Hana, Hai attempted to fill JD and his companions in on what had transpired thus far. When Hai explained Jum Y's role in helping JD's mother, JD asked Hana to express his sincere gratitude.

"It is nothing," Jum Y replied. "Your mother was so kind and friendly to me ... a business girl. She even bought me dinner. And, she said she would ask Dish to help me, and here I am." Jum Y now had tears running down her cheeks. "I am so glad to be out of Ho Chi Minh City. I didn't want to be a ..." Jum Y paused and, embarrassed, looked down at her feet before going on, "a whore."

Chanmali put her arm around Jum Y's shoulders. "You are not and never were a whore. Your father betrayed you. Now, you will put that behind you and start a new life."

JD caught the look on Hana's face. He could see real pain in her eyes.

"Hana, tell Jum Y that we, all of us here, will do whatever we can to help. She has many friends now."

Hana looked at JD, an odd look on her face, then turned to Jum Y and repeated what he'd said. Then, excusing herself, Hana walked off toward the little pavilion that comprised the center of the small village.

Vivas started to go after her, but JD caught his arm. "Hey Vivas, let me talk to her, just a few minutes."

Vivas glanced back at JD, a questioning look on his face.

"It's okay," JD assured him. "But I think if you give me a minute, I can help."

Vivas nodded and watched as JD, after telling Ajax to stay, headed off after Hana. He found her sitting on a bench under the small roofed pavilion.

"Are you okay?" he asked.

Hana looked up, trying to paste a smile on her face. It didn't work, so she gave up. "No, not really."

"Jum Y's story got to you, didn't it?"

Hana nodded. "I have always made excuses for what I do; that I was somehow helping the ladyboys working in my club." She paused. "But I've been lying to myself. I am no better than any of the pimps in

Ho Chi Minh City. I don't see how you, Pallie, and Vivas can even look at me."

"Can I sit down?" JD asked. Hana nodded. JD sat down on the bench next to her before continuing. "First, we would not be here today without your help. And, if we pull this off, me, my mother, a lot of people, are going to owe you so much."

Hana continued to stare down at the ground, and JD paused, searching for the right words. "I am not a Bible-thumper, but I know what I believe. I'm a sailor, and I've done a lot of things for which many people would be quick to condemn me. But I was raised a Christian, and I do believe in God, and I believe we have a higher purpose."

Hana looked up and turned to face JD, but said nothing.

"The things I've done ... well, let's say I am willing to stand before God and account for them because I believe they were justified or at least done for the right reasons."

JD paused again and put his hand on Hana's shoulder.

"You told me during the drive to Sisaket that the people who work in your club would still be doing what they do, but they'd be doing it somewhere else, somewhere less safe. Was that true?"

Hana nodded.

"And, you hire them as go-go dancers and pay them to dance. Anything else they do is up to them. You look out for them, protect them, keep them off drugs. Is that also true?"

Hana again nodded.

"Then I think they are much better off working for you than out on the streets. And I think things happen for a reason. Just maybe ... God has a plan."

"What are you talking about?" Hana asked.

"You are in a great position to do something good, Hana. You have the connections and many of the resources. And, people willing to help."

"Help with what, JD? What are you talking about?"

"How many girls are there like Jum Y? Or, even ladyboys, for that matter. What if you could find a way to get them on track to a better life."

Hana laughed at that, but JD could tell she was intrigued.

"How could I do that?"

"Think about it, Hana. Your father has connections. You have money, the club, connections in Thailand, Laos, and Vietnam. I'd guess even Cambodia."

Hana nodded. "That's all true."

"So, help girls like Jum Y, those who are willing to do something to help themselves. Get them cleaned up, maybe some basic work skills. I bet you could find sponsors in the U.S. to take them in and help them get started. I will help if I can. Look at it as a natural extension of what you are already doing." JD paused, then laughed. "But ... you might have to give up the gun smuggling."

Hana smiled at that. "But damn, JD. Gun smuggling is so much fun." She paused. "Do you think I could do that?"

"Yes, I do. And, I think I know someone else who'd like to help you."

"Who?"

"Vivas, that's who."

"Why would he help? He has a job. He loves being a SEAL."

"Maybe he does," JD agreed. "But, I think that crazy Puerto Rican loves you even more."

"That's silly," Hana replied. "Don't tease me like that. Why would he love me?"

"Why don't you let him tell you." JD stood and walked off toward the veranda.

Hana sat there for a few minutes, thinking about what JD had said. *Was he right?* She knew men considered her to be pretty, and she certainly had money. Many men had shown interest in her because of her looks and her finances, but she couldn't picture Carlos worrying about such material things. *And what about JD's idea? Could I do that?* She wondered.

She had to admit; it was a great idea. She knew her father would approve. Money was not a problem and with the right connections...?

"Are you alright?" It was Vivas. "I saw you talking to JD. Is everything okay?"

"I'm okay, Carlos. JD was just worried about me ... that thing with Jum Y hit me hard. I had to get away and think a bit, but I'm okay now." Hana paused. At that moment, she made the decision. "I am going to help her start a new life."

"That's great, Hana. I hate seeing lost kids like that." Vivas paused. "I see too much of it, in too many countries; a drawback, I guess, in my line of work. Sometimes I wish I could help, but what can I do?"

Hana smiled, but it was now dark, and Vivas didn't notice. "Well, to start, you could sit down and talk with me."

"Uh, sure." Vivas sat down on the bench next to Hana. "Beautiful night," he offered. "Not so damn hot."

"Yes, it's enjoyable sitting here," Hana replied. "You can see the stars from up here."

"You sure can."

There were a few moments of uncomfortable silence before Vivas spoke again. "I'm glad you're okay, Hana. I was worried when you walked off."

"Worried? Why?"

"I don't know, I just was."

"JD said it's because you're in love with me."

It took Vivas a second to process that. "Why that son-of-a ...!" He paused, then laughed. "You know what, Hana? I think JD might be right about that."

Hana stood up and turned around to face Vivas. He could see the smile on her face in the moonlight.

My god, she is so beautiful, he thought.

Hana held out her hand. "Take a walk with me, Carlos?"

Vivas took her hand and stood. "I'd love to, Hana." He smiled. "Let's just be sure we keep well away from the edge of that cliff."

The next morning, JD, Vivas, Hana, and Pallie were seated with Dish and Hai on the veranda of Dish's longhouse. Several of the younger village children were quite interested in Ajax, and chattered quietly among themselves, pointing at the dog and laughing. Ajax, taking it all in stride, found a comfortable spot to lie down near JD, keeping one eye on the youngsters and the other on his team.

Chanmali, aided by Jum Y, served a breakfast of hot Cháo, rice cakes, and steaming cups of black coffee. Mai had made Cháo for JD when he was a young boy, but he had to admit, Chanmali's version was excellent. Neither Vivas nor Pallie had tried the rice porridge before. They were a bit dubious at first, but both found it to be quite delicious.

During breakfast, JD noticed Hana and Vivas chatting away happily. He smiled to himself. That is great, he thought. The teams would miss Vivas, but he was damn sure Vivas would not be re-upping now. JD tried to remember if Vivas had mentioned how much time he had left in his current commitment. He didn't think it was very long.

For now, though, Vivas, all of them, had to stay frosty. It would not do for one of them to get killed now.

After breakfast, Hana and Chanmali, with Pallie's help, collected the dishes while Jum Y refilled the odd assortment of coffee mugs and canteen cups from a large old tea kettle now used to make boiled coffee. A few minutes later, while Jum Y helped Chanmali clean up, the rest settled on the veranda.

Dish looked over at JD and began to speak. "I will tell you about my plan to rescue your mother." He laid out a map of the old Michelin plantation he'd brought back from Xayden the previous night, as well as several hand-drawn sketches of the house and grounds. Then he paused, looking to Hana. "Please help me make things clear, so there is no question about what I say." Hana nodded, and with her help, he began to lay out his rescue plan.

Dish had modified his plans a bit to take advantage of the arrival of JD and the two other Americans. The idea was simple and direct. They would leave Dak To the next morning in two light cargo trucks. The trucks would travel separately to two different locations, to the north and west of the old plantation house. The sites were on old roads formerly used to access the vast groves of rubber trees on the plantation, a short hike from the house itself.

"The trucks will be ready to pick us up at the plantation house after the attack. I think maybe after ten minutes from when the attack begins," Dish explained.

"What if this Trần is ready for us?" Pallie asked.

"I sent a message to Trần. He should believe I am headed to Ho Chi Minh City to arrange a trade for Mai. I think they will not expect an attack tomorrow night."

"What kind of trade is he expecting?" JD asked.

Dish quickly explained about the opium shipment his men had intercepted, and the message he'd sent to Trần.

"Could we make the trade?" Vivas asked.

Dish shook his head. "The opium is gone... destroyed. Trần wants me dead. He will set up a trade only to kill me." He turned his gaze to JD. "He will not let your mother go either. He will kill her, but I think he will hurt her badly first. I believe she is safe until Trần realizes there will be no trade." He paused. "We must take her back and kill Trần."

JD nodded. Vivas and Pallie indicated they understood as well.

"The position to the north allows for a direct attack on the front of the house. There is a hidden position here," Dish indicated another spot on the map. "One of my people has been hiding there and watching the house for several days. This person also drew the sketches of the grounds and the house layout for me."

"Who is this person?" Pallie asked.

Dish nodded. "The woman's name is Hoa. She worked as a housekeeper for Trần until he beat and raped her. Her older brother is a loyal friend and came to me for help. I agreed to help her. And, I now asked her for help."

"She went back there?" Hana asked, amazed.

"Yes. She wants Trần dead." He continued. "Here is a second hidden position." Dish indicated another spot on his map. "This is farther back from the house, maybe eight hundred yards. From this spot is an excellent view through the large windows to the room Mai is in. Hoa has arranged for one of the other housekeepers to pass a note to Mai tomorrow." He glanced at JD. "The note will tell your mother to leave her lights on tomorrow night and, when the shooting starts, to lie down in this corner." Dish pointed to the outer left corner of the room. "That way, anyone entering the room or trying to reach Mai must pass in front of these windows. A good man with a rifle in this location can shoot anyone trying to get to your mother."

According to the plan, JD, Pallie, and Vivas, with five of Dish's men, would travel by truck to the northern location while Dish and eight others would proceed to the point west of the plantation house. Each team would then move to the areas Dish had indicated on the map.

JD considered this. "We don't have a suitable rifle for long-range shots like that. Just our MP-4s. At that range, it would be a challenging shot."

Dish looked at JD. "I have such a rifle. You can see it. It will work well."

JD nodded. "If that's the case, how about you, Pallie. You're our heavy weapons guy and a pretty good shot.

Pallie shook his head. "Needs to be you, JD."

"No way. I'm going in."

"I agree with Pallie," Vivas cut in. "I understand your wanting to go in. It's your mother. But you will have to trust Pallie and me to get her out. You're our best sniper, JD, and better trained for that kind of shooting. Your mother needs you on that rifle."

JD thought quickly. Vivas was right. He didn't like it, but JD had to admit it made the best tactical sense. He had no choice but to agree.

"Okay. But you guys take Ajax in with you."

Vivas nodded.

"Absolutely," Pallie added.

"Good," Dish stated. "At the chosen time, my group will begin our assault on the house from the west, to draw their attention. Wait just long enough for Trần's men to move to fight us, then you hit the house hard and fast, and get Mai out of there."

Dish indicated a man who had been sitting quietly in the background. "This is Poh." Poh nodded. "He's a good man, killed many VC in the war, and speaks good English. He and four others will go with you. They will follow your orders and can go in with you or cover your withdrawal. You decide."

"Thank you, Poh," JD nodded to him. "We appreciate your help. I would suggest we start the assault at 0300 hours. Many will be asleep, and their bodies will be in a low state of readiness. It will take time for them to adjust, even after they're awake."

Dish nodded. "That is good."

JD turned back to his uncle. "How do we coordinate in real-time? We don't have any of our usual communication equipment with us."

"I have several small radios. One for you, one for each team, a few extra if we need." Dish looked around at everyone present. "Once JD sees everything is okay, and Mai has the light on in the room, he will say when we go.

When Dish had completed laying out his plan, all three SEALs were impressed. There was a bit of discussion to clear up minor points here and there, but it was a solid plan.

"Once we're on-site and can see what we're up against, we can make any needed minor adjustments," JD commented. He turned to Vivas. "Ajax will take you straight to my mother. It's up to you, but I'd have Pallie cover your back with the M-27 and some help from a few others on your team. They can secure your way out while you, Ajax, and..." he glanced over at Poh, "... maybe Poh, get her out of that room."

Poh nodded.

Pallie looked from JD to Vivas. "Don't worry. I'll have you covered."

Vivas nodded. "Of course. One question... I know Ajax is a hell of a dog, but how will he know where your mother is?"

"Don't worry," JD replied. "I've got that covered."

When the discussion ended and the gathering started to break up, Vivas leaned over to Pallie. "No wonder the commies hated JD's uncle so much. He'd be one tough adversary; knows his shit. I bet he was one bad dude during the war."

Pallie nodded. "Sure enough. I'd say he still is." He paused, then added, "It's a solid plan. I wonder what kind of rifle he has for JD to use. Hopefully, not some old Chinese piece of crap."

"We shall see."

Spotting Hana talking to Chanmali near the end of the veranda, Vivas said, "Excuse me," and headed off in her direction. Pallie just grinned.

"Come with me, JD," Dish called as soon as the group dispersed. He led the way into his longhouse. In the back, a bench stood against a section of the wall. Dish lifted the cover from a long wooden crate sitting on the bench and indicated that JD should look in the container. JD approached and peered in, discovering it held a Barrett M107 .50 caliber, recoil-operated, semi-automatic sniper rifle. JD could tell it had been sitting for a while, but it looked well maintained. In the crate with the Barrett were three 10-round magazines. However, for proper functioning, eight or nine rounds were the preferred load. Then he spotted something wrapped in a clean cloth rag, in another corner of the crate. Lifting it out of the box, JD unwrapped the cloth to reveal a well-used but functional AN/PVS-10 Sniper Night Sight. He grinned.

"This rifle good?" Dish asked.

JD nodded, turning to his uncle. "This rifle is perfect. I will need to test fire it."

"Tomorrow morning, I take you to a place to test. Long shot ... like at the plantation house." Dish pointed to metal ammo cans on the floor under the bench. "I have maybe one hundred rounds for this rifle. Is it enough?"

"That would be great, and that should be plenty of ammunition for the rescue mission as well as any test firing. Shouldn't take more than six or nine rounds, unless there is a problem."

"No problems. I shoot once ... but some time ago." Dish paused. "Your mother will be okay."

JD nodded.

"It is good to meet my American family," Dish continued. "Your father?"

"He got sick and died a few months ago. Liver cancer."

"I am sorry to hear this. Good man."

"Yes, he was. He always told us you were a good man too."

There was a brief silence.

Dish smiled. "Your Nguyen-Ryu very good. I see on the trail."

JD decided not to mention the blend of Isshin-ryu and Nguyen-Ryu, not being sure he could explain adequately without Hana's help. "Thank you."

"Your father teaches?"

JD laughed. "He tried. Mostly, it was my mother."

Dish grinned at this. "Mai is excellent. Almost as good as me."

JD smiled. "Mom always said the same thing. She said you were good, but she was better."

Dish laughed. "Maybe so."

"You have a brother... sister?" Dish asked.

"A sister, Annie. She is married and has two little boys."

"And you have a woman?"

JD nodded. "I have a woman. Her name is Ellen."

Dish nodded. "It is good. Now, we rest. Tomorrow a busy day."

"Yes. Tomorrow is a busy day."

CHAPTER 40
VIETNAM

It was barely light when Dish led JD to a long hollow between two ridges, where JD could test the M107 rifle. Vivas, Hana, Poh, and Ajax came along to watch. Pallie decided to stay in the village and clean the M-27 IAR.

"Hell, I know JD can shoot. I want to make sure the 27 will be there when we need it," Pallie stated.

Dish carried a piece of cardboard with a three-inch black circle painted on it to use as a target. "You see on map, a position a few hundred yards from the house. Hoa has been hiding there to watch," Dish explained. "But I think it is too close to be a good position from which to shoot. Too easy for Trần's man to find. You use the other position, maybe 800 yards from the house. It is better, I think."

JD agreed. He paced off the 800 yards himself, setting the target. The M107 could reach out and touch someone much farther than that with a maximum range of 7,450 yards, but that was unnecessary for tonight's work. It took six rounds for JD to zero the Barrett. Three to establish a solid shot group, after which he adjusted the windage and elevation. The next three rounds made one large hole that obliterated the center of the black painted circle on the cardboard.

Poh nodded at JD. He was impressed.

"Wow," exclaimed Hana. "That's good shooting."

"Yep," Vivas replied. "That's why JD needs to be the one doing it."

From there, things moved fast. At 0800, Dish led the three SEALs, followed by fourteen of the men from his village, into the jungle. He set a fast pace. It was a bit of a trek, a little over fifteen kilometers to the location on a dirt track just west of Dak To, where they would meet the two light cargo trucks.

Just before they moved out, JD overheard Hana talking to Vivas, who'd expressed concern about Hana's situation if anything were to happen to him. It gratified JD to hear her admonish Vivas, saying, "Carlos, I can take care of myself. Don't worry about me. You need to focus on the mission. That's the best way to make sure you get back to me in one piece."

JD nodded his head, thinking of Ellen. He knew Hana was right. He knew Vivas knew it as well; however, it did not hurt to get an occasional reminder.

One hour and twenty minutes later, the two teams were in their trucks, trying to make themselves comfortable for the twelve-hour ride to their respective drop-off points near the old Michelin plantation. As the vehicle traveled along dirt roads surrounded by rice paddies and the sounds and smells of rural Vietnam, JD's thoughts turned to his mother. *I sure hope she's okay.*

JD knew his mother was a strong and capable woman, but she had to be terrified. He hoped his uncle was right in believing that Trần would not dare harm her until he had Dish out of the way. It made sense. If Trần were to hurt Mai and Dish were to hear of it, there would be no trade. It would be open season on the drug lord and his men. Trần knew that. He also knew from the war that Dish was a deadly enemy.

Even so, JD couldn't help thinking of what she must be going through, taken, and held hostage by thugs. He wished she had waited and let him come with her to Vietnam, but it was futile to think that now.

As if he was reading JD's mind, Vivas spoke quietly. "She'll be okay."

JD nodded. It was the only way he could see it.

Hoa waited for ten minutes near the latrine used by the women employed by Trần. The housekeeper, Bian, did not appear. Scared, Hoa was uncertain what to do next. She was sure Bian would not betray her.

Something must have happened, Hoa thought, fingering the folded slip of paper hidden in the pocket of her pants.

She hesitated only a few more seconds, then Hoa took a step away from the latrine and toward the plantation house.

"Hoa?" A familiar voice called her name from somewhere to her left. She froze. A man stepped out from behind a tree a few yards off, zipping his fly as he did. "What are you doing here?"

It was Long, one of Huỳnh's security team. Hoa knew Long liked her, at least until that animal, Trần, had beaten and raped her. Long had spoken to her several times, making his interest known. Hoa thought fast. She'd gently rebuffed his previous advances. Did he still like her? He would know what Trần did to her; that she was now damaged goods.

"I was looking for Bian," Hoa replied. "I wanted to talk to her about maybe getting my job back... to see if she thought it was possible."

Hoa waited. *Would he fall for it?*

"After what the boss did? Why would you do that?" Long asked. Hoa could hear the shock and amazement in his voice.

"What else can I do? He ruined me. Who would take me?" Hoa paused. "The boss had his fun with me. I think maybe he would leave me alone now. I need to make a living. How else can I survive?"

Long looked down at the ground. "I would take you, Hoa." He looked back up at her. "We could leave here. We could go to Laos or Thailand. I have saved money. We could start over together."

Hoa caught her breath. She'd not expected that. "You would still take me, Long? After what the boss did?"

Long nodded. "I would. I am in love with you, Hoa. But, I think, maybe," he paused, "you feel differently."

Shocked, Hoa searched for something to say. Finally, she settled on, "I still have to see Bian."

"I saw her going to the house a few minutes ago. She will be there."

Hoa nodded and started toward the house. She stopped and looked back at Long.

"Do you know the foundation between the house and the trees? The old storage building that is gone?"

"I know of it," Long replied.

"Meet me there once everyone settles down for the night. We can talk."

Surprise registered on Long's face; then he smiled. "I will meet you, Hoa."

Hoa reached up and placed her palm gently on Long's cheek. Her touch felt so pleasant to the young man. Then, just as quickly, the sensation was gone as she turned away and continued toward the house. Going around to the kitchen entrance in the back, she listened at the door. Everything was quiet. Hoa opened the door and slipped inside.

Huỳnh, if following his habit, would now be eating dinner with men in the outbuilding converted to sleeping quarters. Hoa hoped this would be the case this evening.

Silently making her way to the back stairway that led from the kitchen to the upstairs hallway and bedrooms, she started up the stairs. Reaching the top, Hoa glanced down the hall. There was nobody in sight; the corridor was quiet and dark. The room Mai was imprisoned in was the last room on the right, near the top of the main staircase. Cautiously, she began to make her way down the hall.

Hoa was nearly at the end of the hall when she heard a loud slap, then a scream coming from the door to her left. It was the master bedroom used by Trần, and the cry, she was sure, sounded like Bian.

The bastard, she thought. Hoa paused, wanting to help Bian but afraid. She realized there was nothing she could do. The door would be locked, and Trần always went armed. The odds were she would get Bian and herself killed. At least, Trần's men would not be loitering around the house. Even they tried to be out of earshot whenever Trần decided to satisfy his sadistic urges. However, Huỳnh would still be returning from dinner soon.

Trying to block the sounds coming from beyond the door, Hoa reached the room Mai was in and slipped the note under the door.

Be strong, Bian, Hoa thought. *You will survive the night.* But, if tonight went as planned, that monster, Trần, would not. Hoa turned and quietly made her way back out of the house and into the night.

Mai sat in the chair in her locked room. While it was comfortable as far as prison cells go, that is what it was. Like Hoa, she was doing her best to block out the sounds coming from across the hall. Mai had no idea who the girl was, but what was happening was plain enough. The screams, the sobbing, the sounds of violence left little to the imagination. She wondered if Trần did this to scare her, a preview of what he had in store for her. The thought didn't frighten her as much as it angered her.

That poor girl, she thought. *This man is indeed an evil monster.* Mai had already decided she would not submit to the same treatment. *He will die, or I will. He will never use me like that.*

There was a slight creak just outside the locked door to her room. Mai only noticed because it coincided with a break between the sobs from the young woman across the hall. Standing, Mai moved closer to the door. When Trần was beating his victims, people typically stayed downstairs. She wondered who it could be?

To her amazement, a folded slip of paper slid in from under the door. Mai stood where she was for a few seconds, then realized whoever had slid the note under the door was now gone. She bent down and picked up the paper, then walked over to the chair and sat down before unfolding it. When she looked down and her eyes focused on the writing, it was in Jarai.

Mai,
Tonight, turn on the lights, then go to the front outside corner and lie down there. No matter what happens, you must stay in that corner.
Dish

Sitting back in the chair, Mai suddenly felt like she could breathe. She was relieved, yet at the same time, terrified. Her brother was coming for her.

It was dark when the truck rolled to a stop. JD checked his watch; twelve hours and seven minutes from when they left Dak To. *Well, the darkness certainly helps*, he thought, slinging the heavy Barrett over his right shoulder. It would make getting into position for the rescue without being discovered a much easier task. The night sky was clear, providing just enough visibility for maneuvering to their assigned positions. After a quick equipment check, JD keyed the handheld radio.

"Heading toward position one." The response came immediately. The receiving radio keyed its mic twice.

Poh took the lead, followed by JD with Ajax on his leash, Vivas, and then Pallie falling in behind. The other four men, chosen by Poh, brought up the rear. It was not hard going. About one kilometer in, the jungle foliage gave way to old rubber tree groves. Poh led the team on for another kilometer before squatting down. The men halted and spread out to cover their immediate area. JD was pleased to see that the men Poh had chosen knew what to do and did it without hesitation. Poh waved JD forward.

JD moved up to where Poh waited.

"You see hill?" Poh asked, pointing to a small hill just visible about seventy-five meters to their front and left.

JD nodded.

"You shoot there."

JD understood. Looking back, he waved Vivas forward. Vivas crouched down beside JD, who handed him Ajax's leash.

"Take Ajax with you."

"I don't know all the commands."

JD reached inside his jacket and pulled out a sealed ziplock bag. "You'll only need one command."

"What's this?" Vivas asked as JD handed him the bag.

"One of my mother's old blouses. I brought it from home and kept it sealed in this bag the whole time. When the shooting starts, let him smell the shirt for a few seconds and give the command 'Zoeken.' Just hold on to the leash. Ajax knows what to do. Trust him." JD paused to pat Ajax on the head. "Let him off-leash just before you enter the house."

Vivas nodded. "Got it."

JD gave Ajax one more pat on the head. "You're going with Vivas, old buddy!" He gave the command, "Blijven," and pointed at Vivas! Ajax gave a slight whine but stayed put as JD started toward the hill.

Once JD was on his way, Poh led the rest of the team carefully forward toward their initial position, in a grove of trees about forty yards from the house. Maneuvering carefully to avoid detection, it took the team thirty minutes to reach the trees. Once there, they set up a defensive perimeter.

Both Vivas and Pallie nodded their approval. The position provided excellent concealment and offered a complete view of the front of the house. The forty yards could be covered quickly enough by Ajax, Pallie, Vivas, and Poh once Dish's assault team drew the attention of Trần's men. The four remaining team members would provide covering fire on the front of the house from the grove. Pallie checked his watch and signaled Vivas. It was 0230 hours.

JD had no trouble locating an excellent firing position on the higher ground his uncle had indicated on the map. There was no cover, but excellent concealment in the scrub brush covering the little rise.

Uncle Dish certainly knows his stuff, JD thought. The plantation was just visible in the light provided by the moon overhead and looked to be a little less than 800 meters away. In no time, JD had the Barrett with its AN/PVS-10 night sight set up and dialed in on the second-story windows of the room where Tran held his mother. His thoughts turned to her and whether she was alright or not. He quickly shut that down. Tonight, his mother needed him to be the stone-cold professional, not a worried son. Her life depended on it.

Thanks to the sights integrated day/night functionality, he had a clear view of the room through the two windows. The AN/PVS-10 had a maximum range of 600 meters at night and 800 meters in daylight, but with lights on in the room, JD could make the shots. Putting his eye to the sight, he surveyed the situation. He had a direct line of sight on the bedroom door through the window on the right. If his mother positioned herself as Dish had spelled out in the note, in the left front corner, anyone approaching her would pass in front of the left window as well. JD checked his watch. It was 0247 hours. Thirteen minutes until Dish initiated the diversionary attack from the west.

Holding the handheld radio close to his mouth, he keyed the mic and spoke in a whisper, "In position. Bedroom covered. Ready to go."

There was the sound of a mic keying twice, indicating Dish had received the message. A second later, the keying repeated three times. Vivas and Pallie. JD rechecked his watch. It was 0250 hours.

There was a slight sound; someone was approaching. Then a voice whispered.

"Hoa, are you here?"

"Shh!" Hoa answered. "I am here."

Long saw an opening in the old foundation wall and worked his way over to where Hoa sat, waiting. He looked around. Though it was night, he could still make out a great deal in the moonlight. Someone had been hiding in this place for several days.

"How long have you been hiding here?" Long asked, amazed.

"Three days, but I leave after dark and return before dawn."

"But why?"

Hoa looked at Long's face a few seconds before replying, searching for signs of any ulterior motive. Finally, taking a chance, she replied.

"Because after what that bastard did to me, I want him dead. I watch the house for a friend. He is here now. It will all end tonight. Trần will be dead."

"Who do you watch the house for?" Long asked, shocked by her response.

"The brother of the woman Trần has locked in the house. The Montagnard, Dish."

Long shook his head in amazement. "Dish is here?"

Hoa nodded. "He and his men are here to rescue his sister. He will kill Trần." She paused, placing her hand tentatively on Long's shoulder. "He will help us start a new life together. That is if you truly want to be with me."

Long was quick to respond. "Hoa, I do want that. But this is all so crazy. What do we do now? What if Dish fails?"

"Dish will succeed," Hoa replied firmly. "We wait. When it starts, we will go. You must follow me and stay close."

Long wasn't quite sure what to say, so he nodded. Hoa could tell, however, that he was thinking about it.

Then, a moment later, he added, "We will wait, and I will follow."

Dish fished the old pocket watch from his trouser pocket. He rarely carried a watch, but there were times when it was necessary. This night was one of those times. The watch read 2:56 a.m. or 0256 hours. The eight men with him lay concealed in the brush, four on each side. Dish carried his Browning semi-automatic pistol in its old leather holster on his right hip. On his left was the Buck General bowie-style knife JD's father had given him many years ago. While he was not sure of his exact age, he figured he had to be at least seventy. *I am too old to be leading assaults against drug smugglers and kidnappers*, he thought.

Hopefully, this would be the last time this would be necessary. It would be nice to relax and enjoy Chanmali's company for his remaining years. He looked at his watch again. It was 3:00 a.m.

Dish rose from the ground in a crouch and started forward. On each flank, four loyal warriors rose like ghosts from the mist and followed their leader.

From the reports provided by Hoa, Dish knew that Trần posted a minimal guard at his plantation house and that his guards rarely strayed beyond the main house area. They typically stood around near the entrance to their sleeping quarters, smoking. According to Hoa, Trần's head of security, a man named Huỳnh, was reputed to be very tough and by all accounts, a man to be feared.

Fortunately, Dish thought, *not a man big on maintaining discipline.*

That fact became increasingly evident as Dish and his men drew closer to the house and its outbuilding without a challenge. When they reached the first outbuilding, Dish unholstered his Browning and fired a shot into the air. Immediately, his men fired a volley of gunshots in return, designed to startle and draw the attention of Trần's men. It had the desired effect.

Trần sat bolt upright in his bed. *What the hell was that?* Still in his bedclothes and ignoring the sobbing young woman huddled in the corner, Trần strode to his bedroom door and flung it open. Huỳnh was already coming up the stairs.

"What is happening?" Trần demanded.

"We are under attack... the west side of the compound," Huỳnh replied, catching his breath. "My men are holding them back. It looks like about ten attackers."

"It is Dish. He has come for the woman." Trần paused, thinking. "How many men do we have here now?"

"About thirty-five."

"Pull half your men back to the house. This attack may be a diversion. I think others will attempt to grab the woman. I am getting dressed." Trần turned and stormed back into his room.

Huỳnh headed down the hall toward the back stairs, the quickest route to where the firefight was taking place. From the sound of things, his men were now returning fire.

"Get out," Trần growled at the frightened woman in the corner. He went quickly to his wardrobe and began to dress.

Bian wasted no time. Lunging painfully to her feet, she fled through the open door and hurried after Huỳnh, down the hall toward the back stairs. Once she was through the kitchen door, she turned and headed toward the trees, searching for a place to hide.

When the crack of Dish's old Browning BDA .45 shattered the quiet night, Vivas reacted quickly and opened the sealed zip-lock bag he'd been holding. Removing the blouse, he held it to Ajax's nose. Ajax grew visibly excited as he thrust his nose into the bunched shirt. It was clear the dog recognized the scent. Ajax let out an expectant whine.

"Okay, Ajax, old buddy. Good boy!" Vivas placed the blouse back into the bag and stuffed it into the front of his shirt. Slinging his MP-4 over his right shoulder, he glanced over at Pallie, who nodded. He was ready to move.

"Ajax, Zoeken," Vivas commanded, pointing toward the house. The dog started toward the house at a fast trot with Vivas giving him the lead. Pallie and Poh fanned out on either side, each man alert for trouble. It only took a few seconds to cross the forty yards to the front porch. Pallie covered their six, the M-27 IAR moving in concert with his eyes. Poh positioned himself to the right of the door as Vivas prepared to try the handle.

Ajax let out a growl; his attention suddenly focused toward the right side of the house. A guard came around the corner of the house, his AK-47 blazing away. One bullet struck the action of Vivas' MP-4. The rifle took the impact leaving Vivas unhurt, but the bolt was damaged, the carbine now useless except as a club. Two bullets struck Poh, hitting him in the left leg and hip. Immediately, Pallie let loose with the M-27. The man went down under a withering hail of 5.56mm rounds.

"Move!" Pallie yelled. Vivas wasted no time. He stood and kicked down the door, following Ajax into the house with Poh hopping along on one leg right behind him. Pallie backed in through the doorway, eyes searching for any sign of an attacker. Once inside, Vivas helped Poh into a corner and handed him his rifle.

"Poh, can you help Pallie cover this room? "

Poh nodded, his teeth clenched in pain. Vivas gently slapped Poh's shoulder, then turned and removed Ajax's leash. He again gave the command, "Ajax, Zoeken."

CHAPTER 41
VIETNAM

Mai heard the single shot from Dish's Browning semi-automatic, followed by the volley fired by his man as they advanced toward the house. She lay in the corner, following the instructions Dish had written in his note, listening as the sounds of gunfire increased in intensity.

Huỳnh followed the eighteen men he'd ordered back to the house. Reaching their destination, he split the men into two groups, sending nine around to the front.

"Kill anyone you see who is not one of us!" Huỳnh ordered.

The first to round the corner had fired on Vivas and Pallie, hitting Vivas' MP-4 and Poh, before Pallie took him out with the IAR.

Huỳnh led the remaining men in through the kitchen. He would make sure nobody rescued the woman upstairs; she would die first.

Dividing his men into three groups, he sent three to the top of the stairs with orders to stop anyone attempting to gain access to the second floor. Keeping three men with him to cover the hallway, he sent the last three men down the hall to the room Trần had Mai locked in, handing the key to the closest man.

"Nobody gets into that room! If it looks like the attack will succeed, and the woman will get away, kill her. "

All three men nodded before hurrying down the hall. The man with the key inserted it into the lock and flung the door open.

JD, watching through the scope mounted on the Barrett rifle, saw the door swing open and the man stepping into the room. It took a fraction of a second to determine the man was neither Vivas nor Pallie. JD exhaled slowly, paused, and squeezed the Barrett's trigger.

The .50 caliber slug struck the man squarely in the chest, slamming him into the wall across the hall from the open door. Barely feeling the recoil from the .50 caliber rifle, JD kept his eye glued to the scope, looking for another target.

Both Pallie and Vivas heard the report of the Barrett rifle. Pallie tapped Vivas on the shoulder.

"Go, I got you covered here." Pallie dropped to a kneeling position at the base of the stairs, calm and steady, the barrel of his M-27 continuously sweeping the front entrance and first-floor hallway to his left. The corner of his eye caught movement, the barrel swung back, and his finger gently squeezed as two men carrying Ak-47s burst through the door. Poh, too, opened fire from his corner. Both men ran into a wall of 5.56 mm bullets and dropped to the floor. Pallie looked over at Poh, giving him a thumbs up. Poh nodded.

"Go, Vivas!" Pallie repeated.

Ajax started up the stairs with Vivas right behind him, then froze, his tail down and wagging. The dog gave a low growl and continued slowly up the stairs, hackles raised.

The low wag, Vivas knew, was Ajax signaling him that there was someone near the top of the stairs. Unholstering the Glock .45 MOS, he continued up the stairs after Ajax.

Huỳnh, enraged, shouted to the two men crouched beside the open door. "Get in there, move fast, kill her!"

Mai, hearing Huỳnh's orders, looked up to see two men rush through the open doorway, keeping low to try and avoid being shot. Eight hundred yards away, JD squeezed the Barrett's trigger a second time. The slug hit the first man in the head, showering the man behind him in a splatter of brains and gore. Diving for the floor, the second man landed between the windows, out of JD's line of sight. Wiping the other man's blood from his face, he started to get up.

Mai, in a mix of fear, anger, and frustration, let out a scream as she jumped to her feet, her eyes darting around the room, searching for a weapon.

Ajax was at the top of the stairs when Mai's scream of rage filled the air. The dog, letting out a loud, ferocious canine roar, cleared the top of the stairs and rounded the corner. Vivas had heard the scream as well.

"Pallie!" he shouted as he followed Ajax up the remaining stairs into the hallway. Pallie turned to Poh, who nodded. He started up the stairs.

Ajax hurtled into the man closest to the top of the stairs, knocking him off his feet. The two other men, shocked at seeing the snarling dog charging directly at them, jumped out of the Ajax's way. Farther down the hall, the men with Huỳnh also saw Ajax and opened fire. One bullet struck Ajax in the chest. As he turned into the room, another shot hit the dog in the rear hip. Neither slowed him down.

Vivas cleared the top of the stairs just as Ajax ran right over the first man. Firing his Glock, he sent two rounds into the first man. The two men who had dived out of Ajax's path reacted, starting to bring their weapons up. Vivas fired two shots at each man, then repeated. Both men dropped to the floor.

Vivas then fired at the men down the hall, who ducked into a doorway. The slide on his .45 locked back. Dropping the magazine from his Glock, he reached for another. Huỳnh's three men, seeing the magazine hit the floor, jumped out with guns raised.

"Hit the floor, you crazy Puerto Rican!" Pallie yelled. Vivas dove for the floor as Pallie sent a storm of lead down the long hallway. All three men fell, each shot to doll-rags.

The man in the room with Mai, now back on his feet, his face covered in blood and brains, grinned as he leveled his Chinese-made SKS at Mai.

"Stupid woman. Now you will die."

Mai faced the man. She had no weapon, and he was too far away. It was over.

Hearing the dog's roar, the man turned just in time to see eighty-seven pounds of canine fury descend upon him. Ajax leaped and seized the would-be killer's right arm in his powerful jaws.

Through the scope, JD saw Ajax charge into the room and leap. He held his breath, waiting for an opportunity to make the shot.

Ajax chomped on the man's arm and dropped his weight, attempting to drag him to the floor. The man resisted and tripped, spinning to his left and, in doing so, came into the view of JD's scope.

Instantly squeezing the trigger, the Barrett fired a third time. The .50 caliber bullet struck the man in the chest, slamming him back into the wall and pulling his arm from Ajax's grip. The man slowly slid down the wall and remained still.

"Ajax?" Mai called. "Is that you?" She did not understand how this could be. "Ajax?"

The dog softly whined.

Mai dropped beside the dog and ran her hand over his head. "Ajax, it is you." Something was wrong. Mai drew her hand back. Warm blood covered her fingers.

"Oh, no! Ajax."

Mai reached around the dog and sitting back, pulled the dog over and into her lap. She bent down to examine the dog's chest. It was bleeding badly.

Ajax shifted his head and sniffed Mai's fingers. He whined softly, licked her fingers twice, and was still.

"Ajax!"

Out in the hallway, Vivas and Pallie heard Mai call the dog's name. Pallie started for the room. Vivas looked up to see Huỳnh coming down the hall. The man appeared to be unarmed at first. Then Vivas noticed a wicked-looking karambit in the man's right hand.

"Pallie, check on JD's mom. I've got this."

The sound of gunfire was becoming less frequent. Hoa nodded to Long. "It is time to go. We must get to the house. The trucks will be coming. Stay close to me; we must be cautious."

Long nodded and followed Hoa out from the concealment of the old stone foundation. Keeping low, the two made their way toward the house.

Huỳnh did not care for guns. He preferred a more intimate instrument of death and was very good with his little hooked blade. Now, driven past sense or reason by this turn of events, Huỳnh's only thought was to cut this man in the hall to ribbons; and the man's gun was empty.

Vivas dropped his Glock and slid the Flesheater from its sheath on his right thigh, moving to meet Huỳnh. Huỳnh never slowed down, barreling into Vivas and aiming a low slash at his left leg. Vivas shifted his leg back and countered with a cut down at Huỳnh's shoulder.

Huỳnh nimbly jumped back to avoid the blade, then slashed high at Vivas' face.

Damn, he's quick, Vivas thought, just managing to parry the slash with the edge of his blade, passing Huỳnh's knife to the right and down.

Reversing the cut, the SEAL sliced across at Huỳnh's midsection, slicing the man's shirt and leaving a trail of blood. However, the wound was not deep, and it did not slow Huỳnh down at all.

Huỳnh faked a thrust toward Vivas' midsection, then deftly flicked the knife to his left hand and slashed upward. Vivas winced as the blade laid open his right cheek. The salty iron taste of blood filled his mouth.

Sonofabitch, Vivas cursed silently. *I need to kill this guy before he hurts me.*

The karambit back in his right hand, Huỳnh shifted back slightly and then darted in, slashing again toward Vivas' midsection. Vivas ignored the knife and, angling the Flesheater's razor-sharp blade, caught Huỳnh's thrusting arm just above the wrist. The Flesheater cut to the bone, fileting skin and flesh from Huỳnh's forearm to his elbow, causing him to drop the karambit to the floor. There was a look of shock on Huỳnh's face as Vivas drew the blade back hard, slicing deep across his chest and abdomen. Reversing the movement once more, Vivas thrust the Flesheater's blade upward and into Huỳnh's throat, then twisting sharply to the left, jerked it free.

Already moving through the door after Pallie, Vivas did not look back as Huỳnh fell to the floor, dead.

"All clear," Vivas called out as he entered the room. He found Pallie standing next to Mai, who was sitting on the floor with Ajax cradled in her lap. Pallie had his hand placed on Mai's shoulder, and Vivas was shocked to see a tear running down the big man's cheek.

Mai looked up as Vivas entered the room. The grief on her face was unmistakable. Ajax was dead.

"He saved my life." Mai was gently stroking the big dog's head. "This is the second time Ajax has done that."

Vivas nodded, understanding. "Ajax was one hell of a SEAL," he said quietly. "When Ajax heard you yell, nothing could have stopped him from getting to you. He knew your voice right away."

Mai nodded, then looked up. "Where's JD?"

"JD's outside." Pallie paused, then added. "He shot the men coming into this room. He wanted to be the first one here, but he's our best sniper. We decided he was the best choice to protect you from anyone before we could get in here."

Vivas pulled the small radio from his pocket and keyed the mic. "Mai Cordell is safe. All clear. We'll meet you out in front."

Vivas offered Mai his hand. "We have to go."

Mai hesitated.

Pallie glanced at the bloody slash on Vivas' right cheek but said nothing.

"I'll bring Ajax," Pallie offered. Standing, he handed Vivas the M-27, then gently lifted the big dog from Mai's lap and turning, headed to the door where he paused, waiting.

Mai took Vivas' extended hand, stood, and followed Vivas to the door. The shooting had stopped.

"Sounds like it's over. But we'd better move carefully," Vivas advised. "We haven't seen any sign of Trần."

Pallie nodded. "My bet is he flew the coop, but you are right. Better keep our eyes peeled."

A voice came over the radio in Vivas' hand.

"The trucks are coming, maybe five minutes. Trần's men are either dead or gone. My men control the area." Mai recognized the voice; it was her brother, Dish.

Dish put the radio back in his pocket and moved off to intercept the lone figure he had observed, making its way toward the tree-line south of the house.

JD, the Barrett rifle still held at the ready, had covered half the distance between his shooting position and the house where his mother waited with Vivas and Pallie. He'd seen both men enter the room, a moment later he'd seen Pallie lift Ajax and head to the door. Then, JD saw his mother step into the view through the window and follow Vivas toward the door. She was safe.

CHAPTER 42
VIETNAM

Trần knew it was time to go. After quickly dressing, he hurried down the back stairs to his office to collect his ledger and the cash he kept on hand. Stuffing the book and money into a leather satchel, he retrieved the Makarov from his desk and shoved the pistol into his belt.

From the diminishing sounds of gunfire, he knew the situation was hopeless. While his men fought back, they were not the battle-hardened Viet Cong fighters he'd led during the war. These men, hired in the bars and brothels of Ho Chi Minh City, were considered by some to be hard men. But they were no match for the men Dish had at his side. Besides, they fought for money, money they could not spend if they were dead. As the firefight continued, Trần's men began to disappear into the night.

He slipped out the kitchen door and hurried to a spot near the tree line south of the house. From there, he could see the situation deteriorate rapidly.

No matter, he thought. *I have my ledger and enough cash to set up again.*

Trần decided he would go to Lai Khe and take a cab to Ho Chi Minh City. This loss was merely a setback.

Dish will pay dearly for this, he swore to himself. *And, that damn woman as well.*

Trần turned and started into the trees.

"Leaving so soon?"

Trần stopped dead in his tracks and turned to see an older man standing there, clearly a Degar. The man held an old Browning loosely in his right hand. It was Dish.

"You have much to atone for, Colonel Trần. My sister's family, my village, so many war crimes and acts of cruelty. And, I understand now that you are also a rapist and an abuser of women."

Trần spat. His eyes darted around, looking for a way out. Licking his dry lips, he finally found his voice.

"You are nothing; you are moi! You are a savage, nothing more."

Dish smiled. "Perhaps I am a savage. But I do not turn our women into prostitutes or poison our young with drugs." He paused. "And, in a few moments, I will still be alive."

Trần's eyes widened. Dropping the satchel, he clawed for the gun he'd shoved into his waistband.

Dish raised his right arm smoothly. The Browning .45 spoke twice. Trần rocked back onto his heels, then collapsed to the ground. There were two bullet holes in his chest, directly over his heart.

Dish stood silent for a moment as if to make sure justice had indeed been served. Then, holstering the Browning, he walked over to where Trần lay and kicked the dead man over with his foot. Dish knelt and examined the satchel, seeing that it contained Trần's account ledger and a great deal of cash. The old Montagnard stood, and without giving the dead man another glance, he turned and walked back toward the plantation house.

Vivas and Pallie were waiting with Mai when JD approached the front porch. Poh had hobbled out and was seated on a bench, his wounded leg stretched out in front of him.

Several of Dish's men had formed a perimeter around the house, and JD could see the two trucks coming down the dirt road toward them.

Slinging the Barrett over his shoulder, JD made his way to his mother, who, kneeling over Ajax, had not seen him approach.

"Mom?"

Mai looked up. "JD!" There were tears on her cheeks as she stood to meet her son. "Oh, God! JD! I am so sorry. Ajax ..." Her voice trailed off.

"It's okay, Mom. It's okay. As long as you're safe." JD embraced his mother, holding her tightly for several long seconds.

"That man was going to kill me," Mai shuddered, remembering the moment she knew she was going to die. "Ajax saved my life… again. He stopped that man."

JD glanced down to where Pallie had laid Ajax as they waited for the trucks. A lump formed in his throat.

"It okay. Ajax was a warrior, a SEAL doing his job. He gave his life to save you. He would have given his life for any of us."

Thank you, partner, JD thought, as he looked back down at his dog again. *Thank you!*

JD turned back to Vivas, noting the slice on his friend's right cheek, and shook his head.

"What happened to you?"

"Cut myself shaving," Vivas replied with a grin. "It'll keep until we're out of here."

"And you, Poh?" JD asked.

"Bullets go through," Poh replied. "No problem. He stopped bleeding," Poh continued, indicating Pallie.

Pallie shrugged. "I had a couple of field dressings in my cargo pocket. Used them to plug the holes."

"My wife fix later," Poh added. "Now, we must go."

Hearing two shots, they all looked at each other.

"Sounds like a .45," Pallie commented.

Vivas glanced over at JD. "Your uncle carried an old Browning 45."

JD nodded. "I have a feeling Trần won't be smuggling drugs anymore."

The two cargo trucks slowed to a stop near the porch. JD knelt next to his dog. Vivas crouched down next to him. "He got hit twice," Vivas explained softly. "Once in the rear hip. The bad one passed through the front leg opening into his chest. He was moving so fast, trying to get to your mother."

JD nodded, seeing the wounds.

"It never slowed Ajax down," Vivas continued. "He heard your mother's yell and charged. It was the damndest thing I've ever seen. He went right through them and took down the guy who was getting ready to shoot her."

JD nodded. "I saw some of it, but the man was out of my view. It was almost like Ajax dragged him back in front of the window so I could get the shot."

JD handed Vivas the Barrett. "Can you grab this?"

Vivas nodded and took the rifle. JD reached down and gently lifted his dog into his arms, then stood.

"Time to load up." JD turned and started toward the first truck.

Dish was approaching the trucks, accompanied by Hoa and another man. He noticed the dog in JD's arms and frowned but said nothing. Walking straight to Mai, Dish embraced his sister warmly. "You are safe? He did not hurt you?"

"No," Mai replied. "I am not hurt. He did not hurt me, but I was terrified." Tears were streaming down his mother's face. "And I am so happy to see you at last."

JD thought he saw a tear in Dish's eye as well.

Finally, Dish broke the embrace and stepped back to place his hands on his sister's shoulders. "You crazy to come here to Vietnam. Too dangerous." Dish paused. "But I too am so happy to see you, little sister."

Mai looked up at Dish's face. "Is Trần dead?"

Dish nodded but said nothing.

"I wanted to kill him," Mai continued looking down at her feet. "He was an evil, horrible, vile man."

Again, Dish nodded. "I understand, Mai. And I believe you would have. But I would not have that man's blood on my sister's hands. You are too good a woman. It is finished." With that, Dish turned and indicated the man and woman who had returned to the trucks with him.

"This is Hoa, and she says this man is with her; that he helped her, and she asks us to take him with us. I have agreed."

JD, still holding Ajax, nodded. "We should get going."

"Yes," Dish agreed.

Dish spoke to two of his men. Handing the satchel he'd taken from Trần's dead body to one of them, the two men quickly headed into the house. Dish then indicated the rest should load up into the trucks.

JD handed Ajax up to Pallie, who'd helped Poh up into the truck bed and then climbed up into the back of the first truck after him. JD then helped his mother into the truck bed and climbed up after her. Reaching back, he took the Barrett back from Vivas, who quickly joined them. Dish's men began loading up into the second truck. Finally, Dish clambered up into the back of the same truck, settling down between Mai and JD.

Once everyone had piled in, JD unbuttoned the left cargo pocket of his jacket and pulled out a small tube of antibiotic gel and a tube of super glue. He tossed them to Vivas.

"This should hold you for now."

Vivas nodded and began to open the antibiotic.

"Let me help." Mai shifted closer to Vivas and, taking the two tubes from him, gently checked the gash in his cheek.

JD spoke quietly to Dish. "What was in the satchel your men took into the house?"

"It was Trần's business books and much money. I told my men to burn it with the house."

"How much money?" Pallie asked, having overheard the conversation. "Maybe you could use it for some good."

Dish shrugged. "It does not matter. I have much money. I would not take money made from poisoning and death of my people."

Pallie nodded. He understood.

A moment later, the two men Dish had sent into the house reappeared and headed toward the back of the second truck. JD looked back as the trucks pulled away, starting down the road toward the main highway. The fire quickly spread, the glow from the burning plantation house lighting up the night sky.

CHAPTER 43
VIETNAM

Once everyone was back at the village on the shelf, Hana had quickly whisked Vivas into Dish's longhouse, to get a better look at the gash on his cheek.

Jum Y greeted Mai with a hug. "I am so happy you are here!" the young woman exclaimed. "And, so happy you are okay."

"So am I, " Mai replied with a tired smile. "Thank you so much for everything you did."

Chanmali came out to greet Mai, then hurried back to see what she could do to help Hana with Vivas. While exhausted from her ordeal, Mai followed along to see if her nursing skills could help.

Two of Dish's men helped Poh out of the truck and, one on each side, supported him as he hobbled toward his longhouse. They were met halfway by Poh's wife, who immediately took charge of the situation.

Pallie helped JD get Ajax's body out of the truck. JD carried the dog over to the little pavilion at the village's center and laid him down on a bench. He gently removed the tactical harness, set it aside, and took a seat beside Ajax's body, his hand gently stroking the dog's head. Looking around, JD spotted Dish talking to Pallie a few yards away. They spoke quietly; he could not hear what was said. Then, Dish nodded his head and walked over to JD, sitting down beside him on the bench.

"It is sad. I knew this was a great dog when we met on the trail." Dish paused. "Your dog saved Mai's... your mother's... life. Your friend told me what happened."

JD nodded. "Yes, Ajax always came through when it counted."

"If you like," Dish continued. "We bury your dog here in village — an honored warrior's grave."

Again, JD nodded. "Thank you, Uncle. I think Ajax would like that."

Everyone was dead tired, but sleep did not come to any of them quickly. There was much to do.

Vivas' cheek, now thoroughly cleaned and bandaged, was going to be okay. The superglue had worked well; however, the wound would leave a significant scar. Hana joked that it would give him a roguish flair.

JD had spoken to Hoa with some translation help from Hana, thanking her for the role she played in saving his mother.

"I was happy to do it," she replied, as Hana translated. "That bastard was evil. I wanted him dead, and now it is so. Many Vietnamese girls will be happy." Hoa began to turn to go, then stopped. "I am glad your mother is okay."

Hoa wandered off in search of Long, who had been trying to make himself useful.

Hana stepped closer to JD. "I'm so sorry about Ajax. He was a great dog, and I got pretty attached to him myself over these last few days. But you have your mother back because of what he did. Never forget that."

JD nodded. "I know that. Thank you, Hana. You are right."

Hana paused a moment, watching the various people going about their tasks, then continued.

"I thought about what you said the other day; about these girls, and the people in my club. I talked to your mother, too. She is an amazing woman. We are going to help Jum Y get to America. Your mother told me that she also met a relative, a young woman named Xuan, who is the daughter of her cousin. Xuan also wants to go to America, and your mother thinks Xuan's father will support the idea. We're going to help these two first."

Hana looked happy. JD could see she was excited about the prospect.

"It's a place to start," she finally added.

"It is indeed," JD replied. "I'm happy for you, Hana. What about

Vivas? Is he going to help?"

Hana smiled. "He is! Carlos must finish his term of service. He has a little over four months left. Then he is coming to Thailand to help. We are getting married." As she said this, Hana couldn't contain the joy on her face. Her smile made her glow.

JD smiled too. "That's so great. I'm happy for both of you."

Hana placed her hand on JD's cheek. "Thank you, JD. For everything you did."

"I didn't do anything," he protested.

"Yes. Yes, you did," Hana insisted. "You showed me what I couldn't see, even though it was right in front of me. I have Carlos, and I have a new life. That is because of you."

Hana leaned over and kissed JD's cheek. Then, without another word, she turned and walked off.

The sun was pleasantly warm the next morning, absent the typical early fog. Mai found JD standing near the edge of the ledge, looking out over the wild expanse of the rugged border region.

"It's beautiful, isn't it," Mai commented.

JD looked up. "Yes, it is."

"Did you sleep okay, JD?"

"Not really. I was pretty wound up last night, a lot on my mind."

Mai nodded. "Dish told me last night that he will bury Ajax here in the village."

"Yes," JD replied. "I told him I think Ajax would like that."

"I think he would, at that," Mai agreed. "I am so sorry about what happened. I know how much you loved that dog."

"It's okay, Mom. He was a SEAL, as much as any of us. Ajax did his job. And, like Hana said last night, I still have my mother because of what he did."

Mai said nothing for a moment, then continued. "I like Hana. I am going to help her with her plans. I owe Jum Y my life, and I met a family member, Xuan, who wants to come to America. She is my cousin's daughter. I met them when visiting my father's old village. It has changed a lot."

"That must have been nice. Meeting distant family like that, after what happened before."

"It was..." Mai then let out a long sigh. "Dish will not come to America. He and Chanmali are going to move to Thailand and help

Hana as well. Hana offered him a job, and he can use his many connections to help her succeed." She paused. "I guess it is for the best. This is his world."

"I think you're right, Mom. I'm not sure Uncle Dish would be happy in America now." JD smiled. "Vivas is going to help Hana, too."

His mother laughed. "I am not surprised. He is head-over-heels in love with her."

JD joined in, laughing too. "Yep. He sure is."

"Chanmali has breakfast almost ready. I guess we will start the hike back to Xayden after we eat?"

JD nodded. "I think we should. I want to get back to where I can give Ellen a call, and I'm sure Annie will be greatly relieved to hear from you, Mom."

"Yes, you need to call Ellen, and I will call Annie. Don't be too long. We don't want the food to get cold."

Mai turned and headed back to help Chanmali get breakfast on the table.

Dish, who had been keeping his distance, saw Mai head back toward the longhouse. He picked up the object sitting beside him on the bench and walked over to JD.

"You leave for Xayden after we eat?" he asked.

JD turned toward Dish. "Yes, I think that would be best. We need to get back."

Dish nodded, smiling. "You need to get back to your woman. Chanmali and I will go to Thailand and help Hana. What she does to help… it will be good."

JD nodded. "I think so too."

Dish seemed to have something on his mind. There was a moment of uncomfortable silence before he spoke.

"I am proud to meet Mai's son. You are a good man, JD. Your father, too, is pleased, I think."

JD didn't know quite how to respond, so he nodded.

"I want you to take this knife. Your father gave it to me many years ago. It is a good knife, saved my life many times. His son should have it now." Dish handed JD the old Buck General in its worn but well cared for sheath.

JD turned the knife over and over in his hand, examining it. It was well-used, but his uncle had taken excellent care of it. He knew better than to try and refuse the gift. He could see it meant a great deal to his uncle.

"I'm honored, Uncle, if you are sure you will not need it."

"I will not need it in Thailand," Dish laughed. "You take. Let's go eat."

Pallie was already into his second bowl of steamed rice and vegetables when Dish and JD approached. "Hungry, Pallie?" JD asked, grinning.

"Yep. Hey, are we leaving after breakfast?"

"Yes, I think we should get back, don't you?"

"Hell, yes, I'm ready when you are. This vacation has been fun, but I miss the good old USA."

"Mostly the food," Vivas added, grinning, as he and Hana stepped onto the veranda.

"Well," Pallie laughed, "that, and I was sparking this cute girl named Kathy just before we left on this little escapade."

"Let me guess," Vivas laughed. "A tall, blond Swedish girl."

EPILOGUE

JD took a sip from the coffee mug and set it back down on the table. It was too quiet. He looked at his watch. Nearly 6:00 p.m., *Ellen will be here soon. I need to get ready.*

He and Ellen were going out to dinner, meeting Mai at The Bistro on Gay Street at 7:30. JD was having a little trouble getting moving. *I miss that damn dog*, he observed silently.

Ajax had been an enormous part of JD's life for so long, and he couldn't have asked for a better or more loyal partner. The firefight at the plantation house in Vietnam happened almost three weeks ago, but Ajax's sacrifice in saving his mother still weighed heavily on JD's mind.

JD heard the door to the condo open. It was Ellen.

"Hey, JD! Can you come out here for a second? I want to show you something."

"Be right there." Getting up, he poured the remainder of his coffee into the kitchen sink and setting the cup down on the counter, walked over to the open front door. Ellen was standing near the back door of her Volvo.

"What is it?"

"Well, I know you've been kind of down, and with good reason. So, I wanted to get something to help cheer you up."

Ellen reached into the back seat of her car and came out with a furry little bundle. "This is Sophie. She's nine weeks old." Ellen held the cutest little German Shepherd puppy JD had ever seen.

"She's what they call a sable German Shepherd." Ellen paused, seeing the look on JD's face. "I hope it's not too soon?"

Surprised, JD wasn't sure how he felt.

"Do you want to hold her?"

JD hesitated a moment before walking forward and holding out his hands to take the puppy from Ellen. Sophie, beside herself, joyfully began licking JD's face until overcome with excitement, she piddled all over the front of his shirt.

Ellen clapped her hand over her mouth, not sure whether to laugh or scold the excited little puppy.

JD stood there for a moment, a stunned look on his face. Then, suddenly, he began to laugh. Ellen smiled. She hadn't heard JD laugh like that since he returned from Thailand.

"No, Ellen. It's not too soon. She's perfect. Thank you."

He paused, still laughing. "Ah, here! You hold Sophie. I need to change my shirt before we go to meet Mom."

ABOUT THE AUTHOR

Darren C Gilbert was born in Ilion, NY, but grew up in North Adams, Massachusetts, a small town nestled in the heart of the Berkshire Mountains.

An avid reader, he particularly enjoys military history, epic sagas, spy novels, and historical fiction. In addition to serving in the U.S. Army from 1979 to 1983, Darren has 35 plus years of martial arts training, including managing his own karate dojo for 12 years.

He has earned both undergraduate and graduate degrees from the University of Tennessee and Western Governors University, respectively. Darren is also a graduate of Executive Security International's Executive Protection Program and is a Certified Protection Specialist.

Reviews are critical to the success of any successful author. If you enjoyed **Montagnard**, please take a few minutes to leave a review with the online retailer of your choice.

If you would like to learn more about DC Gilbert:

Website: darrencgilbert.com
Email: darren@darrencgilbert.com
Instagram: darrencgilbert
Twitter: @darrencgilbert

CPSIA information can be obtained
at www.ICGtesting.com
Printed in the USA
LVHW082033050820
662365LV00012B/162/J

9 781734 602326